Unleavened Bread

Robert Grant

Table of Contents

UNLEAVENED BREAD

BOOK I.

THE EMANCIPATION

CHAPTER I.

Babcock and Selma White were among the last of the wedding guests to take their departure. It was a brilliant September night with a touch of autumn vigor in the atmosphere, which had not been without its effect on the company, who had driven off in gay spirits, most of them in hay-carts or other vehicles capable of carrying a party. Their songs and laughter floated back along the winding country road. Selma, comfortable in her wraps and well tucked about with a rug, leaned back contentedly in the chaise, after the goodbyes had been said, to enjoy the glamour of the full moon. They were seven miles from home and she was in no hurry to get there. Neither festivities nor the undisguised devotion of a city young man were common in her life. Consideration she had been used to from a child, and she knew herself to be tacitly acknowledged the smartest girl in Westfield, but perhaps for that very reason she had held aloof from manhood until now. At least no youth in her neighborhood had ever impressed her as her equal. Neither did Babcock so impress her; but he was different from the rest. He was not shy and unexpressive; he was buoyant and self-reliant, and yet he seemed to appreciate her quality none the less.

They had met about a dozen times, and on the last six of these occasions he had come from Benham, ten miles to her uncle's farm, obviously to visit her. The last two times her Aunt Farley had made him spend the night, and it had been arranged that he would drive her in the Farley chaise to Clara Morse's wedding. A seven-mile drive is apt to promote or kill the germs of intimacy, and on the way over she had been conscious of enjoying herself. Scrutiny of Clara's choice had been to the advantage of her own cavalier. The bridegroom had seemed to her what her Aunt Farley would call a mouse-in-the-cheese young man. Whereas Babcock had been the life of the affair.

She had been teaching now in Wilton for more than a year. When, shortly after her father's death, she had obtained the position of school teacher, it seemed to her that at last the opportunity had come to display her capabilities, and at the same time to fulfil her aspirations. But the task of grounding a class of small children in the rudiments of simple knowledge had already begun to pall and to seem unsatisfying. Was she to spend her life in this? And if not, the next step, unless it were marriage, was not obvious. Not that she mistrusted her ability to shine in any educational capacity, but neither Wilton nor the neighboring Westfield offered better, and she was conscious of a lack of influential friends in the greater world, which was embodied for her in Benham. Benham was a western city of these United States, with an eastern exposure; a growing, bustling city according to rumor, with an eager population restless with new ideas and stimulating ambitions. So at least Selma thought of it, and though Boston and New York and a few other places were accepted by her as authoritative, she accepted them, as she accepted Shakespeare, as a matter of course and so far removed from her immediate outlook as almost not to count. But Benham with its seventy-five thousand inhabitants and independent ways was a fascinating possibility. Once established there the world seemed within her grasp, including Boston. Might it not be that Benham, in that it was newer, was nearer to truth and more truly American than that famous city? She was not prepared to believe this an absurdity.

At least the mental atmosphere of Westfield and even of the somewhat less solemn Wilton suggested this apotheosis of the adjacent city to be reasonable. Westfield had stood for Selma as a society of serious though simple souls since she could first remember and had been one of them. Not that she arrogated to her small native town any unusual qualities of soul or mind in distinction from most other American communities, but she regarded it as inferior in point of view to none, and typical of the best national characteristics. She had probably never put into words the reasons of her confidence, but her daily consciousness was permeated with them. To be an American meant to be more keenly alive to the responsibility of life than any other citizen of civilization, and to be an American woman meant to be something finer, cleverer, stronger, and purer than any other daughter of Eve. Under the agreeable but sobering influence of this faith she had grown to womanhood, and the heroic deeds of the civil war had served to intensify a belief, the truth of which she had never heard questioned. Her mission in life had promptly been recognized by her as the development of her soul along individual lines, but until the necessity for a choice had arisen she had been content to contemplate a little longer. Now the world was before her, for she was twenty-three and singularly free from ties. Her mother had died when she was a child. Her father, the physician of the surrounding country, a man of engaging energy with an empirical education and a speculative habit of mind, had been the companion of her girlhood. During the last few years since his return from the war an invalid from a wound, her care for him had left her time for little else.

No more was Babcock in haste to reach home; and after the preliminary dash from the door into the glorious night he suffered the farm-horse to pursue its favorite gait, a deliberate jog. He knew the creature to be docile, and that he could bestow his attention on his companion without peril to her. His own pulses were bounding. He was conscious of having made the whirligig of time pass merrily for the company by his spirits and jolly quips, and that in her presence, and he was groping for an appropriate introduction to the avowal he had determined to make. He would never have a better opportunity than this, and it had been his preconceived intention to take advantage of it if all went well. All had gone well and he was going to try. She had been kind coming over; and had seemed to listen with interest as he told her about himself: and somehow he had felt less distant from her. He was not sure what she would say, for he realized that she was above him. That was one reason why he admired her so. She symbolized for him refinement, poetry, art, the things of the spirit—things from which in the same whirligig of time he had hitherto been cut off by the vicissitudes of the varnish business; but the value of which he was not blind to. How proud he would be of such a wife! How he would strive and labor for her! His heart was in his mouth and trembled on his lip as he thought of the possibility. What a joy to be sitting side by side with her under this splendid moon! He would speak and know his fate.

"Isn't it a lovely night?" murmured Selma appreciatively. "There they go," she added, indicating the disappearance over the brow of a hill of the last of the line of vehicles of the rest of the party, whose songs had come back fainter and fainter.

"I don't care. Do you?" He snuggled toward her a very little.

"I guess they won't think I'm lost," she said, with a low laugh.

"What d'you suppose your folks would say if you *were* lost? I mean if I were to run away with you and didn't bring you back?" There was a nervous ring in the guffaw which concluded his question.

"My friends wouldn't miss me much; at least they'd soon get over the shock; but I might miss myself, Mr. Babcock."

Selma was wondering why it was that she rather liked being alone with this man, big enough, indeed, to play the monster, yet half school-boy, but a man who had done well in his calling. He must be capable; he could give her a home in Benham; and it was plain that he loved her.

"I'll tell you something," he said, eagerly, ignoring her suggestion. "I'd like to run away with you and be married to-night, Selma. That's what I'd like, and I guess you won't. But it's the burning wish of my heart that you'd marry me some time. I want you to be my wife. I'm a rough fellow along-side of you, Selma, but I'd do well by you; I would. I'm able to look after you, and you shall have all you want. There's a nice little house building now in Benham. Say the word and I'll buy it for us to-morrow. I'm crazy after you, Selma."

The rein was dangling, and Babcock reached his left arm around the waist of his lady-love. He had now and again made the same demonstration with others jauntily, but this was a different matter. She was not to be treated like other women. She was a goddess to him, even in his ardor, and he reached gingerly. Selma did not wholly withdraw from the spread of his trembling arm, though this was the first man who had ever ventured to lay a finger on her.

"I'd have to give up my school," she said.

"They could get another teacher."

"*Could* they?"

"Not one like you. You see I'm clumsy, but I'm crazy for you, Selma." Emboldened by the obvious feebleness of her opposition, he broadened his clutch and drew her toward him. "Say you will, sweetheart."

This time she pulled herself free and sat up in the chaise. "Would you let me do things?" she asked after a moment.

"Do things," faltered Babcock. What could she mean? She had told him on the way over that her mother had chosen her name from a theatrical playbill, and it passed through his unsophisticated brain that she might be thinking of the stage.

"Yes, do something worth while. Be somebody. I've had the

idea I could, if I ever got the chance." Her hands were folded in her lap; there was a wrapt expression on her thin, nervous face, and a glitter in her keen eyes, which were looking straight at the moon, as though they would outstare it in brilliancy.

"You shall be anything you like, if you'll only marry me. What is it you're wishing to be?"

"I don't know exactly. It isn't anything especial yet. It's the whole thing. I thought I might find it in my school, but the experience so far hasn't been—satisfying."

"Troublesome little brats!"

"No, I dare say the fault's in me. If I went to Benham to live it would be different. Benham must be interesting—inspiring."

"There's plenty of go there. You'd like it, and people would think lots of you."

"I'd try to make them." She turned and looked at him judicially, but with a softened expression. Her profile in her exalted mood had suggested a beautiful, but worried archangel; her full face seemed less this and wore much of the seductive embarrassment of sex. To Babcock she seemed the most entrancing being he had ever seen. "Would you really like to have me come?"

He gave a hoarse ejaculation, and encircling her eagerly with his strong grasp pressed his lips upon her cheek. "Selma! darling! angel! I'm the happiest man alive."

"You mustn't do that—yet," she said protestingly.

"Yes, I must; I'm yours, and you're mine,—mine. Aren't you, sweetheart? There's no harm in a kiss."

She had to admit to herself that it was not very unpleasant after all to be held in the embrace of a sturdy lover, though she had never intended that their relations should reach this stage of familiarity so promptly. She had known, of course, that girls were to look for endearments from those whom they promised to marry, but her person had hitherto been so sacred to man and to herself that it was difficult not to shrink a little from what was taking place. This then was love, and love was, of course, the sweetest thing in the world. That was one of the truths which she had accepted as she had accepted the beauty of Shakespeare, as something not to be disputed, yet remote. He was a big, affectionate fellow, and she must make up her mind to kiss him. So she turned her face toward him and their lips met eagerly, forestalling the little peck which she had intended. She let her head fall back at his pressure on to his shoulder, and gazed up at the moon.

"Are you happy, Selma?" he asked, giving her a fond, firm squeeze.

"Yes, Lewis."

She could feel his frame throb with joy at the situation as she uttered his name.

"We'll be married right away. That's if you're willing. My business is going first-rate and, if it keeps growing for the next year as it has for the past two, you'll be rich presently. When shall it be, Selma?"

"You're in dreadful haste. Well, I'll promise to give the selectmen notice to-morrow that they must find another teacher."

"Because the one they have now is going to become Mrs. Lewis J. Babcock. I'm the luckiest fellow, hooray! in creation. See here," he added, taking her hand, "I guess a ring wouldn't look badly there—a real diamond, too. Pretty little fingers."

She sighed gently, by way of response. It was comfortable nestling in the hollow of his shoulder, and a new delightful experience to be hectored with sweetness in this way. How round and bountiful the moon looked. She was tired of her present life. What was coming would be better. Her opportunity was at hand to show the world what she was made of.

"A real diamond, and large at that," he repeated, gazing down at her, and then, as though the far away expression in her eyes suggested kinship with the unseen and the eternal, he said, admiringly but humbly, "It must be grand to be clever like you, Selma. I'm no good at that. But if loving you will make up for it, I'll go far, little woman."

"What I know of that I like, and—and if some day, I can make you proud of me, so much the better," said Selma.

"Proud of you? You are an angel, and you know it."

She closed her eyes and sighed again. Even the bright avenues of fame, which her keen eyes had traversed through the golden moon, paled before this tribute from the lips of real flesh and blood. What woman can withstand the fascination of a lover's faith that she is an angel? If a man is fool enough to believe it, why undeceive him? And if he is so sure of it, may it even not be so? Selma was content to have it so, especially as the assertion did not jar with her own prepossessions; and thus they rode home in the summer night in the mutual contentment of a betrothal.

CHAPTER II.

The match was thoroughly agreeable to Mrs. Farley, Selma's aunt and nearest relation, who with her husband presided over a flourishing poultry farm in Wilton. She was an easy-going, friendly spirit, with a sharp but not wide vision, who did not believe that a likelier fellow than Lewis Babcock would come wooing were her niece to wait a lifetime. He was hearty, comical, and generous, and was said to be making money fast in the varnish business. In short, he seemed to her an admirable young man, with a stock of common-sense and high spirits eminently serviceable for a domestic venture. How full of fun he was, to be sure! It did her good to behold the tribute his appetite paid to the buckwheat cakes with cream and other tempting viands she set before him—a pleasing contrast to Selma's starveling diet—and the hearty smack with which he enforced his demands upon her own cheeks as his mother-in-law apparent, argued an affectionate disposition. Burly, rosy-cheeked, good-natured, was he not the very man to dispel her niece's vagaries and turn the girl's morbid cleverness into healthy channels?

Selma, therefore, found nothing but encouragement in her choice at home; so by the end of another three months they were made man and wife, and had moved into that little house in Benham which had attracted Babcock's eye. Benham, as has been indicated, was in the throes of bustle and self-improvement. Before the war it had been essentially unimportant. But the building of a railroad through the town and the discovery of oil wells in its neighborhood had transformed it in a twinkling into an active and spirited centre. Selma's new house was on the edge of the city, in the van of real estate progress, one of a row of small but ambitious-looking dwellings, over the dark yellow clapboards of which the architect had let his imagination run rampant in scrolls and flourishes. There was fancy colored glass in a sort of rose-window over the front door, and lozenges of fancy glass here and there in the facade. Each house had a little grass-plot, which Babcock in his case had made appurtenant to a metal stag, which seemed to him the finishing touch to a cosey and ornamental home. He had done his best and with all his heart, and the future was before them.

Babcock found himself radiant over the first experiences of married life. It was just what he had hoped, only better. His imagination in entertaining an angel had not been unduly literal, and it was a constant delight and source of congratulation to him to reflect over his pipe on the lounge after supper that the charming piece of flesh and blood sewing or reading demurely close by was the divinity of his domestic hearth. There she was to smile at him when he came home at night and enable him to forget the cares and dross of the varnish business. Her presence across the table added a new zest to every meal and improved his appetite. In marrying he had expected to cut loose from his bachelor habits, and he asked for nothing better than to spend every evening alone with Selma, varied by an occasional evening at the theatre, and a drive out to the Farleys' now and then for supper. This, with the regular Sunday service at Rev. Henry Glynn's church, rounded out the weeks to his perfect satisfaction. He was conscious of feeling that the situation did not admit of improvement, for though, when he measured himself with Selma, Babcock was humble-minded, a cheerful and uncritical optimism was the ruling characteristic of his temperament. With health, business fortune, and love all on his side, it was natural to him to regard his lot with complacency. Especially as to all appearances, this was the sort of thing Selma liked, also. Presently, perhaps, there would be a baby, and then their cup of domestic happiness would be overflowing. Babcock's long ungratified yearning for the things of the spirit were fully met by these cosey evenings, which he would have been glad to continue to the crack of doom. To smoke and sprawl and read a little, and exchange chit-chat, was poetry enough for him. So contented was he that his joy was apt to find an outlet in ditties and whistling—he possessed a slightly tuneful, rollicking knack at both—a proceeding which commonly culminated in his causing Selma to sit beside him on the sofa and be made much of, to the detriment of her toilette.

As for the bride, so dazing were the circumstances incident to the double change of matrimony and adaptation to city life, that her judgment was in suspension. Yet though she smiled and sewed demurely, she was thinking. The yellow clapboarded house and metal stag, and a maid-of-all-work at her beck and call, were gratifying at the outset and made demands upon her energies. Selma's position in her father's house had been chiefly ornamental and social. She had been his companion and nurse, had read to him and argued with him, but the mere household work had been performed by an elderly female relative who recognized that her mind was bent on higher things. Nevertheless, she had never doubted that when the time arrived to show her capacity as a housewife, she would be more than equal to the emergency. Assuredly she would, for one of the distinguishing traits of American womanhood was the ability to perform admirably with one's own hand many menial duties and yet be prepared to shine socially with the best. Still the experience was not quite so easy as she expected; even harassing and mortifying. Fortunately, Lewis was more particular about quantity than quality where the table was concerned; and, after all, food and domestic details were secondary considerations in a noble outlook. It would have suited her never to be obliged to eat, and to be able to leave the care of the house to the hired girl; but that being out of the question, it became incumbent on her to make those obligations as simple as possible. However, the possession of a new house and gay fittings was an agreeable realization. At home everything had been upholstered in black horse-hair, and regard for material appearances had been obscured for her by the tension of her introspective tendencies. Lewis was very kind, and she had no reason to reproach herself as yet for her choice. He had insisted that she should provide herself with an ample and more stylish wardrobe, and though the invitation had interested her but mildly, the effect of shrewdly-made and neatly fitting garments on her figure had been a revelation. Like the touch of a man's hand, fine raiment had seemed to her hitherto almost repellant, but it was obvious now that anything which enhanced her effectiveness could not be dismissed as valueless. To arrive at definite conclusions in regard to her social surroundings was less easy for Selma. Benham, in its rapid growth, had got beyond the level simplicity of Westfield and Wilton, and was already confronted by the stern realities which baffle the original ideal in every American city. We like as a nation to cherish the illusion that extremes of social condition do not exist even in our large communities, and that the plutocrat and the saleslady, the learned professions and the proletariat associate on a common basis of equal virtue, intelligence, and culture. And yet, although Benham was a comparatively young and an essentially American city, there were very marked differences in all these respects in its community.

Topographically speaking the starting point of Benham was

its water-course. Twenty years before the war Benham was merely a cluster of frame houses in the valley of the limpid, peaceful river Nye. At that time the inhabitants drank of the Nye taken at a point below the town, for there was a high fall which would have made the drawing of water above less convenient. This they were doing when Selma came to Benham, although every man's hand had been raised against the Nye, which was the nearest, and hence for a community in hot haste, the most natural receptacle for dyestuffs, ashes and all the outflow from woollen mills, pork factories and oil yards, and it ran the color of glistening bean soup. From time to time, as the city grew, the drawing point had been made a little lower where the stream had regained a portion of its limpidity, and no one but wiseacres and busybodies questioned its wholesomeness. Benham at that time was too preoccupied and too proud of its increasing greatness to mistrust its own judgment in matters hygienic, artistic, and educational. There came a day later when the river rose against the city, and an epidemic of typhoid fever convinced a reluctant community that there were some things which free-born Americans did not know intuitively. Then there were public meetings and a general indignation movement, and presently, under the guidance of competent experts, Lake Mohunk, seven miles to the north, was secured as a reservoir. Just to show how the temper of the times has changed, and how sophisticated in regard to hygienic matters some of the good citizens of Benham in these latter days have become, it is worthy of mention that, though competent chemists declare Lake Mohunk to be free from contamination, there are those now who use so-called mineral spring-waters in preference; notably Miss Flagg, the daughter of old Joel Flagg, once the miller and, at the date when the Babcocks set up their household gods, one of the oil magnates of Benham. He drank the bean colored Nye to the day of his death and died at eighty; but she carries a carboy of spring-water with her personal baggage wherever she travels, and is perpetually solicitous in regard to the presence of arsenic in wall-papers into the bargain.

Verily, the world has wagged apace in Benham since Selma first looked out at her metal stag and the surrounding landscape. Ten years later the Benham Home Beautifying Society took in hand the Nye and those who drained into it, and by means of garbage consumers, disinfectants, and filters and judiciously arranged

18

shrubbery converted its channel and banks into quite a respectable citizens' paradise. But even at that time the industries on either bank of the Nye, which flowed from east to west, were forcing the retail shops and the residences further and further away. To illustrate again from the Flagg family, just before the war Joel Flagg built a modest house less than a quarter of a mile from the southerly bank of the river, expecting to end his days there, and was accused by contemporary censors of an intention to seclude himself in magnificent isolation. About this time he had yielded to the plea of his family, that every other building in the street had been given over to trade, and that they were stranded in a social Sahara of factories. So like the easy going yet soaring soul that he was, he had moved out two miles to what was known as the River Drive, where the Nye accomplishes a broad sweep to the south. There an ambitious imported architect, glad of such an opportunity to speculate in artistic effects, had built for him a conglomeration of a feudal castle and an old colonial mansion in all the grisly bulk of signal failure.

Considering our ideals, it is a wonder that no one has provided a law forbidding the erection of all the architecturally attractive, or sumptuous houses in one neighborhood. It ought not to be possible in a republic for such a state of affairs to exist as existed in Benham. That is to say all the wealth and fashion of the city lay to the west of Central Avenue, which was so literally the dividing line that if a Benhamite were referred to as living on that street the conventional inquiry would be "On which side?" And if the answer were "On the east," the inquirer would be apt to say "Oh!" with a cold inflection which suggested a ban. No Benhamite has ever been able to explain precisely why it should be more creditable to live on one side of the same street than on the other, but I have been told by clever women, who were good Americans besides, that this is one of the subtle truths which baffle the Gods and democracies alike. Central Avenue has long ago been appropriated by the leading retail dry-goods shops, huge establishments where everything from a set of drawing-room furniture to a hair-pin can be bought under a single roof; but at that time it was the social artery. Everything to the west was new and assertive; then came the shops and the business centre; and to the east were Tom, Dick, and Harry, Michael, Isaac and Pietro, the army of citizens who worked in the mills, oil yards, and pork factories. And to the north, across the river, on the further side of more manufacturing establishments, was Poland, so-called—a settlement of the Poles—to reach whom now there are seven bridges of iron. There were but two bridges then, one of wood, and journeys across them had not yet been revealed to philanthropic young women eager to do good.

Selma's house lay well to the south-west of Central Avenue, far enough removed from the River Drive and the Flagg mansion to be humble and yet near enough to be called looking up. Their row was complete and mainly occupied, but the locality was a-building, and in the process of making acquaintance. So many strangers had come to Benham that even Babcock knew but few of their neighbors. Without formulating definitely how it was to happen, Selma had expected to be received with open arms into a society eager to recognize her salient qualities. But apparently, at first glance, everybody's interest was absorbed by the butcher and grocer, the dressmaker and the domestic hearth. That is, the other people in their row seemed to be content to do as they were doing. The husbands went to town every day—town which lay in the murky distance—and their wives were friendly enough, but did not seem to be conscious either of voids in their own existence or of the privilege of her society. To be sure, they dressed well and were suggestive in that, but they looked blank at some of her inquiries, and appeared to feel their days complete if, after the housework had been done and the battle fought with the hired girl, they were able to visit the shopping district and pore over fabrics, in case they could not buy them. Some were evidently looking forward to the day when they might be so fortunate as to possess one of the larger houses of the district a mile away, and figure among what they termed "society people." There were others who, in their satisfaction with this course of life, referred with a touch of self-righteousness to the dwellers on the River Drive as deserving reprobation on account of a lack of serious purpose. This criticism appealed to Selma, and consoled her in a measure for the half mortification with which she had begun to realize that she was not of so much account as she had expected; at least, that there were people not very far distant from her block who were different somehow from her neighbors, and who took part in social proceedings in which she and her husband were not invited to participate. Manifestly they were unworthy and un-American. It was a comfort to come to this conclusion, even though her immediate surroundings, including the society of those who had put the taunt into her thoughts, left her unsatisfied.

Some relief was provided at last by her church. Babcock was by birth an Episcopalian, though he had been lax in his interest during early manhood. This was one of the matters which he had expected marriage to correct, and he had taken up again, not merely with resignation but complacency, the custom of attending service regularly. Dr. White had been a controversial Methodist, but since his wife's death, and especially since the war, he had abstained from religious observances, and had argued himself somewhat far afield from the fold of orthodox belief. Consequently Selma, though she attended church at Westfield when her father's ailments did not require her presence at home, had been brought up to exercise her faculties freely on problems of faith and to feel herself a little more enlightened than the conventional worshipper. Still she was not averse to following her husband to the Rev. Henry Glynn's church. The experience was another revelation to her, for service at Westfield had been eminently severe and unadorned. Mr. Glynn was an Englishman; a short, stout, strenuous member of the Church of England with a broad accent and a predilection for ritual, but enthusiastic and earnest. He had been tempted to cross the ocean by the opportunities for preaching the gospel to the heathen, and he had fixed on Benham as a vineyard where he could labor to advantage. His advent had been a success. He had awakened interest by his fervor and by his methods. The pew taken by Babcock was one of the last remaining, and there was already talk of building a larger church to replace the chapel where he ministered. Choir boys, elaborate vestments, and genuflections, were novelties in the Protestant worship of Benham, and attracted the attention of many almost weary of plainer forms of worship, especially as these manifestations of color were effectively supplemented by evident sincerity of spirit on the part of their pastor. Nor were his energy and zeal confined to purely spiritual functions. The scope of his church work was practical and social. He had organized from the congregation societies of various sorts to relieve the poor; Bible classes and evening reunions which the members of the parish were urged to attend in order to become acquainted. Mr. Glynn's manner was both hearty and pompous. To him there was no Church in the world but the Church of England, and it was obvious that as one of the clergy of that Church he considered himself to be no mean man; but apart from this serious intellectual foible with respect to his own relative importance, he was a stimulating Christian and citizen within his lights. His active, crusading, and emotional temperament just suited the seething propensities of Benham.

His flock comprised a few of the residents of the River Drive district, among them the Flaggs, but was a fairly representative mixture of all grades of society, including the poorest. These last were specimens under spiritual duress rather than free worshippers, and it was a constant puzzle to the reverend gentleman why, in the matter of attendance, they, metaphorically speaking, sickened and died. It had never been so in England. "Bonnets!" responded one day Mrs. Hallett Taylor, who had become Mr. Glynn's leading ally in parish matters, and was noted for her executive ability. She was an engaging but clear-headed soul who went straight to the point.

"I do not fathom your meaning," said the pastor, a little loftily, for the suggestion sounded flippant.

"It hurts their feelings to go to a church where their clothes are shabby compared with those of the rest of the congregation."

"Yes, but in God's chapel, dear lady, all such distinctions should be forgotten."

"They can't forget, and I don't blame them much, poor things, do you? It's the free-born American spirit. There now, Mr. Glynn, you were asking me yesterday to suggest some one for junior warden. Why not Mr. Babcock? They're new comers and seem available people."

Mr. Glynn's distress at her first question was merged in the interest inspired by her second, for his glance had followed hers until it rested on the Babcocks, who had just entered the vestry to attend the social reunion. Selma's face wore its worried archangel aspect. She was on her good behavior and proudly on her guard against social impertinence. But she looked very pretty, and her compact, slight figure indicated a busy way.

"I will interrogate him," he answered. "I have observed them before, and—and I can't quite make out the wife. It is almost a spiritual face, and yet—"

"Just a little hard and keen," broke in Mrs. Taylor, upon his hesitation. "She is pretty, and she looks clever. I think we can get some work out of her."

Thereupon she sailed gracefully in the direction of Selma. Mrs. Taylor was from Maryland. Her husband, a physician, had come to Benham at the close of the war to build up a practice, and his wife had aided him by her energy and graciousness to make friends. Unlike some Southerners, she was not indolent, and yet she possessed all the ingratiating, spontaneous charm of well-bred women from that section of the country. Her tastes were æsthetic and ethical rather than intellectual, and her special interest at the moment was the welfare of the church. She thought it desirable that all the elements of which the congregation was composed should be represented on the committees, and Selma seemed to her the most obviously available person from the class to which the Babcocks belonged.

"I want you to help us," she said. "I think you have ideas. We need a woman with sense and ideas on our committee to build the new church."

Selma was not used to easy grace and sprightly spontaneity. It affected her at first much as the touch of man; but just as in that instance the experience was agreeable. Life was too serious a thing in her regard to lend itself casually to lightness, and yet she felt instinctively attracted by this lack of self-consciousness and self-restraint. Besides here was an opportunity such as she had been yearning for. She had met Mrs. Taylor before, and knew her to be the presiding genius of the congregation; and it was evident that Mrs. Taylor had discovered her value.

"Thank you," she said, gravely, but cordially. "That is what I should like. I wish to be of use. I shall be pleased to serve on the committee."

"It will be interesting, I think. I have never helped build anything before. Perhaps you have?"

"No," said Selma slowly. Her tone conveyed the impression that, though her abilities had never been put to that precise test, the employment seemed easily within her capacity.

"Ah! I am sure you will be suggestive" said Mrs. Taylor. "I am right anxious that it shall be a credit in an architectural way, you know."

Mr. Glynn, who had followed with more measured tread, now mingled his hearty bass voice in the conversation. His mental attitude was friendly, but inquisitorial; as seemed to him to befit one charged with the cure of souls. He proceeded to ask questions, beginning with inquiries conventional and domestic, but verging presently on points of faith. Babcock, to whom they were directly addressed, stood the ordeal well, revealing himself as flattered, contrite, and zealous to avail himself of the blessings of the church. He admitted that lately he had been lax in his spiritual duties.

"We come every Sunday now," he said buoyantly, with a glance at Selma as though to indicate that she deserved the credit of his reformation.

"The holy sacrament of marriage has led many souls from darkness into light, from the flesh-pots of Egypt to the table of the Lord" Mr. Glynn answered. "And you, my daughter," he added, meaningly, "guard well your advantage."

It was agreeable to Selma that the clergymen seemed to appreciate her superiority to her embarrassed husband, especially as she thought she knew that in England women were not expected to have opinions of their own. She wished to say something to impress him more distinctly with her cleverness, for though she was secretly contemptuous of his ceremonials, there was something impressive in his mandatory zeal. She came near asking whether he held to the belief that it was wrong for a man to marry his deceased wife's sister, which was the only proposition in relation to the married state which occurred to her at the moment as likely to show her independence, but she contented herself instead with saying, with so much of Mrs. Taylor's spontaneity as she could reproduce without practice, "We expect to be very happy in your church."

Selma, however, supplemented her words with her tense spiritual look. She felt happier than she had for weeks, inasmuch as life seemed to be opening before her. For a few moments she listened to Mr. Glynn unfold his hopes in regard to the new church, trying to make him feel that she was no common woman. She considered it a tribute to her when he took Lewis aside later and asked him to become a junior warden.

24

CHAPTER III.

At this time the necessity for special knowledge as to artistic or educational matters was recognized grudgingly in Benham. Any reputable citizen was considered capable to pass judgment on statues and pictures, design a house or public building, and prescribe courses of study for school-children. Since then the free-born Benhamite, little by little, through wise legislation or public opinion, born of bitter experience, has been robbed of these prerogatives until, not long ago, the un-American and undemocratic proposition to take away the laying out of the new city park from the easy going but ignorant mercies of the so-called city forester, who had been first a plumber and later an alderman, prevailed. An enlightened civic spirit triumphed and special knowledge was invoked.

That was twenty-five years later. Mrs. Hallett Taylor had found herself almost single-handed at the outset in her purpose to build the new church on artistic lines. Or rather the case should be stated thus: Everyone agreed that it was to be the most beautiful church in the country, consistent with the money, and no one doubted that it would be, especially as everyone except Mrs. Taylor felt that in confiding the matter to the leading architect in Benham the committee would be exercising a wise and intelligent discretion. Mr. Pierce, the individual suggested, had never, until recently, employed the word architect in speaking of himself, and he pronounced it, as did some of the committee, "arshitect," shying a little at the word, as though it were caviare and anything but American. He was a builder, practised by a brief but rushing career in erecting houses, banks, schools, and warehouses speedily and boldly. He had been on the spot when the new growth of Benham began, and his handiwork was writ large all over the city. The city was proud of him, and had, as it were, sniffed when Joel Flagg went elsewhere for a man to build his new house. Surely, if it were necessary to pay extra for that sort of thing, was not home talent good enough? Yet it must be confessed that the ugly splendor of the Flagg mediæval castle had so far dazed the eye of Benham that its "arshitect" had felt constrained, in order to keep up with the times, to try fancy flights of his own. He had silenced any doubting Thomases by his latest effort, a new school-house, rich in rampant angles and scrolls, on the brown-stone front of which the name *Flagg School* appeared in ambitious, distorted hieroglyphics.

Think what a wealth of imagery in the tossing of the second O on top of the L. If artistic novelty and genius were sought for the new church, here it was ready to be invoked. Besides, Mr. Pierce was a brother-in-law of one of the members of the committee, and, though the committee had the fear of God in their hearts in the erection of his sanctuary, it was not easy to protest against the near relative of a fellow member, especially one so competent.

The committee numbered seven. Selma had been chosen to fill a vacancy caused by death, but at the time of her selection the matter was still in embryo, and the question of an architect had not been mooted. At the next meeting discussion arose as to whether Mr. Pierce should be given the job, under the eagle eyes of a sub-committee, or Mrs. Taylor's project of inviting competitive designs should be adopted. It was known that Mr. Glynn, without meaning disrespect to Mr. Pierce, favored the latter plan as more progressive, a word always attractive to Benham ears when they had time to listen. Its potency, coupled with veneration, for the pastor's opinion, had secured the vote of Mr. Clyme, a banker. Another member of the committee, a lawyer, favored Mrs. Taylor's idea because of a grudge against Mr. Pierce. The chairman and brother-in-law, and a hard-headed stove dealer, were opposed to the competitive plan as highfalutin and unnecessary. Thus the deciding vote lay with Selma.

Now that they were on the same committee, Mrs. Taylor could not altogether make her out. She remembered that Mr. Glynn had said the same thing. Mrs. Taylor was accustomed to conquests. Without actual premeditation, she was agreeably conscious of being able to convert and sweep most opponents off their feet by the force of her pleasant personality. In this case the effect was not so obvious. She was conscious that Selma's eyes were constantly fixed upon her, but as to what she was thinking Mrs. Taylor felt less certain. Clearly she was mesmerized, but was the tribute admiration or hostility? Mrs. Taylor was piqued, and put upon her metal. Besides she needed Selma's vote. Not being skilled in psychological analyses, she had to resort to practical methods, and invited her to afternoon tea.

Selma had never been present at afternoon tea as a domestic function in her life. Nor had she seen a home like Mrs. Taylor's. The house was no larger than her own, and had cost less. Medicine had not been so lucrative as the manufacture of varnish. Externally the house displayed stern lines of unadorned brick—the custom-made style of Benham in the first throes of expansion before Mr. Pierce's imagination had been stirred. Mr. Taylor had bought it as it stood, and his wife had made no attempt to alter the outside, which was, after all, inoffensively homely. But the interior was bewildering to Selma's gaze in its suggestion of cosey comfort. Pretty, tasteful things, many of them inexpensive knick-knacks of foreign origin—a small picture, a bit of china, a mediæval relic—were cleverly placed as a relief to the conventional furniture. Selma had been used to formalism in household garniture—to a best room little used and precise with the rigor of wax flowers and black horse-hair, and to a living room where the effect sought was purely utilitarian. Her new home, in spite of its colored glass and iron stag, was arranged in much this fashion, as were the houses of her neighbors which she had entered.

Selma managed to seat herself on the one straight-backed chair in the room. From this she was promptly driven by Mrs. Taylor and established in one corner of a lounge with a soft silk cushion behind her, and further propitiated by the proffer of a cup of tea in a dainty cup and saucer. All this, including Mrs. Taylor's musical voice, easy speech, and ingratiating friendliness, alternately thrilled and irritated her. She would have liked to discard her hostess from her thought as a light creature unworthy of intellectual seriousness, but she found herself fascinated and even thawed in spite of herself.

"I'm glad to have the opportunity really to talk to you," said Mrs. Taylor. "At the church reunions one is so liable to interruptions. If I'm not mistaken, you taught school before you were married?"

"For a short time."

"That must have been interesting. It is so practical and definite. My life," she added deprecatingly, "has been a thing of threads and patches—a bit here and a bit there."

She paused, but without forcing a response, proceeded blithely to touch on her past by way of illustration. The war had come just when she was grown up, and her kin in Maryland were divided on the issue. Her father had taken his family abroad, but her heart was in the keeping of a young officer on the Northern side—now her husband. Loss of property and bitterness of spirit had kept her parents expatriated, and she, with them, had journeyed from place to place in Europe. She had seen many beautiful places and beautiful things. At last Major Taylor had come for her and carried her off as his bride to take up again her life as an American.

"I am interested in Benham," she continued, "and I count on you, Mrs. Babcock, to help make the new church what it ought to be artistically—worthy of all the energy and independence there is in this place."

Selma's eye kindled. The allusion to foreign lands had aroused her distrust, but this patriotic avowal warmed her pulses.

"Every one is so busy with private affairs here, owing to the rapid growth of the city," pursued Mrs. Taylor, "that there is danger of our doing inconsiderately things which cannot easily be set right hereafter. An ugly or tawdry-looking building may be an eyesore for a generation. I know that we have honest and skilful mechanics in Benham, but as trustees of the church funds, shouldn't we at least make the effort to get the best talent there is? If we have the cleverest architect here, so much the better. An open competition will enable us to find out. After all Benham is only one city among many, and a very new city. Why shouldn't we take advantage of the ideas of the rest of the country—the older portion of the country?"

"Mr. Pierce built our house, and we think it very satisfactory and pretty."

Selma's tone was firm, but she eyed her hostess narrowly. She had begun of late to distrust the æsthetic worth of the colored glass and metal stag, and, though she was on her guard against effrontery, she wished to know the truth. She knew that Mr. Pierce, with fine business instinct, had already conveyed to her husband the promise that he should furnish the varnish for the new church in case of his own selection, which, as Babcock had remarked, would be a nice thing all round.

Mrs. Taylor underwent the scrutiny without flinching. "I have nothing to say against Mr. Pierce. He is capable within his lights. Indeed I think it quite possible that we shall get nothing more satisfactory elsewhere. Mr. Flagg's grim pile is anything but encouraging. That may sound like an argument against my plan, but in the case of the Flagg house there was no competition; merely unenlightened choice on the one side and ignorant experimenting on the other."

"You don't seem to think very highly of the appearance of Benham," said Selma. The remark was slightly interrogative, but was combative withal. She wished to know if everything, from the Flagg mansion down, was open to criticism, but she would fain question the authority of the censor—this glib, graceful woman whose white, starched cuffs seemed to make light of her own sober, unadorned wrists.

This time Mrs. Taylor flushed faintly. She realized that their relations had reached a critical point, and that the next step might be fatal. She put down her teacup, and leaning forward, said with smiling confidential eagerness, "I don't. I wouldn't admit it to anyone else. But what's the use of mincing matters with an intelligent woman like you? I might put you off now, and declare that Benham is well enough. But you would soon divine what I really think, and that would be the end of confidence between us. I like honesty and frankness, and I can see that you do. My opinion of Benham architecture is that it is slip-shod and mongrel. There! You see I put myself in your hands, but I do so because I feel sure you nearly agree with me already. You know it's so, but you hate to acknowledge it."

Selma's eyes were bright with interest. She felt flattered by the appeal, and there was a righteous assurance in Mrs. Taylor's manner which was convincing. She opened her mouth to say something—what she did not quite know—but Mrs. Taylor raised her hand by way of interdiction.

"Don't answer yet. Let me show you what I mean. I'm as proud of Benham as anyone. I am absorbed by the place, I look to see it fifty years hence—perhaps less—a great city, and a beautiful city too. Just at present everything is commercial and—and ethical; yes, ethical. We wish to do and dare, but we haven't time to adorn as we construct. That is, most of us haven't. But if a few determined spirits—women though they be—cry 'halt,' art may get a chance here and there to assert herself. Look at this," she said, gliding across the room and holding up a small vase of exquisite shape and coloring, "I picked it up on the other side and it stands almost for a lost art. The hands and taste which wrought it represent the transmitted patience and skill of hundreds of years. We like to rush things through in a few weeks on a design hastily conceived by a Mr.

Pierce because we are so earnest. Now, we won't do it this time, will we?"

"No, we won't," said Selma. "I see what you mean. I was afraid at first that you didn't give us credit for the earnestness—for the ethical part. That's the first thing, the great thing according to my idea, and it's what distinguishes us from foreigners,—the foreigners who made that vase, for instance. But I agree with you that there's such a thing as going too fast, and very likely some of the buildings here aren't all they might be. We don't need to model them on foreign patterns, but we must have them pretty and right."

"Certainly, certainly, my dear. What we should strive for is originality—American originality; but soberly, slowly. Art is evolved painfully, little by little; it can't be bought ready-made at shops for the asking like tea and sugar. If we invite designs for the new church, we shall give the youths of the country who have ideas seething in their heads a chance to express themselves. Who knows but we may unearth a genius?"

"Who knows?" echoed Selma, with her spiritual look. "Yes, you are right, Mrs. Taylor. I will help you. As you say, there must be hundreds of young men who would like to do just that sort of thing. I know myself what it is to have lived in a small place without the opportunity to show what one could do; to feel the capacity, but to be without the means and occasion to reveal what is in one. And now that I understand we really look at things the same way, I'm glad to join with you in making Benham beautiful. As you say, we women can do much if we only will. I've the greatest faith in woman's mission in this new, interesting nation of ours. Haven't you, Mrs. Taylor? Don't you believe that she, in her new sphere of usefulness, is one of the great moving forces of the Republic?" Selma was talking rapidly, and had lost every trace of suspicious restraint. She spoke as one transfigured.

"Yes, indeed," answered Mrs. Taylor, checking any disposition she may have felt to interpose qualifications. She could acquiesce generally without violence to her convictions, and she could not afford to imperil the safety of the immediate issue—her church. "I felt sure you would feel so if you only had time to reflect," she added. "If you vote with us, you will have the pleasant consciousness of knowing that you have advanced woman's cause just so much."

"You may count on my vote."

Selma stopped on her way home, although it was late, to purchase some white cuffs. As she approached, her husband stood on the grass-plot in his shirt sleeves with a garden-hose. He was whistling, and when he saw her he kissed his hand at her jubilantly,

"Well, sweetheart, where you been?"

"Visiting. Taking tea with Mrs. Taylor. I've promised her to vote to invite bids for the church plans."

Babcock looked surprised. "That'll throw Pierce out, won't it?"

"Not unless some one else submits a better design than he."

Lewis scratched his head. "I considered that order for varnish as good as booked."

"I'm not sure Mr. Pierce knows as much as he thinks he does," said Selma oracularly. "We shall get plans from New York and Boston. If we don't like them we needn't take them. But that's the way to get an artistic thing. And we're going to have the most artistic church in Benham. I'm sorry about the varnish, but a principle is involved."

Babcock was puzzled but content. He cared far more for the disappointment to Pierce than for the loss of the order. But apart from the business side of the question, he never doubted that his wife must be right, nor did he feel obliged to inquire what principle was involved. He was pleased to have her associate with Mrs. Taylor, and was satisfied that she would be a credit to him in any situation where occult questions of art or learning were mooted. He dropped his hose and pulled her down beside him on the porch settee. There was a beautiful sunset, and the atmosphere was soft and refreshing. Selma felt satisfied with herself. As Mrs. Taylor had said, it was her vote which would turn the scale on behalf of progress. Other things, too, were in her mind. She was not ready to admit that she had been instructed, but she was already planning changes in her own domestic interior, suggested by what she had seen.

She let her husband squeeze her hand, but her thoughts were wandering from his blandishments. Presently she said: "Lewis, I've begun lately to doubt if that stag is really pretty."

"The stag? Well, now, I've always thought it tasty—one of the features of our little place."

"No one would mistake it for a real deer. It looks to me almost comical."

Babcock turned to regard judicially the object of her criticism.

"I like it," he said somewhat mournfully, as though he were puzzled. "But if you don't, we'll change the stag for something else. I wish you to be pleased first of all. Instead we might have a fountain; two children under an umbrella I saw the other day. It was cute. How does that strike you?"

"I can't tell without seeing it. And, Lewis, promise me that you won't select anything new of that sort until I have looked at it."

"Very well," Babcock answered submissively. But he continued to look puzzled. In his estimate of his wife's superiority to himself in the subtleties of life, it had never occurred to him to include the choice of every-day objects of art. He had eyes and could judge for himself like any other American citizen. Still, he was only too glad to humor Selma in such an unimportant matter, especially as he was eager for her happiness.

CHAPTER IV.

Seven designs for the new church were submitted, including three from Benham architects. The leaven of influence exercised by spirits like Mrs. Taylor was only just beginning to work, and the now common custom of competing outside one's own bailiwick was still in embryo. Mr. Pierce's design was bold and sumptuous. His brother-in-law stated oracularly not long before the day when the plans were to be opened: "Pierce is not a man to be frightened out of a job by frills. Mark my words; he will give us an elegant thing." Mr. Pierce had conceived the happy thought of combining a Moorish mosque and New England meeting-house in a conservative and equitable medley, evidently hoping thereby to be both picturesque and traditional. The result, even on paper, was too bold for some of his admirers. The chairman was heard to remark: "I shouldn't feel as though I was in church. That dome set among spires is close to making a theatre of the house of God."

The discomfiture of the first architect of Benham cleared the way for the triumph of Mrs. Taylor's taste. The design submitted by Wilbur Littleton of New York, seemed to her decidedly the most meritorious. It was graceful, appropriate, and artistic; entirely in harmony with religious associations, yet agreeably different from every day sanctuaries. The choice lay between his and that presented by Mr. Cass, a Benham builder—a matter-of-fact, serviceable, but very conventional edifice. The hard-headed stove dealer on the committee declared in favor of the native design, as simpler and more solid.

"It'll be a massive structure" he said, "and when it's finished no one will have to ask what it is. It'll speak for itself. Mr. Cass is a solid business man, and we know what we'll get. The other plan is what I call dandified."

It was evident to the committee that the stove dealer's final criticism comprehended the architect as well as his design. Several competitors—Littleton among them—had come in person to explain the merits of their respective drawings, and by the side of solid, red-bearded, undecorative Mr. Cass, Littleton may well have seemed a dandy. He was a slim young man with a delicate, sensitive face and intelligent brown eyes. He looked eager and interesting. In his case the almost gaunt American physiognomy was softened by a suggestion of poetic impulses. Yet the heritage of nervous energy was apparent. His appearance conveyed the impression of quiet trigness and gentility. His figure lent itself to his clothes, which were utterly inconspicuous, judged by metropolitan standards, but flawless in the face of hard-headed theories of life, and aroused suspicion. He spoke in a gentle but earnest manner, pointing out clearly, yet modestly, the merits of his composition.

Selma had never seen a man just like him before, and she noticed that from the outset his eyes seemed to be fastened on her as though his words were intended for her special benefit. She had never read the lines—indeed they had not been written—

"I think I could be happy with a gentleman like you."

Nor did the precise sentiment contained in them shape itself in her thought. Yet she was suddenly conscious that she had been starving for lack of intellectual companionship, and that he was the sort of man she had hoped to meet—the sort of man who could appreciate her and whom she could appreciate.

It did not become necessary for Selma to act as Mr. Littleton's champion, for the stove dealer's criticism found only one supporter. The New Yorker's design for the church was so obviously pretty and suitable that a majority of the Committee promptly declared in its favor. The successful competitor, who had remained a day to learn the result, was solemnly informed of the decision, and then elaborately introduced to the members. In shaking hands with him, Selma experienced a shade of embarrassment. It was plain that his words to her, spoken with a low bow—"I am very much gratified that my work pleases you" conveyed a more spiritual significance than was contained in his thanks to the others. Still he seemed more at his ease with Mrs. Taylor, who promptly broke the ice of the situation by fixing him as a close relative of friends in Baltimore. Straightway he became sprightly and voluble, speaking of things and people beyond Selma's experience. This social jargon irritated Selma. It seemed to her a profanation of a noble character, yet she was annoyed because she could not understand.

Mrs. Taylor, having discovered in Mr. Littleton one who should have been a friend long before, succeeded in carrying him off to dinner. Yet, before taking his leave, he came back to Selma for a few words. She had overheard Mrs. Taylor's invitation, and she asked herself why she too might not become better acquainted with this young man whose attitude toward her was that of respectful admiration. To have a strange young man to dine off-hand struck her as novel. She had a general conviction that it would seem to Lewis closely allied to light conduct, and that only foreigners or frivolous people let down to this extent the bars of family life. Now that Mrs. Taylor had set her the example, she was less certain of the moral turpitude of such an act, but she concluded also that her husband would be in the way at table. What she desired was an opportunity for a long, interesting chat about high things.

While she reflected, he was saying to her, "I understand that your committee is to supervise my work until the new church is completed, so I shall hope to have the opportunity to meet you occasionally. It will be necessary for me to make trips here from time to time to see that everything is being done correctly by the mechanics."

"Do you go away immediately?"

"It may be that I shall be detained by the arrangements which I must make here until day after to-morrow."

"If you would really like to see me, I live at 25 Onslow Avenue."

"Thank you very much." Littleton took out a small memorandum book and carefully noted the address. "Mrs. Babcock, 25 Onslow Avenue. I shall make a point of calling to-morrow afternoon if I stay—and probably I shall."

He bowed and left Selma pleasantly stirred by the interview. His voice was low and his enunciation sympathetically fluent. She said to herself that she would give him afternoon tea and they would compare ideas together. She felt sure that his must be interesting.

Later in the evening at Mrs. Taylor's, when there was a pause in their sympathetic interchange of social and æsthetic convictions, Littleton said abruptly:

"Tell me something, please, about Mrs. Babcock. She has a suggestive as well as a beautiful face, and it is easy to perceive that she is genuinely American—not one of the women of whom we were speaking, who seem to be ashamed of their own institutions, and who ape foreign manners and customs. I fancy she would illustrate what I was saying just now as to the vital importance of our clinging to our heritage of independent thought—of accepting the truth of the ancient order of things without allowing its lies and demerits to enslave us."

"I suppose so," said Mrs. Taylor. "She certainly does not belong to the dangerous class of whom you were speaking. I was flattering myself that neither did I, for I was agreeing with all you said as to the need of cherishing our native originality. Yet I must confess that now that you compare me with her (the actual comparison is my own, but you instigated it), I begin to feel more doubts about myself—that is if she is the true species, and I'm inclined to think she is. Pray excuse this indirect method of answering your inquiry; it is in the nature of a soliloquy; it is an airing of thoughts and doubts which have been harassing me for a fortnight—ever since I knew Mrs. Babcock. Really, Mr. Littleton, I can tell you very little about her. She is a new-comer on the horizon of Benham; she has been married very recently; I believe she has taught school and that she was brought up not far from here. She is as proud as Lucifer and sometimes as beautiful; she is profoundly serious and—and apparently very ignorant. I fancy she is clever and capable in her way, but I admit she is an enigma to me and that I have not solved it. I can see she does not approve of me altogether. She regards me with suspicion, and yet she threw the casting vote in favor of my proposal to open the competition for the church to architects from other places. I am trying to like her, for I wish to believe in everything genuinely American if I can. There, I have told you all I know, and to a man she may seem altogether attractive and inspiring."

"Thank you. I had no conception that I was broaching such a complex subject. She sounds interesting, and my curiosity is whetted. You have not mentioned the husband."

"To be sure. A burly, easy-going manufacturer of varnish, without much education, I should judge. He is manifestly her inferior in half a dozen ways, but I understand that he is making money, and he looks kind."

Wilbur Littleton's life since he had come to man's estate had been a struggle, and he was only just beginning to make headway. He had never had time to commiserate himself, for necessity on the one hand and youthful ambition on the other had kept his energies tense and his thoughts sane and hopeful. He and his sister Pauline, a year his senior, had been left orphans while both were students by the death of their father on the battlefield. To persevere in their

36

respective tastes and work out their educations had been a labor of love, but an undertaking which demanded rigorous self-denial on the part of each. Wilbur had determined to become an architect. Pauline, early interested in the dogma that woman must no longer be barred from intellectual companionship with man, had sought to cultivate herself intelligently without sacrificing her brother's domestic comfort. She had succeeded. Their home in New York, despite its small dimensions and frugal hospitality, was already a favorite resort of a little group of professional people with busy brains and light purses. Wilbur was in the throes of early progress. He had no relatives or influential friends to give him business, and employment came slowly. He had been an architect on his own account for two years, but was still obliged to supplement his professional orders by work as a draughtsman for others. Yet his enthusiasm kept him buoyant. In respect to his own work he was scrupulous; indeed, a stern critic. He abhorred claptrap and specious effects, and aimed at high standards of artistic expression. This gave him position among his brother architects, but was incompatible with meteoric progress. His design for the church at Benham represented much thought and hope, and he felt happy at his success.

Littleton's familiarity with women, apart from his sister, had been slight, but his thoughts regarding them were in keeping with a poetic and aspiring nature. He hoped to marry some day, and he was fond of picturing to himself in moments of reverie the sort of woman to whom his heart would be given. In the shrine of his secret fancy she appeared primarily as an object of reverence, a white-souled angel of light clad in the graceful outlines of flesh, an Amazon and yet a winsome, tender spirit, and above all a being imbued with the stimulating intellectual independence he had been taught to associate with American womanhood. She would be the loving wife of his bosom and the intelligent sharer of his thoughts and aspirations—often their guide. So pure and exacting was his ideal that while alive to the value of coyness and coquetry as elements of feminine attraction for others, Wilbur had chosen to regard the maiden of his faith as too serious a spirit to condescend to such vanities; and from a similar vein of appreciation he was prone to think of her as unadorned, or rather untarnished, by the gewgaws of fashionable dressmaking and millinery. His first sight of

Selma had made him conscious that here was a face not unlike what he had hoped to encounter some day, and he had instinctively felt her to be sympathetic. He was even conscious of disappointment when he heard her addressed as Mrs. Babcock. Evidently she was a free-born soul, unhampered by the social weaknesses of a large city, and illumined by the spiritual grace of native womanliness. So he thought of her, and Mrs. Taylor's diagnosis rather confirmed than impaired his impression, for in Mrs. Taylor Wilbur felt he discerned a trace of antagonism born of cosmopolitan prejudice—an inability to value at its true worth a nature not moulded on conventional lines. Rigorous as he was in his judgments, and eager to disown what was cheap or shallow, mere conventionalism, whether in art or daily life, was no less abhorrent to him. Here, he said to himself, was an original soul, ignorant and unenlightened perhaps, but endowed with swift perception and capable of noble development.

The appearance of Selma's scroll and glass bedizened house did not affect this impression. Wilbur was first of all appreciatively an American. That is he recognized that native energy had hitherto been expended on the things of the spirit to the neglect of things material. As an artist he was supremely interested in awakening and guiding the national taste in respect to art, but at the same time he was thoroughly aware that the peculiar vigor and independence of character which he knew as Americanism was often utterly indifferent to, or ignorant of, the value of æsthetics. After all, art was a secondary consideration, whereas the inward vision which absorbed the attention of the thoughtful among his countrymen and countrywomen was an absolute essential without which the soul must lose its fineness. He himself was seeking to show that beauty, in external material expression, was not merely consistent with strong ideals but requisite to their fit presentment. He recognized too that the various and variegated departures from the monotonous homely pattern of the every-day American house, which were evident in each live town, were but so many indicators that the nation was beginning to realize the truth of this. His battle was with the designers and builders who were guiding falsely and flamboyantly, not with the deceived victims, nor with those who were still satisfied merely to look inwardly, and ignored form and color. Hence he would have been able to behold the Babcocks' iron stag without rancor had the animal still occupied the grass-plot.

Selma, when she saw the figure of her visitor in the door-way, congratulated herself that it had been removed. It would have pleased her to know that Mr. Littleton had already placed her in a niche above the level of mere grass-plot considerations. That was where she belonged of course; but she was fearful on the score of suspected shortcomings. So it was gratifying to be able to receive him in a smarter gown, to be wearing white cuffs, and to offer him tea with a touch of Mrs. Taylor's tormenting urbanity. Not so unreservedly as she. That would never do. It was and never would be in keeping with her own ideas of serious self-respect. Still a touch of it was grateful to herself. She felt that it was a grace and enhanced her effectiveness.

A few moments later Selma realized that for the first time since she had lived in Benham she was being understood and appreciated. She felt too that for the first time she was talking to a kindred spirit—to be sure, to one different, and more technically proficient in concrete knowledge, possibly more able, too, to express his thoughts in words, but eminently a comrade and sympathizer. She was not obliged to say much. Nor were, indeed, his actual words the source of her realization. The revelation came from what was left unsaid—from the silent recognition by him that she was worthy to share his best thoughts and was herself a serious worker in the struggle of life. No graceful but galling attitude of superiority, no polite indifference to her soul-hunger, no disposition to criticise. And yet he was no less voluble, clever, and spirited than Mrs. Taylor. She listened with wrapt interest to his easy talk, which was ever grave in tone, despite his pleasant sallies. He spoke of Benham with quick appreciation of its bustling energy, and let her see that he divined its capacity for greatness. This led him to refer with kindling eyes to the keen impulse toward education and culture which was animating the younger men and women of the country; to the new beginnings of art, literature, and scientific investigation. At scarcely a hint from her he told briefly of his past life and his hopes, and fondly mentioned his sister and her present absorption in some history courses for women.

"And you?" he said. "You are a student, too. Mrs. Taylor has told me, but I should have guessed it. Duties even more interesting claim you now, but it is easy to perceive that you have known that other happiness, 'To scorn delights and live laborious days.'"

His words sounded musical, though the quotation from Lycidas was unfamiliar to her ears. Her brain was thrilling with the import of all he had told her—with his allusions to the intellectual and ethical movements of Boston and New York, in which she felt herself by right and with his recognition a partner and peer.

"You were teaching school when you married, I believe?" he added.

"Yes."

"And before that, if I may ask?"

"I lived at Westfield with my father. It is a small country town, but we tried to be in earnest."

"I understand—I understand. You grew up among the trees, and the breezes and the brooks, those wonderful wordless teachers. I envy you, for they give one time to think—to expand. I have known only city life myself. It is stimulating, but one is so easily turned aside from one's direct purpose. Do you write at all?"

"Not yet. But I have wished to. Some day I shall. Just now I have too many domestic concerns to—"

She did not finish, for Babcock's heavy tread and whistle resounded in the hall and at the next moment he was calling "Selma!"

She felt annoyed at being interrupted, but she divined that it would never do to show it.

"My husband," she said, and she raised her voice to utter with a sugared dignity which would have done credit to Mrs. Taylor,

"I am in the parlor, Lewis."

"Enter your chief domestic concern," said Littleton blithely. "A happy home is preferable to all the poems and novels in the world."

Babcock, pushing open the door, which stood ajar, stopped short in his melody.

"This is Mr. Littleton, Lewis. The architect of our new church."

"Pleased to make your acquaintance." And by way of accounting for the sudden softening of his brow, Babcock added, "I

40

set you down at first as one of those lightning-rod agents. There was one here last week who wouldn't take 'no' for an answer."

"He has an advantage over me," answered Littleton with a laugh. "In my business a man can't solicit orders. He has to sit and wait for them to come to him."

"I want to know. My wife thinks a lot of your drawings for the new church."

"I hope to make it a credit to your city. I've just been saying to your wife, Mr. Babcock, that Benham has a fine future before it. The very atmosphere seems charged with progress."

Babcock beamed approvingly. "It's a driving place, sir. The man in Benham who stops by the way-side to scratch his head gets left behind. When we moved into this house a year ago looking through that window we were at the jumping-off place; now you see houses cropping up in every direction. It's going to be a big city. Pleased to have you stop to supper with us," he added with burly suavity as their visitor rose.

Littleton excused himself and took his leave. Babcock escorted him to the front door and full of his subject delayed him on the porch to touch once more on the greatness of Benham. There was a clumsy method too in this optimistic garrulity, for at the close he referred with some pride to his own business career, and made a tender of his business card, "Lewis Babcock & Company, Varnishes," with a flourish. "If you do anything in my line, pleased to accommodate you."

Littleton departing, tickled by a pleasant sense of humor, caught through the parlor window a last glimpse of Selma's inspired face bowing gravely, yet wistfully, in acknowledgment of his lifted hat, and he strode away under the spell of a brain picture which he transmuted into words: "There's the sort of case where the cynical foreigner fails to appreciate the true import of our American life. That couple typifies the elements of greatness in our every-day people. At first blush the husband's rough and material, but he's shrewd and enterprising and vigorous—the bread winner. He's enormously proud of her, and he has reason to be, for she is a constant stimulus to higher things. Little by little, and without his knowing it, perhaps, she will smoothe and elevate him, and they will develop together, growing in intelligence and cultivation as they wax in worldly goods. After all, woman is our most marvellous native product—that sort of woman. Heigho!" Having given vent to this sigh, Littleton proceeded to recognize the hopelessness of the personal situation by murmuring with a slightly forced access of sprightliness

"If she be not fair for me,
What care I how fair she be?"

Still he intended to see more of Mrs. Babcock, and that without infringing the tenth or any other commandment. To flirt with a married woman savored to him of things un-American and unworthy, and Littleton had much too healthy an imagination to rhapsodize from such a stand-point. Yet he foresaw that they might be mutually respecting friends.

CHAPTER V.

Selma knew intuitively that an American woman was able to cook a smooth custard, write a poem and control real society with one and the same brain and hand, and she was looking forward to the realization of the apotheosis; but, though she was aware that children are the natural increment of wedlock, she had put the idea from her ever since her marriage as impersonal and vaguely disgusting. Consequently her confinement came as an unwelcome interruption of her occupations and plans.

Her connection with the committee for the new church had proved an introduction to other interests, charitable and social. One day she was taken by Mrs. Taylor to a meeting of the Benham Woman's Institute, a literary club recently established by Mrs. Margaret Rodney Earle, a Western newspaper woman who had made her home in Benham. Selma came in upon some twenty of her own sex in a hotel private parlor hired weekly for the uses of the Institute. Mrs. Earle, the president, a large florid woman of fifty, with gray hair rising from the brow, fluent of speech, endowed with a public manner, a commanding bust and a vigorous, ingratiating smile, wielded a gavel at a little table and directed the exercises. A paper on Shakespeare's heroines was read and discussed. Selections on the piano followed. A thin woman in eye-glasses, the literary editor of the *Benham Sentinel*, recited "Curfew must not ring to-night," and a visitor from Wisconsin gave an exhibition in melodious whistling. In the intervals, tea, chocolate with whipped cream and little cakes were dispensed.

Selma was absorbed and thrilled. What could be more to her taste than this? At the close of the whistling exercise, Mrs. Earle came over and spoke to her. They took a strong fancy to each other on the spot. Selma preferred a person who would tell you everything about herself and to whom you could tell everything about yourself without preliminaries. People like Mrs. Taylor repressed her, but the motherly loquacity and comprehension of Mrs. Earle drew her out and thawed at once and forever the ice of acquaintanceship. Before she quite realized the extent of this fascination she had promised to recite something, and as in a dream, but with flushing cheeks, she heard the President rap the table and announce "You will be gratified to hear that a talented friend who is with us has kindly consented to favor us with a recital. I have the honor to introduce

Mrs. Lewis Babcock."

After the first flush of nervousness, Selma's grave dignity came to her support, and justified her completely in her own eyes. Her father had been fond of verse, especially of verse imbued with moral melancholy, and at his suggestion she had learned and had been wont to repeat many of the occasional pieces which he cut from the newspapers and collected in a scrap-book. Her own preference among these was the poem, "O why should the spirit of mortal be proud?" which she had been told was a great favorite of Abraham Lincoln. It was this piece which came into her mind when Mrs. Earle broached the subject, and this she proceeded to deliver with august precision. She spoke clearly and solemnly without the trace of the giggling protestation which is so often incident to feminine diffidence. She treated the opportunity with the seriousness expected, for though the Institute was not proof against light and diverting contributions, as the whistling performance indicated, levity of spirit would have been out of place.

"'Tis a twink of the eye, 'tis a draught of the breath
From the blossom of health to the paleness of death;
From the gilded saloon to the bier and the shroud,
O why should the spirit of mortal be proud?"

Selma enjoyed the harmony between the long, slow cadence of the metre and the important gravity of the theme. She rolled out the verses with the intensity of a seer, and she looked a beautiful seer as well. Liberal applause greeted her as she sat down, though the clapping woman is apt to be a feeble instrument at best. Selma knew that she had produced an impression and she was moved by her own effectiveness. She was compelled to swallow once or twice to conceal the tears in her voice while listening to the congratulations of Mrs. Earle. The words which she had just recited were ringing through her brain and seemed to her to express the pitch at which her life was keyed.

Selma was chosen a member of the Institute at the next meeting, and forthwith she became intimate with the president. Mrs. Margaret Rodney Earle was, as she herself phrased it, a live woman. She supported herself by writing for the newspapers articles of a morally utilitarian character—for instance a winter's series, published every Saturday, "Hints on Health and Culture," or again, "Receipts for the Parlor and the Kitchen." She also contributed poetry of a pensive cast, and chatty special correspondence flavored with personal allusion. She was one of the pioneers in modern society journalism, which at this time, however, was comparatively veiled and delicate in its methods. Besides, she was a woman of tireless energy, with theories on many subjects and an ardor for organization. She advocated prohibition, the free suffrage of woman, the renunciation of corsets, and was interested in reforms relating to labor, the pauper classes and the public schools. In behalf of any of these causes she was ready from time to time to dash off an article at short notice or address an audience. But her dearest concern was the promotion of woman's culture and the enlargement of woman's sphere of usefulness through the club. The idea of the woman's club, which was taking root over the country, had put in the shade for the time being all her other plans, including the scheme of a society for making the golden-rod the national flower. As the founder and president of the Benham Institute, she felt that she had found an avocation peculiarly adapted to her capacities, and she was already actively in correspondence with clubs of a similar character in other cities, in the hope of forming a national organization for mutual enlightenment and support.

Mrs. Earle received Selma by invitation at her lodgings the following day, and so quickly did their friendship ripen that at the end of two hours each had told the other everything. Selma was prone instinctively to regard as aristocratic and un-American any limitations to confidence. The evident disposition on the part of Mrs. Earle to expose promptly and without reserve the facts of her past and her plans for the future seemed to Selma typical of an interesting character, and she was thankful to make a clean breast in her turn as far as was possible. Mrs. Earle's domestic experience had been thorny.

"I had a home once, too," she said, "a happy home, I thought. My husband said he loved me. But almost from the first we had trouble. It went on so from month to month, and finally we agreed to part. He objected, my dear, to my living my own life. He didn't like me to take an interest in things outside the house—public matters. I was elected on the school-board—the only woman—and he ought to have been proud. He said he was, at first, but he was too fond of declaring that a woman's place is in her kitchen. One day I said to him, 'Ellery, this can't go on. If we can't agree we'd better separate. A cat-and-dog life is no life at all.' He answered back, 'I'm not asking you to leave me, but if you're set on it don't let me hinder you, Margaret. You don't need a man to support you. You're as good as a man yourself.' He meant that to be sarcastic, I suppose. 'Yes,' said I, 'thank God, I think I can take care of myself, even though I am a woman.' That was the end of it. There was no use for either of us to get excited. I packed my things, and a few mornings later I said to him, 'Good-by, Ellery Earle: I wish you well, and I suppose you're my husband still, but I'm going to live my own life without let or hindrance from any man. There's your ring.' My holding out the ring was startling to him, for he said, 'Aren't you going to be sorry for this, Margaret?' 'No,' said I, 'I've thought it all out, and it's best for both of us. There's your ring.' He wouldn't take it, so I dropped it on the table and went out. Some people miss it, and misbelieve I was ever married. That was close on to twenty years ago, and I've never seen him since. When the war broke out I heard he enlisted, but what's become of him I don't know. Maybe he got a divorce. I've kept right on and lived my own life in my own way, and never lacked food or raiment. I'm forty-five years old, but I feel a young woman still."

Notwithstanding Mrs. Earle's business-like directness and the protuberance of her bust in conclusion, by way of reasserting her satisfaction with the results of her action, there was a touch of plaintiveness in her confession which suggested the womanly author of "Hints on Culture and Hygiene," rather than the man-hater. This was lost on Selma, who was fain to sympathize purely from the stand-point of righteousness.

"It was splendid," she said. "He had no right to prevent you living your own life. No husband has that right."

Mrs. Earle brushed her eyes with her handkerchief. "You musn't think, my dear, that I'm not a believer in the home because mine has been unhappy—because my husband didn't or couldn't understand. The true home is the inspirer and nourisher of all that is best in life—in our American life; but men must learn the new lesson. There are many homes—yours, I'm sure—where the free-born American woman has encouragement and the opportunity to expand."

"Oh, yes. My husband lets me do as I wish. I made him promise before I accepted him that he wouldn't thwart me; that he'd let me live my own life."

Selma was so appreciative of Mrs. Earle, and so energetic and suggestive in regard to the scope of the Institute, that she was presently chosen a member of the council, which was the body charged with the supervision of the fortnightly entertainments. It occurred to her as a brilliant conception to have Littleton address the club on "Art," and she broached the subject to him when he next returned to Benham and appeared before the church committee. He declared that he was too busy to prepare a suitable lecture, but he yielded finally to her plea that he owed it to himself to let the women of Benham hear his views and opinions.

"They are wives and they are mothers," said Selma sententiously. "It was a woman's vote, you remember, which elected you to build our church. You owe it to Art; don't you think so?"

A logical appeal to his conscience was never lost on Littleton. Besides he was glad to oblige Mrs. Babcock, who seemed so earnest in her desire to improve the æsthetic taste of Benham. Accordingly, he yielded. The lecture was delivered a few weeks later and was a marked success, for Littleton's earnestness of theme and manner was relieved by a graceful, sympathetic delivery. Selma, whose social aplomb was increasing every day, glided about the rooms with a contented mien receiving felicitations and passing chocolate. She enjoyed the distinction of being the God behind the curtain.

A few days later the knowledge that she herself was to become a mother was forced upon her attention, and was a little irksome. Of necessity her new interests would be interrupted. Though she did not question that she would perform maternal duties fitly and fully, they seemed to her less peculiarly adapted to her than concerns of the intellect and the spirit. However, the possession of a little daughter was more precious to her than she had expected, and the consciousness that the tiny doll which lay upon her breast, was flesh of her flesh and bone of her bone affected her agreeably and stirred her imagination. It should be reared, from the start, in the creed of soul independence and expansion, and she herself would find a new and sacred duty in catering to the needs of this budding intelligence. So she reflected as she lay in bed, but the outlook was a little marred by the thought that the baby was the living image of its father—broad-featured and burly—not altogether desirable cast of countenance for a girl. What a pity, when it might just as well have looked like her.

Babcock, on his part, was transported by paternity. He was bubbling over with appreciation of the new baby, and fondly believed it to be a human wonder. He was solicitous on the score of its infantile ailments, and loaded it with gifts and toys beyond the scope of its enjoyment. He went about the house whistling more exuberantly than ever. There was no speck on his horizon; no fly in his pot of ointment. It was he who urged that the child should be christened promptly, though Dr. Glynn was not disposed to dwell on the clerical barbarism as to the destiny of unbaptized infants. Babcock was cultivating a conservative method: He realized that there was no object in taking chances. Illogical as was the theory that a healthy dog which had bitten him should be killed at once, lest it subsequently go mad and he contract hydrophobia, he was too happy and complacent to run the risk of letting it live. So it was with regard to baby. But Selma chose the name. Babcock preferred in this order another Selma, Sophia, after his mother, or a compliment to the wife of the President of the United States. But Selma, as the result of grave thought, selected Muriel Grace. Without knowing exactly why, she asked Mrs. Taylor to be godmother. The ceremony was solemn and inspiring to her. She knew from the glass in her room that she was looking very pretty. But she was weak and emotional. The baby behaved admirably, even when Lewis, trembling with pride, held it out to Mr. Glynn for baptism and held it so that the blood rushed to its head. "I baptize thee in the name of the Father, the Son, and the Holy Ghost." She was happy and the tears were in her eyes. The divine blessing was upon her and her house, and, after all, baby was a darling and her husband a kind, manly soul. With the help of heaven she would prove herself their good angel.

When they returned home there was a whistle of old silver of light, graceful design, a present from Mrs. Taylor to Muriel. Her aunt, Mrs. Farley, compared this to its disparagement with one already purchased by Lewis, on the gaudily embossed stem of which perched a squirrel with a nut in its mouth. But Selma shook her head. "Both of you are wrong," she said with authority. "This is a beauty."

"It doesn't look new to my eyes," protested Mrs. Parley.

"Of course it isn't new. I shouldn't wonder if she bought it while travelling abroad in Europe. It's artistic, and—and I shan't let baby destroy it."

Babcock glanced from one gift to the other quizzically. Then by way of disposing of the subject he seized his daughter in his arms and dandling her toward the ceiling cried, "If it's artistic things we must have, this is the most artistic thing which I know of in the wide world. Aren't you, little sugar-plum?"

Mrs. Farley, with motherly distrust of man, apprehensively followed with her eyes and arms the gyrations of rise and fall; but Selma, though she saw, pursued the current of her own thought which prompted her to examine her wedding-ring. She was thinking that, compared with Mrs. Taylor's, it was a cart wheel—a clumsy, conspicuous band of metal, instead of a delicate hoop. She wondered if Lewis would object to exchange it for another.

With the return of her strength, Selma took up again eagerly the tenor of her former life, aiding and abetting Mrs. Earle in the development of the Institute. The president was absorbed in enlarging its scope by the enrollment of more members, and the establishment of classes in a variety of topics—such as literature, science, philosophy, current events, history, art, and political economy. She aimed to construct a club which should be social and educational in the broadest sense by mutual co-operation and energy. Selma, in her eagerness to make the most of the opportunities for culture offered, committed herself to two of the new topic classes—"Italian and Grecian Art," and "The Governments of Civilization," and as a consequence found some difficulty in accommodating her baby's nursing hours to these engagements. It was indeed a relief to her when the doctor presently pronounced the supply of her breast-milk inadequate. She was able to assuage Lewis' regret that Muriel should be brought up by hand with the information that a large percentage of Benham and American mothers were similarly barren and that bottle babies were exceedingly healthy. She had gleaned the first fact from the physician, the second from Mrs. Earle, and her own conclusion on the subject was that a lack of milk was an indication of feminine evolution from the status of the brute creation, a sign of spiritual as opposed to animal quality. Selma found Mrs. Earle sympathetic on this point, and also practical in her suggestions as to the rearing of infants by artificial means, recommendations concerning which were contained in one of her series of papers entitled "Mother Lore."

The theory of the new classes was co-operation. That is, the members successively, turn by turn, lectured on the topic, and all were expected to study in the interim so as to be able to ask questions and discuss the views of the lecturer. Concerning both Italian and Grecian Art and the Governments of Civilization, Selma knew that she had convictions in the abstract, but when she found herself face to face with a specific lecture on each subject, it occurred to her as wise to supplement her ideas by a little preparation. The nucleus of a public library had been recently established by Joel Flagg and placed at the disposal of Benham. Here, by means of an encyclopædia and two hand-books, Selma was able in three forenoons to compile a paper satisfactory to her self-esteem on the dynasties of Europe and their inferiority to the United States, but her other task was illumined for her by a happy incident, the promise of Littleton to lend her books. Indeed he seemed delightfully interested in both of her classes, which was especially gratifying in view of the fact that Mrs. Taylor, who was a member of the Institute, had combated the new programme on the plea that they were attempting too much and that it would encourage superficiality. But Littleton seemed appreciative of the value of the undertaking, and he made his promise good forthwith by forwarding to her a package of books on art, among them two volumes of Ruskin. Selma, who had read quotations from Ruskin on one or two occasions and believed herself an admirer of, and tolerably familiar with, his writings, was thrilled. She promptly immersed herself in "Stones of Venice" and "Seven Lamps of Architecture," sitting up late at night to finish them. When she had read these and the article in the encyclopædia under the head of Art, she felt bursting with her subject and eager to air her knowledge before the class. Her lecture was acknowledged to be the most stirring and thorough of the course.

Reports of its success came back to her from Littleton, who offered to assist his pupil further by practical demonstration of the eternal architectural fitness and unfitness of things—especially the latter—in walks through the streets of Benham. But six times in as many months, however. There was no suggestion of coquetry on either side in these excursions, yet each enjoyed them. Littleton's own work was beginning to assume definite form, and his visits to Benham became of necessity more frequent; flying trips, but he generally managed to obtain a few words with Selma. He continued to lend her books, and he invited her criticism on the slowly growing church edifice. The responsibility of critic was an absorbing sensation to her, but the stark glibness of tongue which stood her in good stead before the classes of the Institute failed her in his presence—the presence of real knowledge. She wished to praise, but to praise discriminatingly, with the cant of æsthetic appreciation, so that he should believe that she knew. As for the church itself, she was interested in it; it was fine, of course, but that was a secondary consideration compared with her emotions. His predilection in her favor, however, readily made him deaf in regard to her utterances. He scarcely heeded her halting, solemn, counterfeit transcendentalisms; or rather they passed muster as subtle and genuine, so spell bound was he by the Delphic beauty of her criticising expression. It was enough for him to watch her as she stood with her head on one side and the worried archangel look transfiguring her profile. What she said was lost in his reverie as to what she was—what she represented in his contemplation. As she looked upon his handiwork he was able to view it with different eyes, to discern its weaknesses and to gain fresh inspiration from her presence. He felt that it was growing on his hands and that he should be proud of it, and though, perhaps, he was conscious in his inner soul that she was more to him than another man's wife should be, he knew too, that no word or look of his had offended against the absent husband.

CHAPTER VI.

By the end of another six months Littleton's work was practically completed. Only the finishing touches to the interior decoration remained to be done. The members of Rev. Mr. Glynn's congregation, including Mrs. Hallett Taylor, were thoroughly satisfied with the appearance of the new church. It was attractive in its lines, yet it was simple and, consequently, in keeping with the resources of the treasury. There was no large bill for extras to be audited, as possibly would have been the case had a hard-headed designer like Mr. Pierce been employed. The committee felt itself entitled to the congratulations of the community. Nor was the community on the whole disposed to grumble, for home talent had been employed by the architect; under rigorous supervision, to be sure, so that poor material and slap-dash workmanship were out of the question. Still, payments had been prompt, and Benham was able to admire competent virtue. The church was a monument of suggestion in various ways, artistic and ethical, and it shone neatly with Babcock varnish.

One morning Selma set forth by agreement with Littleton, in order to inspect some fresco work. Muriel Grace was ailing slightly, but as she would be home by mid-day, she bade the hired girl be watchful of baby, and kept her appointment. The child had grown dear to her, for Muriel was a charming little dot, and Selma had already begun to enjoy the maternal delight of human doll dressing, an extravagance in which she was lavishly encouraged by her husband. Babcock was glad of any excuse to spend money on his daughter, who seemed to him, from day to day, a greater marvel of precocity—such a child as became Selma's beauty and cleverness and his own practical common-sense.

Selma was in a pensive frame of mind this morning. Two days before she had read a paper at the Institute on "Motherhood," which had been enthusiastically received. Mrs. Earle had printed a flattering item concerning it in the *Benham Sentinel*. It was agreeable to her to be going to meet Littleton, for he was the most interesting masculine figure in her life. She was sure of Lewis. He was her husband and she knew herself to be the apple of his eye; but she knew exactly what he was going to say before he said it, and much of what he said grated on her. She was almost equally sure of Littleton; that is of his admiration. His companionship was a constant pleasure to her. As a married woman, and as a Christian and American woman, she desired no more than this. But on the other hand, she would fain have this admiring companionship continue; and yet it could not. Littleton had told her the day before that he was going back to New York and that it was doubtful if he would return. She would miss him. She would have the Institute and Mrs. Earle still, but her life would be less full.

Littleton was waiting for her at the church entrance. She followed him down the nave to the chancel where she listened dreamily to his presentation of the merits of the new decoration. He seemed inclined to talk, and from this presently branched off to describe with enthusiasm the plates of a French book on interior architecture, which he had recently bought as a long-resisted but triumphant piece of extravagance. Mechanically, they turned from the chancel and slowly made the round of the aisles. A short silence succeeded his professional ardor. His current of thought, in its reversion to home matters, had reminded him afresh of what was perpetually this morning uppermost in his consciousness—his coming departure.

"Now," he said, abruptly, "is the most favorable opportunity I shall have, Mrs. Babcock, to tell you how much I am your debtor. I shan't despair of our meeting again, for the world is small, and good friends are sure to meet sooner or later. But the past is secure to me at any rate. If this church is in some measure what I have dreamed and wished it to be, if my work with all its faults is a satisfaction to myself, I wish you to know how much you have contributed to make it what it is."

The words were as a melody in Selma's ears, and she listened greedily. Littleton paused, as one seriously moved will pause before giving the details of an important announcement. She, thinking he had finished, interjected with a touch of modesty, "I'm so glad. But my suggestions and criticisms have not been what I meant them to be. It was all new to me, you know."

"Oh, yes. It hasn't been so much what you have said in words which has helped me, though that has been always intelligent and uplifting. I did not look for technical knowledge. You do not possess that, of course. There are women in New York who would be able to confuse you with their familiarity with these things. And yet it is by way of contrast with those very women—fine women, too, in their way—that you have been my good angel. There is no harm in saying that. I should be an ingrate, surely, if I would not let you know that your sane, simple outlook upon life, your independent vision, has kept my brain clear and my soul free. I am a better artist and a better man for the experience. Good-by, and may all happiness attend you. If once in a while you should find time to write to a struggling architect named Littleton, he will be charmed to do your bidding—to send you books and to place his professional knowledge at your service. Good-by."

He held out his hand with frank effusion. He was obviously happy at having given utterance to his sense of obligation. Selma was tingling from head to foot and a womanly blush was on her cheek, though the serious seraph spoke in her words and eyes. She felt moved to a wave of unreserved speech.

"What you have said is very interesting to me. I wish to tell you how much I, too, have enjoyed our friendship. The first time we met I felt sure we should be sympathetic, and we have been, haven't we? One of the fine things about friendships between men and women in this country is that they can really get to know each other without—er—harm to either. Isn't it? It's such a pleasure to know people really, and I feel as if I had known you, as if we had known each other really. I've never known any man exactly in that way, and I have always wanted to. Except, of course, my husband. And he's extremely different—that is, his tastes are not like yours. It's a happiness to me to feel that I have been of assistance to you in your work, and you have been equally helpful to me in mine. As you say, I have never had the opportunity to learn the technical parts of art, and your books have instructed me as to that. I have never been in New York, but I understand what you meant about your friends, those other women. I suppose society people must be constantly diverted from serious work—from the intellectual and spiritual life. Oh yes, we ought to write. Our friendship mustn't languish. We must let each other know what we are thinking and doing. Good-by."

As Selma walked along the street her heart was in her mouth. She felt pity for herself. To just the right person she would have confessed the discovery that she had made a mistake and tied herself for life to the wrong man. It was not so much that she fancied Littleton which distressed her, for, indeed, she was but mildly conscious of infatuation. What disturbed her was the contrast between him and Babcock, which definite separation now forced upon her attention. An indefinable impression that Littleton might think less of her if she were to state this soul truth had restrained her at the last moment from disclosing the secret. Not for an instant did she entertain the idea of being false to Lewis. Her confession would have been but a dissertation on the inexorable irony of fate, calling only for sympathy, and in no way derogating from her dignity and self-respect as a wife. Still, she had restrained herself, and stopped just short of the confidence. He was gone, and she would probably not see him again for years. That was endurable. Indeed, a recognition of the contrary would not have seemed to her consistent with wifely virtue. What brought the tears to her eyes was the vision of continued wedlock, until death intervened, with a husband who could not understand. Could she bear this? Must she endure it? There was but one answer: She must. At the thought she bit her lip with the intensity and sternness of a martyr. She would be faithful to her marriage vows, but she would not let Lewis's low aims interfere with the free development of her own life.

It was after noon when she reached home. She was met at the door by the hired girl with the worried ejaculation that baby was choking. The doctor was hastily summoned. He at once pronounced that Muriel Grace had membranous croup, and was desperately ill. Remedies of various sorts were tried, and a consulting physician called, but when Babcock returned from his office her condition was evidently hopeless. The child died in the early night. Selma was relieved to hear the doctor tell her husband that it was a malignant case from the first, and that nothing could have averted the result. In response to questions from Lewis, however, she was obliged to admit that she had not been at home when the acute symptoms appeared. This afforded Babcock an outlet for his suffering. He spoke to her roughly for the first time in his life, bitterly suggesting neglect on her part.

"You knew she wasn't all right this morning, yet you had to go fiddle-faddling with that architect instead of staying at home where you belonged. And now she's dead. My little girl, my little girl!" And the big man burst out sobbing.

Selma grew deadly pale. No one had ever spoken to her like that before in her life. To the horror of her grief was added the consciousness that she was being unjustly dealt with. Lewis had heard the doctor's statement, and yet he dared address her in such terms. As if the loss of the child did not fall equally on her.

"If it were to be done over again, I should do just the same," she answered, with righteous quietness. "To all appearances she had nothing but a little cold. You have no right to lay the blame on me, her mother." At the last word she looked ready to cry, too.

Babcock regarded her like a miserable tame bull. "I didn't mean to," he blubbered. "She's taken away from me, and I'm so wretched that I don't know what I'm saying. I'm sorry, Selma."

He held out his arms to her. She was ready to go to them, for the angel of death had entered her home and pierced her heart, where it should be most tender. She loved her baby. Yet, when she had time to think, she was not sure that she wished to have another. When the bitterness of his grief had passed away, that was the hope which Lewis ventured to express, at first in a whisper, and later with reiterated boldness. Selma acquiesced externally, but she had her own opinions. Certain things which were not included in "Mother Lore," had been confided by Mrs. Margaret Rodney Earle by word of mouth in the fulness of their mutual soul-scourings, and had remained pigeon-holed for future reference in Selma's inner consciousness. Another baby just at this time meant interference with everything elevating. There was time enough. In a year or two, when she had established herself more securely in the social sphere of Benham, she would present her husband with a second child. It was best for them both to wait, for her success was his success; but it would be useless to try to make that clear to him in his present mood.

So she put away her baby things, dropping tears over the little socks and other reminders of her sorrow, and took up her life again, keeping her own counsel. The sympathy offered her was an interesting experience. Mrs. Earle came to her at once, and took her to her bosom; Mrs. Taylor sent her flowers with a kind note, which set Selma thinking whether she ought not to buy mourning note-paper; and within a week she received a visit of condolence from Mr. Glynn, rather a ghastly visit. Ghastly, because Lewis sat through it all with red eyes, very much as though he were listening to a touching exhortation in church. To be sure, he gripped the pastor's hand like a vice, at the end, and thanked him for coming, but his silent, afflicted presence had interfered with the free interchange of thought which would have been possible had she been alone with the clergyman. The subject of death, and the whole train of reflections incident to it, were uppermost in her mind, and she would have been glad to probe the mysteries of the subject by controversial argument, instead of listening to hearty, sonorous platitudes. She listened rather contemptuously, for she recognized that Mr. Glynn was saying the stereotyped thing in the stereotyped way, without realizing that it was nothing but sacerdotal pap, little adapted to an intelligent soul. What was suited to Lewis was not fit for her. And yet her baby's death had served to dissipate somewhat the immediate discontent which she felt with her husband. His strong grief had touched her in spite of herself, and, though she blamed him still for his inconsiderate accusation, she was fond of him as she might have been fond of some loving Newfoundland, which, splendid in awkward bulk, caressed her and licked her hand. It was pleasant enough to be in his arms, for the touch of man—even the wrong man—was, at times, a comfort.

She took up again with determined interest her relations to the Institute, joining additional classes and pursuing a variety of topics of study, in regard to some of which she consulted Littleton. She missed his presence less than she had expected, especially after they had begun to correspond and were able to keep in touch by letter. His letters were delightful. They served her in her lecture courses, for they so clearly and concisely expressed her views that she was able to use long extracts from them word for word. And every now and then they contained a respectful allusion which showed that he still retained a personal interest in her. So the weeks slipped away and she was reasonably happy. She was absorbed and there was nothing new to mar the tenor of her life, though she was vaguely conscious that the loss of their little girl had widened the breach between her and her husband—widened it for the reason that now, for the first time, he perceived how lonely he was. The baby had furnished him with constant delight and preoccupation. He had looked forward all day to seeing it at night, and questions relating to it had supplied a never-ceasing small change of conversation between him and her. He had let her go her way with a smile on his face. Selma did not choose to dwell on the situation, but it was obvious that Lewis continued to look glum, and that there were apt to be long silences between them at meals. Now and again he would show some impatience at the continuous recurrence of the Institute classes as a bar to some project of domesticity or recreation, as though she had not been an active member of the Institute before baby was born.

One of the plans in which Mrs. Earle was most interested was a Congress of Women's Clubs, and in the early summer of the same year—some four months subsequent to the death of Muriel Grace—a small beginning toward this end was arranged to take place in Chicago. There were to be six delegates from each club, and Selma was unanimously selected as one of the delegation from the Benham Women's Institute. The opinion was generally expressed that a change would do her good, and there was no question that she was admirably fitted to represent the club. Selma, who had not travelled a hundred miles beyond Benham in her life, was elated at the prospect of the expedition; so much so that she proudly recounted to Lewis the same evening the news of her appointment. It never occurred to her that he would wish to accompany her, and when he presently informed her that he had been wishing to go to Chicago on business for some time, and that the date proposed would suit him admirably, she was dumfounded. Half of the interest of the expedition would consist in travelling as an independent delegation. A husband would be in the way and spoil the savor of the occasion. It would never do, and so Selma proceeded to explain. She wished to go alone.

"A pack of six women travel by themselves?" blurted Lewis. "Suppose there were an accident?" he added, after searching his brain for a less feeble argument.

"We should either be killed or we shouldn't be," said Selma firmly. "We are perfectly well able to take care of ourselves. Women travel alone everywhere every-day—that is, intelligent American women."

Lewis looked a little sad. "I thought, perhaps, it would seem nice for you to go with me, Selma. We haven't been off since we were married, and I can get away now just as well as not."

"So it would have been if I weren't one of the delegation. I should think you would see, Lewis, that your coming is out of the question."

So it proved. Selma set forth for Chicago on the appointed

day, made many new acquaintances among the delegates, and was pleased to be introduced and referred to publicly as Mrs. Selma Babcock—a form of address to which she was unaccustomed at Benham. On the night before her departure, being in pleasant spirits, she told Lewis that her absence would do him good, and that he would appreciate her all the more on her return.

She was to be gone a week. The first twenty-four hours passed gloomily for Babcock. Then he began to take notice. He noticed that the county fair was fixed for the following days. He had hoped to carry Selma there, but, as she was not to be had, it seemed to him sensible to get what enjoyment from it he could alone. Then it happened that a former companion of his bachelor days and his bachelor habits, a commercial traveller, whom he had not seen since his marriage, appeared on the scene.

"The very man for me!" he ejaculated, jubilantly.

The obscurity of this remark was presently made clear to his friend, who had hoped perhaps to enjoy a snug evening at Babcock's domestic hearth, but who was not averse to playing a different part—that of cheering up a father who had lost his baby, and whose wife had left him in the lurch. He assured Babcock that a regular old time outing—a shaking up—would do him good, and Babcock was ready to agree with him, intending thereby a free-handed two days at the fair. As has been intimated, his manner of life before marriage had not been irreproachable, but he had been glad of an opportunity to put an end to the mildly riotous and coarse bouts which disfigured his otherwise commonplace existence. He had no intention now of misbehaving himself, but he felt the need of being enlivened. His companion was a man who delighted in what he called a lark, and whose only method of insuring a lark was by starting in with whiskey and keeping it up. That had been also Babcock's former conception of a good time, and though he had dimly in mind that he was now a husband and church-member, he strove to conduct himself in such a manner as to maintain his self-respect without becoming a spoil sport.

During the first day at the fair Babcock managed to preserve this nice distinction. On the second, he lost account of his conduct, and by the late afternoon was sauntering with his friend among the booths in the company of two suspicions looking women. With these same women the pair of revellers drove off in top buggies just before dusk, and vanished in the direction of the open country.

CHAPTER VII.

Babcock returned to his home twenty-four hours later like a whipped cur. He was disgusted with himself. It seemed to him incredible that he should have fallen so low. He had sinned against his wife and his own self-respect without excuse; for it was no excuse that he had let himself be led to drink too much. His heart ached and his cheek burned at the recollection of his two days of debauchery. What was to be done? If only he were able to cut this ugly sore in his soul out with a knife and have done with it forever! But that was impossible. It stared him in the face, a haunting reality. In his distress he asked himself whether he would not go to Mr. Glynn and make a clean breast of it; but his practical instincts answered him that he would none the less have made a beast of himself. He held his head between his hands, and stared dejectedly at his desk. Some relief came to him at last only from the reflection that it was a single fault, and that it need never—it should never be repeated. Selma need not know, and he would henceforth avoid all such temptations. Terrible as it was, it was a slip, not a deliberate fault, and his love for his wife was not in question.

Thus reasoning, he managed by the third day after his return to reach a less despondent frame of mind. While busy writing in his office a lady was announced, and looking up he encountered the meretricious smile of the courtesan with whom he had forgotten himself. She had taken a fancy to her victim, and having learned that he was well to do, she had come in order to establish, if possible, on a more permanent basis, her relations with him. She was a young woman, who had been drifting from place to place, and whose professional inclination for a protector was heightened by the liking which she had conceived for him. Babcock recalled in her smile merely his shame, and regarded her reappearance as effrontery. He was blind to her prettiness and her sentimental mood. He asked her roughly what she wanted, and rising from his chair, he bade her be gone before she had time to answer. Nine out of ten women of her class would have taken their dismissal lightly. Some might have answered back in tones loud enough to enlighten the clerks, and thus have accomplished a pretty revenge in the course of retreat. This particular Lesbian was in no humor to be harshly treated. She was a little desperate and Babcock had pleased her. It piqued her to be treated in such a fashion; accordingly, she held her ground and sat down. She tried upon him, alternately, irony and pathos. He was angry but confused under the first, he became savage and merciless under the second, throwing back in her teeth the suggestion of her fondness, and stigmatizing her coarsely. Then she became angry in her turn—angry as a woman whose proffered love is spurned. The method for revenge was obvious, and she told him plainly what she intended. His wife should know at once how her husband passed his time during her absence. She had posted herself, and she saw that her shaft hurt. Babcock winced, but mad and incredulous, he threatened her with arrest and drove her from the room. She went out smiling, but with an ominous look in her eyes, the remembrance of which made him ask himself now and again if she could be vicious enough, or fool enough, to keep her promise. He dismissed the idea as improbable; still the bare chance worried him. Selma was to arrive early the next morning, and he had reconciled himself to the conclusion that she need never know, and that he would henceforth be a faithful husband. Had he not given an earnest of his good faith in his reception of his visitor? Surely, no such untoward and unnatural accident would dash the cup of returning happiness from his lips. A more clever man would have gone straight to police headquarters, instead of trusting to chance.

A night's rest reassured him as to the idleness of the threat, so that he was able to welcome Selma at the railroad station with a comparatively light heart. She was in high spirits over the success of her expedition, and yet graciously ready to admit that she was glad to return home—meaning thereby, to her own bed and bathing facilities; but the general term seemed to poor Lewis a declaration of wifely devotion. He went to his business with the mien of a man who had passed through an ordeal and is beginning life again; but when he returned at night, as soon as he beheld Selma, he suspected what had happened.

She was awaiting him in the parlor. Though he saw at a glance that she looked grave, he went forward to kiss her, but she rose and, stepping behind the table, put out her hand forbiddingly.

"What is the matter?" he faltered.

"That woman has been here," was her slow, scornful response.

"Selma, I—" A confusing sense of hopelessness as to what to say choked Babcock's attempt to articulate. There was a brief silence, while he looked at her imploringly and miserably.

"Is it true what she says? Have you been false to your marriage vows? Have you committed adultery?"

"My God! Selma, you don't understand."

"It is an easy question to answer, yes or no?"

"I forgot myself, Selma. I was drunk and crazy. I ask your pardon."

She shook her head coldly. "I shall have nothing more to do with you. I cannot live with you any longer."

"Not live with me?"

"Would you live with me if it were I who had forgotten myself?"

"I think I would, Selma. You don't understand. I was a brute. I have been wretched ever since. But it was a slip—an accident. I drank too much, and it happened. I love you, Selma, with all my heart. I have never been false to you in my affection."

"It is a strange time to talk of affection. I went away for a week, and in my absence you insulted me by debauchery with a creature like that. Love? You have no conception of the meaning of the word. Oh no, I shall never live with you again."

Babcock clinched his palms in his distress and walked up and down. She stood pale and determined looking into space. Presently he turned to her and asked with quiet but intense solicitude, "You don't mean that you're going to leave me for one fault, we being husband and wife and the little girl in her grave? I said you don't understand and you don't. A man's a man, and there are times when he's been drinking when he's liable to yield to temptation, and that though he's so fond of his wife that life without her would be misery. This sounds strange to a woman, and it's a poor excuse. But it ought to count, Selma, when it comes to a question of our separating. There would be happy years before us yet if you give me another chance."

"Not happy years for me," she replied concisely. "The American woman does not choose to live with the sort of man you describe. She demands from her husband what he demands from her, faithfulness to the marriage tie. We could never be happy again. Our ideal of life is different. I have made excuses for you in other things, but my soul revolts at this."

Babcock looked at her for a moment in silence, then he said, a little sternly, "You shouldn't have gone away and left me. I'm not blaming you, but you shouldn't have gone." He walked to the window but he saw nothing. His heart was racked. He had been eager to humiliate himself before her to prove his deep contrition, but he had come to the end of his resources, and yet she was adamant. Her charge that she had been making excuses for him hitherto reminded him that they had not been really sympathetic for some time past. With his back turned to her he heard her answer:

"It was understood before I agreed to marry you that I was to be free to follow my tastes and interests. It is a paltry excuse that, because I left you alone for a week in pursuit of them, I am accessory to your sin."

Babcock faced her sadly. "The sin's all mine," he said. "I can't deny that. But, Selma, I guess I've been pretty lonely ever since the baby died."

"Lonely?" she echoed. "Then my leaving you will not matter so much. Here," she said, slipping off her wedding-ring, "this belongs to you." She remembered Mrs. Earle's proceeding, and though she had not yet decided what course to pursue in order to maintain her liberty, she regarded this as the significant and definite act. She held out the ring, but Babcock shook his head.

"The law doesn't work as quick as that, nor the church either. You can get a divorce if you're set on it, Selma. But we're husband and wife yet."

"Only the husk of our marriage is left. The spirit is dead," she said sententiously. "I am going away. I cannot pass another night in this house. If you will not take this ring, I shall leave it here."

Babcock turned to hide the tears which blinded his eyes. Selma regarded him a moment gravely, then she laid her wedding-ring on the table and went from the room.

She put her immediate belongings into a bag and left the house. She had decided to go to Mrs. Earle's lodgings where she would be certain to find shelter and sympathy. Were she to go to her aunt's she would be exposed to importunity on her husband's behalf from Mrs. Farley, who was partial to Lewis. Her mind was entirely made up that there could be no question of reconciliation. Her duty was plain; and she would be doing herself an injustice were she to continue to live with one so weak and regardless of the honor which she had a right to demand of the man to whom she had given her society and her body. His gross conduct had entitled her to her liberty, and to neglect to seize it would be to condemn herself to continuous unhappiness, for this overt act of his was merely a definite proof of the lack of sympathy between them, of which she had for some time been well aware at heart. As she walked along the street she was conscious that it was a relief to her to be sloughing off the garment of an uncongenial relationship and to be starting life afresh. There was nothing in her immediate surroundings from which she was not glad to escape. Their house was full of blemishes from the stand-point of her later knowledge, and she yearned to dissociate herself, once and for all, from the trammels of her pitiful mistake. She barely entertained the thought that she was without means. She would have to support herself, of course, but it never occurred to her to doubt her ability to do so, and the necessity added a zest to her decision. It would be plain sailing, for Mrs. Earle had more than once invited her to send copy to the *Benham Sentinel*, and there was no form of occupation which would be more to her liking than newspaper work. It was almost with the mien of a prisoner escaped from jail that she walked in upon her friend and said:

"I have left my husband. He has been unfaithful to me."

In Mrs. Earle, conventional feminine instincts were apt, before she had time to think, to get the upper hand of her set theories. "You, poor, poor child," she cried extending her arms.

Selma had not intended to weep. Still the opportunity was convenient, and her nerves were on edge. She found herself sobbing with her head on Mrs. Earle's, bosom, and telling her sad story.

"He was never good enough for you. I have always said so," Mrs. Earle murmured stroking her hair.

"I ought to have known from the first that it was impossible for us to be happy. Why did I ever marry him? He said he loved me, and I let myself be badgered into it," Selma answered through her tears. "Well, it's all over now," she added, sitting up and drying her eyes. "He has given me back my liberty. I am a free woman."

"Yes, dear, if you are perfectly sure of yourself, there is only one course to pursue. Only you should consider the matter solemnly. Perhaps in a few days, after he has apologized and shown proper contrition, you might feel willing to give him another chance."

Selma was unprepared for Mrs. Earle's sentimentality. "Surely," she exclaimed with tragic earnestness, "you wouldn't have me live with him after what occurred? Contrition? He said everything he could think of to get me to stay, but I made my decision then and there."

Mrs. Earle put her own handkerchief to her eyes. "Women have forgiven such things; but I respect you all the more for not being weak. I know how you feel. It is hard to do, but if I had it to do over again, I would act just the same—just the same. It's a serious responsibility to encourage any one to desert a home, but under the circumstances I would not live with him another minute, my child—not another minute." Thereupon Mrs. Earle protruded her bosom to celebrate the triumph of justice in her own mental processes over conventional and maudlin scruples. "You will apply for a divorce, I suppose?"

"I have not considered that. All I care for is never to see him again."

"Oh yes, you must get a divorce. It is much better, you know. In my case I couldn't, for he did nothing public. A divorce settles matters, and puts you back where you were before. You might wish some day to marry again."

"I have had enough of marriage."

"It isn't any harm to be a free woman—free in the eye of the law as well as of conscience. I know an excellent lawyer—a Mr. Lyons, a sympathetic and able man. Besides your husband is bound to support you. You must get alimony."

"I wouldn't touch a dollar of his money," Selma answered with scorn. "I intend to support myself. I shall write—work."

"Of course you will, dear; and it will be a boon and a blessing to me to have you in our ranks—one of the new army of self-supporting, self-respecting women. I suppose you are right. I have never had a sixpence. But your husband deserves to be punished. Perhaps it is punishment enough to lose you."

"He will get over that. It is enough for me," she exclaimed, ardently, after a dreamy pause, "that I am separated from him forever—that I am free—free—free."

A night's sleep served to intensify Selma's determination, and she awoke clearly of the opinion that a divorce was desirable.

Why remain fettered by a bare legal tie to one who was a husband only in name? Accordingly, in company with Mrs. Earle, she visited the office of James O. Lyons, and took the initiatory steps to dissolve the marriage.

Mr. Lyons was a large, full-bodied man of thirty-five, with a fat, cleanly-shaven, cherubic countenance, an aspect of candor, and keen, solemn eyes. His manner was impressive and slightly pontifical; his voice resonant and engaging. He knew when to joke and when to be grave as an owl. He wore in every-day life a shiny, black frock-coat, a standing collar, which yawned at the throat, and a narrow, black tie. His general effect was that of a cross between a parson and a shrewd Yankee—a happy suggestion of righteous, plain, serious-mindedness, protected against the wiles of human society—and able to protect others—by a canny intelligence. For a young man he had already a considerable clientage. A certain class of people, notably the hard-headed, God-fearing, felt themselves safe in his hands. His magnetic yet grave manner of conducting business pleased Benham, attracting also both the distressed and the bilious portions of the community, and the farmers from the surrounding country. As Mrs. Earle informed Selma, he was in sympathy with all progressive and stimulating ideas, and he already figured in the newspapers politically, and before the courts as a friend of the masses, and a fluent advocate of social reforms. His method of handling Selma's case was smooth. To begin with, he was sympathetic within proper limits, giving her tacitly to understand that, though as a man and brother, he deplored the necessity of extreme measures, he recognized that she had made up her mind, and that compromise was out of the question. To put it concisely, his manner was grieved, but practical. He told her that he would represent to Babcock the futility of contesting a cause, which, on the evidence, must be hopeless, and that, in all probability, the matter could be disposed of easily and without publicity. He seemed to Selma a very sensible and capable man, and it was agreeable to her to feel that he appreciated that, though divorce in the abstract was deplorable, her experience justified and called for the protection of the law.

In the meantime Babcock was very unhappy, and was casting about for a method to induce his wife to return. He wrote to her a pitiful letter, setting forth once more the sorry facts in the best light which he could bring to bear on them, and implored her forgiveness. He applied to her aunt, Mrs. Farley, and got her to supplement his plea with her good-natured intervention. "There are lots of men like that," she confided to Selma, "and he's a kind, devoted creature." When this failed, he sought Rev. Mr. Glynn as a last resort, and, after he had listened to a stern and fervid rating from the clergyman on the lust of the flesh, he found his pastor on his side. Mr. Glynn was opposed to divorce on general ecclesiastical principles; moreover, he had been educated under the law of England, by which a woman cannot obtain a divorce from her husband for the cause of adultery unless it be coupled with cruelty—a clever distinction between the sexes, which was doubtless intended as a cloak for occasional lapses on the part of man. It was plain to him, as a Christian and as a hearty soul, that there had been an untoward accident—a bestial fault, a soul-debasing carnal sin, but still an accident, and hence to be forgiven by God and woman. It was his duty to interfere; and so, having disciplined the husband, he essayed the more delicate matter of propitiating the wife. And he essayed it without a thought of failure.

"I'm afraid she's determined to leave me, and that there's not much hope," said Babcock, despondently, as he gripped the clergyman's hand in token of his gratitude.

"Nonsense, my man," asserted Mr. Glynn briskly. "All she needs is an exhortation from me, and she will take you back."

Selma was opposed to divorce in theory. That is, she had accepted on trust the traditional prejudice against it as she had accepted Shakespeare and Boston. But theory stood for nothing in her regard before the crying needs of her own experience. She had not the least intention of living with her husband again. No one could oblige her to do that. In addition, the law offered her a formal escape from his control and name. Why not avail herself of it? She recollected, besides, that her husband's church recognized infidelity as a lawful ground of release from the so-called sacrament of marriage. This had come into her mind as an additional sanction to her own decision. But it had not contributed to that decision. Consequently, when she was confronted in Mrs. Earle's lodgings by the errand of Mr. Glynn, she felt that his coming was superfluous. Still, she was glad of the opportunity to measure ideas with him in a thorough interview free from interruption.

68

Mr. Glynn's confidence was based on his intention to appeal to the ever womanly quality of pity. He expected to encounter some resistance, for indisputably here was a woman whose sensibilities had been justly and severely shocked—a woman of finer tissue than her husband, as he had noted in other American couples. She was entitled to her day in court—to a stubborn, righteous respite of indignation. But he expected to carry the day in the end, amid a rush of tears, with which his own might be mingled. He trusted to what he regarded as the innate reluctance of the wife to abandon the man she loved, and to the leaven of feminine Christian charity.

As a conscientious hater of sin, he did not attempt to minimize Babcock's act or the insult put upon her. That done, he was free to intercede fervently for him and to extol the virtue and the advisability of forgiveness. This plea, however cogent, was narrow, and once stated admitted merely of duplication in the same form. It was indeed no argument, merely an appeal, and, in proportion as it failed to move the listener, became feeble. Selma listened to him with a tense face, her hands clasped before her in the guise of an interested and self-scrutinizing spirit. But she betrayed no sign of yielding, or symptom of doubt. She shook her head once or twice as he proceeded, and, when he paused, asked why she should return to a man who had broken faith with her; asked it in such a genuine tone of conviction that Dr. Glynn realized the weakness of his own case, and became slightly nettled at the same time.

"True," he said, rather sternly, "your husband has committed a hideous, carnal sin, but he is genuinely repentant. Do you wish to ruin his life forever?"

"His life?" said Selma. "It would ruin my life to return to him. I have other plans—plans which will bring me happiness. I could never be happy with him."

The clergyman was baffled. Other plans! The words offended him, and yet he could not dispute her right to do as she chose. Still he saw fit to murmur: "He that findeth his life shall lose it, and he that loseth his life for my sake shall find it."

Selma flushed. To be accused of acting contrary to Christian precepts was painful and surprising to her. "Mr. Glynn," she said, "I see you don't understand. My husband and I ought never to have married. It has all been a dreadful mistake. We have not the same tastes and interests. I am sorry for him, but I can never consent to return to him. To do so would condemn us both to a life of unhappiness. We were not intended for husband and wife, and it is best—yes, more Christian—for us to separate. We American women do not feel justified in letting a mistake ruin our lives when there is a chance to escape."

Mr. Glynn regarded her in silence for a moment. He was accustomed to convince, and he had not succeeded, which to a clergyman is more annoying than to most men. Still what she said made his plea seem doubtful wisdom.

"Then you do not love your husband?" he said.

"No," said Selma quietly, "I do not love him. It is best to be frank with one's self—with you, in such a matter, isn't it? So you see that what you ask is out of the question."

Mr. Glynn rose. Clearly his mission had failed, and there was nothing more to be said. Being a just man, he hesitated to pass an unkind judgment on this bright-faced, pensive woman. She was within her moral rights, and he must be careful to keep within his. But he went away bewildered and discomfited. Selma would have liked to dismiss the subject and keep him longer. She would have been glad to branch off on to other ethical topics and discuss them. She was satisfied with the result of the interview, for she had vindicated her position and spiked Lewis's last gun.

So, indeed, it proved. Mr. Glynn sent for Babcock and told him the naked truth, that his wife's love for him was dead and reconciliation impossible. He properly refrained from expressing the doubt lurking in his own mind as to whether Selma had ever loved her husband. Thus convinced of the hopelessness of his predicament, Babcock agreed to Mr. Lyons's suggestion not to contest the legal proceedings. The lawyer had been diligent, and the necessary evidence—the testimony of the woman—was secure. She was ready to carry her revenge to the end, hoping, perhaps, that the victim of it would return to her when he had lost his wife. Accordingly, a few weeks later, Selma was granted a divorce nisi and the right to resume her maiden name. She had decided, however, to retain the badge of marriage as a decorous social prefix, and to call herself Mrs. Selma White.

CHAPTER VIII.

The consciousness that she was dependent for the means of support solely on her own exertions was a genuine pleasure to Selma, and she applied herself with confidence and enthusiasm to the problem of earning her livelihood. She had remained steadfast to her decision to accept nothing from her husband except the legal costs of the proceedings, though Mr. Lyons explained to her that alimony was a natural and moral increment of divorce. Still, after her refusal, he informed her as a man and a friend that he respected and admired the independence of her action, which was an agreeable tribute. She had fixed definitely on newspaper work as the most inviting and congenial form of occupation. She believed herself to be well fitted for it. It would afford her an immediate income, and it would give her the opportunity which she craved for giving public expression to her ideas and fixing attention on herself. There was room for more than one Mrs. Earle in Benham, for Benham was growing and wide-awake and on the alert for originality of any kind—especially in the way of reportorial and journalistic cleverness. Selma had no intention of becoming a second Mrs. Earle. That is, she promised herself to follow, but not to follow blindly; to imitate judiciously, but to improve on a gradually diverging line of progress. This was mere generalization as yet. It was an agreeable seething brain consciousness for future development. For the moment, however, she counted on Mrs. Earle to obtain for her a start by personal influence at the office of the *Benham Sentinel.* This was provided forthwith in the form of an invitation to prepare a weekly column under the caption of "What Women Wear;" a summary of passing usages in clothes. The woman reporter in charge of it had just died. Selma's first impulse was to decline the work as unworthy of her abilities, yet she was in immediate need of employment to avoid running in debt and she was assured by Mrs. Earle that she would be very foolish to reject such an offer. Reflection caused her to think more highly of the work itself. It would afford her a chance to explain to the women of Benham, and indirectly to the country at large, that taste in dress was not necessarily inconsistent with virtue and serious intentions—a truth of which she herself had become possessed since her marriage and which it seemed to her might be utilized delightfully in her department. She would endeavor to treat dress from the standpoint of ethical responsibility to society, and to show that both extravagance and dowdy homeliness were to be avoided. Clothes in themselves had grown to be a satisfaction to her, and any association of vanity would be eliminated by the introduction of a serious artistic purpose into a weekly commentary concerning them. Accordingly she accepted the position and entered upon its duties with grave zeal.

For each of these contributions Selma was to receive eight dollars—four hundred a year, which she hoped to expand to a thousand by creative literary production—preferably essays and poetry. She hired a room in the same neighborhood as Mrs. Earle, in the boarding-house district appurtenant to Central Avenue—that is to say, on the ragged edge of Benham's social artery, and set up her new household gods. The interest of preparing the first paper absorbed her to the exclusion of everything else. She visited all the dress-making and dry-goods establishments in town, examined, at a hint from Mrs. Earle, the fashion departments of the New York papers, and then, pen in hand, gave herself up to her subject. The result seemed to her a happy blending of timely philosophy and suggestions as to toilette, and she took it in person to the editor. He saw fit to read it on the spot. His brow wrinkled at first and he looked dubious. He re-read it and said with some gusto, "It's a novelty, but I guess they'll like it. Our women readers have been used to fashion notes which are crisp and to the point, and the big houses expect to have attention called to the goods they wish to sell. If you'll run over this again and set your cold facts in little paragraphs by themselves every now and then, I shouldn't wonder if the rest were a sort of lecture course which will catch them. It's a good idea. Next time you could work in a pathetic story—some references to a dead baby—verses—anecdotes—a little variety. You perceive the idea?"

"Oh, yes," said Selma, appropriately sober at the allusion yet ecstatic. "That's just what I should like to do. It would give me more scope. I wish my articles to be of real use—to help people to live better, and to dress better."

"That's right, that's right; and if they make the paper sell, we'll know that folks like them," responded the editor with Delphic urbanity.

The first article was a success. That is, Selma's method was not interfered with, and she had the satisfaction of reading in the

Sentinel during the week an item calling gratified attention to the change in its "What Women Wear" column, and indicating that it would contain new features from week to week. It gave her a pleasant thrill to see her name, "Selma White," signed at the end of the printed column, and she set to work eagerly to carry out the editor's suggestions. At the same time she tried her hand at a short story—the story of an American girl who went to Paris to study art, refused to alter her mode of life to suit foreign ideas of female propriety, displayed exceptional talent as an artist, and finally married a fine-spirited young American, to the utter discomfiture of a French member of the nobility, who had begun by insulting her and ended with making her an offer of marriage. This she sent to the *Eagle*, the other Benham newspaper, for its Sunday edition.

It took her a month to compose this story, and after a week she received it back with a memorandum to the effect that it was one-half too long, but intimating that in a revised form it would be acceptable. This was a little depressing, especially as it arrived at a time when the novelty of her occupation had worn off and she was realizing the limitations of her present life. She had begun to miss the advantages of a free purse and the importance of a domestic establishment. She possessed her liberty, and was fulfilling her mission as a social force, but her life had been deprived of some of its savor, and, though she was thankful to be rid of Babcock, she felt the lack of an element of personal devotion to herself, an element which was not to be supplied by mere admiration on the part of Mrs. Earle and the other members of the Institute. It did not suit her not to be able to gratify her growing taste in clothes and in other lines of expenditure, and there were moments when she experienced the need of being petted and made much of by a man. She was conscious of loneliness, and in this mood she pitied herself as a victim of untoward circumstances, one who had wasted the freshness of her young life, and missed the happiness which the American wife is apt to find waiting for her. Under the spell of this nostalgia she wrote a poem entitled "The Bitter Sweets of Solitude," and disposed of it for five dollars to the *Sentinel*. The price shocked her, for the verses seemed flesh of her flesh. Still, five dollars was better than nothing, and she discerned from the manner of the newspaper editor that he cared little whether she left them or not. It was on that evening that she received a letter from Littleton, stating that he was on the eve of leaving New York for Benham. He was coming to consult concerning certain further interior decorations which the committee had decided to add to the church.

Selma's nerves vibrated blissfully as she read the news. For some reason, which she had never seen fit definitely to define, she had chosen not to acquaint Littleton with the fact of her divorce. Their letters had been infrequent during the last six months, for this visit had been impending, having been put off from time to time because the committee had been dilatory and he otherwise engaged. Perhaps her secret motive had been to surprise him, to let him find himself confronted with an accomplished fact, which would obviate argument and reveal her established in her new career, a happy, independent citizen, without ties. At any rate she smiled now at the address on the envelope—Mrs. Lewis Babcock. Obviously he was still in the dark as to the truth, and it would be her privilege to enlighten him. She began to wonder what would be the upshot of his coming, and tears came to her eyes, tears of self-congratulation that the narrow tenor of her daily life was to be irradiated by a sympathetic spirit.

When Littleton duly appeared at the committee meeting on the following day, Selma saw at a glance that he was unaware of what had happened. He looked slightly puzzled when one of the members addressed her as Mrs. White, but evidently he regarded this as a slip of the tongue. Selma looked, as she felt, contented and vivacious. She had dressed herself simply, but with effective trigness. To those who knew her experience, her appearance indicated courage and becoming self-respect. Public opinion, even as embodied in the church committee, while deploring the necessity, was not disposed to question the propriety of her action. That is, all except Mrs. Taylor. In her, Selma thought she had detected signs of coldness, a sort of suspicious reservation of judgment, which contrasted itself unpleasantly with the sympathetic attitude of the others, who were fain to refer to her, in not altogether muffled whispers, as a plucky, independent, little woman. Hence, she was glad that Mrs. Taylor happened to be detained at home by illness on this afternoon, and that, accordingly, she was free to enjoy unreservedly the dramatic nature of the situation. Her heart beat a little faster as the chairman, turning to her to ask a question, addressed her unmistakably as Mrs. White. She could not refrain from casting half-amused, half-pathetic sheep's eyes at Littleton. He started visibly, regarded her for, a moment in obvious amazement, then flushed to the roots of his hair. She felt the blood rising to her own cheeks, and a sensation of mild triumph. The meeting was over and the members were merely lingering to tie up the loose threads of the matter arranged for. In a few moments Selma found herself with the architect sufficiently apart from the others for him to ask:

"Two persons have addressed you this afternoon as Mrs. White. I do not understand."

She cast down her eyes, as a woman will when a question of modesty is involved, then she raised them and said: "You did not know, then, that I had left my husband?"

"Left him?"

"Yes. I have obtained a divorce. He was unfaithful to me."

"I see"—said Littleton with a sort of gasp—"I see. I did not know. You never wrote to me."

"I did not feel like writing to any body. There was nothing to be done but that."

Littleton regarded her with a perturbed, restless air.

"Then you live no longer at 25 Onslow Avenue?"

"Oh, no. I left there more than six months ago. I live in lodgings. I am supporting myself by literary work. I am Mrs. Selma White now, and my divorce has been absolute more than a month."

She spoke gravely and quietly, with less than her usual assurance, for she felt the spell of his keen, eager scrutiny and was not averse to yield at the moment to the propensity of her sex. She wondered what he was thinking about. Did he blame her? Did he sympathize with her?

"Where are you going when you leave here?" he asked.

"Home—to my new home. Will you walk along with me?"

"That is what I should like. I am astonished by what you have told me, and am anxious to hear more about it, if to speak of it would not wound you. Divorced! How you must have suffered! And I did not have the chance to offer you my help—my sympathy."

"Yes, I have suffered. But that is all over now. I am a free woman. I am beginning my life over again."

It was a beautiful afternoon, and by mutual consent, which neither put into words, they diverged from the exact route to Selma's lodging house and turned their steps to the open country beyond the city limits—the picturesque dell which has since become the site of Benham's public park. There they seated themselves where they would not be interrupted. Selma told him on the way the few vital facts in her painful story, to which he listened in a tense silence, broken chiefly by an occasional ejaculation expressive of his contempt for the man who had brought such unhappiness upon her. She let him understand, too, that her married life, from the first, had been far less happy than he had imagined—wretched makeshift for the true relation of husband and wife. She spoke of her future buoyantly, yet with a touch of sadness, as though to indicate that she was aware that the triumphs of intelligence and individuality could not entirely be a substitute for a happy home.

"And what do you expect to do?" he inquired in a

76

bewildered fashion, as though her delineation of her hopes had been lost on him.

"Do? Support myself by my own exertions, as I have told you. By writing I expect. I am doing very well already. Do you question my ability to continue?"

"Oh, no; not that. Only—"

"Only what? Surely you are not one of the men who grudge women the chance to prove what is in them—who would treat us like china dolls and circumscribe us by conventions? I know you are not, because I have heard you inveigh against that very sort of narrow mindedness. Only what?"

"I can't make up my mind to it. And I suppose the reason is that it means so much to me—that you mean so much to me. What is the use of my dodging the truth, Selma—seeking to conceal it because such a short time has elapsed since you ceased to be a wife? Forgive me if I hurt you, if it seem indelicate to speak of love at the very moment when you are happy in your liberty. I can't help it; it's my nature to speak openly. And there's no bar now. The fact that you are free makes clear to me what I have not dared to countenance before, that you are the one woman in the world for me—the woman I have dreamed of—and longed to meet—the woman whose influence has blessed me already, and without whom I shall lack the greatest happiness which life can give. Selma, I love you—I adore you."

Selma listened with greedy ears, which she could scarcely believe. It seemed to her that she was in dream-land, so unexpected, yet entrancing, was his avowal. She had been vaguely aware that he admired her more than he had allowed himself to disclose, and conscious, too, that his presence was agreeable to her; but in an instant now she recognized that this was love—the love she had sought, the love she had yearned to inspire and to feel. Compared with it, Babcock's clumsy ecstasy and her own sufferance of it had been a sham and a delusion. Of so much she was conscious in a twinkling, and yet what she deemed proper self-respect restrained her from casting herself into his arms. It was, indeed, soon, and she had been happy in her liberty. At least, she had supposed herself so; and she owed it to her own plans and hopes not to act hastily, though she knew what she intended to do. She had been lonely, yes starving, for lack of true companionship, and here was the soul which would be a true mate to hers.

They were sitting on a grassy bank. He was bending toward her with clasped hands, a picture of fervor. She could see him out of the corner of her glance, though she looked into space with her gaze of seraphic worry. Yet her lips were ready to lend themselves to a smile of blissful satisfaction and her eyes to fill with the melting mood of the thought that at last happiness had come to her.

The silence was very brief, but Littleton, as would have seemed fitting to her, feared lest she were shocked.

"I distress you," he said. "Forgive me. Listen—will you listen?" Selma was glad to listen. The words of love, such love as this, were delicious, and she felt she owed it to herself not to be won too easily. "I am listening," she answered softly with the voice of one face to face with an array of doubts.

"Before I met you, Selma, woman but was a name to me. My life brought me little into contact with them, except my dear sister, and I had no temptation to regret that I could not support a wife. Yet I dreamed of woman and of love and of a joy which might some day come to me if I could meet one who fulfilled my ideal of what a true woman should be. So I dreamed until I met you. The first time I saw you, Selma, I knew in my heart that you were a woman whom I could love. Perhaps I should have recognized more clearly as time went on that you were more to me even then than I had a right to allow; yet I call heaven to witness that I did not, by word or sign, do a wrong to him who has done such a cruel wrong to you."

"Never by word or sign," echoed Selma solemnly. The bare suggestion that Babcock had cause to complain of either of them seemed to her preposterous. Yet she was saying to herself that it was easy to perceive that he had loved her from the first.

"And since I love you with all my soul must I—should I in justice to myself—to my own hopes of happiness, refrain from speaking merely because you have so recently been divorced? I must speak—I am speaking. It is too soon, I dare say, for you to be willing to think of marriage again—but I offer you the love and protection of a husband. My means are small, but I am able now to support a wife in decent comfort. Selma, give me some hope. Tell me, that in time you may be willing to trust yourself to my love. You wish to work—to distinguish yourself. Would I be a hindrance to that? Indeed, you must know that I would do every thing in my power to promote your desire to be of service to the world."

The time for her smile and her tears had come. He had argued his case and her own, and it was clear to her mind that delay would be futile. Since happiness was at hand, why not grasp it? As for her work, he need not interfere with that. And, after all, now that she had tried it, was she so sure that newspaper work—hack work, such as she was pursuing, was what she wished? As a wife, re-established in the security of a home, she could pick and choose her method of expression. Perhaps, indeed, it would not be writing, except occasionally. Was not New York a wide, fruitful field, for a reforming social influence? She saw herself in her mind's eye a leader of movements and of progress. And that with a man she loved—yes, adored even as he adored her.

So she turned to Littleton with her smile and in tears—the image of bewitching but pathetic self-justification and surrender. Her mind was made up; hence why procrastinate and coyly postpone the desirable, and the inevitable? That was what she had the shrewdness to formulate in the ecstasy of her transport; and so eloquent was the mute revelation of her love that Littleton, diffident reverencer of the modesty of woman as he was, without a word from her clasped her to his breast, a victor in a breath. As, regardless of the possible invasion of interlopers, he took her in his embrace, she felt with satisfaction once more the grasp of masculine arms. She let her head fall on his shoulder in delighted contentment. While he murmured in succession inarticulate terms of endearment, she revelled in the thrill of her nerves and approved her own sagacious and commendable behavior.

"Dearest," she whispered, "you are right. We are right. Since we love each other, why should we not say so? I love you—I love you. The ugly hateful past shall not keep us apart longer. You say you loved me from the first; so did I love you, though I did not know it then. We were meant for each other—God meant us—did he not? It is right, and we shall be so happy, Wilbur."

"Yes, Selma." Words seemed to him an inadequate means for expressing his emotions. He pressed his lips upon hers with the adoring respect of a worshipper touching his god, yet with the energy of a man. She sighed and compared him in her thought with Babcock. How gentle this new lover! How refined and sensitive and appreciative! How intelligent and gentlemanly!

"If I had my wish, darling," he said, "we should be married to-night and I would carry you away from here forever."

She remembered that Babcock had uttered the same wish on the occasion when he had offered himself. To grant it then had been out of the question. To do so now would be convenient—a prompt and satisfactory blotting out of her past and present life—a happy method of solving many minor problems of ways and means connected with waiting to be married. Besides it would be romantic, and a delicious, fitting crowning of her present blissful mood.

He mistook her silence for womanly scruples, and he recounted with a little laugh the predicament in which he should find himself on his own account were they to be so precipitate. "What would my sister think if she were to get a telegram—'Married to-night. Expect us to-morrow?' She would think I had lost my senses. So I have, darling; and you are the cause. She knows about you. I have talked to her about you."

"But she thinks I am Mrs. Babcock."

"Oh yes. Ha! ha! It would never do to state to whom I was married, unless I sent a telegram as long as my arm. Dear Pauline! She will be radiant. It is all arranged that she is to stay where she is in the old quarters, and I am to take you to a new house. We've decided on that, time and again, when we've chanced to talk of what might happen—of 'the fair, the chaste and unexpressive she'—my she. Dearest, I wondered if I should ever find her. Pauline has always said that she would never run the risk of spoiling everything by living with us."

"It would be very nice—and very simple," responded Selma, slowly. "You wouldn't think any the worse of me, Wilbur, if I were to marry you to-night?"

"The worse of you? It is what I would like of all things. Whom does it concern but us? Why should we wait in order to make a public spectacle of ourselves?"

"I shouldn't wish that. I should insist on being married very quietly. Under all the circumstances there is really no reason—it seems to me it would be easier if we were to be married as soon as possible. It would avoid explanations and talk, wouldn't it? That is, if you are perfectly sure."

"Sure? That I love you? Oh Selma!"

80

She shut her eyes under the thrill which his kiss gave her. "Then we will be married whenever you wish," she said.

It was already late in the afternoon, so that the prospects of obtaining a license did not seem favorable. Still it happened that Littleton knew a clergyman of his own faith—Unitarian—in Benham, a college classmate, whom he suggested as soon as he understood that Selma preferred not to be married by Mr. Glynn. They found him at home, and by diligent personal effort on his part the necessary legal forms were complied with and they were made husband and wife three hours before the departure of the evening train for New York. After the ceremony they stepped buoyantly, arm in arm in the dusk, along the street to send the telegram to Miss Littleton, and to snatch a hasty meal before Selma went to her lodgings to pack. There were others in the restaurant, so having discovered that they were not hungry, they bought sandwiches and bananas, and resumed their travels. The suddenness and surprise of it all made Selma feel as if on wings. It seemed to her to be of the essence of new and exquisite romance to be walking at the side of her fond, clever lover in the democratic simplicity of two paper bags of provender and an open, yet almost headlong marriage. She felt that at last she was yoked to a spirit who comprehended her and who would stimulate instead of repress the fire of originality within her. She had found love and she was happy. Meanwhile she had decided to leave Benham without a word to anyone, even Mrs. Earle. She would write and explain what had happened.

BOOK II.

THE STRUGGLE

CHAPTER I.

Littleton had not expected that Selma would accede to his request to be married at once, but he was delighted at her decision. He had uttered his wish in sincerity, for there was really no reason for waiting, and by an immediate marriage they would escape the tedium of an engagement during which they could hope to see each other but rarely. He was able to support a wife provided they were to live simply and economically. He felt sure that Selma understood his circumstances and was no less ready than he to forego luxuries in order that they might be all in all to each other spiritually as husband and wife. Besides he had hopes that his clientage would continue to grow so that he would be able to provide all reasonable comforts for his new home. Consequently he drove up from the station in New York with a light heart, fondly pointing out to his wife this and that building and other objects of interest. He mistook her pensive silence for diffidence at the idea of descending suddenly on another woman's home—a matter which in this instance gave him no concern, for he had unlimited confidence in Pauline's executive ability and her tendency not to get ruffled. She had been his good angel, domestically speaking, and, indeed, in every way, since they had first begun to keep house together, and it had rather amused him to let fall such a bombshell as the contents of his telegram upon the regularity of her daily life.

"Don't be nervous, darling," he said gayly. "You will find Pauline bubbling over with joy at our coming, and everything arranged as though we were expected to live there all our lives."

Selma looked at him blankly and then remembered. She was not feeling nervous, and Pauline was not in her thoughts. She had been lost in her own reflections—lost in the happy consciousness of the contrast between her new and her old husband, and in the increasing satisfaction that she was actually in New York. How bright and busy the streets looked! The throng of eager passers and jostling vehicles against the background of brilliant shop-windows bewildered and stimulated her. She was saying to herself that here was the place where she was suited to live, and mutely acknowledging its superiority to Benham as a centre of life. This was a rash, swift conclusion, but Selma prided herself on her capacity to arrive at wise judgments by rapid mental processes. So absorbed was she in the glittering, stirring panorama that Wilbur's efforts at enlightenment were practically wasted. She was in no humor for details; she was glorying in the exalted impression which the whole vivid scene produced upon her.

His remark caused her to realize that they must be near their destination. She had no misgivings on the score of her own reception, but she was interested and curious to see Pauline, this wonderful sister of whom Wilbur was so fond and so proud. Then her husband cried, "Here we are!" and in another moment she found herself in the hearty embrace of a large, comely woman who met her at the door. This of course must be Pauline. Selma was just a little shocked by the fervor of the greeting; for though she delighted in rapid intimacies, unexpected liberties with her person were contrary to her conceptions of propriety. Still it was delightful to be welcomed so heartily. She returned the embrace warmly but with dignity, and allowed herself to be convoyed into the house arm in arm with her new relation who seemed, indeed, to be bubbling over with joy. It was not until they were in the same room that Selma could get a good look at her.

Pauline Littleton was fine looking rather than pretty. She was tall and substantial, with an agreeable face, an intelligent brow, a firm yet sweet mouth, and steady, honest eyes which now sparkled with pleasure. Her physique was very different from her brother's. Selma noticed that she was taller than herself and only a little shorter than Wilbur. She had Wilbur's smile too, suggesting a disposition to take things humorously; but her expression lacked the poetic cast which made him so attractive and congenial to herself and excused the existence of the lighter vein. Selma did not admire women who were inclined to be stout. She associated spareness of person with high thinking, and an abundance of flesh as an indication of material or commonplace aims. She reflected that Pauline was presumably business-like and a good house-keeper, and, very likely, an industrious teacher in her classes, but she set her down in her mind as deficient in the finer sensibilities of the spirit belonging to herself and Wilbur. It was instinctive with Selma to form a prompt estimate of every one she met, and it was a relief to her to come to the agreeable conclusion that there was nothing in her sister-in-law's appearance to make her discontented with herself. This warmed her heart at once toward Pauline. To be sure Pauline manifested the same sort of social grace which distinguished Mrs.

Hallett Taylor, but Selma, though she still regarded this with suspicion, for the reason that she had not yet become mistress of it, was secretly content to know that she had married into a family which possessed it. Altogether she was agreeably impressed by her scrutiny of her new sister, who, in her opinion, would not be an irritating rival either in looks or character, and yet who was a pleasing and sufficiently serious-minded person—in short just the sort of sister-in-law which she yearned to have.

Pauline, on her part, was duly fascinated by the delicate and inspiring beauty of her brother's wife. She understood at once why Wilbur had chosen her in preference to any one of his own circle. Selma obviously symbolized by her grave, tense, thin face the serious ideals of living and womanhood, which had been dear to his meditation as a youth and a part of his heritage from his New England ancestors. It made her joyous to feel that he had found a wife who would be a constant source of inspiration to him, for she knew that Wilbur would not be happy with any one who fell short of his ideal as to what a woman should be. She knew her brother well, and she understood how deeply in earnest he was to make the most of his life, and what an exalted vision he entertained as to the possibilities for mutual sympathy and help between husband and wife.

Partly as a consequence of their limited means, partly owing to absorption in their respective studies and interests, the Littletons, though of gentle stock, lived simple lives according to New York standards. They were aware of the growth of luxury resulting from the accumulation of big fortunes since the war. As an architect, Wilbur saw larger and more elaborate public and private buildings being erected on every side. As a house-keeper and a woman with social interests, Pauline knew that the power of money was revolutionizing the public taste in the matter of household expenditure; that in the details of domestic life there was more color and more circumstance, and that people who were well-to-do, and many who were not, were requiring as daily comforts all sorts of things to which they had been unaccustomed. But though they both thus knew vaguely that the temper of society had changed, and that sober citizens and their wives, who, twenty years before, would have prated solemnly against a host of gay, enlivening or pretty customs as incompatible with American virtue, were now adopting these as rapidly as money could procure them—the brother and sister had remained comparatively unaffected by the consequences of the transformation scene. Certainly their home had. It was old-fashioned in its garniture and its gentility. It spoke of a day, not so many years before, when high thinking had led to blinking where domestic decoration was concerned, and people had bought ugly wooden and worsted things to live with because only the things of the spirit seemed of real importance. Still time, with its marvellous touch, has often the gift of making furniture and upholstery, which were hideous when bought, look interesting and cosey when they have become old-fashioned. In this way Pauline Wilbur's parlor was a delightful relic of a day gone by. There was scarcely a pretty thing in it, as Wilbur himself well knew, yet, as a whole, it had an atmosphere—an atmosphere of simple unaffected refinement. Their domestic belongings had come to them from their parents, and they had never had the means to replenish them. When, in due time, they had realized their artistic worthlessness, they had held to them through affection, humorously conscious of the incongruity that two such modern individuals as themselves should be living in a domestic museum. Then, presto! friends had begun to congratulate them on the uniqueness of their establishment, and to express affection for it. It had become a favorite resort for many modern spirits—artists, literary men, musicians, self-supporting women—and Pauline's oyster suppers, cooked in her grandmother's blazer, were still a stimulus to high thinking.

So matters stood when Selma entered it as a bride. Her coming signified the breaking up of the household and the establishment. Pauline had thought that out in her clear brain over night since receiving Wilbur's telegram. Wilbur must move into a modern house, and she into a modern flat. She would keep the very old things, such as the blazer and some andirons and a pair of candlesticks, for they were ancient enough to be really artistic, but the furniture of the immediate past, her father and mother's generation, should be sold at auction. Wilbur and she must, if only for Selma's sake, become modern in material matters as well as in their mental interests.

Pauline proceeded to unfold this at the dinner-table that evening. She had heard in the meanwhile from her brother, the story of Selma's divorce and the explanation of his sudden marriage; and in consequence, she felt the more solicitous that her sister-in-law's new venture should begin propitiously. It was agreed that Wilbur should make inquiries at once about houses further uptown, and that his present lease from year to year should not be renewed. She said to Selma:

"You have saved us from becoming an old-fashioned bachelor and maid. Our friends began to leave this neighborhood five years ago, and there is no one left. We are surrounded by boarding-houses and shops. We were comfortable, and we were too busy to care. But it would never do for a young married couple to begin house-keeping here. You must have a brand new house uptown, Selma. You must insist on that. Don't be alarmed, Wilbur. I know it will have to be small, but I noticed the other day several blocks of new houses going up on the side streets west of the Park, which looked attractive and cheap."

"I will look at them," said Wilbur. "Since you seem determined not to live with us, and we are obliged to move, we will follow the procession. But Selma and I could be happy anywhere." He turned from his sister to her as he spoke with a proud, happy look.

Selma said nothing to mar his confidence. She had no intention of living either with Pauline or in their present house, and she felt that her sister-in-law had shown good sense in recognizing that neither was possible. She necessarily had vague ideas as to New York houses and locations, but she had seen enough in her drive from the station to understand that it was a wonderful and decorative place. Although her experience of Benham had taught her that some old things—such as Mrs. Hallett Taylor's gleanings from Europe—were desirable, she associated new things with progress—especially American progress. Consequently the Littleton household possessions had puzzled her, for though she thought them ugly, she was resolved not to commit herself too hastily. But now that Pauline had sounded a note of warning, the situation was clear. They had suffered themselves to fall behind the times, and she was to be her husband's good angel by helping him to catch up with them. And it was evident that Pauline would be her ally. Selma for the first time asked herself whether it might be that Wilbur was a little visionary.

Meanwhile he was saying: "Pauline is right, Selma. I had

88

already asked myself if it would not be fairer to you to move uptown where we should be in the van and in touch with what is going on. Pauline is gently hinting to you that you must not humor me as she has done, and let me eat bread and milk out of a bowl in this old curiosity shop, instead of following in the wake of fashion. She has spoiled me and now she deserts me at the critical moment of my life. Selma, you shall have the most charming modern house in New York within my means. It must be love in a cottage, but the cottage shall have the latest improvements—hot and cold water, tiles, hygienic plumbing and dados."

"Bravo!" said Pauline. "He says I have spoiled him, Selma. Perhaps I have. It will be your turn now. You will fail to convert him as I have failed, and the world will be the better for it. There are too few men who think noble thoughts and practice them, who are true to themselves and the light which is in them through thick and thin. But you see, he admits himself that he needs to mix with the world a little more. Otherwise he is perfect. You know that perhaps, already, Selma. But I wish to tell it to you before him. Take care of him, dear, won't you?"

"It was because I felt that his thoughts were nobler than most men's that I wished to marry him," Selma replied, seraphically. "But I can see that it is sensible to live where your friends live. I shall try not to spoil him, Pauline." She was already conscious of a mission which appealed to her. She had been content until now in the ardor of her love to regard Wilbur as flawless—as in some respects superior to herself; but it was a gratification to her to detect this failing, and to perceive her opportunity for usefulness. Surely it was important for her husband to be progressive and not merely a dreamer.

Littleton looked from one to the other fondly. "Not many men are blessed with the love of two such women," he said. "I put myself in your hands. I bow my neck to the yoke."

In New York in the early seventies the fashionable quarter lay between Eighth and Fortieth Streets, bounded on either side by Fourth and Sixth Avenues. Central Park was completed, but the region west of it was, from the social stand-point, still a wilderness, and Fifth Avenue in the neighborhood of Twenty-third Street was the centre of elegant social life. Selma took her first view of this brilliant street on the following day on her way to hunt for houses in the outlying district. The roar and bustle of the city, which thrilled yet dazed her, seemed here softened by the rows of tall, imposing residences in brown stone. Along the sunny sidewalks passed with jaunty tread an ever-hurrying procession of stylishly clad men and women; and along the roadbed sped an array of private carriages conducted by coachmen in livery. It was a brilliant day, and New Yorkers were making the most of it.

Selma had never seen such a sight before. Benham faded into insignificance in comparison. She was excited, and she gazed eagerly at the spectacle. Yet her look, though absorbed, was stern. This sort of thing was unlike anything American within her personal experience. This avenue of grand houses and this procession of fine individuals and fine vehicles made her think of that small section of Benham into which she had never been invited, and the thought affected her disagreeably.

"Who are the people who live in these houses?" she asked, presently.

Littleton had already told her that it was the most fashionable street in the city.

"Oh, the rich and prosperous."

"Those who gamble in stocks, I suppose." Selma wished to be assured that this was so.

"Some of them," said Littleton, with a laugh. "They belong to people who have made money in various ways or have inherited it—our well-to-do class, among them the first families in New York, and many of them our best citizens."

"Are they friends of yours?"

Littleton laughed again. "A few—not many. Society here is divided into sets, and they are not in my set. I prefer mine, and fortunately, for I can't afford to belong to theirs."

"Oh!"

The frigidity and dryness of the exclamation Littleton ascribed to Selma's intuitive enmity to the vanities of life.

"You mustn't pass judgment on them too hastily," he said. "New York is a wonderful place, and it's likely to shock you before you learn to appreciate what is interesting and fine here. I will tell you a secret, Selma. Every one likes to make money. Even clergymen feel it their duty to accept a call from the congregation which offers the best salary, and probing men of science do not hesitate to reap the harvest from a wonderful invention. Yet it is the fashion with most of the people in this country who possess little to prate about the wickedness of money-getters and to think evil of the rich. That proceeds chiefly from envy, and it is sheer cant. The people of the United States are engaged in an eager struggle to advance themselves—to gain individual distinction, comfort, success, and in New York to a greater extent than in any other place can the capable man or woman sell his or her wares to the best advantage—be they what they may, stocks, merchandise, law, medicine, pictures. The world pays well for the things it wants—and the world is pretty just in the long run. If it doesn't like my designs, that will be because they're not worth buying. The great thing—the difficult thing to guard against in the whirl of this great city, where we are all striving to get ahead—is not to sell one's self for money, not to sacrifice the thing worth doing for mere pecuniary advantage. It's the great temptation to some to do so, for only money can buy fine houses, and carriages and jewels—yes, and in a certain sense, social preferment. The problem is presented in a different form to every man. Some can grow rich honestly, and some have to remain poor in order to be true to themselves. We may have to remain poor, Selma mia." He spoke gayly, as though that prospect did not disturb him in the least.

"And we shall be just as good as the people who own these houses." She said it gravely, as if it were a declaration of principles, and at the same moment her gaze was caught and disturbed by a pair of blithe, fashionably dressed young women gliding by her with the quiet, unconscious grace of good-breeding. She was inwardly aware, though she would never acknowledge it by word or sign, that such people troubled her. More even than Mrs. Taylor had troubled her. They were different from her and they tantalized her.

At the same moment her husband was saying in reply, "Just as good, but not necessarily any better. No—other things being equal—not so good. We mustn't deceive ourselves with that piece of cant. Some of them are frivolous enough, and dishonest enough, heaven knows, but so there are frivolous and dishonest people in every class. But there are many more who endeavor to be good citizens—are good citizens, our best citizens. The possession of money gives them the opportunity to become arbiters of morals and taste, and to seek culture under the best advantages. After all, an

91

accumulation of money represents brains and energy in some one. Look at this swell," he continued, indicating an attractive looking young man who was passing. "His grandfather was one of the ablest men in the city—an intelligent, self-respecting, shrewd, industrious, public-spirited citizen who made a large fortune. The son has had advantages which I have never had, and I happen to know that he is a fine fellow and a very able one. If it came to comparisons, I should be obliged to admit that he's a more ornamental member of society than Jones, Brown, or Robinson, and certainly no less useful. Do I shock you—you sweet, unswerving little democrat of the democrats?"

It always pleased Selma to be called endearing names, and it suited her in her present frame of mind to be dubbed a democrat, for it did not suit her to be painfully realizing that she was unable, at one brilliant swoop, to take her place as a leader in social influence. Somehow she had expected to do this, despite her first difficulties at Benham, for she had thought of New York as a place where, as the wife of Littleton, the architect, she would at once be a figure of importance. She shook her head and said, "It's hard to believe that these people are really in earnest; that they are serious in purpose and spirit." Meanwhile she was being haunted by the irritating reflection that her clothes and her bearing were inferior to those of the women she was passing. Secretly she was making a resolve to imitate them, though she believed that she despised them. She put her hand through her husband's arm and added, almost fiercely, as she pressed closer to him, "We needn't trouble our heads about them, Wilbur. We can get along without being rich and fashionable, you and I. In spite of what you say, I don't consider this sort of thing American."

"Get along? Darling, I was merely trying to be just to them; to let you see that they are not so black as they're painted. We will forget them forever. We have nothing in common with them. Get along? I feel that my life will be a paradise living with you and trying to make some impression on the life of this big, striving city. But as to its not being American to live like these people—well you know they are Americans and that New York is the Mecca of the hard-fisted sons of toil from all over the country who have made money. But you're right, Selma. Those who go in for show and extravagance are not the best Americans—the Americans whom you and I believe in. Sometimes I get discouraged when I stop to think, and now I shall have you to keep me steadfast to our faith."

"Yes, Wilbur. And how far from here are we to live?"

"Oh, a mile or more. On some side street where the land is cheap and the rent low. What do we care for that, Selma mia?"

CHAPTER II.

Shortly before Selma Littleton took up her abode in New York, Miss Florence, or, as she was familiarly known, Miss Flossy Price, was an inhabitant of a New Jersey city. Her father was a second cousin of Morton Price, whose family at that time was socially conspicuous in fashionable New York society. Not aggressively conspicuous, as ultra fashionable people are to-day, by dint of frequent newspaper advertisement, but in consequence of elegant, conservative respectability, fortified by and cushioned on a huge income. In the early seventies to know the Morton Prices was a social passport, and by no means every one socially ambitious knew them. Morton Price's great-grandfather had been a peddler, his grandfather a tea merchant, his father a tea merchant and bank organizer, and he himself did nothing mercantile, but was a director in diverse institutions, representing trusts or philantrophy, and was regarded by many, including himself, as the embodiment of ornamental and admirable citizenship. He could talk by the hour on the degeneracy of state and city politics and the evil deeds of Congress, and was, generally speaking, a conservative, fastidious, well-dressed, well-fed man, who had a winning way with women and a happy faculty of looking wise and saying nothing rash in the presence of men. Some of the younger generation were apt, with the lack of reverence belonging to youth, to speak of him covertly as "a stuffed club," but no echo of this epithet had ever reached the ear of his cousin, David Price, in New Jersey. For him, as for most of the world within a radius of two hundred miles, he was above criticism and a monument of social power.

David Price, Miss Flossy's father, was the president of a small and unprogressive but eminently solid bank. Respectable routine was his motto, and he lived up to it, and, as a consequence, no more sound institution of the kind existed in his neighborhood. He and his directors were slow to adopt innovations of any kind; they put stumbling blocks in the path of business convenience whenever they could; in short, David Price in his humble way was a righteous, narrow, hide-bound retarder of progress and worshipper of established local custom. Therefore it was a constant source of surprise and worry to him that he should have a progressive daughter. There were four other children, patterns of quiet, plodding conservatism, but—such is the irony of fate—the

94

youngest, prettiest, and his favorite, was an independent, opinionated young woman, who seemed to turn a deaf ear to paternal and maternal advice of safest New Jersey type. In her father's words, she had no reverence for any thing or any body, which was approximately true, for she did not hesitate to speak disrespectfully even of the head of the house in New York.

"Poppa," she said one day, "Cousin Morton doesn't care for any of us a little bit. I know what you're going to say," she added; "that he sends you two turkeys every Thanksgiving. The last were terribly tough. I'm sure he thinks that we never see turkeys here in New Jersey, and that he considers us poor relations and that we live in a hole. If one of us should call on him, I know it would distress him awfully. He's right in thinking that this is a hole. Nothing ever happens here, and when I marry I intend to live in New York."

This was when she was seventeen. Her father was greatly shocked, especially as he suspected in his secret soul that the tirade was true in substance. He had been the recipient of Thanksgiving turkeys for nearly twenty years on the plea that they had been grown on the donor's farm in Westchester county, and he had seen fit to invite his fellow-directors annually to dine off one of them as a modest notice that he was on friendly terms with his aristocratic New York cousin. But in all these twenty years turkeys had been the only medium of intercourse between them. David Price, on the few occasions when he had visited New York, had not found it convenient to call. Once he had walked by on the other side of Fifth avenue and looked at the house, but shyness and the thought that he had no evening clothes in his valise had restrained him from ringing the doorbell.

"You do your cousin Morton great injustice—great injustice, Florence," he answered. "He never forgets to send the turkeys, and as to the rest of your speech, I have only to say that it is very disrespectful and very foolish. The next time I go to New York I will take you to call on your cousins."

"And what would I say to them? No thank you, poppa." The young woman shook her head decisively, and then she added, "I'm not going to call on them, until I'm fit to. There!"

The ambiguity of this remark gave Mr. Price the opportunity to say that, in view of her immediate shortcomings, it was a wise conclusion, but he knew what she really meant and was distressed.

His feeling toward his cousin, though mildly envious, did not extend to self-depreciation, nor had it served to undermine his faith in the innate dignity and worth of New Jersey family life. He could not only with a straight face, but with a kindling eye inveigh against the perils of New York fashionable life, and express gratification that no son or daughter of his had wandered so far from the fold. It distressed him to think that Florence should be casting sheep's eyes at the flesh-pots of Gotham, and so failing to appreciate the blessings and safety of a quiet American home.

Miss Flossy continued to entertain and to express opinions of her own, and as a result became socially interesting. At eighteen, by her beauty, her engaging frankness and lack of self-consciousness, she spread havoc among the young men of her native city, several of whom offered her marriage. But marriage was far from her thoughts. Life seemed too interesting and she wished to see the world. She was erect and alert looking, with a compact figure of medium height, large brown eyes and rich red hair, and a laughing mouth; also an innocent demeanor, which served to give her, by moonlight, the effect of an angel. She succeeded in visiting Bar Harbor, where she promptly became a bright particular star among the galaxy of young women who at that period were establishing the reputation of the summer girl. She continued to be a summer girl for four seasons without injury to her own peace of mind. At the end of the fourth summer she appeared on close scrutiny to be a little worn, and her innocent air seemed a trifle deliberate. She returned to her home in New Jersey in not quite her usual spirits. In fact she became pensive. She had seen the world, and lo! she found it stuffed with sawdust. She was ready to settle down, but the only man with whom she would have been willing to settle had never asked her. He was the brother of one of the girls who had been forbidden by her mother to stay out in canoes with young men after nine at night. The rumor had reached Flossy that this same mother had referred to her in "the fish pond" at Rodick's as "that dreadful girl." It would have pleased her after that to have wrung an offer of marriage from the son and heir, who knew her cousins, the Morton Prices, and to whom she would have been willing to engage herself temporarily at all events. He was very devoted; they stayed out in his canoe until past midnight; he wrote verses to her and told her his innermost thoughts; but he stopped there. He went away without committing himself, and she was left to chew the cud of reflection. It was bitter, not because she was in love with him, for she was not. In her heart she knew he bored her a little. But she was piqued. Evidently he had been afraid to marry "that dreadful girl." She was piqued and she was sad. She recognized that it was another case of not being fit. When would she be fit? What was she to do in order to become fit—fit like the girl who was not allowed to stay on the water after nine o'clock? She had ceased to think of the young man, but the image of his sister haunted her. How stylish she was, yet how simple and quiet! "I wonder," thought Flossy to herself, "if I could ever become like her." The reflection threw her into a brown study in which she remained for weeks, and during which she refused the hand of a staid and respectable townsman, who, in her father's words, was ready to take her with all her follies. David Price was disappointed. He loved this independent daughter, and he had hopes that her demure and reticent deportment signified that the effervescence of youth had evaporated. But it was only an effort on Flossy's part to imitate the young man's sister.

At this juncture and just when she was bored and dispirited by the process, Gregory Williams appeared on the scene. Flossy met him at a dancing party. He had a very tall collar, a very friendly, confident, and (toward her) devoted manner, and good looks. It was whispered among the girls that he was a banker from New York. He was obviously not over thirty, which was young for a banker, but so he presently described himself to Flossy with hints of impending prosperity. He spoke glibly and picturesquely. He had a convincing eloquence of gesture—a wave of the hand which suggested energy and compelled confidence. He had picked her out at once to be introduced to, and sympathy between them was speedily established. Her wearing, as a red-headed girl, a white horse in the form of a pin, in order to prevent the attention of the men to whom she talked from wandering, delighted him. He said to himself that here was a girl after his own heart. He had admired her looks at the outset, but he gazed at her now more critically. He danced every dance with her, and they sat together at supper, apart from everybody else. Flossy's resolutions were swept away. That is, she had become in an instant indifferent to the fact that the New York girl she had yearned to imitate would not have made herself so conspicuous. Her excuse was that she could not help herself. It was a case of genuine, violent attraction, which she made no effort to straggle against.

The attraction was violent on both sides. Gregory Williams was not seeking to be married. He had been, until within six months, a broker's clerk, and had become a banker on the strength of ten thousand dollars bequeathed to him by a grandmother. He and a clerk from another broker's office, J. Willett VanHorne, had recently formed a partnership as Williams & VanHorne, Bankers and Dealers in Stocks and Bonds. He was not seeking to be married, but he intended to be married some day, and it was no part of his scheme of life to deny himself anything he wished. Support a wife? Of course he could; and support her in the same grandiose fashion which he had adopted for himself since he had begun business on his own account. He had chosen as a philosophy of life the smart paradox, which he enjoyed uttering, that he spent what he needed first and supplied the means later; and at the same time he let it be understood that the system worked wonderfully. He possessed unlimited confidence in himself, and though he was dimly aware that a very small turn of the wheel of fortune in the wrong direction would ruin him financially, he chose to close his eyes to the possibilities of disaster and to assume a bold and important bearing before the world. He had implicit faith in his own special line of ability, and he appreciated the worth of his partner, VanHorne. He had joined forces with VanHorne because he knew that he was the opposite of himself—that he was a delving, thorough, shrewd, keen office man—and able too. How genuinely able Williams did not yet know. He himself was to be the showy partner, the originator of schemes and procurer of business, the brilliant man before the world. So there was some method in his madness. And with it all went a cheery, incisive, humorous point of view which was congenial and diverting to Flossy.

He went away, but he came back once—twice—thrice in quick succession. On business, so he said casually to Mr. and Mrs. Price, but his language to their daughter was a declaration of personal devotion. It remained for her to say whether she would marry him or no. Of one thing she was sure without need of reflection, that she loved him ardently. As a consequence she surrendered at once, though, curiously enough, she was conscious when she permitted him to kiss her with effusion that he was not the sort of man she had intended to marry—that he was not fit in her sense of the word. Yet she was determined to marry him, and from the moment their troth was plighted she found herself his eager and faithful ally, dreaming and scheming on their joint account. She would help him to succeed; they would conquer the world together; she would never doubt his ability to conquer it. And in time—yes, in time they would make even the Morton Prices notice them.

And so after some bewildered opposition on the part of Mr. Price, who was alternately appalled and fascinated by the magniloquent language of his would-be son-in-law, they were married. Flossy gave but a single sign to her husband that she understood him and recognized what they really represented. It was one evening a few months after they had set up housekeeping while they were walking home from the theatre. They had previously dined at Delmonico's, and the cost of the evening's entertainment, including a bottle of champagne at dinner, their tickets and a corsage bouquet of violets for Flossy, had been fifteen dollars. Flossy wore a resplendent theatre hat and fashionable cape—one of the several stylish costumes with which her husband had hastened to present her, and Gregory was convoying her along the Avenue with the air of a man not averse to have the world recognize that they were a well set up and prosperous couple. Flossy had put her arm well inside his and was doing her best to help him produce the effect which he desired, when she suddenly said:

"I wonder, Gregory, how long it will be before we're really anybody. Now, of course, we're only make believe swell."

Gregory gave an amused laugh. "What a clever little woman! That's just what we are. We'll keep it a secret, though, and won't advertise it to the world."

"Mum's the word," she replied, giving his arm a squeeze. "I only wished you to know that I was not being fooled; that I understood."

Fate ordained that the Williamses and the Littletons should take houses side by side in the same block. It was a new block, and at first they were the sole occupants. Williams bought his house, giving a mortgage back to the seller for all the man would accept, and obtaining a second mortgage from a money lender in consideration of a higher rate of interest, for practically the remaining value. He furnished his house ornately from top to bottom in the latest fashion, incurring bills for a portion of the effects, and arranging to pay on the instalment plan where he could not obtain full credit. His reasoning was convincing to himself and did not alarm Flossy, who was glad to feel that they were the owners of the house and attractive furniture. It was that the land was sure to improve in value before the mortgage became due, and as for the carpets and curtains and other outlays, a few points in the stock market would pay for them at any time.

Wilbur Littleton did not possess the ready money to buy; consequently he took a lease of his new house for three years, and paid promptly for the furniture he bought, the selection of which was gradual. Gregory Williams had a marvellous way of entering a shop and buying everything which pleased his eye at one fell swoop, but Wilbur, who desired to accomplish the best æsthetic effects possible consistent with his limited means, trotted Selma from one shop to another before choosing. This process of selecting slowly the things with which they were to pass their lives was a pleasure to him, and, as he supposed, to Selma. She did enjoy keenly at first beholding the enticing contents of the various stores which they entered in the process of procuring wall-papers, carpets, and the other essentials for house-keeping. It was a revelation to her that such beautiful things existed, and her inclination was to purchase the most showy and the most costly articles. In the adornment of her former home Babcock had given her a free hand. That is, his disposition had been to buy the finest things which the shopkeepers of Benham called to his attention. She understood now that his taste and the taste of Benham, and even her's, had been at fault, but she found herself hampered now by a new and annoying limitation, the smallness of their means. Almost every thing was very expensive, and she was obliged to pass by the patterns and materials she desired to possess, and accept articles of a more sober and less engaging character. Many of these, to be sure, were declared by Wilbur to be artistically charming and more suitable than many which she preferred, but it would have suited her better to fix on the rich upholstery and solid furniture, which were evidently the latest fashion in household decoration, rather than go mousing from place to place, only at last to pick up in the back corner of some store this or that object which was both reasonably pretty and reasonably cheap. When it was all over Selma was pleased with the effect of her establishment, but she had eaten of the tree of knowledge. She had visited the New York shops. These, in her capacity of a God-fearing American, she would have been ready to anathematize in a speech or in a newspaper article, but the memory of them haunted her imagination and left her domestic yearnings not wholly satisfied.

Wilbur Littleton's scheme of domestic life was essentially spiritual, and in the development of it he felt that he was consulting his wife's tastes and theories no less than his own. He knew that she understood that he was ambitious to make a name for himself as an architect; but to make it only by virtue of work of a high order; that he was unwilling to become a time-server or to lower his professional standards merely to make temporary progress, which in the end would mar a success worth having. He had no doubt that he had made this clear to her and that she sympathized with him. As a married man it was his desire and intention not to allow his interest in this ambition to interfere with the enjoyment of the new great happiness which had come into his life. He would be a professional recluse no longer. He would cast off his work when he left his office, and devote his evenings to the æsthetic delights of Selma's society. They would read aloud; he would tell her his plans and ask her advice; they would go now and then to the theatre; and, in justice to her, they would occasionally entertain their friends and accept invitations from them. With this outlook in mind he had made such an outlay as would render his home attractive and cosey—simple as became a couple just beginning life, yet the abode of a gentleman and a lover of inspiring and pretty things.

As has been mentioned, Littleton was a Unitarian, and one effect of his faith had been to make his point of view broad and straightforward. He detested hypocrisy and cant, subterfuge and self-delusion. He was content to let other people live according to their own lights without too much distress on their account, but he was too honest and too clear-headed to be able to deceive himself as to his own motives and his own conduct. He had no intention to be morbid, but he saw clearly that it was his privilege and his duty to be true to both his loves, his wife and his profession, and that if he neglected either, he would be so far false to his best needs and aspirations. Yet he felt that for the moment it was incumbent on him to err on the side of devotion to his wife until she should become accustomed to her new surroundings.

The problem of the proper arrangement and subdivision of life in a large city and in these seething, modern times is perplexing to all of us. There are so many things we would like to do which we cannot; so many things which we do against our wills. We are perpetually squinting at happiness, but just as we get a delightful vision before our eyes we are whisked off by duty or ambition or the force of social momentum to try a different view. Consequently our perennial regret is apt to be that we have seen our real interests and our real friends as in a panorama, for a fleeting moment, and then no more until the next time. For Littleton this was less true than for most. His life was deep and stable rather than many-sided. To be sure his brain experienced, now and then, the dazing effects of trying to confront all the problems of the universe and adapt his architectural endeavors to his interpretation of them; and he knew well the bewildering difficulties of the process of adjusting professional theories to the sterile conditions which workaday practice often presented. But this crowding of his mental canvas was all in the line of his life purpose. The days were too short, and sometimes left him perplexed and harassed by their rush; yet he was still pursuing the tenor of his way. The interest of marriage was not, therefore, in his case a fresh burden on a soul already laden with a variety of side pursuits. He was neither socially nor philanthropically active; he was not a club man, nor an athletic enthusiast; he was on no committees; he voted on election days, but he did not take an active part in politics. For Selma's sake all this must be changed; and he was glad to acknowledge that he owed it to himself as well as to her to widen his sympathies.

As a first step in reform he began to leave his office daily at five instead of six, and, on Saturdays, as soon after two as possible. For a few months these brands of time snatched from the furnace of his professional ardor were devoted to the shopping relative to house-furnishing. When that was over, to walking with Selma; sometimes as a sheer round of exercise in company, sometimes to visit a print-shop, exhibition of pictures, book-store, or other attraction of the hour. But the evening was for him the ideal portion of the day; when, after dinner was done, they made themselves comfortable in the new library, their living room, and it became his privilege to read aloud to her or to compare ideas with her regarding books and pictures and what was going on in the world. It had been a dream of Littleton's that some day he would re-read consecutively the British poets, and as soon as the furniture was all in place and the questions of choice of rugs and chairs and pictures had been settled by purchase, he proposed it as a definite occupation whenever they had nothing else in view. It delighted him that Selma received this suggestion with enthusiasm. Accordingly, they devoted their spare evenings to the undertaking, reading aloud in turn. Littleton's enunciation was clear and intelligent, and as a happy lover he was in a mood to fit poetic thoughts to his own experience, and to utter them ardently. While he read, Selma knew that she was ever the heroine of his imagination, which was agreeable, and she recognized besides that his performance in itself was æsthetically attractive. Yet in spite of the personal tribute, Selma preferred the evenings when she herself was the elocutionist. She enjoyed the sound of her own voice, and she enjoyed the emotions which her utterance of the rhythmic stanzas set coursing through her brain. It was obvious to her that Wilbur was captivated by her reading, and she delighted in giving herself up to the spirit of the text with the reservations appropriate to an enlightened but virtuous soul. For instance, in the case of Shelley, she gloried in his soaring, but did not let herself forget that fire-worship was not practical; in the case of Byron, though she yielded her senses to the spell of his passionate imagery, she reflected approvingly that she was a married woman.

But Littleton appreciated also that his wife should have the society of others beside himself. Pauline introduced her promptly to her own small but intelligent feminine circle, and pending Pauline's removal to a flat, the Saturday evening suppers were maintained at the old establishment. Here Selma made the acquaintance of her husband's and his sister's friends, both men and women, who dropped in often after the play and without ceremony for a weekly interchange of thought and comradeship. Selma looked forward to the first of these occasions with an eager curiosity. She expected a renewal of the Benham Institute, only in a more impressive form, as befitted a great literary centre; that papers would be read, original compositions recited, and many interesting people of both sexes perform according to their specialties. She confidently hoped to have the opportunity to declaim, "Oh, why should the spirit of mortal be proud?" "Curfew must not ring to-night," or some other of her literary pieces.

Therefore, it was almost a shock to her that the affair was so informal, and that the company seemed chiefly occupied in behaving gayly—in making sallies at each other's expense, which were greeted with merriment. They seemed to her like a lot of children let loose from school. There were no exercises, and no allusion was made to the attainments of the various guests beyond an occasional word of introduction by Pauline or Wilbur; and this word was apt to be of serio-comic import. Selma realized that among the fifteen people present there were representatives of various interesting crafts—writers, artists, a magazine editor, two critics of the stage, a prominent musician, and a college professor—but none of them seemed to her to act a part or to have their accomplishments in evidence, as she would have liked. Every one was very cordial to her, and appeared desirous to recognize her as a permanent member of their circle, but she could not help feeling disappointed at the absence of ceremony and formal events. There was no president or secretary, and presently the party went into the dining-room and sat around a table, at either end of which Pauline and Wilbur presided over a blazer. Interest centred on the preparation of a rabbit and creamed oysters, and pleasant badinage flew from tongue to tongue. Selma found herself between the magazine editor and a large, powerfully built man with a broad, rotund, strong face, who was introduced to her as Dr. Page, and who was called George by every one else. He had arrived late, just as they were going in to supper, and his appearance had been greeted with a murmur of satisfaction. He had placed himself between Pauline and her, and he showed himself, to Selma's thinking, one of the least dignified of the company.

"My dear Mrs. Littleton," he said, with a counterfeit of great gravity, "you are now witnessing an impressive example of the politeness of true friendship. There are cynics who assert that the American people are lacking in courtesy, and cast in our teeth the superiority of Japanese manners. I wish they were here to-night. There is not a single individual present, male or female, married or single, who does not secretly cherish the amiable belief that he or she can cook things on a blazer better than any one else. And yet we abstain from criticism; we offer no suggestions; we accept, without a

104

murmur, the proportions of cheese and beer and butter inflicted upon us by our hostess and her brother, and are silent. We shall even become complimentary later. Can the Japanese vie with this?"

The contrast between his eager, grave gaze, and the levity of his words, puzzled Selma. He looked interesting, but his speech seemed to her trivial and unworthy of the occasion. Still she appreciated that she must not be a spoil-sport, and that it was incumbent on her to resign herself to the situation, so she smiled gayly, and said: "I am the only one then not suffering from self-restraint. I never made a Welsh rabbit, nor cooked on a blazer." Then, in her desire for more serious conversation, she added: "Do you really think that we, as a people, are less polite than the Japanese?"

The doctor regarded her with solemn interest for an instant, as though he were pondering the question. As a matter of fact, he was thinking that she was remarkably pretty. Then he put his finger on his lips, and in a hoarse whisper, said, "Sh! Be careful. If the editorial ear should catch your proposition the editorial man would appropriate it. There!" he added, as her left-hand neighbor bent toward them in response to the summons, "he has heard, and your opportunity to sell an idea to the magazine is lost. It is all very fine for him to protest that he has heard nothing. That is a trick of his trade. Let us see now if he will agree to buy. If he refuses, it will be a clear case that he has heard and purloined it. Come, Dennison, here's a chance for a ten thousand-word symposium debate, 'Are we, as a nation, less polite than the Japanese?' We offer it for a hundred and fifty cash, and cheap at the price."

Mr. Dennison, who was a keen-eyed, quiet man, with a brown, closely-cut beard, had paused in his occupation of buttering hot toast for the impending rabbit, and was smiling quizzically. "If you have literary secrets to dispose of, Mrs. Littleton, let me warn you against making a confidant of Dr. Page. Had you spoken to me first, there is no knowing what I might have—"

"What did I tell you?" broke in the doctor. "A one hundred and fifty-dollar idea ruthlessly appropriated. These editors, these editors!"

It was tantalizing to Selma to be skirting the edge of themes she would have enjoyed to hear treated seriously. She hoped that Mr. Dennison would inquire if she really wrote, and at least he would tell her something about his magazine and literary life in New York. But he took up again his task of buttering toast, and sought to interest her in that. Presently she was unable to resist the temptation of remarking that the editorship of a magazine must be one of the most interesting of all occupations; but he looked at her with his quizzical smile, and answered:

"Between you and me, Mrs. Littleton, I will confide to you that a considerable portion of the time it is a confounded bore. To tell the truth, I much prefer to sit next to you and butter toast."

This was depressing and puzzling to Selma; but after the consumption of the rabbit and the oysters there was some improvement in the general tone of the conversation. Yet, not so far as she was concerned. Mr. Dennison neglected to confide to her the secrets of his prison house, and Dr. Page ruthlessly refused to discuss medicine, philosophy, or the Japanese. But here and there allusion was made by one or another of the company to something which had been done in the world of letters, or art, or music, which possessed merit or deserved discouragement. What was said was uttered simply, often trenchantly and lightly, but never as a dogma, or with the solemnity which Mrs. Earle had been wont to impart to her opinions. Just as the party was about to break up, Dr. Page approached Selma and offered her his hand. "It is a great pleasure to me to have met you," he said, looking into her face with his honest eyes. "A good wife was just what Wilbur needed to insure him happiness and a fine career. His friends have great confidence in his ability, and we intrust him to you in the belief that the world will hear from him—and I, for one, shall be very grateful to you."

He spoke now with evident feeling, and his manner suggested the desire to be her friend. Selma admired his large physique and felt the attraction of his searching gaze.

"Perhaps he did need a wife," she answered with an attempt at the sprightliness which he had laid aside. "I shall try not to let him be too indifferent to practical considerations."

CHAPTER III.

"Who is Dr. Page?" asked Selma of her husband when they left the house.

"One of our best friends, and one of the leading physicians in the city. The energy of that man is tireless. He is absorbed in his profession. The only respite he allows himself are these Saturday evenings, and his devotion to his little son who has hip disease. He told me to-night that he had finished his day's work only just before he came in. What did you think of him? He likes to tease."

"Then he is married?"

"He is a widower."

"He seems interested in you. He was good enough to say that he thought you needed a wife."

"Then he must have admired you, Selma. Poor fellow! I wish he might have that happiness himself. I'll tell you a secret: He has desired to marry Pauline for years. They are devoted friends—but until now that is all. His wife was an actress—a handsome creature. Two years after they were married she ran away with another man and left him. Left him with one little boy, a cripple, on whom he lavishes all the love of his big nature."

"How dreadful!"

"Yes, it is a sad story. That was ten years ago. He was very young and the woman was very beautiful. It has been the making of him, though, in one way. He had the pride and confidence of ability, but he lacked sympathy. His experience and the appealing presence of his son have developed his nature and given him tenderness. He has not been imbittered; he has simply become gentle. And how he works! He is already famous in his profession."

"Does Pauline care for him?"

"I don't know her feelings. I am sure she is fond of him, and admires him. I fancy, though, that she hesitates to renounce her own ambitions. As you are aware, she is greatly interested in her classes, and in matters pertaining to the higher education of women. George Page knew her at the time of his marriage. I do not mean that he paid her serious attention then, but he had the opportunity to ask her instead of the other. Now, when she has become absorbed in her life-work, she would naturally decline to give it up unless she felt sure that she could not be happy without him."

"I would not marry him if I were she," said Selma. "He has

given his best to the other woman. He is the one at fault, not Pauline. Why should she sacrifice her own career in order to console him?"

"She might love him sufficiently to be willing to do so, Selma. Love makes women blind to faults. But poor George was scarcely at fault. It was a misfortune."

"He made his choice and was deceived. It would be weak of her to give up her own life merely because he is lonely. We modern women have too much self-respect for that. Love is love, and it is not to be trifled with."

"Yes, love is love," murmured Littleton, "and I am happy in mine."

"That is because neither of us has loved before, you foolish boy. But as to this evening, it wasn't at all what I expected. Are your friends always like that?"

Littleton laughed. "Did they seem to you frivolous and undignified, then?"

"Almost. They certainly said nothing serious."

"It is their holiday—their evening out. They have to be serious during the rest of the week—busy with problems and cares, for they are a set of hard workers. The stress of life is so rigorous and constant here in New York that we have learned not to take our pleasure sadly. When you become accustomed to their way you will realize that they are no less serious at heart because they frolic now and then."

Selma was silent a moment; then she said, "That reminds me; have you found out about our next-door neighbors yet?"

"He is a banker named Williams, I believe."

"I saw his wife pass the window this morning. She was beautifully dressed. They must be rich."

"I dare say."

"But they live in the same style of house as ours."

"Bankers have mysterious ways of making money. We cannot compete with those."

"I suppose not. I was thinking that she had the same manner as some of your friends this evening, only more pronounced. She stopped to speak to some one just in front of the house, so I could observe her. I should think she was frivolous, but fascinating. That must be the New York manner, and, consequently, she may be very much in earnest."

"It isn't given to every woman to be attractive all the time just because she looks in earnest, as it is to you, dearest. But you musn't be too severe on the others."

"On the contrary, I think I shall like Mrs. Williams. She may teach us to be practical. You know that is what your friends would like to have me help you to be, Wilbur."

"Then they did talk a word or two of sense?"

"They said that. Do you think it is true that you are visionary?"

"It is your duty to tell me so, Selma, when you think it, just as I have told you that we can afford to laugh now and then. Come, begin."

"I haven't been your wife long enough yet. I shall know better by the end of another six months."

A fortnight elapsed before Selma made the acquaintance of Mrs. Gregory Williams. It was not a chance meeting. Flossy rang the bell deliberately one afternoon and was ushered in, thereby bridging over summarily the yawning chasm which may continue to exist for an indefinite period between families in the same block who are waiting to be introduced.

"I said to my husband last night, Mrs. Littleton, that it was ridiculous for us to be living side by side without knowing one another, and that I was going to call. We moved in three weeks before you, so I'm the one who ought to break the ice. Otherwise we might have stared at each other blankly for three months, looked at each other sheepishly out of the corner of our eyes for another three, half bowed for six months, and finally, perhaps, reached the stage where we are now. Neighbors should be neighborly, don't you think so?"

"Indeed I do. Of course I knew you by sight; and I felt I should like to make your acquaintance." Selma spoke with enthusiasm. Here was some one whose social deftness was no less marked than Mrs. Hallett Taylor's, and, to her mind, more brilliant, yet whom she felt at once to be congenial. Though she perceived that her neighbor's clothes made her own apparel seem dull, and was accordingly disposed to be on her guard, she realized instinctively that she was attracted by the visitor.

"That is very nice of you," said Flossy. "I told my

husband—Gregory—the other day that I was sure you were something literary—I mean Mr. Littleton, of course—and when he found out that he was I said we must certainly cultivate you as an antidote to the banking business. Gregory's a banker. It must be delightful to plan houses. This room is so pretty and tasteful."

"It isn't wholly furnished yet. We are buying things by degrees, as we find pieces which we like."

"We bought all our things in two days at one fell swoop," said Flossy with a gay laugh. "Gregory gave the dealers carte blanche. That's his way," she added with a touch of pride. "I dare say the house would have been prettier if we could have taken more time. However, it is all paid for now. Some of it was bought on the instalment plan, but Gregory bought or sold something in stocks the next week which covered the furniture and paid for a present for me of this besides," she said, indicating her seal-skin cape. "Wasn't he a dear?"

Selma did not know precisely what the instalment plan was, but she understood that Mr. Williams had been distinctly clever in his wife's estimation. She perceived that Mrs. Williams had the same light, half jocular manner displayed by Wilbur's friends, and that she spoke with bubbling, jaunty assurance, which was suggestive of frivolity. Still Wilbur had intimated that this might be the New York manner, and clearly her neighbor had come in a friendly spirit and was duly appreciative of the distinction of being literary. Besides, her ready disposition to talk about herself and her affairs seemed to Selma the sign of a willingness to be truly friendly. The seal-skin cape she wore was very handsome, and she was more conspicuously attired from head to foot than any woman with whom Selma had ever conversed. She was pretty, too—a type of beauty less spiritual than her own—with piquant, eager features, laughing, restless gray eyes, and light hair which escaped from her coquettish bonnet in airy ringlets. If they had met three years earlier Selma would certainly have regarded her as an incarnation of volatility and servility to foreign fashions. Now, though she classed her promptly as a frivolous person, she regarded her with a keen curiosity not unmixed with self-distress, and the reflection came to her that a little of the New York manner might perhaps be desirable when in New York.

"Yes, it's beautiful," she replied, referring to the cape.

110

"Gregory is always making me presents like that. He gave me this bracelet yesterday. He saw it in the shop-window and went in and bought it. Speaking of husbands, you won't mind my saying that I think Mr. Littleton is very distinguished looking? I often see him pass the window in the morning."

"Of course *I* think so," said Selma. "I suppose it would seem flat if I were to say that I admired Mr. Williams's appearance also."

"The truth is no harm. Wouldn't it be nice if we should happen to become friends? We are the pioneers in this block, but I hear three other houses have been sold. I suppose you own your house?"

"I believe not. We have a lease of it."

"That's a pity, because Gregory bought ours on a mortgage, thinking the land is sure to become more valuable. He hopes to be able to sell some day for a great deal more than he paid for it. May I ask where you lived before you were married?"

Selma told her briefly.

"Then you are almost Western. I felt sure you weren't a New Yorker, and I didn't think you were from Boston. You have the Boston earnest expression, but somehow you're different. You don't mind my analyzing you, do you? That's a Boston habit by the way. But I'm not from Boston. I've lived all my life in New Jersey. So we are both strangers in New York. That is, I'm the same as a stranger, though my father is a cousin of the Morton Prices. We sent them wedding cards and they called one day when I was out. I shall return the call and find them out, and that will be the last move on either side until Gregory does something remarkable. I'm rather glad I wasn't at home, because it would have been awkward. They wouldn't have known what to say to me, and they might have felt that they ought to ask me to dinner, and I don't care to have them ask me until they're obliged to. Do I shock you running on so about my own affairs?" Flossy asked, noticing Selma draw herself up sternly.

"Oh no, I like that. I was only thinking that it was very strange of your cousins. You are as good as they, aren't you?"

"Mercy, no. We both know it, and that's what makes the situation so awkward. As Christians, they had to call on me, but I really think they are justified in stopping there. Socially I'm nobody."

"In this country we are all free and equal."

"You're a dear—a delicious dear," retorted Flossy, with a caressing laugh. "There's something of the sort in the Declaration of Independence, but, as Gregory says, that was put in as a bluff to console salesladies. Was everybody equal in Benham, Mrs. Littleton?"

"Practically so," said Selma, with an air of haughtiness, which was evoked by her recollection of the group of houses on Benham's River Drive into which she had never been invited. "There were some people who were richer than others, but that didn't make them better than any one else."

"Well, in New York it's different. Of course, every body has the same right to vote or to be elected President of the United States, but equality ends there. People here are either in society or out of it, and society itself is divided into sets. There's the conservative aristocratic set, the smart rapid set, the set which hasn't much money, but has Knickerbocker or other highly respectable ancestors, the new millionaire set, the literary set, the intellectual philanthropic set, and so on, according to one's means or tastes. Each has its little circle which shades away into the others, and every now and then there is a big entertainment to which they all go."

"I see," said Selma, coldly.

"Now, to make it plain, I will confide to you in strictest confidence that Gregory and I aren't yet really in any set. We are trying to get a footing and are holding on by our teeth to the fringe of the social merry-go-round. I wouldn't admit it to any one but you; but as you are a stranger like myself and in the same block, I am glad to initiate you into the customs of this part of the country," Flossy gave a merry toss to her head which set her ringlets bobbing, and rose to go.

"And in what set are your cousins?" asked Selma.

"If you wish to hear about them, I shall have to sit down again. The Morton-Prices belong to the ultra-conservative, solid, stupid, aristocratic set—the most dignified and august of all. They are almost as sacred as Hindoo gods, and some people would walk over red-hot coals to gain admission to their house. And really, it's quite just in one way that incense should be burnt before them. You mustn't look so disgusted, because there's some sense in it all. As Gregory says, it's best to look things squarely in the face. Most of the people in these different sets are somebodies because either their grandfathers or they have done something well—better than other people, and made money as a consequence. And when a family has made money or won distinction by its brains and then has brushed its teeth twice a day religiously for two generations, the members of it, even though dull, are entitled to respect, don't you think so?"

Selma, who brushed her teeth but once a day, looked a little sharp at Flossy.

"It makes money of too much importance and it establishes class distinctions. I don't approve of such a condition of affairs at all."

Flossy shrugged her shoulders. "I have never thought whether I approve of it or not. I am only telling you what exists. I don't deny that money counts for a great deal, for, as Gregory says, money is the measure of success. But money isn't everything. Brains count and refinement, and nice honorable ways of looking at things. Of course, I'm only telling you what my ambition is. People have different kinds of bees in their bonnets. Some men have the presidential bee; I have the social bee. I should like to be recognized as a prominent member of the charmed circle on my own merits and show my cousins that I am really worthy of their attention. There are a few who are able to be superior to that sort of thing, who go on living their own lives attractively and finely, without thinking of society, and who suddenly wake up some day to find themselves socially famous—to find that they have been taken up. That's the best way, but one requires to be the right sort of person and to have a lot of moral courage. I can imagine it happening to you and your husband. But it would never happen to Gregory and me. We shall have to make money and cut a dash in order to attract attention, and by-and-by, if we are persistent and clever enough, we may be recognized as somebodies, provided there is something original or interesting about us. There! I have told you my secret and shocked you into the bargain. I really must be going. But I'll tell you another secret first: It'll be a pleasure to me to see you, if I may, because you look at things differently and haven't a social bee. I wish I were like that—really like it. But then, as Gregory would say, I shouldn't be myself, and not to be one's self is worse than anything else after all, isn't it? You and your husband must come and dine with us soon."

After Mrs. Williams had gone, Selma fell into a brown study. She had listened to sentiments of which she thoroughly disapproved, and which were at variance with all her theories and conceptions. What her friendly, frivolous visitor had told her with engaging frankness offended her conscience and patriotism. She did not choose to admit the existence of these class-distinctions, and she knew that even if they did exist, they could not possibly concern Wilbur and herself. Even Mrs. Williams had appreciated that Wilbur and her literary superiority put them above and beyond the application of any snobbish, artificial, social measuring-tape. And yet Selma's brow was clouded. Her thought reverted to the row of stately houses on either side of Fifth Avenue, into none of which she had the right of free access, in spite of the fact that she was leading her life attractively and finely, without regard to society. She thought instinctively of Sodom and Gomorrah, and she saw righteously with her mind's eye for a moment an angel with a flaming sword consigning to destruction these offending mansions and their owners as symbols of mammon and contraband to God.

That evening she told Wilbur of Mrs. Williams's visit. "She's a bright, amusing person, and quite pretty. We took a fancy to each other. But what do you suppose she said? She intimated that we haven't any social position."

"Very kind of her, I'm sure. She must be a woman of discrimination—likewise something of a character."

"She's smart. So you think it's true?"

"What? About our social position? Ours is as good as theirs, I fancy."

"Oh yes, Wilbur. She acknowledges that herself. She admires us both and she thinks it fine that we don't care for that sort of thing. What she said was chiefly in connection with herself, but she intimated that neither they, nor we, are the—er—equals of the people who live on Fifth Avenue and thereabouts. She's a cousin of the Morton Prices, whoever they may be, and she declared perfectly frankly that they were better than she. Wasn't it funny?"

"You seem to have made considerable progress for one visit."

"I like that, you know, Wilbur. I prefer people who are willing to tell me their real feelings at once."

"Morton Price is one of the big bugs. His great grandfather

114

was among the wise, shrewd pioneers in the commercial progress of the city. The present generation are eminently respectable, very dignified, mildly philanthropic, somewhat self-indulgent, reasonably harmless, decidedly ornamental and rather dull."

"But Mrs. Williams says that she will never be happy until her relations and the people of that set are obliged to take notice of her, and that she and her husband are going to cut a dash to attract attention. It's her secret."

"The cat which she let out of the bag is a familiar one. She must be amusing, provided she is not vulgar."

"I don't think she's vulgar, Wilbur. She wears gorgeous clothes, but they're extremely pretty. She said that she called on me because she thought that we were literary, and that she desired an antidote to the banker's business, which shows she isn't altogether worldly. She wishes us to dine with them soon."

"That's neighborly."

"Why was it, Wilbur, that you didn't buy our house instead of hiring it?"

"Because I hadn't money enough to pay for it."

"The Williamses bought theirs. But I don't believe they paid for it altogether. She says her husband thinks the land will increase in value, and they hope some day to make money by the rise. I imagine Mr. Williams must be shrewd."

"He's a business man. Probably he bought, and gave a mortgage back. I might have done that, but we weren't sure we should like the location, and it isn't certain yet that fashion will move in just this direction. I have very little, and I preferred not to tie up everything in a house we might not wish to keep."

"I see. She appreciates that people may take us up any time. She thinks you are distinguished looking."

"If she isn't careful, I shall make you jealous, Selma. Was there anything you didn't discuss?"

"I regard you as the peer of any Morton Price alive. Why aren't you?"

"Far be it from me to discourage such a wifely conclusion. Provided you think so, I don't care for any one else's opinion."

"But you agree with her. That is, you consider because people of that sort don't invite us to their houses, they are better than we."

"Nothing of the kind. But there's no use denying the existence of social classes in this city, and that, though I flatter myself you and I are trying to make the most of our lives in accordance with the talents and means at our disposal, we are not and are not likely to become, for the present at any rate, socially prominent. That's what you have in mind, I think. I don't know those people; they don't know me. Consequently they do not ask me to their beautiful and costly entertainments. Some day, perhaps, if I am very successful as an architect, we may come more in contact with them, and they will have a chance to discover what a charming wife I have. But from the point of view of society, your neighbor Mrs. Williams is right. She evidently has a clear head on her shoulders and knows what she desires. You and I believe that we can get more happiness out of life by pursuing the even tenor of our way in the position in which we happen to find ourselves."

"I don't understand it," said Selma, shaking her head and looking into space with her spiritual expression. "It troubles me. It isn't American. I didn't think such distinctions existed in this country. Is it all a question of money, then? Do intelligence and—er—purpose count for nothing?"

"My dear girl, it simply means that the people who are on top—the people who, by force of success, or ability, or money, are most prominent in the community, associate together, and the world gives a certain prominence to their doings. Here, where fortunes have been made so rapidly, and we have no formal aristocracy, money undoubtedly plays a conspicuous part in giving access to what is known as society. But it is only an entering wedge. Money supplies the means to cultivate manners and the right way of looking at things, and good society represents the best manners and, on the whole, the best way of looking at things."

"Yes. But you say that we don't belong to it."

"We do in the broad, but not in the narrow sense. We have neither the means nor the time to take part in fashionable society. Surely, Selma, you have no such ambition?"

"I? You know I disapprove of everything of the sort. It is like Europe. There's nothing American in it."

"I don't know about that. The people concerned in it are Americans. If a man has made money there is no reason why he shouldn't build a handsome house, maintain a fine establishment, give his children the best educational advantages, and choose his own friends. So the next generation becomes more civilized. It isn't the best Americanism to waste one's time in pursuing frivolities and excessive luxury, as some of these people do; but there's nothing un-American in making the most of one's opportunities. As I've said to you before, Selma, it's the way in which one rises that's the important thing in the individual equation, and every man must choose for himself what that shall be. My ambition is to excel in my profession, and to mould my life to that end without neglecting my duties as a citizen or a husband. If, in the end, I win fame and fortune, so much the better. But there's no use in worrying because other people are more fashionable than we."

"Of course. You speak as if you thought I was envious of them, Wilbur. What I don't understand is why such people should be allowed to exist in this country."

"We're a free people, Selma. I'm a good democrat, but you must agree that the day-laborer in his muddy garb would not find himself at ease in a Fifth Avenue drawing-room. On that account shall we abolish the drawing-room?"

"We are not day-laborers."

"Not precisely; but we have our spurs to win. And, unlike some people in our respectable, but humble station, we have each other's love to give us courage to fight the battle of life bravely. I had a fresh order to-day—and I have bought tickets for to-night at the theatre."

CHAPTER IV.

Almost the first persons at the theatre on whom Selma's eyes rested were the Gregory Williamses. They were in a box with two other people, and both Flossy and her husband were talking with the festive air peculiar to those who are willing to be noticed and conscious that their wish is being gratified. Flossy wore a gay bonnet and a stylish frock, supplemented by a huge bunch of violets, and her husband's evening dress betrayed a slight exaggeration of the prevailing fashion in respect to his standing collar and necktie. Selma had never had a thorough look at him before, and she reflected that he was decidedly impressive and handsome. His face was full and pleasant, his mustache large and gracefully curved, and his figure manly. His most distinguishing characteristic was a dignity of bearing uncommon in so young a man, suggesting that he carried, if not the destiny of republics on his shoulders, at least, important financial secrets in his brain. The man and woman with them were almost elderly and gave the effect of being strangers to the city. They were Mr. and Mrs. Silas S. Parsons. Mr. Parsons was a prosperous Western business man, who now and then visited New York, and who had recently become a customer of Williams's. He had dealt in the office where Williams was a clerk, and, having taken a fancy to him, was disposed to help the new firm. Gregory had invited them to dinner and to the theatre, by way of being attentive, and had taken a box instead of stalls, in order to make his civility as magnificent as the occasion would permit. A box, besides being a delicate testimonial to his guest, would cause the audience to notice him and his wife and to ask who they were.

In the gradual development of the social appetite in this country a certain class has been evolved whose drawing-room is the floor of the leading theatres. Society consists for them chiefly in being present often at theatrical performances in sumptuous dress, not merely to witness the play, but to be participants in a social function which enhances their self-esteem. To be looked at and to look on these occasions takes the place with them of balls and dinner parties. They are not theatregoers in the proper sense, but social aspirants, and the boxes and stalls are for them an arena in which for a price they can show themselves in their finery and attractions, for lack of other opportunities.

Our theatres are now in the full blaze of this harmless

118

appropriation for quasi-ballroom uses. At the time when Selma was a New York bride the movement was in its infancy. The people who went to the theatre for spectacular purposes no less than to see the actors on the stage were comparatively few in number. Still the device was practised, and from the very fact that it was not freely employed, was apt to dazzle the eyes of the uninitiated public more unreservedly than to-day. The sight of Mrs. Williams in a box, in the glory of her becoming frock and her violets, caused even so stern a patriot and admirer of simplicity as Selma to seize her husband's arm and whisper:

"Look." What is more she caught herself a moment later blushing with satisfaction on account of the friendly bow which was bestowed on her.

Wilbur Littleton's ambitions were so definite and congenial that the sight of his neighbors' splendor neither offended nor irritated him. He did not feel obliged to pass judgment on them while deriving amusement from their display, nor did he experience any qualms of regret that he was not able to imitate them. He regarded Flossy and her husband with the tolerant gaze of one content to allow other people to work out their salvation, without officious criticism, provided he were allowed the same privilege, and ready to enjoy any features of the situation which appealed to his sense of humor or to his human sympathy. Flossy's frank, open nod and ingenuous face won his favor at once, especially as he appreciated that she and Selma had found each other attractive, and though he tabooed luxury and fashionable paraphernalia where he was immediately concerned, it occurred to him that this evidently wide-awake, vivacious-looking couple might, as friends, introduce just the right element of variety into their lives. He had no wish to be a banker himself, nor to hire boxes at the theatre, but he was disposed to meet half-way these entertaining and gorgeous neighbors.

Selma, in spite of her wish to watch the play, found her glance returning again and again to the occupants of the box, though she endeavored to dispose of the matter by remarking presently that she could not understand why people should care to make themselves so conspicuous, particularly as the seats in the boxes were less desirable for seeing the stage than their own.

"We wouldn't care for it, but probably it's just what they

like," said Wilbur. "Some society reporter may notice them; in which case we shall see in the Sunday newspaper that Mr. Gregory Williams and party occupied a private box at the Empire Theatre last Tuesday evening, which will be another straw toward helping them to carry out their project of attracting attention. I like the face of your new friend, my dear. I mean to say that she looks unaffected and honest, and as if she had a sense of humor. With those three virtues a woman can afford to have some faults. I suppose she has hers."

Littleton felt that Selma was disposed to fancy her neighbor, but was restrained by conscientious scruples due to her dislike for society concerns. He had fallen in love with and married his wife because he believed her to be free from and superior to the petty weaknesses of the feminine social creed; but though extremely proud of her uncompromising standards, he had begun to fear lest she might indulge her point of view so far as to be unjust. Her scornful references from time to time to those who had made money and occupied fine houses had wounded his own sense of justice. He had endeavored to explain that virtue was not the exclusive prerogative of the noble-minded poor, and now he welcomed an opportunity of letting her realize from personal experience that society was not so bad as it was painted.

Selma returned Mrs. Williams's call during the week, but did not find her at home. A few days later arrived a note stamped with a purple and gold monogram inviting them to dinner. When the evening arrived they found only a party of four. A third couple had given out at the last minute, so they were alone with their hosts. The Williams house in its decoration and upholstery was very different from their own. The drawing-room was bright with color. The furniture was covered with light blue plush; there were blue and yellow curtains, gay cushions, and a profusion of gilt ornamentation. A bear-skin, a show picture on an easel, and a variety of florid bric-à-brac completed the brilliant aspect of the apartment. Selma reflected at once that that this was the sort of drawing-room which would have pleased her had she been given her head and a full purse. It suggested her home at Benham refurnished by the light of her later experience undimmed by the shadow of economy. On the way down to dinner she noticed in the corner of the hall a suit of old armor, and she was able to perceive that the little room on one

120

side of the front door, which they learned subsequently was Mr. Williams's den, contained Japanese curiosities. The dinner-table shone with glass and silver ware, and was lighted by four candles screened by small pink shades. By the side of Flossy's plate and her own was a small bunch of violets, and there was a rosebud for each of the men. The dinner, which was elaborate, was served by two trig maids. There were champagne and frozen pudding. Selma felt almost as if she were in fairy-land. She had never experienced anything just like this before; but her exacting conscience was kept at bay by the reflection that this must be a further manifestation of the New York manner, and her self-respect was propitiated by the cordiality of her entertainers. The conversation was bubbling and light-hearted on the part of both Mr. and Mrs. Williams. They kept up a running prattle on the current fads of the day, the theatre, the doings of well-known social personages, and their own household possessions, which they naïvely called to the attention of their guests, that they might be admired. But Selma enjoyed more than the general conversation her talk with the master of the house, who possessed all the friendly suavity of his wife and also the valuable masculine trait of seeming to be utterly absorbed in any woman to whom he was talking. Gregory had a great deal of manner and a confidential fluency of style, which gave distinction even to commonplace remarks. His method did not condescend to nudging when he wished to note a point, but it fell only so far short of it as he thought social elegance required. His conversation presently drifted, or more properly speaking, flowed into a graphic and frank account of his own progress as a banker. He referred to past successful undertakings, descanted on his present roseate responsibilities, and hinted sagely at impending operations which would eclipse in importance any in which he had hitherto been engaged. In answer to Selma's questions he discoursed alluringly concerning the methods of the Stock Exchange, and gave her to understand that for an intelligent and enterprising man speculation was the high road to fortune. No doubt for fools and for people of mediocre or torpid abilities it was a dangerous trade; but for keen and bold intellects what pursuit offered such dazzling opportunities?

Selma listened, abhorrent yet fascinated. It worried her to be told that what she had been accustomed to regard as gambling should be so quickly and richly rewarded. Yet the fairy scene around her manifestly confirmed the prosperous language of her host and left no room for doubt that her neighbors were making brilliant progress. Apparently, too, this business of speculation and of vast combinations of railroad and other capital, the details of which were very vague to her, was, in his opinion, the most desirable and profitable of callings.

"Do you know," she said, "that I have been taught to believe that to speculate in stocks is rather dreadful, and that the people of the country don't approve of it." She spoke smilingly, for the leaven of the New York manner was working, but she could not refrain from testifying on behalf of righteousness.

"The people of the country!" exclaimed Gregory, with a smile of complacent amusement. "My dear Mrs. Littleton, you must not let yourself be deceived by the Sunday school, Fourth of July, legislative or other public utterances of the American people. It isn't necessary to shout it on the house-tops, but I will confide to you that, whatever they may declaim or publish to the contrary, the American people are at heart a nation of gamblers. They don't play little horses and other games in public for francs, like the French, for the law forbids it, but I don't believe that any one, except we bankers and brokers, realizes how widely exists the habit of playing the stock-market. Thousands of people, big and little, sanctimonious and highly respectable, put up their margins and reap their profits or their losses. Oh no, the country doesn't approve of it, especially those who lose. I assure you that the letters which pass through the post-office from the godly, freeborn voters in the rural districts would tell an eloquent story concerning the wishes of the people of the country in regard to speculation."

Flossy was rising from table as he finished, so he accompanied the close of his statement with a sweeping bow which comported with his jaunty dignity.

"I am afraid you are a wicked man. You ought not to slander the American people like that," Selma answered, pleased as she spoke at the light touch which she was able to impart to her speech.

"It's true. Every word of it is true," he said as she passed him. He added in a low tone—"I would almost even venture to wager a pair of gloves that at some time or other your husband has had a finger in the pie."

"Never," retorted Selma.

"What is that Gregory is saying?" interrupted Flossy, putting her arm inside Selma's. "I can see by his look that he has been plaguing you."

"Yes, he has been trying to shatter my ideals, and now he is trying to induce me to make an odious bet with him."

"Don't, for you would be certain to lose. Gregory is in great luck nowadays."

"That is evident, for he has had the good fortune to make the acquaintance of Mrs. Littleton," said Williams gallantly.

The two men were left alone with their cigars. After these were lighted, as if he were carrying out his previous train of thought, Gregory remarked, oracularly, at the end of a puff: "Louisville and Nashville is certain to sell higher."

Littleton looked blank for a moment. He knew so little of stocks that at first he did not understand what was meant. Then he said, politely: "Indeed!"

"It is good for a ten-point rise in my opinion," Williams continued after another puff. He was of a liberal nature, and was making a present of this tip to his guest in the same spirit of hospitality as he had proffered the dinner and the champagne. He was willing to take for granted that Littleton, as a gentleman, would give him the order in case he decided to buy, which would add another customer to his list. But his suggestion was chiefly disinterested.

"I'm afraid I know very little about such matters," Littleton responded with a smile. "I never owned but ten shares of stock in my life." Then, by way, perhaps, of showing that he was not indifferent to all the good things which the occasion afforded, he said, indicating a picture on the opposite wall: "That is a fine piece of color."

Williams, having discharged his obligations as a host, was willing to exchange the stock-market as a topic for his own capacity as a lightning appreciator and purchaser of objects of art.

"Yes," he said, urbanely, "that is a good thing. I saw it in the shop-window, asked the price and bought it. I bought two other pictures at the same time. 'I'll take that, and that, and that,' I said, pointing with my cane. The dealer looked astonished. He was used, I suppose, to having people come in and look at a picture every day for a fortnight before deciding. When I like a thing I know it. The three cost me eighteen hundred dollars, and I paid for them within a week by a turn in the market."

"You were very fortunate," said Littleton, who wished to seem sympathetic.

Meanwhile the two wives had returned to the drawing-room arm in arm, and established themselves on one of those small sofas for two, constructed so that the sitters are face to face. They had taken a strong fancy to each other, especially Flossy to Selma, and in the half hour which followed they made rapid progress toward intimacy. Before they parted each had agreed to call the other by her Christian name, and Selma had confided the story of her divorce. Flossy listened with absorbed interest and murmured at the close:

"Who would have thought it? You look so pure and gentle and refined that a man must have been a brute to treat you like that. But you are happy now, thank goodness. You have a husband worthy of you."

Each had a host of things still unsaid when Littleton and Williams joined them.

"Well, my dear," said Wilbur as they left the house, "that was a sort of Arabian Nights entertainment for us, wasn't it? A little barbaric, but handsome and well intentioned. I hope it didn't shock you too much."

"It struck me as very pleasant, Wilbur. I think I am beginning to understand New York a little better. Every thing costs so much here that it seems necessary to make money, doesn't it? I don't see exactly how poor people get along. Do you know, Mr. Williams wished to bet me a pair of gloves that you buy stocks sometimes."

"He would have lost his bet."

"So I told him at once. But he didn't seem to believe me. I was sure you never did. He appears to be very successful; but I let him see that I knew it was gambling. You consider it gambling, don't you?"

"Not quite so bad as that. Some stock-brokers are gamblers; but the occupation of buying and selling stocks for a commission is a well recognized and fashionable business."

"Mr. Williams thinks that a great many Americans make money in stocks—that we are gamblers as a nation."

"I am, in my heart, of the same opinion."

"Oh, Wilbur. I find you are not so good a patriot as I supposed."

"I hate bunkum."

"What is that?"

"Saying things for effect, and professing virtue which we do not possess."

Selma was silent a moment. "What does champagne cost a bottle?"

"About three dollars and a half."

"Do you really think their house barbaric?"

"It certainly suggests to me heterogeneous barbaric splendor. They bought their upholstery as they did their pictures, with free-handed self-confidence. Occasionally they made a brilliant shot, but oftener they never hit the target at all."

"I think I like brighter colors than you do, Wilbur," mused Selma. "I used to consider things like that as wrong; but I suppose that was because our fathers wished Europe to understand that we disapproved of the luxury of courts and the empty lives of the nobility. But if people here with purpose have money, it would seem sensible to furnish their houses prettily."

"Subject always to the crucifying canons of art," laughed Littleton. "I'm glad you're coming round to my view, Selma. Only I deny the ability of the free-born American, with the overflowing purse, to indulge his newly acquired taste for gorgeous effects without professional assistance."

"I suppose so. I can see that their house is crude, though I do think that they have some handsome things. It must be interesting to walk through shops and say: 'I'll take that,' just because it pleases you."

During her first marriage Selma had found the problem of dollars and cents a simple one. The income of Lewis Babcock was always larger than the demands made upon it, and though she kept house and was familiar with the domestic disbursements, questions of expenditure solved themselves readily. She had never been obliged to ask herself whether they could afford this or that outlay. Her husband had been only too eager to give her anything she desired. Consideration of the cost of things had seemed to her beneath her notice, and as the concern of the providing man rather than the thoughtful American wife and mother. After she had been divorced the difficulty in supplying herself readily with money had been a dismaying incident of her single life. Dismaying because it had seemed to her a limitation unworthy of her aspirations and abilities. She had married Littleton because she believed him her ideal of what a man should be, but she had been glad that he would be able to support her and exempt her from the necessity of asking what things cost.

By the end of their first year and a half of marriage, Selma realized that this necessity still stood, almost like a wolf at the door, between her and the free development of her desires and aspirations. New York prices were appalling; the demands of life in New York still more so. They had started house-keeping on a more elaborate scale than she had been used to in Benham. As Mrs. Babcock she had kept one hired girl; but in her new kitchen there were two servants, in deference to the desire of Littleton, who did not wish her to perform the manual work of the establishment. Men rarely appreciate in advance to the full extent the extra cost of married life, and Littleton, though intending to be prudent, found his bills larger than he had expected. He was able to pay them promptly and without worry, but he was obliged to make evident to Selma that the margin over and above their carefully considered expenses was very small. The task of watching the butcher's book and the provision list, and thinking twice before making any new outlay, was something she had not bargained for. All through her early life as a girl, the question of money had been kept in the background by the simplicity of her surroundings. In her country town at home they had kept no servants. A woman relative had done the work, and she had been free to pursue her mental interests and devote herself to her father. She had thought then that the existence of domestic servants was an act of treason against the institutions of the country by those who kept them. Yet she had accepted, with glee, the hired-girl whom Babcock had provided, satisfying her own democratic scruples by dubbing her "help," and by occasionally offering her a book to read or catechising her as to her moral needs. There is probably no one in the civilized world more proud of the possession of a domestic servant than the American woman who has never had one, and no one more prompt to consign her to the obscurity of the kitchen after a feeble pretense at making her feel at home. Selma was delighted to have two instead

126

of one, and, after beholding Mrs. Williams's trig maids, was eager to see her own arrayed in white caps and black alpaca dresses. Yet, though she had become keen to cultivate the New York manner, and had succeeded in reconciling her conscience to the possession of beautiful things by people with a purpose, it irked her to feel that she was hampered in living up to her new-found faith by the bugbear of a lean purse. She had expected, as Wilbur's wife, to figure quickly and gracefully in the van of New York intellectual and social progress. Instead, she was one among thousands, living in a new and undeveloped locality, unrecognized by the people of whom she read in the newspapers, and without opportunities for displaying her own individuality and talents. It depressed her to see the long lines of houses, street after street, and to think that she was merely a unit, unknown by name, in this great sea of humanity—she, Selma Littleton, free-born American, conscious of virtue and power. This must not be; and she divined clearer and clearer every day that it need not be if she had more money.

It began to be annoying to her that Wilbur's professional progress was not more rapid. To be sure he had warned her that he could not hope to reach the front rank at once; that recognition must be gradual; and that he must needs work slowly in order to do himself justice. She had accepted this chiefly as a manifestation of modesty, not doubting that many orders would be forthcoming, especially now that he had the new stimulus of her love and inspiration. Instead there had been no marked increase in the number of his commissions; moreover he had been unsuccessful in two out of three competitions for minor public buildings for which he had submitted designs. From both the pecuniary and professional point of view these failures had been a disappointment. He was in good spirits and obviously happy, and declared that he was doing as well as he could reasonably expect; yet on his discouraged days he admitted that the cost of retaining his draughtsmen was a drain on the profit side of his ledger.

In contrast with this the prosperity of her neighbors the Williamses was a little hard to bear. The sudden friendship developed into neighborly intimacy, and she and Flossy saw much of each other, dropping in familiarly, and often walking and shopping together. The two men were on sufficiently cordial terms, each being tolerant of the other's limitations, and seeking to recognize his good points for the sake of the bond between their wives. The return dinner was duly given, and Selma, hopeless of imitating the barbaric splendor, sought refuge in the reflection that the æsthetic and intellectual atmosphere of her table would atone for the lack of material magnificence, and limited her efforts to a few minor details such as providing candles with colored shades and some bonbon dishes. It was plain that Flossy admired her because she recognized her to be a fine and superior soul, and the appreciation of this served to make it more easy not to repine at the difference between their entertainments. Still the constant acquisition of pretty things by her frank and engaging friend was an ordeal which only a soul endowed with high, stern democratic faith and purpose could hope to endure with equanimity. Flossy bought new adornments for her house and her person with an amiable lavishness which required no confession to demonstrate that her husband was making money. She made the confession, though, from time to time with a bubbling pride, never suspecting that it could harass or tempt her spiritual looking friend. She prattled artlessly of theatre parties followed by a supper at one of the fashionable restaurants, and of new acquaintances whom she entertained, and through whom her social circle was enlarged, without divining that the sprightly narration was a thorn in the flesh of her hearer. Selma was capricious in her reception of these reports of progress. At times she listened to them with grave, cold eyes, which Flossy took for signals of noble disdain and sought to deprecate by wooing promises to be less worldly. At others she asked questions with a feverish, searching curiosity, which stimulated Mrs. Williams's free and independent style into running commentaries on the current course of social events and the doings and idiosyncracies of contemporary leaders of fashion whom she had viewed from afar. One afternoon Selma saw from her window Flossy and her husband drive jubilantly away in a high cart with yellow wheels drawn by a sleek cob, and at the same moment she became definitely aware that her draught from the cup of life had a bitter taste. Why should these people drive in their own vehicle rather than she? It seemed clear to her that Wilbur could not be making the best use of his talents, and that she had both a grievance against him and a sacred duty to perform in his and her own behalf. Justice and self-respect demanded that their mutual light should no longer be hid under a bushel.

CHAPTER V.

Pauline Littleton was now established in her new lodgings. Having been freed by her brother's marriage from the responsibilities of a housewife, she was able to concentrate her attention on the work in which she was interested. Her classes absorbed a large portion of her time. The remainder was devoted to writing to girls in other cities who sought her advice in regard to courses of study, and to correspondence, consultation, and committee meetings with a group of women in New York and elsewhere, who like herself were engrossed in educational matters. She was glad to have the additional time thus afforded her for pursuing her own tastes, and the days seemed too short for what she wished to accomplish. She occupied two pleasant rooms within easy walking distance of her brother's house. Her classes took her from home four days in the week, and two mornings in every seven were spent at her desk with her books and papers, in the agreeable labor of planning and correspondence.

Naturally one of her chief desires was to be on loving terms with her brother's wife, and to do everything in her power to add to Selma's happiness. She summoned her women friends to meet her sister-in-law at afternoon tea. All of these called on the bride, and some of them invited her to their houses. They were busy women like Pauline herself, intent in their several ways on their vocations or avocations. They were disposed to extend the right hand of fellowship to Mrs. Littleton, whom they without exception regarded as interesting in appearance, but they had no leisure for immediate intimacy with her. Having been introduced to her and having scheduled her in their minds as a new and desirable acquaintance, they went their ways, trusting chiefly to time to renew the meeting and to supply the evidence as to the stranger's social value. Busy people in a large city are obliged to argue that new-comers should win their spurs, and that great minds, valuable opinions, and moving social graces are never crushed by inhumanity, but are certain sooner or later to gain recognition. Therefore after being very cordial and expressing the hope of seeing more of her in the future, every one departed and left Selma to her duties and her opportunities as Littleton's wife, without having the courtesy to indicate that they considered her a superior woman.

Pauline regarded this behavior on the part of her friends as normal, and having done her social duty in the afternoon tea line, without a suspicion that Selma was disappointed by the experience, she gave herself up to the congenial undertaking of becoming intimate with her sister-in-law. She ascribed Selma's reserve, and cold, serious manner partly to shyness due to her new surroundings, and partly to the spiritual rigor of the puritan conscience and point of view. She had often been told that individuals of this temperament possessed more depth of character than more emotional and socially facile people, and she was prepared to woo. In comparison with Wilbur, Pauline was accustomed to regard herself as a practical and easy-going soul, but she was essentially a woman of fine and vigorous moral and mental purpose. Like many of her associates in active life, however, she had become too occupied with concrete possibilities to be able to give much thought to her own soul anatomy, and she was glad to look up to her brother's wife as a spiritual superior and to recognize that the burden lay on herself to demonstrate her own worthiness to be admitted to close intimacy on equal terms. Wilbur was to her a creature of light, and she had no doubt that his wife was of the same ethereal composition.

Pauline was glad, too, of the opportunity really to know a countrywoman of a type so different from her own friends. She, like Wilbur, had heard all her life of these interesting and inspiring beings; intense, marvellously capable, peerless, free-born creatures panoplied in chastity and endowed with congenital mental power and bodily charms, who were able to cook, educate children, control society and write literature in the course of the day's employment. The newspapers and popular opinion had given her to understand that these were the true Americans, and caused her to ask herself whether the circle to which she herself belonged was not retrograde from a nobler ideal. In what way she did not precisely understand, except that she and her friends did not altogether disdain nice social usages and conventional womanly ways. But, nevertheless, the impression had remained in her mind that she must be at fault somehow, and it interested her that she would now be able to understand wherein she was inferior.

She went to see Selma as often as she could, and encouraged her to call at her lodgings on the mornings when she was at home, expecting that it might please her sister-in-law to become familiar with the budding educational enterprises, and that thus a fresh bond of sympathy would be established between them. Selma presented herself three or four times in the course of the next three months, and on the first occasion expressed gratifying appreciation of the cosiness of the new lodgings.

"I almost envy you," she said, "your freedom to live your own life and do just what you like. It must be delightful away up here where you can see over the tops of the houses and almost touch the sky, and there is no one to disturb the current of your thoughts. It must be a glorious place to work and write. I shall ask you to let me come up here sometimes when I wish to be alone with my own ideas."

"As often as you like. You shall have a pass key."

"I should think," said Selma, continuing to gaze, with her far away look, over the vista of roofs which the top story of the apartment house commanded, "that you would be a great deal happier than if you had married him."

The pause which ensued caused her to look round, and add jauntily, "I have heard, you know, about Dr. Page."

A wave of crimson spread over Pauline's face—the crimson of wounded surprise, which froze Selma's genial intentions to the core.

"I didn't think you'd mind talking about it," she said stiffly.

"There's nothing to talk about. Since you have mentioned it, Dr. Page is a dear friend of mine, and will always continue to be, I hope."

"Oh, I knew you were nothing but friends now," Selma answered. She felt wounded in her turn. She had come with the wish to be gracious and companionable, and it had seemed to her a happy thought to congratulate Pauline on the wisdom of her decision. She did not like people who were not ready to be communicative and discuss their intimate concerns.

The episode impaired the success of the first morning visit. At the next, which occurred a fortnight later, Pauline announced that she had a piece of interesting news.

"Do you know a Mr. Joel Flagg in Benham?"

"I know who he is," said Selma. "I have met his daughter."

"It seems he has made a fortune in oil and real estate, and is desirous to build a college for women in memory of his mother,

Sarah Wetmore. One of my friends has just received a letter from a Mrs. Hallett Taylor, to whom Mr. Flagg appears to have applied for counsel, and who wishes some of us who are interested in educational matters to serve as an advisory committee. Probably you know Mrs. Taylor too?"

"Oh yes. I have been at her house, and I served with her on the committee which awarded Wilbur the church."

"Why, then you are the very person to tell us all about her. I think I remember now having heard Wilbur mention her name."

"Wilbur fancied her, I believe."

"Your tone rather implies that you did not. You must tell me everything you know. My friend has corresponded with her before in regard to some artistic matters, but she has never met her. Her letter suggests a lady."

"I dare say you would like Mrs. Taylor," said Selma, gravely. "She is attractive, I suppose, and seemed to know more or less about European art and pictures, but we in Benham didn't consider her exactly an American. If you really wish to know my opinion, I think that she was too exclusive a person to have fine ideas."

"That's a pity."

"If she lived in New York she would like to be one of those society ladies who live on Fifth Avenue; only she hasn't really any conception of what true elegance is. Her house there, except for the ornaments she had bought abroad, was not so well furnished as the one I lived in. I wonder what she would think if she could look into the drawing-room of my friend Mrs. Williams."

"I see," said Pauline, though in truth she was puzzled. "I am sorry if she is a fine lady, but people like that, when they become interested, are often excellent workers. It is a noble gift of Mr. Flagg's—$500,000 as a foundation fund. He's a good American at all events. Wilbur must certainly compete for the buildings, and his having first met you there ought to be an inspiration to him to do fine work."

Selma had been glad of the opportunity to criticise Mrs. Hallett Taylor, whom she had learned, by the light of her superior social knowledge, to regard as an unimportant person. Yet she had been conscious of a righteous impulse in saying what she thought of her. She knew that she had never liked Mrs. Taylor, and she was not pleased to hear that Mr. Flagg had selected her from among the women of Benham to superintend the administration of his splendid gift. Benham had come to seem to her remote and primitive, yet she preferred, and was in the mood, to think that it represented the principles which were dear to her, and that she had been appreciated there far better than in her present sphere. She was still tied to Benham by correspondence with Mrs. Earle. Selma had written at once to explain her sudden departure, and letters passed between them at intervals of a few weeks—letters on Selma's part fluent with dazzled metropolitan condescension, yet containing every now and then a stern charge against her new fellow-citizens on the score of levity and worldliness.

The donation for the establishment of Wetmore College was made shortly after another institution for the education of women in which Pauline was interested—Everdean College—had been opened to students. The number of applicants for admission to Everdean had been larger than the authorities had anticipated, and Pauline, who had been one of the promoters and most active workers in raising funds for and supervising the construction of this labor of love, was jubilant over the outlook, and busy in regard to a variety of new matters presented for solution by the suddenly evolved needs of the situation. Among these was the acquisition of two or three new women instructors; and it occurred to Pauline at once that Selma might know of some desirable candidate. Selma appeared to manifest but little interest in this inquiry at the time, but a few months subsequent to their conversation in regard to Mrs. Taylor she presented herself at Pauline's rooms one morning with the announcement that she had found some one. Pauline, who was busy at her desk, asked permission to finish a letter before listening; so there was silence for a few minutes, and Selma, who wore a new costume of a more fashionable guise than her last, reflected while she waited that the details of such work as occupied her sister-in-law must be tedious. Indeed, she had begun to entertain of late a sort of contempt for the deliberate, delving processes of the Littletons. She was inclined to ask herself if Wilbur and Pauline were not both plodders. Her own idea of doing things was to do them quickly and brilliantly, arriving at conclusions, as became an American, with prompt energy and despatch. It seemed to her that Wilbur, in his work, was slow and elaborate, disposed to hesitate and refine instead of producing boldly and immediately. And his sister, with her studies and letter-writing, suggested the same wearisome tendency. Why should not Wilbur, in his line, act with the confident enterprise and capacity to produce immediate, ostensible results which their neighbor, Gregory Williams, displayed? As for Pauline, of course she had not Wilbur's talent and could not, perhaps, be expected to shine conspicuously, but surely she might make more of herself if only she would cease to spend so much time in details and cogitation, with nothing tangible to show for her labor. Selma remembered her own experience as a small school teacher, and her thankfulness at her escape from a petty task unworthy of her capabilities, and she smiled scornfully to herself, as she sat waiting, at what she regarded Pauline's willingness to spend her energies in such inconspicuous, self-effacing work. Indeed, when Pauline had finished her letter and announced that she was now entirely at leisure, Selma felt impelled to remark:

"I should think, Pauline, that you would give a course of lectures on education. We should be glad to have them at our house, and your friends ought to be able to dispose of a great many tickets." Such a thing had never occurred to Selma until this moment, but it seemed to her, as she heard her own words, a brilliant suggestion, both as a step forward for Pauline and a social opportunity for herself.

"On education? My dear Selma, you have no idea of the depths of my ignorance. Education is an enormous subject, and I am just beginning to realize how little I know concerning it. People have talked and written about education enough. What we need and what some of us are trying to do is to study statistics and observe results. I am very much obliged to you, but I should only make myself a laughing-stock."

"I don't think you would. You have spent a great deal of time in learning about education, and you must have interesting things to say. You are too modest and—don't you think it may be that you are not quite enterprising enough? A course of lectures would call public attention to you, and you would get ahead faster, perhaps. I think that you and Wilbur are both inclined to hide your light under a bushel. It seems to me that one can be conscientious and live up to one's ideals without neglecting one's opportunities."

"The difficulty is," said Pauline, with a laugh, "that I shouldn't regard it as an opportunity, and I am sure it wouldn't help me to get ahead, as you call it, with the people I desire to impress, to give afternoon tea or women-club lectures. I don't know enough to lecture effectively. As to enterprise, I am busy from morning until night. What more can a woman do? You mustn't hurry Wilbur, Selma. All he needs is time to let the world see his light."

"Very likely. Of course, if you don't consider that you know enough there is nothing to be said. I thought of it because I used to lecture in Benham, at the Benham Institute, and I am sure it helped me to get ahead. I used to think a great deal about educational matters, and perhaps I will set you the example by giving some lectures myself."

"That would be very interesting. If a person has new ideas and has confidence in them, it is natural to wish to let the world hear them."

Pauline spoke amiably, but she was disposed to regard her sister with more critical eyes. She felt no annoyance at the patronizing tone toward herself, but the reference to Wilbur made her blood rebel. Still she could not bear to harbor distrust against that grave face with its delicate beauty and spiritualized air, which was becomingly accommodated to metropolitan conditions by a more festive bonnet than any which she herself owned. Yet she noticed that the thin lips had an expression of discontent, and she wondered why.

Recurring to the errand on which she had come, Selma explained that she had just received a letter from Benham—from her friend, Mrs. Margaret Rodney Earle, an authoress and a promulgator of advanced and original ideas in respect to the cause of womanhood, asking if she happened to know of an opening for a gifted young lady in any branch of intellectual work.

"I thought at once of Everdean," said Selma, "and have come to give you the opportunity of securing her."

Pauline expressed her thanks cordially, and inquired if Mrs. Earle had referred to the candidate's experience or special fitness for the duties of the position.

"She writes that she is very clever and gifted. I did not bring the letter with me, but I think Mrs. Earle's language was that Miss Bailey will perform brilliantly any duties which may be intrusted to her."

"That is rather general," said Pauline. "I am sorry that she didn't specify what Miss Bailey's education has been, and whether she has taught elsewhere."

"Mrs. Earle wouldn't have recommended her if she hadn't felt sure that she was well educated. I remember seeing her at the Benham Institute on one of the last occasions when I was present. She delivered a whistling solo which every one thought clever and melodious."

"I dare say she is just the person we are looking for," said Pauline, leniently. "It happens that Mrs. Grainger—my friend to whom Mrs. Taylor wrote concerning Mr. Flagg's gift—is to make Mrs. Taylor a visit at Benham next week, in order to consider the steps to be taken in regard to Wetmore College. She and Miss Bailey can arrange to meet, and that will save Miss Bailey the expense of a journey to New York, at the possible risk of disappointment."

"I thought," said Selma, "that you would consider yourselves fortunate to secure her services."

"I dare say we shall be very fortunate, Selma. But we cannot engage her without seeing her and testing her qualifications."

Selma made no further demur at the delay, but she was obviously surprised and piqued that her offer should be treated in this elaborate fashion. She was obliged to acknowledge to herself that she could not reasonably expect Pauline to make a definite decision without further inquiry, but she had expected to be able to report to Mrs. Earle that the matter was as good as settled—that, if Miss Bailey would give a few particulars as to her accomplishments, the position would be hers. Surely she and Mrs. Earle were qualified to choose a school-teacher. Here was another instance of the Littleton tendency to waste time on unimportant details. She reasoned that a woman with more wide-awake perceptions would have recognized the opportunity as unusual, and would have snapped up Miss Bailey on the spot.

The sequel was more serious. Neither Selma nor Pauline spoke of the matter for a month. Then it was broached by Pauline, who wrote a few lines to the effect that she was sorry to report that the authorities of Everdean, after investigation, had concluded not to engage the services of Miss Bailey as instructor. When Selma read the note her cheeks burned with resentment. She regarded the decision as an affront. Pauline dined with them on the evening of that day, and at table Selma was cold and formal. When the two women were alone, Selma said at once, with an attempt at calmness:

"What fault do you find with my candidate?"

"I think it possible that she might have been satisfactory from the mere point of scholarship," judicially answered Pauline, who did not realize in the least that her sister-in-law was offended, "though Mrs. Grainger stopped short of close inquiry on that score, for the reason that Miss Bailey failed to satisfy our requirements in another respect. I don't wish to imply by what I am going to say anything against her character, or her capacity for usefulness as a teacher under certain conditions, but I confide to you frankly, Selma, that we make it an absolute condition in the choice of instructors for our students that they should be first of all lady-like in thought and speech, and here it was that she fell short. Of course I have never seen Miss Bailey, but Mrs. Grainger reported that she was—er—impossible."

"You mean that your friend does not consider her a lady? She isn't a society lady, but I did not suppose an American girl would be refused a position as a teacher for such a reason as that."

"A lady is a lady, whether she is what you term a society lady or not. Mrs. Grainger told us that Miss Bailey's appearance and manners did not suggest the womanly refinement which we deem indispensable in those who are to teach our college students. Five years ago only scholarship and cleverness were demanded, but experience has taught the educators of women that this was a mistake."

"I presume," said Selma, with dramatic scorn, "that Mrs. Hallett Taylor disapproved of her. I thought there would be some such outcome when I heard that she was to be consulted."

"Mrs. Taylor's name was not mentioned," answered Pauline, in astonishment. "I had no idea, Selma, that you regarded this as a personal matter. You told me that you had seen Miss Bailey but once."

"I am interested in her because—because I do not like to see a cruel wrong done. You do not understand her. You allow a prejudice, a class-prejudice, to interfere with her career and the opportunity to display her abilities. You should have trusted Mrs. Earle, Pauline, She is my friend, and she recommended Miss Bailey because she believed in her. It is a reflection on me and my friends to intimate that she is not a lady."

138

She bent forward from the sofa with her hands clasped and her lips tightly compressed. For a moment she gazed angrily at the bewildered Pauline, then, as though she had suddenly bethought her of her New York manner, she drew herself up and said with a forced laugh—"If the reason you give were not so ridiculous, I should be seriously offended."

"Offended! Offended with Pauline," exclaimed Littleton, who entered the room at the moment. "It cannot be that my two guardian angels have had a falling out." He looked from one to the other brightly as if it were really a joke.

"It is nothing," said Selma.

"It seems," said Pauline with fervor, "that I have unintentionally hurt Selma's feelings. It is the last thing in the world I wish to do, and I trust that when she thinks the matter over she will realize that I am innocent. I am very, very sorry."

CHAPTER VI.

"Why don't you follow the advice of Mr. Williams and buy some shares of stock?" asked Selma lightly, yet coaxingly, of her husband one day in the third year of their marriage. The Williamses were dining with them at the time, and a statement by Gregory, not altogether without motive, as to the profits made by several people who had taken his advice, called forth the question. He and his wife were amiably inclined toward the Littletons, and were proud of the acquaintance. Among their other friends they boasted of the delightful excursions into the literary circle which the intimacy afforded them. They both would have been pleased to see their neighbors more amply provided with money, and Gregory, partly at the instance of Flossy, partly from sheer good-humor in order to give a deserving but impractical fellow a chance to better himself, threw out tips from time to time—crumbs from the rich man's table, but bestowed in a friendly spirit. Whenever they were let fall, Selma would look at Wilbur hoping for a sign of interest, but hitherto they had evoked merely a smile of refusal or had been utterly ignored.

Her own question had been put on several occasions, both in the company of the tempter and in the privacy of the domestic hearth, and both in the gayly suggestive and the pensively argumentative key. Why might they not, by means of a clever purchase in the stock market, occasionally procure some of the agreeable extra pleasures of life—provide the ready money for theatres, a larger wardrobe, trips from home, or a modest equipage? Why not take advantage of the friendly advice given? Mr. Williams had made clear that the purchase of stocks on a sufficient margin was no more reprehensible as a moral proposition than the purchase of cargoes of sugar, cotton, coffee or tea against which merchants borrowed money at the bank. In neither instance did the purchaser own outright what he sought to sell at an advance; merely in one case it was shares, in the other merchandise. Of course it was foolish for inexperienced country folk with small means to dabble in stocks and bonds, but why should not city people who were clever and had clever friends in the business eke out the cost of living by shrewd investments? In an old-fashioned sense it might be considered gambling; but, if it were true, as Wilbur and Mr. Williams both maintained, that the American people were addicted to speculation, was not the existence of the habit strong evidence that the prejudice against it must be ill-founded? The logical and the patriotic conclusion must needs be that business methods had changed, and that the American nation had been clever enough to substitute dealings in shares of stock, and in contracts relating to cereals and merchandise for the methods of their grandfathers who delivered the properties in bulk.

To this condensation of Gregory's glib sophistries on the lips of his wife, Wilbur had seemed to turn a deaf ear. It did not occur to him, at first, that Selma was seriously in earnest. He regarded her suggestions of neglected opportunities, which were often whimsically uttered, as more than half playful—a sort of make-believe envy of the meteoric progress in magnificence of their friendly neighbors. He was even glad that she should show herself appreciative of the merits of civilized comfort, for he had been afraid lest her ascetic scruples would lead her judgments too far in the opposite direction. He welcomed them and encouraged her small schemes to make the establishment more festive and stylish in appearance, in modest imitation of the splendor next door. But constant and more sombre reference to the growing fortunes of the Williamses presently attracted his attention and made him more observant. His income sufficed to pay the ordinary expenses of quiet domestic life, and to leave a small margin for carefully, considered amusements, but he reflected that if Selma were yearning for greater luxury, he could not afford at present to increase materially her allowance. It grieved him as a proud man to think that the woman he loved should lack any thing she desired, and without a thought of distrust he applied himself more strenuously to his work, hoping that the sum of his commissions would enable him presently to gratify some of her hankerings—such, for instance, as the possession of a horse and vehicle. Selma had several times alluded with a sigh to the satisfaction there must be in driving in the new park. Babcock had kept a horse, and the Williamses now drove past the windows daily in a phaeton drawn by two iron gray, champing steeds. He said to himself that he could scarcely blame Selma if she coveted now and then Flossy's fine possessions, and the thought that she was not altogether happy in consequence of his failure to earn more kept recurring to his mind and worried him. No children had been born to them, and he pictured with growing concern his wife lonely at home on this account, yet without extra income to make purchases which might enable her to forget at times that there was no baby in the house. Flossy had two children, a boy and a girl, two gorgeously bedizened little beings who were trundled along the sidewalk in a black, highly varnished baby-wagon which was reputed by the dealer who sold it to Gregory to have belonged to an English nobleman. Wilbur more than once detected Selma looking at the babies with a wistful glance. She was really admiring their clothes, yet the thought of how prettily she would have been able to dress a baby of her own was at times so pathetic as to bring tears to her eyes, and cause her to deplore her own lack of children as a misfortune.

As the weeks slipped away and Wilbur realized that, though he was gaining ground in his profession, more liberal expenditures were still out of the question, he reached a frame of mind which made him yearn for a means of relief. So it happened that, when Selma asked him once more why he did not follow the advice proffered and buy some stocks, he replied by smiling at Gregory and inquiring what he should buy. During the dinner, which had been pleasant, Wilbur's eye had been attracted by the brilliancy of some new jewels which Mrs. Williams wore, and he had been conscious of the wish that he were able to make a present like that to his own wife.

"You take my breath away. Wonders will never cease," responded Gregory, while both the women clapped their hands. "But you musn't buy anything; you must sell," he continued. "VanHorne and I both came to the conclusion to-day that it is time for a turn on the short side of the market. When the public are crazy and will buy any thing, then is the time to let them have all they wish."

"What, then, am I to sell?" asked Wilbur "I am a complete lamb, you know." He was already sorry that he had consented, but Selma's manifest interest restrained him from turning the matter into a joke.

"Leave it all to me," said Williams with a magnificent gesture.

"But you will need some money from me."

"Not at all. If you would feel better, you may send me a check or a bond for a thousand dollars. But it isn't necessary in your case."

"I will bring you in a bond to-morrow—one of the very few I own."

Wilbur having delivered his security the first thing in the morning, heard nothing further from Williams for a fortnight. One day he received a formal account of certain transactions executed by Williams and VanHorne for Wilbur Littleton, Esq., and a check for two thousand dollars. The flush which rose to his cheeks was induced partly by pleasure, partly by shame. His inclination, as he reflected, was to return the check, but he recognized presently that this was a foolish idea, and that the only thing to be done was to deposit it. He wrote a grateful note of acknowledgment to Williams, and then gave himself up to the agreeable occupation of thinking what he should buy for Selma with the money. He decided not to tell her of his good fortune, but to treat her to a surprise. His first fancy was in favor of jewelry—some necklace or lustrous ornament for the hair, which would charm the feminine eye and might make Selma even more beautiful than she already appeared in evening dress. His choice settled on a horse and buggy as more genuinely useful. To be sure there was the feed of the animal to be considered; but he would be able to reserve sufficient money to cover this cost for some months, and by the end of that time he would perhaps be able to afford the outlay from his income. Horse-flesh and vehicles were not in his line, but he succeeded by investigation in procuring a modest equipment for seven hundred dollars, which left him three hundred for fodder, and the other thousand. This he had decided to hand over to Selma as pin money. It was for her sake that he had consented to speculate, and it seemed meet that she should have the satisfaction of spending it.

He carried out his surprise by appearing one afternoon before the door and inviting her to drive. Selma became radiant at the news that the horse and buggy were hers, though, when the particulars of the purchase were disclosed she said to herself that she wished Wilbur had allowed her to choose the vehicle. She would have preferred one more stylish and less domestic looking. She flung her arms about his neck and gave him a kiss on their return to show her satisfaction.

"You see how easy it is, Wilbur," she said as she surveyed the check which he had handed her.

"It was not I, it was Williams."

"No, but you could, if you would only think so. I have the greatest confidence in you, dear," she added, looking eagerly into his face; "but don't you sometimes go out of your way to avoid what is enterprising and—er—modern, just because it is modern?"

"Gambling is as old as the hills, Selma."

"Yes. And if this were gambling—the sort of gambling you mean, do you think I would allow you to do it? Do you think the American people would tolerate it for a minute?" she asked triumphantly.

"It seems to me that your admiration for the American people sometimes makes you a little weak in your logic," he answered with good-humor. He was so pleased by Selma's gratification that he was disposed to exorcise his scruples.

"I have always told you that I was more of a patriot than you, Wilbur."

The bond had not been returned by Williams at the time he sent the money, and some fortnight later—only a few days in fact after this drive, Littleton received another cheque for $500 and a request that he call at the office.

"I thought you would like to see the instruments of torture at work—the process of lamb-shearing in active operation," Williams explained as he shook hands and waved him into his private room. After a few easy remarks on the methods of doing business the broker continued, "I flatter myself that for so small an investment and so short a time, I have done tolerably well for you."

"I scarcely know how to express my thanks and my admiration for your skill. Indeed I feel rather awkwardly about—"

"That's all right, my dear fellow. It's my business; I get my commission. Still I admit friendly regard—and this is why I suggested your dropping in—by introducing the personal equation, makes one nervous. If instead of closing out your account, I had in each instance held on, you would have made more money. I was glad to take this responsibility at first because you were a neophyte at the business, but I think it will be more satisfactory both for you and for me that in future transactions you should give me the word when to reap the profit. Of course you shall have all the information which I possess and my advice will be at your command, but where a man's money is concerned his own head is apt to be the wisest

144

counsellor. Now I took the liberty yesterday of selling for you two hundred shares of Reading railroad. You can cover to-day at a profit of one point—about $200. I do not urge it. On the contrary I believe that the market, barring occasional rallies, is still on the downward track. I wish, however, to put you in a position where you can, if you desire, take advantage of the full opportunities of the financial situation and save myself from feeling that I have robbed you by my friendly caution."

"In other words you don't wish to speculate with my money," said Littleton. "You wish me to paddle my own canoe."

Williams' real desire was to escape the bother of personally superintending an insignificant account. His circumlocution was a suave way of stating that he had done all that could be expected of a neighbor and benevolent friend, and that the ordinary relation of broker and customer ought now be established. As for Littleton, he perceived that he was not free to retire from the market on the profits of friendly regard unless he was prepared to fly in the face of advice and buy in his two hundred Reading railroad. To do so would be pusillanimous; moreover to retire and abstain from further dealings would make Williams' two cheques more obviously a charitable donation, and the thought of them was becoming galling. Above all there were Selma's feelings to be considered. The possession of the means to afford her happiness was already a sweet argument in favor of further experiments.

And so it happened that during the next nine months Littleton became a frequenter of the office of Williams & VanHorne. He was not among those who hung over the tape and were to be seen there daily; but he found himself attracted as the needle by the magnet to look in once or twice a week to ascertain the state of the market. His ventures continued to be small, and were conducted under the ken of Williams, and though the occasional rallies referred to by the broker harassed Wilbur's spirit when they occurred, the policy of selling short proved reasonably remunerative in the course of half a dozen separate speculations. In round figures he added another $2,500 to that which Williams had made for him. The process kept him on pins and needles, and led him to scan the list of stock quotations before reading anything else in the newspaper. Selma was delighted at his success, and though he chose not to tell her the details of his dealings, she watched him furtively, followed the general tendency of the market, and when she perceived that he was in good spirits, satisfied sufficiently her curiosity by questions.

On the strength of this addition to their pecuniary resources, Selma branched out into sundry mild extravagances. She augmented her wardrobe, engaged an additional house-maid and a more expensive cook, and entertained with greater freedom and elaboration. She was fond of going to the theatre and supping afterward at some fashionable restaurant where she could show her new plumage and be a part of the gay, chattering rout at the tables consuming soft-shelled crabs and champagne. She was gradually increasing her acquaintance, chiefly among the friends of the Williamses, people who were fond of display and luxury and who seemed to have plenty of money. In this connection she was glad to avail herself of the reputation of belonging to the literary circle, and she conceived the plan of mingling these new associates with Wilbur's former set—to her thinking a delightful scheme, which she inaugurated by means of a dinner party. She included among the guests Pauline and Dr. Page, and considered that she had acted gracefully in putting them side by side at table, thus sacrificing the theory of her entertainment to her feminine interest in romance. In her opinion it was more than Pauline deserved, and she was proud of her generosity. There were fourteen in the company, and after dinner they were regaled by a young woman who had brought a letter of introduction to Selma from Mrs. Earle, who read from her own poems. The dinner was given for her, and her seat was between Wilbur and Mr. Dennison, the magazine editor. Selma had attended a dinner-party at the Williamses a fortnight earlier where there had been music in the drawing-room by a ballad-singer at a cost of $100 (so Flossy had told her in confidence). A poetess reading from her own works, a guest and not invited in after dinner on a business footing, appealed to Selma as more American, and less expensive. She, in her secret soul, would have liked to recite herself, but she feared to run the gauntlet of the New York manner. The verses were intense in character and were delivered by the young woman with a hollow-eyed fervor which, as one of the non-literary wing of the company stated, made one creep and weep alternately. There was no doubt that the entertainment was novel and acceptable to the commercial element, and to Selma it seemed a delightful reminder of the Benham Institute. She was curious to know what Mr. Dennison thought, though she said to herself that she did not really care. She felt that anything free and earnest in the literary line was likely to be frowned on by the coterie to which her husband's people belonged. Nevertheless she seized an opportunity to ask the editor if he did not think the verses remarkable.

"They are certainly remarkable," answered Mr. Dennison. After a brief pause he added, "Being a strictly truthful person, Mrs. Littleton, I do not wish to seek shelter behind the rampart which your word 'remarkable' affords. A dinner may be remarkable—remarkably good, like the one I have just eaten, or remarkably bad. Some editors would have replied to you as I have done, and yet been capable of a mental reservation unflattering to the ambitious young woman to whom we have been listening. But without wishing to express an opinion, let me remind you that poetry, like point-lace, needs close scrutiny before its merits can be defined. I thought I recognized some ancient and well-worn flowers of speech, but my editorial ear and eye may have been deceived. She has beautiful hair at all events."

"'Fair tresses man's imperial race ensnare;
And beauty draws us by a single hair.'

"You cynical personage! I only hope she may prove a genius and that you will realize when too late that you might have discovered her," said Selma, looking into his face brightly with a knowing smile and tapping her fan against her hand. She was in a gay humor at the success of the entertainment, despite the non-committal attitude of this censor, and pleased at the appositeness of her quotation. Her figure had filled out since her marriage. She was almost plump and she wore a single short fat curl pendent behind her ear.

A few months subsequent to this dinner party Flossy announced one day that Mr. Silas S. Parsons, whom Selma had seen with the Williamses at the theatre nearly three years before, had come to live in New York with his wife and daughter. Flossy referred to him eagerly as one of her husband's most valuable customers, a shrewd, sensible, Western business man, who had made money in patent machinery and was superbly rich. He had gone temporarily to a hotel, but he was intending to build a large house on Fifth Avenue near the park. Selma heard this announcement with keen interest, asking herself at once why Wilbur should not be the architect. Why not, indeed? She promptly reasoned that here was her chance to aid her husband; that he, if left to his own devices, would do nothing to attract the magnate's attention, and that it behooved her, as an American wife and a wide-awake, modern woman, to let Mr. Parsons know his qualifications, and to prepossess him in Wilbur's favor by her own attractions. The idea appealed to her exceedingly. She had been hoping that some opportunity to take an active part in the furtherance of Wilbur's career would present itself, for she felt instinctively that with her co-operation he would make more rapid progress. Here was exactly the occasion longed for. She saw in her mind's eye Mr. Parsons's completed mansion, stately and beautiful, the admired precursor of a host of important edifices—a revolutionizing monument in contemporary architecture. Wilbur would become the fashion, and his professional success be assured, thanks to the prompt ability of his wife to take advantage of circumstances. So she would prove herself a veritable helpmate, and the bond of marital sympathy would be strengthened and refreshed.

To begin with, Selma hinted to Mrs. Williams that Mr. Parsons might do worse than employ Wilbur to design his house. Flossy accepted the suggestion with enthusiasm and promised her support, adding that Mr. Parsons was a person of sudden and strong fancies, and that if he were to take a fancy to Wilbur, the desired result would be apt to follow. Selma quickly decided that Mr. Parsons must be made to like her, for she feared lest Wilbur's quiet, undemonstrative manner would fail to attract him. Evidently he admired the self-confidence and manly assertion of Gregory Williams, and would be liable to regard Wilbur as lacking in force and enterprise. The reflection that she would thus be working—as necessarily she would—for the eternal progress of truth, added a pleasant savor to the undertaking, for it was clear that her husband was an ideal architect for the purpose, and she would be doing a true service to Mr. Parsons in convincing him that this was so. Altogether her soul was in an agreeable flutter, notwithstanding that her neighbor Flossy had recently received invitations to two or three large balls, and been referred to in the society columns of the newspapers as the fascinating and clever wife of the rising banker Gregory Williams.

The Littletons were promptly given by Flossy the opportunity to make the acquaintance of the Parsons family. Mr. Parsons was a ponderous man of over sixty, with a solid, rotund, grave face and a chin whisker. He was absorbed in financial interests, though he had retired from active business, and had come to New York to live chiefly to please his wife and daughter. Mrs. Parsons, who was somewhat her husband's junior, was a devotee, or more correctly, a debauchee, of hotel life. Since the time when they had become exceedingly rich, about ten years before, they had made a grand tour of the hotels of this country and Europe. By so doing Mrs. Parsons and her daughter felt that they became a part of the social life of the cities which they visited. Although they had been used to plain, if not slovenly, house-keeping before the money came, both the wife and daughter had evolved into connoisseurs of modish and luxurious hotel apparatus and garniture. They had learned to revel in many courses, radiantly upholstered parlors, and a close acquaintance with the hotel register. Society for them, wherever they went, meant finding out the names of the other guests and dressing for them, being on easy terms with the head waiter and elevator boy, visiting the theatres, and keeping up a round of shopping in pursuit of articles of apparel. They wore rich garments and considerable jewelry, and plastered themselves—especially the daughter—with bunches of violets or roses self-bestowed. Mrs. Parsons was partial to perfume, and they both were addicted to the free consumption of assorted bonbons. To be sure they had made some acquaintances in the course of their peregrinations, but one reason for moving to New York was that Mrs. Parsons had come to the melancholy conclusion that neither the princes of Europe nor the sons of American leading citizens were paying that attention to her daughter which the young lady's charms seemed to her to merit. If living lavishly in hotels and seeing everybody right and left were not the high-road to elegant existence and hence to a brilliant match for Lucretia, Mrs. Parsons was ready to try the effect of a house on Fifth Avenue, though she preferred the comforts of her present mode of life. Still one advantage of a stable home would be that Mr. Parsons could be constantly with them, instead of an occasional and intermittent visitor communicated with more frequently by electricity than by word of mouth. While Mr. Parsons was selecting the land, she and Lucretia had abandoned themselves to an orgy of shopping, and with an eye to the new house, their rooms at the hotel were already littered with gorgeous fabrics, patterns of wall-paper and pieces of pottery.

Selma's facility in the New York manner was practised on Silas Parsons with flattering success. He was captivated by her—more so than by Flossy, who amused him as a flibbertigibbet, but who seemed to him to lack the serious cast of character which he felt that he discerned beneath the sprightliness of this new charmer. Mr. Parsons was what he called a "stickler" for the dignity of a serious demeanor. He liked to laugh at the theatre, but mistrusted a daily point of view which savored of buffoonery. He was fond of saying that more than one public man in the United States had come to grief politically from being a joker, and that the American people could not endure flippancy in their representatives. He liked to tell and listen to humorous stories in the security of a smoking-room, but in his opinion it behooved a citizen to maintain a dignified bearing before the world. Like other self-made men who had come to New York—like Selma herself—he had shrunk from and deplored at first the lighter tone of casual speech. Still he had grown used to it, and had even come to depend on it as an amusement. But he felt that in the case of Selma there was a basis of ethical earnestness, appropriate to woman, beneath her chatty flow of small talk. That she was comparatively a new-comer accounted partially for this impression, but it was mainly due to the fact that she still reverted after her sallies of pleasantry to a grave method of deportment.

Selma's chief hospitality toward the Parsonses took the form of a theatre party, which included a supper at Delmonico's after the play. It was an expensive kind of entertainment, which she felt obliged to justify to Wilbur by the assertion that the Williamses had been so civil she considered it would be only decent to show attention to their friends. She was unwilling to disclose her secret, lest the knowledge of it might make Wilbur offish and so embarrass her efforts. There were eight in the party, and the affair seemed to Selma to go off admirably. She was enthralled by the idea of using her own personal magnetism to promote her husband's business. She felt that it was just the sort of thing she would like and was fitted for, and that here was an opportunity for her individuality to display itself. She devoted herself with engaging assiduity to Mr.

Parsons, pleased during the active process of propitiation by the sub-consciousness that her table was one of the centres of interest in the large restaurant. She had dressed herself with formal care, and nothing in the way of compliment could have gratified her more than the remark which Mr. Parsons made, as he regarded her appreciatively, when he had finished his supper, that she suggested his idea of Columbia. Selma glowed with satisfaction. The comparison struck her as apt and appropriate, and she replied with a proud erection of her head, which imparted to her features their transcendental look, and caused her short curl to joggle tremulously, "I suppose I see what you mean, Mr. Parsons."

CHAPTER VII.

One evening, four or five days after this supper party, Wilbur laid down the book which he was pretending to read, and said, "Selma, I have come to the conclusion that I must give up dabbling in stocks. I am being injured by it—not financially, for, as you know, I have made a few thousand dollars—but morally."

"I thought you were convinced that it was not immoral," answered Selma, in a constrained voice.

"I do not refer to whether speculation is justifiable in itself, but to its effect on me as an individual—its distraction to my mind and consequent interference with my professional work."

"Oh."

"For a year now, the greater portion of the time, I have had some interest in the market, and as a consequence, have felt impelled to look in on Williams and VanHorne every day—sometimes oftener. I am unable to dismiss my speculations from my thoughts. I find myself wondering what has happened to the stocks I am carrying, and I am satisfied that the practice is thoroughly demoralizing to my self-respect and to my progress. I am going to give it up."

"I suppose you must give it up if it affects you like that," responded Selma drily. "I don't see exactly why it should."

"It may seem foolish to you, but I am unable to put my ventures out of my mind. The consequences of loss would be so serious to me that I suppose my imagination becomes unduly active and apprehensive. Also, I find myself eager to secure large gains. I must renounce Aladdin's lamp from this day forth, my dear, and trust to my legitimate business for my income."

Selma folded her hands and looked grave. "It's disappointing that you feel so just when we are beginning to get on, Wilbur."

"I have realized, Selma, that you have enjoyed and—er—been made happier by the freedom to spend which this extra money has afforded you. But I know, when you reflect, you will understand that I am right, and that it would be disastrous to both of us if I were to continue to do what I believe demoralizing. It is a mortification to me to ask you to retrench, but I said to myself that Selma would be the first to insist on our doing so if she knew my feelings, and it makes me happy to be sure of your approval."

Littleton spoke with a tender plaintiveness which betrayed

that in his secret soul he was less confident on this score than his words declared, or than he himself supposed. "Of course," he added, earnestly, "I shall hope that it will not make much difference. My business is slowly, but steadily, improving, and I am doing more this year than last. I am bending all my energies on my plans for Wetmore College. If I win in that competition, I shall make a reputation and a respectable commission."

"You have been on those plans three months."

"Yes, and shall not finish them for another two. I wish to do my best work, and I shall be glad not to hear quotations of the ticker in my brain. You desire me to be thorough, surely, Selma *mia?*"

"Oh, yes. Only, you know people very often spoil things by pottering over them."

"I never potter. I reject because I am dissatisfied rather than offer a design which does not please me, but I do not waste my time."

"Call it over-conscientiousness then. I wish you to do your best work, of course, but one can't expect to do best work invariably. Everything was going so nicely that you must perceive it will be inconvenient to have to economize as we did before."

Littleton looked at his wife with a glance of loving distress. "You wouldn't really care a button. I know you wouldn't, Selma," he said, stoutly.

"Of course not, if it were necessary," she answered. "Only I don't wish to do so unless it is necessary. I am not controverting your decision about the stocks, though I think your imagination, as you say, is to blame. I would rather cut my right hand off than persuade you to act contrary to your conscience. But it *is* inconvenient, Wilbur, you must admit, to give up the things we have become accustomed to."

"We shall be able to keep the horse. I am certain of that."

"I wish you to see my side of it. Say that you do," she said, with shrill intensity.

"It is because I do see it that I am troubled, Selma. For myself I am no happier now than I was when we lived more simply. I can't believe that you will really find it a hardship to deny yourself such extravagances as our theatre party last week. Being a man," he added, after a pause, "I suppose I may not appreciate how important and seductive some of these social observances appear to a woman, and heaven knows my chief wish in life is to do everything in my power to make you happy. You must be aware of that, dearest. I delight to work hard for your sake. But it seems almost ludicrous to be talking of social interests to you, of all women. Why, at the time we were married, I feared that you would cut yourself off from reasonable pleasures on account of your dislike of everything frivolous. I remember I encouraged you not to take too ascetic a view of such things. So I am bound to believe that your side is my side—that we both will find true happiness in not attempting to compete with people whose tastes are not our tastes, and whose aims are not our aims."

"Then you think I have deteriorated," she said, with a superior smile.

"I think of you as the most conscientious woman I ever met. It was only natural that you should be spurred by our neighbors, the Williamses, to make a better showing socially before the world. I have been glad to see you emulous up to a certain point. You must realize though, that we cannot keep pace with them, even if we so desire. Already they are in the public eye. He appears to have made considerable money, and his views on the stock-market are given prominence by the press. He and his wife are beginning to be recognized by people who were ignorant of their existence four years ago. You told me last week that Mrs. Williams had attended one of the fashionable balls, and I saw in yesterday's newspaper a description of her toilette at another. It begins to look as if, in a few years more, their ambition might be realized, and the doors of the Morton Price mansion open wide to admit this clever country cousin to the earthly paradise. It must be evident to you, Selma, that very shortly we shall see only the dust of their chariot-wheels in the dim social distance. Williams told me to-day that he has bought a house near the park."

"He has bought a new house? They are going to move?" exclaimed Selma, sitting up straight, and with a fierce light in her eyes.

"Yes. He was going home to tell his wife. It seems that they have been talking vaguely of moving for some time. An acquaintance happened to offer him a house, and Williams closed the bargain on the spot in his customary chain-lightning style. I shall

154

be sorry to have them go on some accounts, for they have always been friendly, and you seem fond of the wife, but we shall find it easier, perhaps, when they are gone, to live according to our own ideas."

"Flossy has not been quite so nice lately," said Selma; "I am afraid she is disposed to put on airs."

"Her head may have been turned by her success. She has a kind heart, but a giddy brain in spite of its cleverness."

"Flossy has been getting on, of course. But so are we getting on. Why should they be recognized, as you call it, any more than we? In time, I mean. Not in the same way, perhaps, since you don't approve of the sort of things—"

"Since I don't approve? Why, Selma, surely—"

"Since *we* don't approve, then. I only mean that Gregory Williams has shown initiative, has pushed ahead, and is—er—the talk of the town. I expect you to be successful, too. Is there any reason on earth why the door of the Morton Prices should open wide to her and not to me?"

"I suppose not, if—if you wish it."

She made a gesture of impatience and gazed at him a moment with an imperious frown, then suddenly, with the litheness of a cat, she slipped from her chair to the floor at his feet, and leaning against his knee, looked up into his face.

"You dear boy, I am going to tell you something. You said to me once that if ever the time came when I thought you visionary, I was to let you know. Of course I understand you are worth a thousand *Gregorys*; but don't you think you would get on faster if you were a little more aggressive in your work?—if you weren't so afraid of being superficial or sensational? You were intimating a few minutes ago," she added, speaking rapidly under the stress of the message she burned to deliver, "that I seemed changed. I don't believe I am changed. But, if I seem different, it is because I feel so strongly that those who wish to succeed must assert themselves and seize opportunities. There is where it seems to me that Mr. Williams has the advantage over you, Wilbur. One of the finest and most significant qualities of our people, you know, is their enterprise and aggressiveness. Architecture isn't like the stock business, but the same theory of progress must be applicable to both. Don't you think I may be right, Wilbur? Don't you see what I mean?"

155

He stroked her hair and answered gently, "What is it that I am not doing which you think I might do?"

Selma snuggled close to him, and put her hand in his. She was vibrating with the proud consciousness of the duty vouchsafed to her to guide and assist the man she loved. It was a blissful and a precious moment to her. "If I were you," she said, solemnly, "I should build something striking and original, something which would make everyone who beheld it ask, 'what is the architect's name?' I would strike out boldly without caring too much what the critics and the people of Europe would say. You musn't be too afraid, Wilbur, of producing something American, and you mustn't be too afraid of the American ways of doing things. We work more quickly here in everything, and—and I still can't help feeling that you potter a little. Necessarily I don't know about the details of your business, but if I were you, instead of designing small buildings or competing for colleges and churches, where more than half the time someone else gets the award, I should make friends with the people who live in those fine houses on Fifth Avenue, and get an order to design a splendid residence for one of them. If you were to make a grand success of that, as you surely would, your reputation would be made. You ask me why I like to entertain and am willing to know people like that. It is to help you to get clients and to come to the front professionally. Now isn't that sensible and practical and right, too?"

Her voice rang triumphantly with the righteousness of her plea.

"Selma, dear, if I am not worldly-wise enough, I am glad to listen to your suggestions. But art is not to be hurried. I cannot vulgarize my art. I could not consent to that."

"Of course not, Wilbur. Not worldly-wise enough is just the phrase, I think. You are so absorbed in the theory of fine things that I am sure you often let the practical opportunities to get the fine things to do slip."

"Perhaps, dear. I will try to guard against it." Wilbur took her hands in his and looked down tenderly into her face. His own was a little weary. "Above everything else in life I wish, to make you happy," he said.

"I am happy, you dear boy."

"Truly?"

156

"Yes, truly. And if something happens which I am nearly sure will happen, I shall be happier still. It's a secret, and I mustn't tell you, but if it does happen, you can't help agreeing that your wife has been clever and has helped you in your profession."

"Helped me? Ah, Selma," he said, folding her in his arms, "I don't think you realize how much you are to me. In this modern world, what with self-consciousness, and shyness and contemporary distaste for fulsome expression, it is difficult to tell adequately those we love how we feel toward them. You are my darling and my inspiration. The sun rises and sets with you, and unless you were happy, I could never be. Each man in this puzzling world must live according to his own lights, and I, according to mine, am trying to make the most of myself, consistent with self-respect and avoidance of the low human aims and time-serving methods upon which our new civilization is supposed to frown. If I am neglecting my lawful opportunities, if I am failing to see wisely and correctly, I shall be grateful for counsel. Ah, Selma, for your sake, even more than for my own, I grieve that we have no children. A baby's hands would, I fancy, be the best of counsellors and enlighteners."

"If children had come at first, it would have been very nice. But now—now I think they might stand in the way of my being of help to you. And I am so anxious to help you, Wilbur."

As a result of this conversation Littleton devoted himself more assiduously than ever to his work. He was eager to increase his earnings so that his income should not be curtailed by his decision to avoid further ventures in the stock-market. He was troubled in soul, for Selma's accusation that he was visionary haunted him. Could it be that he was too scrupulous, too uncompromising, and lacked proper enterprise? Self-scrutiny failed to convince him that this was so, yet left a lurking doubt which was harassing. His clear mind was too modest to believe in its own infallibility, for he was psychologist enough to understand that no one can be absolutely sure that his perspective of life is accurate. Possibly he was sacrificing his wife's legitimate aspirations to too rigid canons of behavior, and to an unconscious lack of initiative. On the other hand, as a positive character, he believed that he saw clearly, and he could not avoid the reflection that, if this was the case, he and Selma were drifting apart—the more bitter alternative of the two, and a condition which, if perpetuated, would involve the destruction of the scheme of matrimonial happiness, the ideal communion of two sympathetic souls, in which he was living as a proud partner. Apparently he was in one of two predicaments; either he was self deceived, which was abhorrent to him as a thoughtful grappler with the eternal mysteries, or he had misinterpreted the character of the woman whose transcendent quality was a dearer faith to him than the integrity of his own manhood.

So it was with a troubled heart that he applied himself to more rigorous professional endeavor. Like most architects he had pursued certain lines of work because orders had come to him, and the chances of employment had ordained that his services should be sought for small churches, school-houses and kindred buildings in the surrounding country rather than for more elaborate and costly structures. On these undertakings it was his habit to expend abundant thought and devotion. The class of work was to his taste, for, though the funds at his disposal were not always so large as he desired for artistic effects, yet he enjoyed the opportunity of showing that simplicity need not be homely and disenchanting, but could wear the aspect of grace and poetry. Latterly he had been requested to furnish designs for some blocks of houses in the outlying wards of the city, where the owners sought to provide attractive, modern flats for people with moderate means. Various commissions had come to him, also, to design decorative work, which interested him and gave scope to his refined and aspiring imagination, and he was enthusiastically absorbed in preparing his competitive plans for the building of Wetmore College. His time was already well occupied by the matters which he had in hand. That is, he had enough to do and yet did not feel obliged to deny himself the luxury of deliberate thoroughness in connection with each professional undertaking. Save for the thought that he must needs earn more in order to please Selma, he would have been completely happy in the slow but flattering growth of his business, and in feeling his way securely toward greater success. Now, however, he began to ask himself if it were not possible to hasten this or that piece of work in order to afford himself the necessary leisure for new employment. He began also to consider whether he might not be able, without loss of dignity, to put himself in the way of securing more important clients. To solicit business was not to be thought of, but now and again he put the question to himself whether he had not been too indifferent as to who was who, and what was what, in the development of his business.

While Littleton was thus mulling over existing conditions, and subjecting his conduct to the relentless lens of his own conscience and theories, Selma announced to him jubilantly, about a fortnight subsequent to their conversation, that her secret was a secret no longer, and that Mr. Parsons desired to employ him to build an imposing private residence on Fifth Avenue near the Park. Mr. Parsons confirmed this intelligence on the following day in a personal interview. He informed Littleton that he was going to build in order to please his wife and daughter, and intimated that expense need not stand in the way of the gratification of their wishes. After the business matters were disposed of he was obviously ready to intrust all the artistic details to his architect. Consequently Littleton enjoyed an agreeable quarter of an hour of exaltation. He was pleased at the prospect of building a house of this description, and the hope of being able to give free scope to his architectural bent without molestation made that prospect roseate. He could desire no better opportunity for expressing his ideas and proving his capacity. It was an ideal chance, and his soul thrilled as he called up the shadowy fabric of scheme after scheme to fill the trial canvas of his fantasy. Nor did he fail to award due credit to Selma for her share in the transaction; not to the extent, perhaps, of confessing incapacity on his own part, but by testifying lovingly to her cleverness. She was in too good humor at her success to insist on his humiliation in set terms. The two points in which she was most vitally interested—the advantage of her own interference and the consequent prompt extension of her husband's field of usefulness—had been triumphantly proved, and there was no need that the third—Wilbur's lack of capacity to battle and discriminate for himself—should be emphasized. Selma knew what she thought in her own mind, and she entertained the hope that this lesson might be a lamp to his feet for future illumination. She was even generous enough to exclaim, placing her hands on his shoulders and looking into his face with complacent fervor:

"You might have accomplished it just as well yourself, Wilbur."

Littleton shook his head and smiled. "It was a case of witchery and fascination. He probably divined how eager you were to help me, and he was glad to yield to the agreeable spell of your wifely devotion."

"Oh, no," said Selma. "I am sure he never guessed for one moment of what I was thinking. Of course, I did try to make him like me, but that was only sensible. To make people like one is the way to get business, I believe."

Littleton's quarter of an hour of exaltation was rudely checked by a note from Mrs. Parsons, requesting an interview in regard to the plans. When he presented himself he found her and her daughter imbued with definite ideas on the subject of architects and architecture. In the eyes of Mrs. Parsons the architect of her projected house was nothing but a young man in the employ of her husband, who was to guide them as to measurements, carpentry, party-walls and plumbing, but was otherwise to do her bidding for a pecuniary consideration, on the same general basis as the waiter at the hotel or the theatre ticket-agent. As to architecture, she expected him to draw plans just as she expected dealers in carpets or wall-papers to show her patterns in easy succession. "I don't care for that; take it away." "That is rather pretty, but let me see something else." What she said to Littleton was, "We haven't quite decided yet what we want, but, if you'll bring some plans the next time you call, we'll let you know which we like best. There's a house in Vienna I saw once, which I said at the time to Lucretia I would copy if I ever built. I've mislaid the photograph of it, but I may be able to tell you when I see your drawings how it differed from yours. Lucretia has a fancy for something Moorish or Oriental. I guess Mr. Parsons would prefer brown-stone, plain and massive, but he has left it all to us, and both daughter and I think we'd rather have a house which would speak for itself, and not be mixed up with everybody else's. You'd better bring us half a dozen to choose from, and between me and you and Lucretia, we'll arrive at something elegant and unique."

This was sadly disillusionizing to Littleton, and the second experience was no less so. The refined outline sketches proffered by him were unenthusiastically surveyed and languidly discarded like so many wall-papers. It was evident that both the mother and daughter were disappointed, and Littleton presently divined that their chief objection was to the plainness of the several designs. This was made unmistakably obvious when Mrs. Parsons, after exhibiting a number of photographs of foreign public buildings with which she had

160

armed herself, surveyed the most ornate, holding it out with her head on one side, and exclaimed impressively, "This is more the sort of thing we should like. I think Mr. Parsons has already explained to you that he desired our house to be as handsome as possible."

"I had endeavored to bear that in mind," Littleton retorted with spirit. "I believe that either of these plans would give you a house which would be handsome, interesting and in good taste."

"It does not seem to me that there is anything unique about any of them," said Mrs. Parsons, with a cold sniff intended to be conclusive. Nor did Littleton's efforts to explain that elaboration in a private residence was liable to detract from architectural dignity and to produce the effect of vulgarity fall upon receptive soil. The rich man's wife listened in stony silence, at times raising her lorgnette to examine as a curiosity this young man who was telling her—an American woman who had travelled around the world and seen everything to be seen—how she ought to build her own house. The upshot of this interview was that Littleton was sent away with languid instructions to try again. He departed, thinking melancholy thoughts and with fire in his soul, which, for Selma's sake, he endeavored to keep out of his eyes.

CHAPTER VIII.

The departure of the Williamses to a smarter neighborhood was a trial for Selma. She nursed the dispiriting reflection that she and Wilbur might just as well be moving also; that a little foresight and shrewdness on her husband's part would have enabled him to sell at a handsome profit the house in which they were living; and that there was no reason, except the sheer, happy faculty of making the most of opportunities, to account for the social recognition which Flossy and her husband were beginning to receive. It had not been easy to bear with equanimity during the last year the ingenuous, light-hearted warblings in which Flossy had indulged as an outlet to her triumphant spirits, and to listen to naïve recitals of new progress, as though she herself were a companion or ladies' maid, to whom such developments could never happen. She was weary of being merely a recipient of confidences and a sympathetic listener, and more weary still of being regarded as such by her self-absorbed and successful neighbor. Why should Flossy be so dense? Why should she play second fiddle to Flossy? Why should Flossy take for granted that she did not intend to keep pace with her? Keep pace, indeed, when, if circumstances would only shape themselves a little differently, she would be able speedily to outstrip her volatile friend in the struggle for social preferment.

Not unnaturally their friendship had been somewhat strained by the simmering of these thoughts in Selma's bosom. If a recipient of confidences becomes tart or cold, ingenuous prattle is apt to flow less spontaneously. Though Flossy was completely self-absorbed, and consequently glad to pour out her satisfaction into a sympathetic ear, she began to realize that there was something amiss with her friend which mere conscientious disapproval of her own frivolities did not adequately explain. It troubled her somewhat, for she liked the Littletons and was proud of her acquaintance with them. However, she was conscious of having acquitted herself toward them with liberality, and, especially now that her social vista was widening, she was not disposed at first to analyze too deeply the cause of the lack of sympathy between them. That is, she was struck by Selma's offish manner and frigid silences, but forgot them until they were forced upon her attention the next time they met. But as her friend continued to receive her bubbling announcements with stiff indifference, Flossy, in her perplexity, began to bend her acute

162

mental faculties more searchingly on her idol. A fixed point of view will keep a shrine sacred forever, but let a worshipper's perspective be altered, and it is astonishing how different the features of divinity will appear. Flossy had worshipped with the eyes of faith. Now that her adoration was rejected without apparent cause, her curiosity was piqued, and she sought an interpretation of the mystery from her clever wits. As she observed Selma more dispassionately her suspicion was stirred, and she began to wonder if she had been burning incense before a false goddess. This doubt was agitating her mind at the time when they moved from the street.

Selma was unconscious of the existence of this doubt as she had been largely unconscious of her own sour demeanor. She had no wish to lose the advantages of intimate association with the Williamses. On the contrary, she expected to make progress on her own account by admission into their new social circle. She went promptly to call, and saw fit to show herself tactfully appreciative of the new establishment and more ready to listen to Flossy's volubility. Flossy, who was radiant and bubbling over with fresh experiences which she was eager to impart, was glad to dismiss her doubt and to give herself up to the delights of unbridled speech. She took Selma over her new house, which had been purchased just as it stood, completely furnished, from the previous owner, who had suffered financial reverses. "Gregory bought it because it was really a bargain," she said. "It will do very well for the present, but we intend to build before long. I am keeping my eye on your husband, and am expecting great things from the Parsons house. Do you know, I believe in Mr. Littleton, and feel sure that some day we shall wake up and find him famous."

This was amiable, particularly as Flossy was very busily engaged in contemplating the brilliant progress of Gregory Williams and his wife. But Selma returned home feeling sore and dissatisfied. Flossy had been gracious, but still dense and naïvely condescending. Selma chose to foresee that her friend would neglect her, and her foresight was correct. The call was not returned for many weeks, although Flossy had assured her when they separated that distance would make no difference in their intimacy. But in the first place, her doubts recurred to Flossy after the departure of her visitor, and in the second, the agitations incident to her new surroundings, fortified by these doubts, made neglect easy. When she did call,

Selma happened to be out. A few days later an invitation to dine with the Williamses arrived. Selma would have preferred to remain at home as a rebuke, but she was miserably conscious that Flossy would not perceive the point of the refusal. So she went, and was annoyed when she realized that the guests were only people whom she knew already—the Parsonses, and some of Gregory Williams's former associates, whom she had met at the old house. It was a pleasant dinner, apparently, to all except Selma. The entertainment was flatteringly lavish, and both the host and hostess with suavity put in circulation, under the rose, the sentiment that there are no friends like old friends—a graceful insincerity which most of them present accepted as true. Indeed, in one sense it was not an insincerity, for Gregory and his wife entertained cordial feelings toward them all. But on the other hand, Selma's immediate and bitter conclusion was also true, that the company had been invited together for the reason that, in the opinion of Flossy, they would not have harmonized well with anyone else.

Said Wilbur as they drove away from the house—"Barring a few moments of agony in the society of my tormentor, Mrs. Parsons, I had a pleasant evening. They were obviously potting their old acquaintance in one pie, but to my thinking it was preferable to being sandwiched in between some of their new friends whom we do not know and who know nothing of us. It was a little evident, but on the whole agreeable."

Selma, shrouded in her wraps, made no reply at first. Suddenly she exclaimed, with, fierceness, "I consider it rank impertinence. It was as much as to say that they do not think us good enough to meet their new friends."

Littleton, who still found difficulty in remembering that his wife would not always enjoy the humor of an equivocal situation, was sorry that he had spoken. "Come, Selma," he said, "there's no use in taking that view of the matter. You would not really care to meet the other people."

"Yes, I would, and she knows it. I shall never enter her house again."

"As to that, my dear, the probabilities are that we shall not be asked for some time. You know perfectly well that, in the nature of things, your intimacy with Mrs. Williams must languish now that she lives at a distance and has new surroundings. She may continue to be very fond of you, but you can't hope to see very much of her, unless I am greatly mistaken in her character."

"She is a shallow little worldling," said Selma, with measured intensity.

"But you knew that already. The fact that she invited us to dinner and did not ignore our existence altogether shows that she likes us and wishes to continue the friendship. I've no doubt she believes that she is going to see a great deal of us, and you should blame destiny and the force of fashionable circumstances, not Flossy, if you drift apart."

"She invited us because she wished to show off her new house."

"Not altogether. You musn't be too hard on her."

Selma moved her shoulders impatiently, and there was silence for some moments broken only by the tapping of her foot. Then she asked, "How nearly have you finished the plans for the Parsons house?"

Wilbur's brow clouded under cover of the night. He hesitated an instant before replying, "I am sorry to say that Mrs. Parsons and I do not seem to get on very well together. Her ideas and mine on the subject of architecture are wide apart, as I have intimated to you once or twice. I have modified my plans again, and she has made airy suggestions which from my point of view are impossible. We are practically at loggerheads, and I am trying to make up my mind what I ought to do."

There was a wealth of condensation in the word 'impossible' which brought back unpleasantly to Selma Pauline's use of the same word in connection with the estimate which had been formed of Miss Bailey. "There can be only one thing to do in the end," she said, "if you can't agree. Mrs. Parsons, of course, must have her house as she wishes it. It is her house, Wilbur."

"It is her house, and she has that right, certainly. The question is whether I am willing to allow the world to point to an architectural hotch-potch and call it mine."

"Isn't this another case of neglecting the practical side, Wilbur? I am sure you exaggerate the importance of the changes she desires. If I were building a house, I should expect to have it built to suit me, and I should be annoyed if the architect stood on points and were captious." Selma under the influence of this more congenial theme had partially recovered her equanimity. Her duty was her pleasure, and it was clearly her duty to lead her husband in the right path and save him from becoming the victim of his own shortcomings.

Wilbur sighed. "I have told her," he said, "that I would submit another entirely new sketch. It may be that I can introduce some of her and her daughter's splurgy and garish misconceptions without making myself hopelessly ridiculous."

He entered the house wearily, and as he stood before the hall table under the chandelier, Selma took him by the arm and turning him toward her gazed into his face. "I wish to examine you. Pauline said to me to-day that she thinks you are looking pale. I don't see that you are; no more so than usual. You never were rosy exactly. Do you know I have an idea that she thinks I am working you to death."

"Pauline? What reason has she to think anything of the kind? Besides, I am perfectly well. It is a delight to work for a woman like you, dearest." He took her face between his hands and kissed her tenderly; yet gravely, too, as though the riddle of life did not solve itself at the touch of her lips. "You will be interested to hear," he added, "that I shall finish and send off the Wetmore College plans this week."

"I am glad they are off your hands, for you will have more time for other work."

"Yes. I think I may have done something worth while," he said, wistfully.

"And I shall try not to be annoyed if someone else gets the award," she responded, smoothing down the sheen of her evening dress and regarding herself in the mirror.

"Of course someone else may have taken equal pains and done a better thing. It is necessary always to be prepared for that."

"That is the trouble. That is why I disapprove of competitions."

"Selma, you are talking nonsense," Littleton exclaimed with sudden sternness.

The decision in his tone made her start. The color mounted to her face, and she surveyed him for an instant haughtily, as though he had done her an injury. Then with an oratorical air and her archangel look, she said, "You do not seem to understand, Wilbur, that I am trying to save you from yourself."

Littleton was ever susceptible to that look of hers. It suggested incarnate conscientiousness, and seemed incompatible with human imperfection or unworthy ambitions. He was too wroth to relent altogether, but he compressed his lips and returned her look searchingly, as though he would scrutinize her soul.

"I'm bound to believe, I do believe, that you are trying to help me, Selma. I need your advice and help, even against myself, I dare say. But there are some matters of which you cannot judge so well as I. You must trust my opinion where the development of my professional life is concerned. I shall not forget your caution to be practical, but for the sake of expediency I cannot be false to what I believe true. Come, dear, let us go to bed."

He put his hand on her arm to lead her upstairs, but she turned from it to collect her fan and gloves. Looking, not at him, but at herself in the mirror, she answered, "Of course. I trust, though, that this does not mean you intend to act foolishly in regard to the Parsons house."

"I have already told you," he said, looking back, "that I am going to make another attempt to satisfy that exasperating woman and her daughter."

"And you can satisfy them, I'm sure, if you only choose to," said Selma, by way of a firm, final observation.

Littleton's prophecy in regard to the waning of friendship between his wife and Mrs. Williams proved to be correct. Propinquity had made them intimate, and separation by force of circumstances put a summary end to frequent and cordial intercourse between them. As he had predicted, their first invitation to the new house was still the last at the end of three months, and save for a few words on one occasion in the street, Selma and Flossy did not meet during that period. But during that same three months Selma's attention was constantly attracted to the Williamses by prominent newspaper allusions to their prosperity and growing fashionable prestige. What they did and where they went were chronicled in the then new style journalistic social gossip, and the every-day world was made familiar with his financial opinions and his equipages and her toilettes. The meeting in the street was an ordeal for Selma. Flossy had been shopping and was about to step into her carriage, the door of which was held open by an imposing liveried footman, when the two women nearly collided.

"I have not seen you for an age," Flossy exclaimed, with the genuine ring of regret in her tone, with which busy people partially atone for having left undone the things they ought or would like to have done. "Which way are you going? Can't I take you somewhere?"

Selma glanced sternly at the snug coupe and stylish horses. "No, we don't seem to meet very often," she said drily. "I'm living, though, at the same place," she added, with a determination to be sprightly.

"Yes, I know; I owe you a call. It's dreadful of me. I've been intending to come, but you can't imagine how busy I've been. Such a number of invitations, and new things to be done. I'm looking forward to giving you a full account of my experiences."

"I've read about them in the newspapers."

"Oh, yes. Gregory is always civil to reporters. He says that the newspapers are one of the great institutions of the country, and that it is sensible to keep in touch with them. I will confide to you that I think the whole business vulgar, and I intend some day, when we are firmly established, to be ugly to them. But at present the publicity is rather convenient and amusing," she exclaimed, with a gay shake of her head, which set her ringlets bobbing.

"I should think it would be unpleasant to have the details of one's appearance described by the press."

Flossy's doubts had returned in full force during the conversation. She said to herself, "I wonder if that is true? I wonder if it wouldn't be the very thing she would like?" But she answered blithely, "Oh, one gets used to it. Then I can't take you anywhere? I'm sorry. Some day I hope my round of gayety will cease, so that we can have a quiet evening together. I miss your husband. I always find him suggestive and interesting."

"'Her round of gayety! A quiet evening together!'" murmured Selma as she walked away. "Wilbur is right; purse-proud, frivolous little thing! She is determined to destroy our friendship."

Four weeks subsequent to this meeting the newspapers contained a fulsome account of a dancing party given by Mr. and Mrs. Gregory Williams—"an elegant and recherché entertainment," in the language of the reporter. A list of the company followed, which Selma scrutinized with a brow like a thunder-cloud. She had

168

acquired a feverish habit of perusing similar lists, and she recognized that Flossy's guests—among the first of whom were Mr. and Mrs. Morton Price and the Misses Price—were chiefly confined to persons whom she had learned to know as members of fashionable society. She read, in the further phraseology of the reporter, that "it was a small and select affair." At the end of the list, as though they had been invited on sufferance as a business necessity, were the Parsonses; but these were the only former associates of the Williamses. Selma had just finished her second reading of this news item when her meditation was interrupted by the voice of her husband, who had been silent during dinner, as though he had some matter on his mind, and was at the moment sitting close by, on the other side of the lamp which lighted the library table.

"I fear you will be disappointed, Selma, but I have informed Mr. Parsons definitely this morning, that he must get another architect. The ideas of his wife and daughter are hopelessly at variance with mine. He seemed to be sorry—indeed, I should think he was a reasonable and sensible man—but he said that he was building to please Mrs. Parsons, and we both agreed that under the circumstances it was necessary that she should make a fresh start. He asked me to send my bill, and we parted on the best of terms. So it is all over, and except from the point of view of dollars and cents, I am very glad. Only the remembrance that you had set your heart on my making this my masterpiece, prevented me from throwing over the contract weeks ago. Tell me, Selma *mia*, that you approve of what I have done and congratulate me." He pulled forward his chair so that he might see her face without interference from the lamp and leaned toward her with frank appeal.

"Yes, I had set my heart on it, and you knew it. Yet you preferred to give up this fine opportunity to show what you could do and to get business worth having rather than sacrifice your own ideas as to how a house should be built to the ideas of the women who were to live in it. I dare say I should agree with them, and that the things which they wished and you objected to were things I would have insisted on having."

Littleton started as though she had struck him in the face. "Selma! My wife! Do you realize what you are saying?"

"Perfectly."

"Then—then——. Why, what have I said, what have I done

that you should talk like this?"

"Done? Everything. For one thing you have thrown away the chance for getting ahead in your profession which I procured for you. For another, by your visionary, unpractical ways, you have put me in the position where I can be insulted. Read that, and judge for yourself." She held out to him the newspaper containing the account of the dancing party, pointing with her finger to the obnoxious passage.

With nervous hands Littleton drew the page under the light. "What is all this about? A party? What has it to do with our affairs?"

"It has this to do with them—if you had been more practical and enterprising, our names would have been on that list."

"I am glad they are not there."

"Yes, I know. You would be content to have us remain nobodies all our days. You do not care what becomes of my life, provided you can carry out your own narrow theory of how we ought to live. And I had such faith in you, too! I have refused to believe until now that you were not trying to make the most of your opportunities, and to enable me to make the most of mine."

"Selma, are you crazy? To think that you, the woman I have loved with all my soul, should be capable of saying such things to me! What does it mean?"

She was quick to take advantage of his phrase. "Have loved? Yes, I know that you do not love me as you did; otherwise you could not have refused to build that house, against my wish and advice. It means this, Wilbur Littleton, that I am determined not to let you spoil my life. You forget that in marrying you I gave up my own ambitions and hopes for your sake; because—because I believed that by living together we should be more, and accomplish more, than by living apart. You said you needed me, and I was fool enough to believe it."

The fierce tragedy in her tone lapsed into self-pity under the influence of her last thought, and Littleton, eager in his bewilderment for some escape from the horror of the situation, put aside his anger and dropping on his knees beside her tried to take her hands.

"You are provoked, my darling. Do not say things which you will be sorry for to-morrow. I call God to witness that I have sought above all else to make you happy, and if I have failed, I am

170

utterly miserable. I have needed you, I do need you. Do not let a single difference of opinion spoil the joy of both our lives and divide our hearts."

She pulled her hands away, and shunning his endearment, rose to her feet.

"I am provoked, but I know what I am saying. A single difference of opinion? Do you not see, Wilbur, that none of our opinions are the same, and that we look at everything differently? Even your religion and the God you call to witness are not mine. They are stiff and cold; you Unitarians permit your consciences to deaden your emotions and belittle your outlook on life. When I went with Mr. Parsons the other day to the Methodist church, I could not help thinking how different it was. I was thrilled and I felt I could do anything and be anything. My mother was a Methodist. They sang 'Onward Christian Soldiers,' and it was glorious." She paused a moment and, with an exalted look, seemed to be recalling the movement of the hymn. "With you, Wilbur, and the people like you—Pauline is the same—everything is measured and pondered over, and nothing is spontaneous. I like action, and progress and prompt, sensible conclusions. That is the American way, and the way in which people who succeed get on. But you won't see it—you can't see it. I've tried to explain it to you, and now—now it's too late. We're nobodies, and, if our hearts are divided, that's fate I suppose. It's a very cruel fate for me. But I don't choose to remain a nobody."

Littleton's expression as she talked had changed from astonishment to anger, and from anger to a sternness which gave his words of response the effect of calm and final decision. "You have said so many things with which I do not agree, and which I should have to dispute, that I will not attempt to argue with you concerning them. One thing is clear, both of us have made a horrible mistake. Each has misunderstood the other. You are dissatisfied with me; I realize suddenly that you are utterly different from what I supposed. I am overwhelmed, but your words make plain many things which have distressed and puzzled me." He paused as though in spite of the certainty of his tone, he hoped that she would see fit to deny his conclusions. "We have made a mistake and we shall both be miserable—that must needs be—but we must consider whether there is any method by which we can be less unhappy. What would you like to have me do, Selma? We have no children, thank heaven! Would it be more agreeable to live apart from me and receive support? A divorce does not seem necessary. Besides, our misconception of each other would not be a legal cause."

Selma flushed at the reference to divorce. Littleton's sad, simple statement wore on the surface no sign of a design to hark back to her experience with her first husband, yet she divined that it must be in his thoughts and she resented the recurrence. Moreover, separation, certainly for the present, went beyond her purpose.

"I have no wish for divorce or separation. I see no reason why we should not continue to live as we are," she answered. "To separate would cause scandal. It is not necessary that people should know we have made a mistake. I shall merely feel more free now to live my own life—and there is no telling that you may not some day see things from my point of view and sympathize with me more." She uttered the last words with a mixture of pathos and bright solicitation.

Littleton shook his head. "I agree with you that to go on as we are is our best course. As you say, we ought, if possible, to keep the knowledge of our sorrow to ourselves. God knows that I wish I could hope that our life could ever be as it was before. Too many things have become plain to me in the last half-hour to make that possible. I could never learn to accept or sympathize with your point of view. There can be no half-love with me, Selma. It is my nature to be frank, and as you are fond of saying, that is the American way. I am your husband still, and while I live you shall have my money and my protection. But I have ceased to be your lover, though my heart is broken."

"Very well," said Selma, after a painful pause. "But you know, Wilbur," she added in a tone of eager protestation, "that I do not admit for a moment that I am at fault. I was simply trying to help you. You have only yourself to blame for your unhappiness and—and for mine. I hope you understand that."

"Yes, I understand that you think so," he said sadly.

CHAPTER IX.

The breach between Littleton and his wife was too serious to be healed, for he was confronted by the conviction that Selma was a very different being from the woman whom he had supposed that he was marrying. He had been slow to harbor distrust, and loath, even in the face of her own words, to admit that he had misinterpreted her character; but this last conversation left no room for doubt. Selma had declared to him, unequivocally, that his ideas and theory of life were repugnant to her, and that, henceforth, she intended to act independently of them, so far as she could do so, and yet maintain the semblance of the married state. It was a cruel shock and disappointment to him. At the time of his marriage he would have said that the least likely of possible happenings would be self-deception as to the character of the woman he loved. Yet this was precisely what had befallen him.

Having realized his mistake, he did not seek to flinch from the bitter truth. He saw clearly that their future relations toward each other must be largely formal; that tender comradeship and mutual soul alliance were at an end. At the same time his simple, direct conscience promptly indicated to him that it was his duty to recognize Selma's point of view and endeavor to satisfy it as far as he could without sacrifice of his own principles. He chose to remember that she, too, had made a mistake, and that he was not the kind of husband whom she desired; that his tastes were not her tastes, nor his ambitions her's; that she had tastes and ambitions of her own which he, as the man to whom she was bound by the law, must not disregard. Thus reasoning, he resolved to carry out the scheme of life which she appeared to despise, but also to work hard to provide her with the means to fulfil her own aims. She craved money for social advancement. She should have it from him, for there was no other source from which she could obtain it. The poignancy of his own sorrow should not cause him to ignore that she had given up her own career and pursuits in order to become his wife, and was now disappointed and without independent resources. His pride was sorely wounded, his ideals shattered and his heart crushed; yet, though he could not forbear from judging Selma, and was unconscious of having failed in his obligations to her as a husband and a man, he saw what she called her side, and he took up the thread of life again under the spur of an intention to give her

174

everything but love.

On her part Selma felt aggrieved yet emancipated. She had not looked for any such grave result from her vituperation. She had intended to reprove his surrender of the Parsons's contract, in direct opposition to her own wishes, with the severity it deserved, and to let him understand clearly that he was sacrificing her happiness, no less than his own, by his hysterical folly. When the conversation developed stubborn resistance on his part, and she realized that he was defending and adhering to his purpose, a righteous sense of injury became predominant in her mind over everything else. All her past wrongs cried for redress, and she rejoiced in the opportunity of giving free vent to the pent up grievances which had been accumulating for many months. Even then it was startling to her that Wilbur should suddenly utter the tragic ultimatum that their happiness was at an end, and hint at divorce. She considered that she loved him, and it had never occurred to her that he could ever cease to love her. Rather than retract a word of her own accusations she would have let him leave her, then and there, to live her own life without protection or support from him, but his calmer decision that they should continue to live together, yet apart, suited her better. In spite of his resolute mien she was sceptical of the seriousness of the situation. She believed in her heart that after a few days of restraint they would resume their former life, and that Wilbur, on reflection, would appreciate that he had been absurd.

When it became apparent that he was not to be appeased and that his threat had been genuine, Selma accepted the new relation without demur, and prepared to play her part in the compact as though she had been equally obdurate in her outcry for her freedom. She met reserve with reserve, maintaining rigorously the attitude that she had been wronged and that he was to blame. Meantime she watched him narrowly, wondering what his grave, sad demeanor and solicitous politeness signified. When presently it became plain to her that not merely she was to be free to follow her own bent, but that he was ready to provide her with the means to carry out her schemes, she regarded his liberality as weakness and a sign that he knew in his heart that she was in the right. Immediately, and with thinly concealed triumph, she planned to utilize the new liberty at her disposal, purging any scruples from her conscience by the generous reflection that when Wilbur's brow unbent and his lips moved freely she would forgive him and proffer him once more her conjugal counsel and sympathy. She was firmly of the opinion that, unless he thus acknowledged his shortcomings and promised improvement, the present arrangement was completely to her liking, and that confidence and happiness between them would be utterly impossible. She shed some tears over the thought that unkind circumstances had robbed her of the love by which she had set such store and which she, on her part, still cherished, but she comforted herself with the retort that its loss was preferable to sacrificing weakly the development of her own ideas and life to its perpetuation.

Her flush of triumph was succeeded, however, by a discontented mood, because cogitation constrained her to suspect that her social progress might not be so rapid as her first rosy visions had suggested. She counted on being able to procure the participation of Wilbur sufficiently to preserve the appearance of domestic harmony. This would be for practical purposes a scarcely less effective furtherance of her plans than if he were heartily in sympathy with them. Were there not many instances where busy husbands took part in the social undertakings of their wives, merely on the surface, to preserve appearances? The attitude of Wilbur seemed reasonably secure. That which harassed her as the result of her reflections and efforts to plan was the unpalatable consciousness that she did not know exactly what to do, and that no one, even now that she was free, appeared eager to extend to her the hand of recognition. She was prompt to lay the blame of this on her husband. It was he who, by preventing her from taking advantage of the social opportunities at their disposal, had consigned her to this eddy where she was overlooked. This seemed to her a complete excuse, and yet, though she made the most of it, it did not satisfy her. Her helplessness angered her, and aroused her old feelings of suspicion and resentment against the fashionable crew who appeared to be unaware of her existence. She was glad to believe that the reason they ignored her was because she was too serious minded and spiritual to suit their frivolous and pleasure-loving tastes. Sometimes she reasoned that the sensible thing for her to do was to break away from her present life, where convention and caste trammelled her efforts, and make a name for herself as an independent soul, like Mrs. Margaret Rodney Earle and other free-born women of the Republic. With satisfaction she pictured herself on the lecture platform uttering burning denunciation of the un-American social proclivities of this shallow society, and initiating a crusade which should sweep it from existence beneath the ban of the moral sense of the thoughtful people of the country.

But more frequently she nursed her resentment against Mrs. Williams, to whom she ascribed the blame of her isolation, reasoning that if Flossy had been a true friend, not even Wilbur's waywardness would have prevented her social recognition and success. That, instead, this volatile, fickle prattler had used her so long as she needed her, and then dropped her heartlessly. The memory of Flossy's ball still rankled deeply, and appeared to Selma a more obvious and more exasperating insult as the days passed without a sign of explanation on the part of her late neighbor, and as her new projects languished for lack of a few words of introduction here and there, which, in her opinion, were all she needed to ensure her enthusiastic welcome as a social leader. The appreciation that without those words of introduction she was helpless for the time being focused her resentment, already keen, on the successful Flossy, whose gay doings had disappeared from the public prints in a blaze of glory with the advent of the Lenten season. Refusing to acknowledge her dependence, Selma essayed several spasmodic attempts to assert herself, but they proved unsatisfactory. She made the most of Mr. Parsons's predilection for her society, which had not been checked by Wilbur's termination of the contract. She was thus enabled to affiliate with some of their new friends, but she was disagreeably conscious that she was not making real progress, and that Mr. and Mrs. Parsons and their daughter had, like herself, been dropped by the Williamses—dropped skilfully and imperceptibly, yet none the less dropped. Two dinner parties, which she gave in the course of a fortnight to the most important of these new acquaintances, by way of manifesting to Wilbur her intention to enjoy her liberty at his expense, left her depressed and sore.

It was just at this time that Flossy took it into her head to call on her—one of her first Lenten duties, as she hastened to assure Selma, with glib liveliness, as soon as she entered. Flossy was in too exalted a frame of mind, too bubbling over with the desire to recite her triumphs, to have in mind either her doubts concerning Selma

177

or the need of being more than mildly apologetic for her lack of devotion. She felt friendly, for she was in good humor, and was naïvely desirous to be received in the same spirit, so that she might unbosom herself unreservedly. Sweeping into the room, an animated vision of smiling, stylish cordiality, she sought, as it were, to carry before her by force of her own radiant mood all obstacles to an amiable reception.

"My dear, we haven't met for ages. Thank heaven, Lent has come, and now I may see something of you. I said to Gregory only yesterday that I should make a bee-line for your house, and here I am. Well, dear, how are you? All sorts of things have happened, Selma, since we've had a real chat together. Do you remember my telling you—of course you do—not long after Gregory and I were married that I never should be satisfied until one thing happened? Well, you may congratulate me; it has happened. We dined a week ago to-night with my cousins—the Morton Prices—a dinner of fourteen, all of them just the people I wished to know. Wasn't it lovely? I have waited for it to come, and I haven't moved a finger to bring it about, except to ask them to my dancing party—I had to do that, for after all they are my relations. They accepted and came and I was pleased by it; but they could easily have ignored me afterward if they had wished. What really pleased me, Selma, was their asking me to one of their select dinners, because—because it showed that we are—"

Flossy's hesitation was due partly to the inherent difficulty of expressing her thought with proper regard for modesty. With her rise in life she had learned that unlimited laudation of self was not altogether consistent with "fitness," even in such a confidential interview as the present. But she was also disconcerted by the look in Selma's eyes—a look which, at first startled into momentary friendliness by the suddenness of the onslaught, had become more and more lowering until it was unpleasantly suggestive of scornful dislike. While she thus faltered, Selma drily rounded out the sentence with the words, "Because it showed that you are somebodies now."

Flossy gave an embarrassed little laugh. "Yes, that's what I meant. I see you have a good memory, and it sounds nicer on your lips than it would on mine."

"You have come here to-day on purpose to tell me this?"

said Selma.

"I thought you would be interested to hear that my cousins had recognized me at last. I remember, you thought it strange that they should take so little notice of me." Flossy's festive manner had disappeared before the tart reception of her confidences, and her keen wits, baffled in their search for flattery, recalled the suspicions which were only slumbering. She realized that Selma was seriously offended with her, and though she did not choose to acknowledge to herself that she knew the cause, she had already guessed it. An encounter at repartee had no terrors for her, if necessary, and the occasion seemed to her opportune for probing the accumulating mysteries of Selma's hostile demeanor. Yet, without waiting for a response to her last remark, she changed the subject, and said, volubly, "I hear that your husband has refused to build the new Parsons house because Mrs. Parsons insisted on drawing the plans."

Selma's pale, tense face flushed. She thought for a moment that she was being taunted.

"That was Mr. Littleton's decision, not mine."

"I admire his independence. He was quite right. What do Mrs. Parsons or her daughter know about architecture? Everybody is laughing at them. You know I consider your husband a friend of mine, Selma."

"And we were friends, too, I believe?" Selma exclaimed, after a moment of stern silence.

"Naturally," responded Flossy, with a slightly sardonic air, prompted by the acerbity with which the question was put.

"Then, if we were friends—are friends, why have you ceased to associate with us, simply because you live in another street and a finer house?"

Flossy gave a gasp. "Oh," she said to herself, "it's true. She is jealous. Why didn't I appreciate it before?"

"Am I not associating with you now by calling on you, Selma?" she said aloud. "I don't understand what you mean."

"You are calling on me, and you asked us to dinner to meet—to meet just the people we knew already, and didn't care to meet; but you have never asked us to meet your new friends, and you left us out when you gave your dancing party."

"You do not dance."

"How do you know?"

"I have never associated you with dancing. I assumed that you did not dance."

"What grounds had you for such an assumption?"

"Really, Selma, your catechism is most extraordinary. Excuse my smiling. And I don't know how to answer your questions—your fierce questions any better. I didn't ask you to my party because I supposed that you and your husband were not interested in that sort of thing, and would not know any of the people. You have often told me that you thought they were frivolous."

"I consider them so still."

"Then why do you complain?"

"Because—because you have not acted like a friend. Your idea of friendship has been to pour into my ears, day after day, how you had been asked to dinner by this person and taken up by that person, until I was weary of the sound of your voice, but it seems not to have occurred to you, as a friend of mine, and a friend and admirer of my husband, to introduce us to people whom you were eager to know, and who might have helped him in his profession. And now, after turning the cold shoulder on us, and omitting us from your party, because you assumed I didn't dance, you have come here this morning, in the name of friendship, to tell me that your cousins, at last, have invited you to dinner. And yet you think it strange that I'm not interested. That's the only reason you came—to let me know that you are a somebody now; and you expected me, as a friend and a nobody, to tell you how glad I am."

Flossy's eyes opened wide. Free as she was accustomed to be in her own utterances, this flow of bitter speech delivered with seer-like intensity was a new experience to her. She did not know whether to be angry or amused by the indictment, which caused her to wince notwithstanding that she deemed it slander. Moreover the insinuation that she had been a bore was humiliating.

"I shall not weary you soon again with my confidences," she answered. "So it appears that you were envious of me all the time—that while you were preaching to me that fashionable society was hollow and un-American, you were secretly unhappy because you couldn't do what I was doing—because you weren't invited, too. Oh, I see it all now; it's clear as daylight. I've suspected the truth for some time, but I've refused to credit it. Now everything is explained. I took you at your word; I believed in you and your husband and looked up to you as literary people—people who were interested in fine and ennobling things. I admired you for the very reason that I thought you didn't care, and that you didn't need to care, about society and fashionable position. I kept saying to you that I envied you your tastes, and let you see that I considered myself your real inferior in my determination to attract attention and oblige society to notice us. I was guileless and simpleton enough to tell you of my progress—things I would have blushed to tell another woman like myself—because I considered you the embodiment of high aims and spiritual ideas, as far superior to mine as the poetic star is superior to the garish electric light. I thought it might amuse you to listen to my vanities. Instead, it seems you were masquerading and were eating your heart out with envy of me—poor me. You were ambitious to be like me."

"I wouldn't be like you for anything in the world."

"You couldn't if you tried. That's one of the things which this extraordinary interview has made plain beyond the shadow of a doubt. You are aching to be a social success. You are not fit to be. I have found that out for certain to-day."

"It is false," exclaimed Selma, with a tragic intonation. "You do not understand. I have no wish to be a social success. I should abhor to spend my life after the manner of you and your associates. What I object to, what I complain of, is that, in spite of your fine words and pretended admiration of me, you have preferred these people, who are exclusive without a shadow of right, to me who was your friend, and that you have chosen to ignore me for the sake of them, and behaved as if you thought I was not their equal or your equal. That is not friendship, it is snobbishness—un-American snobbishness."

"It is very amusing. Amusing yet depressing," continued Flossy, without heed to this asseveration. "You have proved one of my ideals to be a delusion, which is sad." She had arisen and stood gently swaying pendent by its crook her gay parasol, with her head on one side, and seeming for once to be choosing her words judicially. "When we met first and I nearly rushed into your arms, I was fascinated, and I said to myself that here was the sort of American woman of whom I had dreamed—the sort of woman I had fondly imagined once that I might become. I saw you were unsophisticated and different from the conventional women to

181

whom I was accustomed, and, even at first, the things you said every now and then gave me a creepy feeling, but you were inspiring to look at—though now that the scales have fallen from my eyes I wonder at my infatuation—and I continued to worship you as a goddess on a pedestal. I used to say to Gregory, 'there's a couple who are to the manner born; they never have to make believe. They are genuinely free and gentle souls.' Your husband? I can't believe that I have been deluded in regard to him, also. I just wonder if you appreciate him—if it is possible that he has been deluded, also. That's rank impertinence, I know; but after all, we are unbosoming our thoughts to each other to-day, and may as well speak openly. You said just now that it was his decision not to go on with the Parsons house. Did you disapprove of it?"

"Yes, I disapproved of it," answered Selma with flashing eyes. "And what if I did?"

She rose and stood confronting her visitor as though to banish her from the house.

"I'm going," said Flossy. "It's none of my concern of course, and I'm aware that I appear very rude. I'm anxious though not to lose faith in your husband, and now that I've begun to understand you, my wits are being flooded with light. I was saying that you were not fit to be a social success, and I'm going to tell you why. No one else is likely to, and I'm just mischievous and frank enough. You're one of those American women—I've always been curious to meet one in all her glory—who believe that they are born in the complete panoply of flawless womanhood; that they are by birthright consummate house-wives, leaders of the world's thought and ethics, and peerless society queens. All this by instinct, by heritage, and without education. That's what you believe, isn't it? And now you are offended because you haven't been invited to become a leader of New York society. You don't understand, and I don't suppose you ever will understand, that a true lady—a genuine society queen—represents modesty and sweetness and self-control, and gentle thoughts and feelings; that she is evolved by gradual processes from generation to generation, not ready made. Oh, you needn't look at me like that. I'm quite aware that if I were the genuine article I shouldn't be talking to you in this fashion. But there's hope for me because I'm conscious of my shortcomings and am trying to correct them; whereas you are satisfied, and fail to see the difference between yourself and the well-bred women whom you envy and sneer at. You're pretty and smart and superficial and—er—common, and you don't know it. I'm rather dreadful, but I'm learning. I don't believe you will ever learn. There! Now I'm going."

"Go!" cried Selma with a wave of her arm. "Yes, I am one of those women. I am proud to be, and you have insulted by your aspersions, not only me, but the spirit of independent and aspiring American womanhood. You don't understand us; you have nothing in common with us. You think to keep us down by your barriers of caste borrowed from effete European courts, but we—I—the American people defy you. The time will come when we shall rise in our might and teach you your place. Go! Envy you? I would not become one of your frivolous and purposeless set if you were all on your bended knees before me."

"Oh, yes you would," exclaimed Flossy, glancing back over her shoulder. "And it's because you've not been given the chance that we have quarrelled now."

CHAPTER X.

The morning after her drastic interview with Mrs. Williams, Selma studied herself searchingly in her mirror. Of all Flossy's candid strictures the intimation that she was not and never would be completely a lady was the only one which rankled. The effrontery of it made her blood boil; and yet she consulted her glass in the seclusion of her chamber in order to reassure herself as to the spiteful falsity of the criticism. Wild horses would not have induced her to admit even to herself that there was the slightest ground for it; still it rankled, thereby suggesting a sub-consciousness of suspicion on the look out for just such a calumny.

She gave Littleton her own version of the quarrel. Her explanation was that she had charged Flossy with a lack of friendship in failing to invite her to her ball, and convicted her of detestable snobbery; that she had denounced this conduct in vigorous language, that they had parted in anger, and that all intercourse between them was at an end.

"We understand each other now," she added. "I have felt for some time that we were no longer sympathetic; and that something of this kind was inevitable. I am glad that we had the chance to speak plainly, for I was able to show her that I had been waiting for an excuse to cut loose from her and her frivolous surroundings. I have wearied my spirit long enough with listening to social inanities, and in lowering my standards to hers for the sake of appearing friendly and conventional. That is all over now, thank heaven."

It did not occur to Selma that there was any inconsistency in these observations, or that they might appear a partial vindication of her husband's point of view. The most salient effect of her encounter with Flossy had been suddenly to fuse and crystallize her mixed and seemingly contradictory ambitions into utter hostility to conventional fashionable society. Even when her heart had been hungering for an invitation to Flossy's ball, she considered that she despised these people, but the interview had served to establish her in the glowing faith that they, by their inability to appreciate her, had shown themselves unworthy of further consideration. The desire which she had experienced of late for a renewal of her intimacy with Mrs. Earle and a reassertion of her former life of independent feminine activity had returned to her, coupled with the crusading intention to enroll herself openly once more in the army of new

American women, whose impending victorious campaign she had prophesied in her retort to Mrs. Williams's maledictions. She had, in her own opinion, never ceased to belong to this army, and she felt herself now more firmly convinced than ever that the course of life of those who had turned a cold shoulder on her was hostile to the spirit of American institutions. So far as her husband was concerned, imaginative enterprise and the capacity to take advantage of opportunities still seemed to her of the essence of fine character. Indeed, she was not conscious of any change in her point of view. She had resented Flossy's charge that she desired to be a social success, and had declared that her wounded feelings were solely due to Flossy's betrayal of friendship, not to balked social ambition. Consequently it was no strain on her conscientiousness to feel that her real sentiments had always been the same.

Nevertheless she scrutinized herself eagerly and long in her mirror, and the process left her serious brow still clouded. She saw in the glass features which seemed to her suggestive of superior womanhood, a slender clear-cut nose, the nostrils of which dilated nervously, delicately thin, compressed lips, a pale, transparent complexion, and clear, steel-like, greenish-brown eyes looking straight and boldly from an anxious forehead surmounted with a coiffure of elaborately and smoothly arranged hair. She saw indisputable evidence that she had ceased to be the ethically attractive, but modishly unsophisticated and physically undeveloped girl, who had come to New York five years before, for her figure was compact without being unduly plump, her cheeks becomingly oval, and her toilette stylish. There were rings on her fingers, and her neck-gear was smart. Altogether the vision was satisfactory, yet she recognized as she gazed that her appearance and general effect were not precisely those of Flossy, Pauline, or Mrs. Hallett Taylor. She had always prided herself on the distinction of her face, and admired especially its freedom from gross or unintellectual lines. She did not intend to question its superiority now; but Flossy's offensive words rang in her ears and caused her to gnaw her lips with annoyance. What was the difference between them? Flossy had dared to call her common and superficial; had dared to insinuate that she never could be a lady. A lady? What was there in her appearance not lady-like? In what way was she the inferior of any of them in beauty, intelligence or character? Rigorous as was the scrutiny, the face in the mirror seemed to her an unanswerable refutation of the slander. What was the difference? Was it that her eyes were keener and brighter, her lips thinner and less fleshly, her general expression more wide-awake and self-reliant? If so, were these not signs of superiority; signs that they, not she, were deficient in the attributes of the best modern womanhood in spite of their affectation of exclusiveness?

The result of this process of self-examination in her looking-glass, which was not limited to a single occasion, established more firmly than ever in Selma's opinion the malignant falsity of the imputation, and yet she was still haunted by it. She was tortured by the secret thought that, though her ambition had been to become just like those other women, she was still distinguishable from them; and moreover, that she was baffled in her attempt to analyze the distinction. Distinguishable even from Flossy—from Flossy, who had slighted and then reviled her! Why had she ever faltered in her distrust of these enemies of true American society? Yet this lingering sense of torture served to whet her new-found purpose to have done with them forever, and to obtain the recognition and power to which she was entitled, in spite of their impertinence and neglect.

The announcement was made to her by Wilbur at about this time that his plans for Wetmore College had been accepted, and that he was to be the architect of the new buildings. As he told her his face showed a tremulous animation which it had not worn for many weeks, and he regarded her for a moment with shy eagerness, as though he half hoped that this vindication of his purposes by success might prompt her to tender some sort of apology, and thus afford him the chance to persuade himself that he had been mistaken after all in his judgment of her.

"You must be very much pleased," she said. "And so am I, of course." Then, after a moment of reflective abstraction, she asked with sudden eagerness, "How long will it take to build them?"

"Two or three years, I suppose."

"And you would be obliged to go frequently to Benham?"

"In order to oversee the work I should have to make short trips there from time to time."

"Yes. Wilbur," she exclaimed, with her exalted expression, "why shouldn't we go to Benham to live? I have been thinking a

186

great deal lately about what we said to each other that time when you felt so badly, and I have come to the conclusion that our living in New York is what is really the trouble. I have the feeling, Wilbur, that in some other place than this cruel, conventional city we should be happier than we are now—indeed, very happy. Has it ever occurred to you? You see, New York doesn't understand me; it doesn't understand you, Wilbur. It sneers at our aspirations. Benham is a growing, earnest city—a city throbbing with the best American spirit and energy. I suggest Benham because we both know it so well. The college buildings would give you a grand start, and I—we both would be in our proper sphere."

Littleton had started at the suggestion. As a drowning man will grasp at a straw, his grieving soul for an instant entertained the plan as a panacea for their woes. But his brow grew grave and sad under the influence of reflection as she proceeded to set forth her reasons in her wrapt fashion. If he had not learned to remain cold under the witchery of her intense moods, he no longer hesitated to probe her fervid assertions with his self-respecting common-sense.

"I would he willing to go to the ends of the earth, Selma," he answered, "if I believed that by so doing you and I could become what we once were to each other. But I cannot see why we should hope to be happier in Benham than here, nor do I agree with you that this is not our proper sphere. I do not share your sentiments in regard to New York; but whatever its faults, New York is the place where I have established myself and am known, and where the abilities which I possess can be utilized and will be appreciated soonest. Benham is twenty-five years behind this city in all things which concern art and my professional life, as you well know."

Selma flushed. "On the contrary, I have reason to believe that Benham has made wonderful progress in the last five years. My friends there write that there are many new streets and beautiful buildings, and that the spirit of the place is enthusiastic and liberal, not luxurious and sneering. You never appreciated Benham at its true worth, Wilbur."

"Perhaps not. But we chose New York."

"Then you insist on remaining here?"

"I see no reason for sacrificing the fruits of the past five years—for pulling myself up by the roots and making a fresh start. From a professional point of view, I think it would be madness."

"Not even to save our happiness?" Selma's eyes swam and her lips trembled as she spoke. She felt very miserable, and she yearned with the desire that her husband would clasp her in his arms in a vast embrace, and tell her that she was right and that he would go. She felt that if he did, the horror of the past would be wiped out and loving harmony be restored.

Wilbur's lips trembled, too. He gazed at her for a moment without speaking, in conflict with himself; then passing his hand across his forehead, as though he would sweep away a misty spell from his eyes, said, "Be sensible, Selma. If we could be happy in Benham, we should be happy here."

"Then you refuse?"

"For the present, yes."

"And I must remain here to be insulted—and a nobody."

"For God's sake, Selma, let us not renew that discussion. What you ask is impossible at present, but I shall remember that it is your wish, and when I begin my work at Benham the circumstances and surroundings may be such that I shall feel willing to move."

Selma turned to the table and took up a book, dissatisfied, yet buoyed by a new hope. She did not observe the tired lines on her husband's face—the weariness of a soul disappointed in its most precious aspirations.

Within the next month it happened that a terrible and unusual fatality was the occasion of the death of both Mrs. Parsons and her daughter. They were killed by a fall of the elevator at the hotel in which they were living—one of those dire casualties which are liable to happen to any one of us in these days of swift and complicated apparatus, but which always seem remote from personal experience. This cruel blow of fate put an end to all desire on the part of the bereaved husband and father to remain in New York, whither he had come to live mainly to please his women folk, as he called them. As soon as he recovered from the bewilderment of the shock, Mr. Parsons sent for the architect who had taken Littleton's place, and who had just begun the subservient task of fusing diverse types of architecture in order to satisfy an American woman's appetite for startling effect, and told him to arrange to dispose of the lot and its immature walls to the highest bidder. His precise plans for the future were still uncertain when Selma called on him, and found comfort for her own miseries in ministering to his solitude, but he expressed an inclination to return to his native Western town, as the most congenial spot in which to end his days. Selma, whose soul was full of Benham, suggested it as an alternative, enlarging with contagious enthusiasm on its civic merits. The crushed old man listened with growing attention. Already the germs of a plan for the disposition of his large property were sprouting in his mind to provide him with a refuge from despondency. He was a reticent man, not in the habit of confiding his affairs until ready to act, but he paid interested heed to Selma's eulogy of the bustling energy and rapid growth of Benham. His preliminary thought had been that it would make him happy to endow his native town, which was a small and inconspicuous place, with a library building. But, as his visitor referred to the attractions and admirable public spirit of the thriving city, which was in the same State as his own home, he silently reasoned that residence there need not interfere with his original project, and that he might find a wide and more important field for his benefactions in a community so representative of American ideas and principles.

Selma's visits of condolence to Mr. Parsons were interrupted by the illness of her own husband. In reflecting, subsequently, she remembered that he had seemed weary and out of sorts for several days, but her conscious attention was invoked by his coming home early in the afternoon, suffering from a violent chill, and manifestly in a state of physical collapse. He went to bed at once; Selma brought blankets and a hot-water bottle, and Dr. George Page was sent for. Dr. Page was the one of Littleton's friends whom Selma had unsuccessfully yearned to know better. She had never been able to understand him exactly, but he fascinated her in spite of—perhaps because of—his bantering manner. She found difficulty in reconciling it with his reputation for hard work and masterly skill in his profession. She was constantly hoping to extract from him something worthy of his large, solid face, with its firm mouth and general expression of reserve force, but he seemed always bent on talking nonsense in her society, and more than once the disagreeable thought had occurred to her that he was laughing at her. He had come to the house after her marriage now and then, but during the past year or two she had scarcely seen him. The last time when they had met, Selma had taxed him with his neglect of her.

His reply had been characteristically elusive and

unsatisfactory. "I will not attempt to frame excuses for my behavior, Mrs. Littleton, for no reason which I could offer would be a justification."

But on the present occasion his greeting was grave and eager.

"Wilbur sick? I feared as much. I warned Pauline two months ago that he was overworking, and only last week I told him that he would break down if he did not go away for a fortnight's rest."

"I wish you had spoken to me."

Selma noted with satisfaction that there was no raillery in his manner now. He bent his gaze on her searchingly.

"Have you not noticed that he looked ill and tired?"

She did not flinch. Why indeed should she? "A little. He tired himself, I think, over the designs for Wetmore College, which he did in addition to his other work. But since the award was made it has seemed to me that he was looking better."

She started to lead the way to Wilbur's room, but the doctor paused, and regarding her again fixedly, as though he had formed a resolution to ferret the secrets of her soul, said laconically:

"Is he happy?"

"Happy?" she echoed.

"Has he anything on his mind, I mean—anything except his work?"

"Nothing—that is," she added, looking up at her inquisitor with bright, interested eyes, "nothing except that he is very conscientious—over-conscientious I sometimes think." To be bandying psychological analyses with this able man was an edifying experience despite her concern for Wilbur.

"I see," he answered dryly, and for an instant there was a twinkle in his eyes. Yet he added, "To make a correct diagnosis it is important to know all the facts of the case."

"Of course," she said solemnly, reassured in her belief that she was being consulted and was taking part in the treatment of her husband's malady.

She accompanied Dr. Page to Wilbur's bed-side. He conversed in a cheery tone with his friend while he took his temperature and made what seemed to her a comparatively brief examination. Selma jumped to the conclusion that there was nothing

190

serious the matter. The moment they had left the room, the doctor's manner changed, and he said with alert concern:

"Your husband is very ill; he has pneumonia. I am going to send for a nurse."

"A nurse? I will nurse him myself, Dr. Page."

It seemed to her the obvious thing to do. She spoke proudly, for it flashed into her mind that here was the opportunity to redeem the situation with Wilbur. She would tend him devotedly and when he had been restored to health by her loving skill, perhaps he would appreciate her at her worth, and recognize that she had thwarted him only to help him.

The doctor's brow darkened, and he said with an emphasis which was almost stern: "Mrs. Littleton, I do not wish to alarm you, but it is right that you should know that Wilbur's symptoms are grave. I hope to save his life, but it can be saved only by trained skill and attendance. Inexperienced assistance, however devoted, would be of no use in a case like this."

"But I only wished to nurse him."

"I know it; I understand perfectly. You supposed that anyone could do that. At least that you could. I shall return in an hour at the latest with a nurse who was trained for three years in a hospital to fit her to battle for valuable lives."

Selma flushed with annoyance. She felt that she was being ridiculed and treated as though she were an incapable doll. She divined that by his raillery he had been making fun of her, and forthwith her predilection was turned to resentment. Not nurse her husband? Did this brow-beating doctor realize that, as a girl, she had been the constant attendant of her invalid father, and that more than once it had occurred to her that her true mission in life might be to become a nurse? Training? She would prove to him that she needed no further training. These were her thoughts, and she felt like crying, because he had humiliated her at a time like this. Yet she had let Dr. Page go without a word. She returned to Wilbur and established herself beside his bed. He tried to smile at her coming.

"I think I shall be better to-morrow. It is only a heavy cold," he said, but already he found difficulty in speaking.

"I have come to nurse you. The blankets and hot-water bottle have made you warmer, haven't they? Nod; you mustn't talk."

"Yes," he whispered huskily.

She felt his forehead, and it was burning. She took his hand and saying, "Sh! You ought not to talk," held it in her own. Then there was silence save for Wilbur's uneasy turning. It was plain that he was very uncomfortable. She realized that he was growing worse, and though she chose to believe that the doctor had exaggerated the seriousness of the case in order to affront her, the thought came that he might die. She had never considered such a possibility before. What should she do? She would be a widow without children and without means, for she knew that Wilbur had laid up little if anything. She would have to begin life over again—a pathetic prospect, yet interesting. Even this conjecture of such a dire result conjured up a variety of possible methods of livelihood and occupation which sped through her mind.

The return of Dr. Page with a nurse cut short these painful yet engrossing speculations. His offensive manner appeared to have exhausted itself, but he proceeded to install his companion in Wilbur's room. Selma would have liked to turn her out of the house, but realized that she could not run the risk of taking issue with him at a time when her husband's life might be in danger. With an injured air yet in silence she beheld the deliberate yet swift preparations. Once or twice Dr. Page asked her to procure for him some article or appliance likely to be in the house, speaking with a crisp, business-like preoccupation which virtually ignored her existence, yet was free from offence. His soul evidently was absorbed by his patient, whom he observed with alert watchfulness, issuing brief directions now and then to his white-capped, methodical, and noiseless assistant. Selma sat with her hands before her in a corner of the bed-room, practically ignored. The shadows deepened and a maid announced dinner. Dr. Page looked at his watch.

"I shall pass the night here," he said.

"Is he worse?"

"The disease is making progress and must run its course. This is only the beginning. You should eat your dinner, for you will need your strength," he added with simple graciousness.

"But I am doing nothing," she blurted.

"If there is anything you can do I will let you know."

Their eyes met. His were gray and steady, but kind. She felt that he chose to treat her like a child, yet that he was trying to be considerate. She was galled, but after all, he was the doctor, and Wilbur had the utmost confidence in him, so she must submit. She ate her dinner, and when she returned preparations were being made for the night. The nurse was to use a lounge at the foot of Wilbur's bed. Dr. Page asked permission to occupy the dressing-room adjoining, so as to be within easy call. He established himself there with a book, returning at short intervals to look at his patient. Selma had resumed her seat. It was dark save for a night lamp. In the stillness the only sounds were the ticking of the clock on the mantel-piece and Wilbur's labored breathing. It seemed as though he were struggling for his life. What should she do if he died? Why was she debarred from tending him? It was cruel. Tears fell on her hand. She stared into the darkness, twisting her fingers, until at last, as though to show her independence, she stepped to the bed on tip-toe. Wilbur's eyes were open. He put out his hand, and, taking hers, touched it to his burning lips.

"Good-night, Selma," he murmured.

She stooped and kissed his brow. "I am here beside you, Wilbur."

A figure stood behind her. She turned, expecting to encounter the white-capped sentinel. It was Dr. Page. He touched her gently on the arm. "We must let him rest now. You can do no good. Won't you go to bed?"

"Oh, no. I shall sit with him all night."

"Very well. But it is important that you should not speak to him," he said with another touch of emphasis.

She resumed her seat and sat out the night, wide-awake and conscious of each movement on Wilbur's part. He was restless and moaning. Twice the nurse summoned the doctor, and two or three times he came to the bed-side of his own accord. She felt slighted, and once, when it seemed to her that Wilbur was in distress and anxious for something, she forestalled the nurse.

"He wishes water," Selma said sternly, and she fetched a glass from the table and let him drink.

Dr. Page took breakfast with her. She was conscious that somehow her vigil had affected his estimate of her, for his speech was frank and direct, as though he considered her now more fit to be treated with confidence.

"He is very ill, but he is holding his own. If you will lie down for a few hours, I will call you to take Miss Barker's place while she rests."

This was gratifying, and tended to assuage her bitterness. But the doctor appeared to her anxious, and spent only a few minutes at table. He said as he rose,

"Excuse me, but Pauline—does she know?"

"I will send her word."

Selma would have been glad to dispense with the presence of her sister-in-law. Their relations had not been sympathetic since the episode of Miss Bailey, and, though Pauline still dined at the house once a week, the intercourse between them had become reserved and perfunctory. She grudged sharing with her what might be Wilbur's last hours. She grudged, too, permitting her to help to nurse him, especially now that her own capabilities were in the way of being recognized, for she remembered Dr. Page's partiality for her. Still, she appreciated that she must let her know.

Pauline arrived speedily, and Selma found herself sobbing in her arms. She was pleased by this rush of feeling on her own part, and, confirmed in her belief that her sister-in-law was cold because she did not break down, and, shrinking from her efforts to comfort her, she quickly regained her self-control. Pauline seemed composed and cheerful, but the unceasing watchfulness and manifest tension of the doctor were disconcerting, and as the afternoon shadows deepened, the two women sat grave and silent, appalled by the suspicion that Wilbur's condition was eminently critical. Yet Dr. Page volunteered to say to them presently:

"If his heart holds out, I am hopeful that he will pull through."

Dr. Page had given up all his duties for the sake of Wilbur. He never left the house, manifestly devoting, as shown by the unflagging, absorbed scrutiny with which he noted every symptom and change, the fullest measure of his professional skill and a heart-felt purpose to save his friend's life if human brain or human concentration could avail. And yet he stated to Pauline in Selma's hearing that, beyond keeping up the patient's strength by stimulants, science was practically helpless, and that all they could do was to wait.

And so they sat, still and unemployed watchers, while day turned into darkness. From time to time, by the night-lamp, Selma

194

saw Pauline smiling at her as though in defiance of whatever fate might have in store. Selma herself felt the inclination neither to smile nor to weep. She sat looking before her with her hands clasped, resenting the powerlessness of the few remedies used, and impatient of the inactivity and relentless silence. Why did not the doctor adopt more stringent measures? Surely there was something to be done to enable Wilbur to combat the disease. Dr. Page had the reputation of being a skilful physician, and, presumably, was doing his best; but was it not possible, was it not sensible, to suppose there was a different and better way of treating pneumonia—a way which was as superior to the conventional and stereotyped method as the true American point of view was superior in other matters?

It came over her as a conviction that if she were elsewhere—in Benham, for instance—her husband could be readily and brilliantly cured. This impassive mode of treatment seemed to her of one piece with the entire Littleton surroundings, the culmination of which was Pauline smiling in the face of death. She yearned to do something active and decided. Yet, how helpless she was! This arbitrary doctor was following his own dictates without a word to anyone, and without suspecting the existence of wiser expedients.

In a moment of rebellion she rose, and swiftly approaching Wilbur's bed, exclaimed, fervently: "Is there not something we can do for you, darling? Something you feel will do you good?"

The sufferer faintly smiled and feebly shook his head, and at the same moment she was drawn away by a firm hand, and Dr. Page whispered: "He is very weak. Entire rest is his only chance. The least exertion is a drain on his vitality."

"Surely there must be some medicine—some powerful application which will help his breathing," she retorted, and she detected again the semblance of laughter in the doctor's eyes.

"Everything which modern science can do is being done, Mrs. Littleton."

What was there but to resume her seat and helpless vigil? Modern science? The word grated on her ears. It savored to her of narrow medical tyranny, and distrust of aspiring individuality. Wilbur was dying, and all modern science saw fit to do was to give him brandy and wait. And she, his wife—the one who loved him best in the world, was powerless to intervene. Nay, she had intervened, and modern science had mocked her.

Selma's eyes, like the glint of two swords, bent themselves on her husband's bed. A righteous anger reinforced her grieving heart and made her spirit militant, while the creeping hours passed. Over and over she pursued the tenor of her protest until her wearied system sought refuge in sleep. She was not conscious of slumbering, but she reasoned later that she must have slept, for she suddenly became conscious of a touch on the shoulder and a vibrant utterance of her name.

"Selma, Selma, you must come at once."

Her returning wits realized that it was Pauline who was arousing her and urging her to Wilbur's bed-side. She sprang forward, and saw the light of existence fading from her husband's eyes into the mute dulness of death. Dr. Page was bending over him in a desperate, but vain, effort to force some restorative between his lips. At the foot of the bed stood the nurse, with an expression which betrayed what had occurred.

"What is it, Wilbur? What have they done to you? What has happened?" Selma cried, looking from one to the other, though she had discerned the truth in a flash. As she spoke, Dr. Page desisted from his undertaking, and stepped back from the bed, and instantly Selma threw herself on her knees and pressed her face upon Littleton's lifeless features. There was no response. His spirit had departed.

"His heart could not stand the strain. That is the great peril in pneumonia," she heard the doctor murmur.

"He is dead," she cried, in a horrified outburst, and she looked up at the pitying group with the gaze of an afflicted lioness. She caught sight of Pauline smiling through her tears—that same unprotesting, submissive smile—and holding out her hands to her. Selma, rising, turned away, and as her sister-in-law sought to put her arm about her, evaded the caress.

"No—no," she said. Then facing her, added, with aggrieved conviction:

"I cannot believe that Wilbur's death was necessary. Why was not something energetic done?"

Pauline flushed, but, ascribing the calumny to distress, she held her peace, and said, simply:

"Sh! dear. You will understand better by and by."

196

BOOK III.

THE SUCCESS

CHAPTER I.

It had never occurred to Selma that she might lose her husband. Even with his shortcomings he was so important to her from the point of view of support, and her scheme of life was so interwoven with his, she had taken for granted that he would live as long as she desired. She felt that destiny had a second time been signally cruel to her, and that she was drinking deeply of the cup of sorrow. She was convinced that Wilbur, had he lived, would have moved presently to Benham, in accordance with her desire, and that they would then have been completely happy again. Instead he was dead and under the sod, and she was left to face the world with no means save $5,000 from his life insurance and the natural gifts and soul which God had given her.

She appreciated that she was still a comparatively young woman, and that, notwithstanding her love for Wilbur, she had been unable as his wife to exhibit herself to the world in her true light. She was free once more to lead her own life, and to obtain due recognition for her ideas and principles. She deplored with a grief which depleted the curve of her oval cheeks the premature end of her husband's artistic career—an aspiring soul cut off on the threshold of success—yet, though of course she never squarely made the reflection, she was aware that the development of her own life was more intrinsically valuable to the world than his, and that of the two it was best that he should be taken. She was sad, sore against Providence, and uncertain as to the future. But she was keenly conscious that she had a future, and she was eager to be stirring. Still, for the moment, the outlook was perplexing. What was she to do? First, and certainly, she desired to shake the dust of New York from her feet at the earliest opportunity. She inclined toward Benham as a residence, and to the lecture platform, supplemented by literature, and perhaps eventually the stage, as a means of livelihood. She believed in her secret soul that she could act. Her supposed facility in acquiring the New York manner had helped to generate that impression. It seemed to her more than probable that with a little instruction as to technical stage business she could gain fame and fortune almost at once as an actress of tragedy or melodrama. Comedy she despised as unworthy of her. But the stage appealed to her only on the ground of income. The life of an actress lacked the ethical character which she liked to associate with whatever she did. To be sure, a great actress was an inspiring influence. Nevertheless she preferred some more obviously improving occupation, provided it would afford a suitable support. Yet was it fitting that she should be condemned to do hack work for her daily bread instead of something to enlighten and uplift the community in which she lived? She considered that she had served her apprenticeship by teaching school and writing for the newspapers, and she begrudged spending further time in subordinate work. Better on the whole a striking success on the stage than this, for after she had made a name and money she could retire and devote herself to more congenial undertakings. Nevertheless her conscience told her that a theatrical career must be regarded as a last resort, and she appreciated the importance of not making a hasty decision as to what she would do. The lease of her house would not expire for six months, and it seemed to her probable that even in New York, where she was not understood, someone would realize her value as a manager of some intellectual or literary movement and make overtures to her. She wrote to Mrs. Earle and received a cordial response declaring that Benham would welcome her with open arms, a complimentary though somewhat vague certificate. She sent a line also to Mr. Dennison, informing him that she hoped soon to submit some short stories for his magazine, and received a guarded but polite reply to the effect that he would be glad to read her manuscripts.

While she was thus deliberating and winding up her husband's affairs, Mr. Parsons, who had been absent from New York at the time of Wilbur's decease, called and bluntly made the announcement that he had bought a house in Benham, was to move there immediately, and was desirous that she should live with him as his companion and housekeeper on liberal pecuniary terms.

"I am an old man," he said, "and my health is not what it used to be. I need someone to look after me and to keep me company. I like your chatty ways, and, if I have someone smart and brisk around like you, I sha'n't be thinking so often that I'm all alone in the world. It'll be dull for you, I guess; but you'll be keeping quiet for the present wherever you are; and when the time comes that you wish to take notice again I won't stand in the way of your amusing yourself."

To this homely plea Selma returned a beatific smile. It struck

200

her as an ideal arrangement; a golden opportunity for him, and convenient and promising for her. In the first place she was accorded the mission of cheering and guarding the declining years of this fine old man, whom she had come to look on with esteem and liking. And at the same time as his companion—the virtual mistress of his house, for she knew perfectly well that as a genuine American he was not offering her a position less than this—she would be able to shape her life gradually along congenial lines, and to wait for the ripe occasion for usefulness to present itself. In an instant a great load was lifted from her spirit. She was thankful to be spared conscientious qualms concerning the career of an actress, and thankful to be freed at one bound from her New York associations—especially with Pauline, whose attitude toward her had been further strained by her continued conviction that Wilbur's life might have been saved. Indeed, so completely alleviating was Mr. Parsons's proposition that, stimulated by the thought that he was to be a greater gainer from the plan than she, Selma gave rein to her emotions by exclaiming with fervor:

"Usually I like to think important plans over before coming to a decision; but this arrangement seems to me so sensible and natural and mutually advantageous, Mr. Parsons, that I see no reason why I shouldn't accept your offer now. God grant that I may be a worthy daughter to you—and in some measure take the place of the dear ones you have lost."

"That's what I want," he said. "I took a liking to you the first time we met. Then it's settled?"

"Yes. I suppose," she added, after a moment's hesitation—speaking with an accent of scorn—"I suppose there may be people—people like those who are called fashionable here—who will criticise the arrangement on the ground—er—of propriety, because I'm not a relation, and you are not very old. But I despise conventions such as that. They may be necessary for foreigners; but they are not meant for self-respecting American women. I fancy my sister-in-law may not wholly approve of it, but I don't know. I shall take pleasure in showing her and the rest that it would be wicked as well as foolish to let a flimsy suggestion of evil interfere with the happiness of two people situated as we are."

Mr. Parsons seemed puzzled at first, as though he did not understand exactly what she meant, but when she concluded he said:

"You come to me, as you have yourself stated, on the footing of a daughter. If folk are not content to mind their own business, I guess we needn't worry because they don't happen to be suited. There's one or two relations of mine would be glad to be in your shoes, but I don't know of anything in the Bible or the Constitution of the United States which forbids an old man from choosing the face he'll have opposite to him at table."

"Or forbids the interchange of true sympathy—that priceless privilege," answered Selma, her liking for a sententious speech rising paramount even to the pleasure caused her by the allusion to her personal appearance. Nevertheless it was agreeable to be preferred to his female cousins on the score of comeliness.

Accordingly, within six months of her husband's death, the transition to Benham was accomplished, and Selma was able to encounter the metaphorically open arms, referred to by Mrs. Earle, without feeling that she was a less important person than when she had been whisked off as a bride by Littleton, the rising architect. She was returning as the confidential, protecting companion of a successful, self-made old man, who was relying on her to make his new establishment a pleasure to himself and a credit to the wide-awake city in which he had elected to pass his remaining days. She was returning to a house on the River Drive (the aristocratic boulevard of Benham, where the river Nye makes a broad sweep to the south); a house not far distant from the Flagg mansion at which, as Mrs. Lewis Babcock, she had looked askance as a monument inimical to democratic simplicity. Wilbur had taught her that it was very ugly, and now that she saw it again after a lapse of years she was pleased to note that her new residence, though slightly smaller, had a more modern and distinguished air.

The new house was of rough-hewn red sandstone, combining solid dignity and some artistic merit, for Benham had not stood still architecturally speaking. The River Drive was a grotesque, yet on the whole encouraging exhibit. Most of the residences had been designed by native talent, but under the spur of experiment even the plain, hard-headed builders had been constrained to dub themselves "architects," and adopt modern methods; and here and there stood evidences that the seed planted by Mrs. Hallett Taylor and Littleton had borne fruit, for Benham possessed at least half a dozen private houses which could defy criticism.

The one selected by Mr. Parsons was not of these half dozen; but the plain, hard-headed builder who had erected it for the original owner was shrewd and imitative, and had avoided ambitious deviations from the type he wished to copy—the red sandstone, swell front variety, which ten years before would have seemed to the moral sense of Benham unduly cheerful. Mr. Parsons was so fortunate as to be able to buy it just after it had been completed, together with a stable and half an acre of ground, from one of the few Benhamites whose financial ventures had ended in disaster, and who was obliged to sell. It was a more ambitious residence than Mr. Parsons had desired, but it was the most available, inasmuch as he could occupy it at once. It had been painted and decorated within, but was unfurnished. Mr. Parsons, as a practical business man, engaged the builder to select and supply the bedroom and solid fittings, but it occurred to him to invite Selma to choose the furnishings for what he called the show rooms.

Selma was delighted to visit once more the New York stores, free from the bridle of Wilbur's criticism and unrestrained by economy. She found to her satisfaction that the internal decoration of the new house was not unlike that of the Williamses' first habitation—that is, gay and bedizened; and she was resolved in the selection of her draperies and ornaments to buy things which suggested by their looks that they were handsome, and whose claim to distinction was not mere sober unobtrusiveness. She realized that some of her purchases would have made Wilbur squirm, but since his death she felt more sure than ever that even where art was concerned his taste was subdued, timid, and unimaginative. For instance, she believed that he would not have approved her choice of light-blue satin for the upholstery of the drawing-room, nor of a marble statue—an allegorical figure of Truth, duly draped, as its most conspicuous ornament.

Selma was spared the embarrassment of her first husband's presence. Divorce is no bar to ordinary feminine curiosity as to the whereabouts of a former partner for life, and she had proved no exception to the rule. Mrs. Earle had kept her posted as to Babcock's career since their separation, and what she learned had tended merely to demonstrate the wisdom and justice of her action. As a divorced man he had, after a time, resumed the free and easy, coarse companionship to which he had been partial before his marriage, and had gradually become a heavy drinker. Presently he had neglected his business, a misfortune of which a rival concern had been quick to take advantage. The trend of his affairs had been steadily downhill, and had come to a crisis three months before Littleton's death, when, in order to avoid insolvency, he sold out his factory and business to the rival company, and accepted at the same hands the position of manager in a branch office in a city further west. Consequently, Selma could feel free from molestation or an appeal to her sensibilities. She preferred to think of Babcock as completely outside her life, as dead to her, and she would have disliked the possibility of meeting him in the flesh while shopping on Central avenue. It had been the only drawback to her proposed return to Benham.

During the years of Selma's second marriage Benham had waxed rapidly in population and importance. People had been attracted thither by the varied industries of the city—alike those in search of fortune, and those offering themselves for employment in the mills, oil-works, and pork factories; and at the date of Littleton's death it boasted over one hundred and fifty thousand inhabitants. It was already the second city of the State in point of population, and was freely acknowledged to be the most wide-awake and enterprising. The civic spirit of Benham was reputed to be constantly and increasingly alert and progressive, notwithstanding the river Nye still ran the color of bean-soup above where it was drawn for drinking purposes, and the ability of a plumber, who had become an alderman, to provide a statue or lay out a public park was still unquestioned by the majority. Even to-day, when trained ability has obtained recognition in many quarters, the Benhamites at large are apt to resent criticism as aristocratic fault-finding; yet at this time that saving minority of souls who refused to regard everything which Benham did as perfection, and whose subsequent forlorn hopes and desperately won victories have little by little taught the community wisdom, if not modesty, was beginning to utter disagreeable strictures.

Mrs. Margaret Rodney Earle, when she opened her arms to Selma and folded her to her bosom with a hug of welcome, was raging inwardly against this minority, and they had not been many minutes together before she gave utterance to her grievance.

204

"You have come just in time to give us your sympathy and support in an important matter, my dear. Miss Bailey has been nominated for the School Board at the instance of the Executive Committee of the Benham Institute. We supposed that she would have plain sailing, for many of the voters have begun to recognize the justice of having one or two women on the School Board, and by hard work we had succeeded in getting her name put on the Democratic ticket. Judge, then, of our feelings when we learned that the Reform Club had decided to blacklist and refuse to support at the polls three of the six names on the ticket, including our Luella Bailey, on the ground of lack of experience in educational matters. The Reform Club has nominated three other persons—one of them a woman. And who do you suppose is the head and front of this unholy crusade?"

"It sounds like Mrs. Hallett Taylor," answered Selma, sternly.

"How did you know? What made you think so? How clever of you, Selma! Yes, she is the active spirit."

"It was she who was at the bottom of Miss Bailey's rejection when she was my candidate for a position at Everdean College."

"To be sure. I remember. This Reform Club, which was started a year or so ago, and which sets itself up as a censor of what we are trying to do in Benham, has nominated a Miss Snow, who is said to have travelled abroad studying the school systems of Europe."

"As if that would help us in any way."

"Precisely. She has probably come home with her head full of queer-fangled notions which would be out of keeping with our institutions. Just the reason why she shouldn't be chosen. We are greatly troubled as to the result, dear, for though we expect to win, the prejudice of some men against voting for a woman under any circumstances will operate against our candidate, so that this action of the Reform Club may possibly be the means of electing one of the men on the Republican ticket instead of Luella. Miss Snow hasn't the ghost of a chance. But that isn't all. These Reform Club nominations are preliminary to a bill before the Legislature to take away from the people the right to elect members of the school committee, and substitute an appointive board of specialists to serve during long terms of good behavior. As Mr. Lyons says, that's the real issue involved. It's quixotic and it isn't necessary. Haven't we always prided ourselves on our ability to keep our public schools the best in the world? And is there any doubt, Selma, that either you or I would be fully qualified to serve on the School Board though we haven't made any special study of primers and geographies? Luella Bailey hasn't had any special training, but she's smart and progressive, and the poor thing would like the recognition. We fixed on her because we thought it would help her to get ahead, for she has not been lucky in obtaining suitable employment. As Mr. Lyons says, a serious principle is involved. He has come out strong against the movement and declares that it is a direct menace to the intelligence of the plain people of the United States and a subtle invasion of their liberties."

"Mr. Lyons? What Mr. Lyons is that?"

"Yes, dear, it is the same one who managed your affair. Your Mr. Lyons. He has become an important man since you left Benham. He speaks delightfully, and is likely to receive the next Democratic nomination for Congress. He is in accord with all liberal movements, and a foe of everything exclusive, unchristian or arbitrary. He has declared his intention to oppose the bill when it is introduced, and I shall devote myself body and soul to working against it in case Luella Bailey is defeated. It is awkward because Mrs. Taylor is a member of the Institute, though she doesn't often come, and the club has never been in politics. But here when there was a chance to do Luella Bailey a good turn, and I'd been able through some of my newspaper friends to get her on the ticket, it seems to me positively unchristian—yes, that's the word—to try to keep her off the board. There are some things of course, Luella couldn't do—and if the position were superintendent of a hospital, for instance, I dare say that special training would be advantageous, though nursing can be picked up very rapidly by a keen intelligence: but to raise such objections in regard to a candidate for the School Board seems to me ridiculous as well as cruel. What we need there are open, receptive minds, free from fads and prejudice—wide-awake, progressive enthusiastic intellects. It worries me to see the Institute dragged into politics, but it is my duty to resist this undemocratic movement."

"Surely," exclaimed Selma, with fire. "I am thankful I have come in time to help you. I understand exactly. I have been passing through just such experiences in New York—encountering and being rebuffed by just such people as those who belong to this Reform Club. My husband was beginning to see through them and to recognize that we were both tied hand and foot by their narrowness and lack of enthusiasm when he died. If he had lived, we would have moved to Benham shortly in order to escape from bondage. And one thing is certain, dear Mrs. Earle," she continued with intensity, "we must not permit this carping spirit of hostility to original and spontaneous effort to get a foothold in Benham. We must crush it, we must stamp it out."

"Amen, my dear. I am delighted to hear you talk like that. I declare you would be very effective in public if you were roused."

"Yes, I am roused, and I am willing to speak in public if it becomes necessary in order to keep Benham uncontaminated by the insidious canker of exclusiveness and the distrust of aspiring souls which a few narrow minds choose to term untrained. Am *I* untrained? Am *I* superficial and common? Do *I* lack the appearance and behavior of a lady?"

Selma accompanied these interrogatories with successive waves of the hand, as though she were branding so many falsehoods.

"Assuredly not, Selma. I consider you"—and here Mrs. Earle gasped in the process of choosing her words—"I consider you one of our best trained and most independent minds—cultured, a friend of culture, and an earnest seeker after truth. If you are not a lady, neither am I, neither is anyone in Benham. Why do you ask, dear?" And without waiting for an answer, Mrs. Earle added with a touch of material wisdom, "You return to Benham under satisfactory, I might say, brilliant auspices. You will be the active spirit in this fine house, and be in a position to promote worthy intellectual and moral movements."

"Thank heavens, yes. And to combat those which are unworthy and dangerous," exclaimed Selma, clasping her fingers, "I can count on the support of Mr. Parsons, God bless him! And it would seem at last as if I had, a real chance—a real chance at last. Mrs. Earle—Cora—I know you can keep a secret. I feel almost as though you were my mother, for there is no one else now to whom I can talk like this. I have not been happy in New York. I thought I was happy at first, but lately we have been miserable. My marriage—er—they drove my husband to the wall, and killed him. He was sensitive and noble, but not practical, and he fell a victim to the mercenary despotism of our surroundings. When I tried to help him they became jealous of me, and shut their doors in our faces."

"You poor, poor child. I have suspected for some time that something was wrong."

"It nearly killed me. But now, thank heaven, I breathe freely once more. I have lost my dear husband, but I have escaped from that prison-house; and with his memory to keep me merciless, I am eager to wage war against those influences which are conspiring to

208

fetter the free-born soul and stifle spontaneity. Luella Bailey must be elected, and these people be taught that foreign ideas may flourish in New York, but cannot obtain root in Benham."

Mrs. Earle wiped her eyes, which were running over as the result of this combination of confidence and eloquence.

"If you don't mind my saying so, Selma, I never saw anyone so much improved as you. You always had ideas, and were well equipped, but now you speak as though you could remove mountains if necessary. It's a blessing for us as well as you that you're back among us once more."

CHAPTER II.

When Selma uttered her edict that Luella Bailey must be elected she did not know that the election was only three days off. When she was told this by Mrs. Earle, she cast about feverishly during a few hours for the means to compass certain victory, then promptly and sensibly disclaimed responsibility for the result, suggesting even that her first appearance as a remover of mountains be deferred to the time when the bill should be before the Legislature. As she aptly explained to Mrs. Earle, the canvass was virtually at an end, she was unacquainted with the practical features of the situation, and was to all intents a stranger in Benham after so long an absence. Mrs. Earle was unable to combat the logic of these representations, but she obtained from Selma a ready promise to accompany the Benham Institute to the final rally on the evening before election day and sit in a prominent place on the platform. The Institute was to attend as a body by way of promoting the cause of its candidate, for though the meeting was called in aid of the entire Democratic municipal ticket, Hon. James O. Lyons, the leading orator of the occasion, had promised to devote special attention to Miss Bailey, whose election, owing to the attitude of the Reform Club, was recognized as in doubt. Selma also agreed to accompany Mrs. Earle in a hack on the day itself, and career through the city in search of recalcitrant or indifferent female voters, for the recently acquired right of Benham women to vote for members of the School Board had not as yet been exercised by any considerable number of the emancipated sex.

As a part of the programme of the meeting the Benham Institute, or the major portion of it (for there were a few who sympathized openly with Mrs. Taylor), filed showily on to the platform headed by Mrs. Earle, who waved her pocket handkerchief at the audience, which was the occasion for renewed hand-clapping and enthusiasm. Selma walked not far behind and took her seat among the forty other members, who all wore white silk badges stamped in red with the sentiment "A vote for Luella Bailey is a vote for the liberty of the people." Her pulses were throbbing with interest and pleasure. This was the sort of thing she delighted in, and which she had hoped would be a frequent incident of her life in New York. It pleased her to think how naturally and easily she had taken her place in the ranks of these earnest, enthusiastic workers, and that she had merely to express a wish in order to have leadership urged upon her. Matters had shaped themselves exactly as she desired. Mr. Parsons not only treated her completely as an equal, but consulted her in regard to everything. He had already become obviously dependent on her, and had begun to develop the tendencies of an invalid.

The exercises were of a partisan cast. The theory that municipal government should be independent of party politics had been an adage in Benham since its foundation, and been disregarded annually by nine-tenths of the population ever since. This was a Democratic love-feast. The speakers and the audience alike were in the best of spirits, for there was no uncertainty in the minds of the party prophets as to the result of the morrow's ballot—excepting with regard to Miss Bailey. The rest of the ticket would unquestionably be elected; accordingly all hands and voices were free to focus their energies in her behalf and thus make the victory a clean sweep. Nevertheless the earlier speakers felt obliged to let their eloquence flow over the whole range of political misgovernment from the White House and the national platform down, although the actual issue was the choice of a mayor, twelve aldermen and a school committee, so that only casual reference was made to the single weak spot on the ticket until the Hon. James O. Lyons rose to address the meeting. The reception accorded him was more spontaneous and effusive than that which had been bestowed on either of his predecessors, and as he stood waiting with dignified urbanity for the applause to subside, some rapturous admirer called for three cheers, and the tumult was renewed.

Selma was thrilled. Her acquaintance with Mr. Lyons naturally heightened her interest, and she observed him eagerly. Time had added to his corporeal weight since he had acted as her counsel, and enhanced the sober yet genial decorum of his bearing. His slightly pontifical air seemed an assurance against ill-timed levity. His cheeks were still fat and smooth shaven, but, like many of the successful men of Benham, he now wore a chin beard—a thick tuft of hair which in his case tapered so that it bore some resemblance to the beard of a goat, and gave a rough-and-ready aspect to his appearance suggestive alike of smart, solid worth and an absence of dandified tendencies. Mr. Parsons had a thicker beard of the same character, which Selma regarded with favor as a badge of serious intentions.

"My friends," he began when the applause had subsided; then paused and surveyed his audience in a manner which left them in doubt as to whether he was struggling with emotion or busy in silent prayer. "My friends, a month ago to-day the citizens of Benham assembled to crown with appropriate and beautiful services the monument which they, the survivors, have erected with pious hands to perpetuate the memory of those who laid down their lives to keep intact our beloved union of States and to banish slavery forever from the confines of our aspiring civilization. A week ago an equally representative assembly, without regard to creed or party, listened to the exercises attending the dedication of the new Court House which we have raised to Justice—that white-robed goddess, the guardian of the liberties of the people. Each was a notable and significant event. On each occasion I had the honor to say a few poor words. We celebrated with bowed heads and with garlands the deeds of the heroic dead, and now have consecrated ourselves to the opportunities and possibilities of peace under the law—to the revelation of the temper of our new civilization which, tried in the furnace of war, is to be a grand and vital power for the advancement of the human race, for the righteous furtherance of the brotherhood of man. What is the hope of the world?" he asked. "America—these United States, a bulwark against tyranny, an asylum for the aspiring and the downtrodden. The eyes of the nations are upon us. In the souls of the survivors and of the sons and daughters of the patriots who have died in defence of the liberties of our beloved country abide the seed and inspiration for new victories of peace. Our privilege be it as the heirs of Washington and Franklin and Hamilton and Lincoln and Grant to set the nations of the earth an example of what peace under the law may accomplish, so that the free-born son of America from the shores of Cape Cod to the western limits of the Golden Gate may remain a synonym for noble aims and noble deeds, for truth and patriotism and fearlessness of soul."

The speaker's words had been uttered slowly at the outset—ponderous, sonorous, sentence by sentence, like the big drops before a heavy shower. As he warmed to his theme the pauses ceased, and his speech flowed with the musical sweep of a master of platform oratory. When he spoke of war his voice choked; in

212

speaking of peace he paused for an appreciable moment, casting his eyes up as though he could discern the angel of national tranquillity hovering overhead. Although this opening peroration seemed scarcely germane to the occasion, the audience listened in absorbed silence, spell-bound by the magnetism of his delivery. They felt sure that he had a point in reserve to which these splendid and agreeable truths were a pertinent introduction.

Proceeding, with his address, Mr. Lyons made a panegyric on these United States of America, from the special standpoint of their dedication to the "God of our fathers," a solemn figure of speech. The sincerity of his patriotism was emphasized by the religious fervor of his deduction that God was on the side of the nation, and the nation on the side of God. Though he abstained from direct strictures, both his manner and his matter seemed to serve a caveat, so to speak, on the other nations by declaring that for fineness of heart and thought, and deed, the world must look to the land "whose wide and well-nigh boundless prairies were blossoming with the buds of truth fanned by the breeze of liberty and fertilized by the aspirations of a God-fearing and a God-led population. What is the hope of the world, I repeat?" he continued. "The plain and sovereign people of our beloved country. Whatever menaces their liberties, whatever detracts from their, power and infringes on their prerogatives is a peril to our institutions and a step backward in the science of government. My friends, we are here to-night to protest against a purpose to invade those liberties—a deliberately conceived design to take away from the sovereign people of this city one of their cherished privileges—the right to decide who shall direct the policy of our free public-school system, that priceless heritage of every American. I beg to remind you that this contest is no mere question of healthy rivalry between two great political parties; nor again is it only a vigorous competition between two ambitious and intelligent women. A ballot in behalf of our candidate will be a vote of confidence in the ability of the plain people of this country to adopt the best educational methods without the patronizing dictation of aboard of specialists nurtured on foreign and uninspiring theories of instruction. A ballot against Miss Luella Bailey, the competent and cultivated lady whose name adds strength and distinction to our ticket, and who has been needlessly and wantonly opposed by those who should be her proud friends, will signify a willingness to renounce one of our most precious liberties—the free man's right to choose those who are to impart to his children mastery of knowledge and love of country. I take my stand to-night as the resolute enemy of this aristocratic and un-American suggestion, and urge you, on the eve of election, to devote your energies to overwhelming beneath the shower of your fearless ballots this insult to the intelligence of the voters of Benham, and this menace to our free and successful institutions, which, under the guidance of the God of our fathers, we purpose to keep perpetually progressive and undefiled."

A salvo of enthusiasm greeted Mr. Lyons as he concluded. His speeches were apt to cause those whom he addressed to feel that they were no common campaign utterances, but eloquent expressions of principle and conviction, clothed in memorable language, as, indeed, they were. He was fond of giving a moral or patriotic flavor to what he said in public, for he entertained both a profound reverence for high moral ideas and an abiding faith in the superiority of everything American. He had arrayed himself on the threshold of his legal career as a friend and champion of the mass of the people—the plain and sovereign people, as he was apt to style them in public. His first and considerable successes had been as the counsel for plaintiffs before juries in accident cases against large corporations, and he had thought of himself with complete sincerity as a plain man, contesting for human rights before the bar of justice, by the sheer might of his sonorous voice and diligent brain. His political development had been on the same side. Latterly the situation had become a little puzzling, though to a man of straightforward intentions, like himself, not fundamentally embarrassing. That is, the last four or five years had altered both the character of his practice and his circumstances, so that instead of fighting corporations he was now the close adviser of a score of them; not the defender of their accident cases, but the confidential attorney who was consulted in regard to their vital interests, and who charged them liberal sums for his services. He still figured in court from time to time in his capacity of the plain man's friend, which he still considered himself to be no less than before, but most of his time was devoted to protecting the legal interests of the railroad, gas, water, manufacturing, mining and other undertakings which, the rapid growth of Benham had forgotten. And as a result

214

of this commerce with the leading men of affairs in Benham, and knowledge of what was going on, he had been able to invest his large fees to the best advantage, and had already reaped a rich harvest from the rapid rise in value of the securities of diverse successful enterprises. When new projects were under consideration he was in a position to have a finger in the pie, and he was able to borrow freely from a local bank in which he was a director.

He was puzzled—it might be said distressed—how to make these rewards of his professional prominence appear compatible with his real political principles, so that the plain and sovereign people would recognize as clearly as he that there was no inconsistency in his having taken advantage of the opportunities for professional advancement thrown in his way. He was ambitious for political preferment, sharing the growing impression that he was well qualified for public office, and he desired to rise as the champion of popular ideas. Consequently he resented bitterly the calumnies which had appeared in one or two irresponsible newspapers to the effect that he was becoming a corporation attorney and a capitalist. Could a man refuse legitimate business which was thrust upon him? How were his convictions and interest in the cause of struggling humanity altered or affected by his success at the bar? Hence he neglected no occasion to declare his allegiance to progressive doctrine, and to give utterance to the patriotism which at all times was on tap in his emotional system. He had been married, but his wife had been dead a number of years, and he made his home with his aged mother, to whom he was apt to refer with pious tremulousness when he desired to emphasize some domestic situation before a jury. As a staunch member of the Methodist Church, he was on terms of intimate association with his pastor, and was known as a liberal contributor to domestic and foreign missions.

Selma was genuinely carried away by the character of his oratory. His sentiments were so completely in accord with her own ideas that she felt he had left nothing unsaid, and had put the case grandly. Here at last was a man who shared with her the convictions with which her brain was seething—a man who was not afraid to give public expression to his views, and who possessed a splendid gift of statement. She had felt sure that she would meet sympathy and kindred spirits in Benham, but her experience in New York had so far depressed her that she had not allowed herself to expect such a thorough-going champion. What a contrast his solid, devotional, yet business-like aspect was to the quizzical lightness of the men in New York she had been told were clever, like Dr. Page and Mr. Dennison! He possessed Wilbur's ardor and reverence, with a robustness of physique and a practical air which Wilbur had lacked—lacked to his and her detriment. If Wilbur had been as vigorous in body as he ought to have been, would he have died? She had read somewhere lately that physical delicacy was apt to react on the mind and make one's ideas too fine-spun and unsubstantial. Here was the advantage which a man like Mr. Lyons had over Wilbur. He was strong and thickset, and looked as though he could endure hard work without wincing. So could she. It was a great boon, an essential of effective manhood or womanhood. These thoughts followed in the wake of the enthusiasm his personality had aroused in her at the close of his address. She scarcely heard the remarks of the next speaker, the last on the programme. Her eyes kept straying wistfully in the direction of Mr. Lyons, and she wondered if there would be an opportunity when the meeting was over to let him know how much she approved of what he had said, and how necessary she felt the promulgation, of such ideas was for the welfare of the country.

She was aroused from contemplation by the voice of Mrs. Earle, who, now that everybody was standing up preliminary to departure, bent over her front bench on the platform to whisper, "Wasn't Mr. Lyons splendid?"

"Yes, indeed," said Selma. "I should like so much to make his acquaintance, to compare notes with him and thank him for his brave, true words."

"I know he'd be pleased to meet you. I'll try to catch his eye. I wish some of those Reform Club people could have heard what he thought of them. There! He's looking this way. I'm going to attract his attention." Whereupon Mrs. Earle began to nod in his direction energetically. "He sees us now, and has noticed you. I shouldn't wonder if he has recognized you. Follow me close, Selma, and we'll be able to shake hands with him."

By dint of squeezing and stertorous declarations of her desire, Mrs. Earle obtained a gradual passage through the crowd. Many from the audience had ascended to the platform for the purpose of accosting the speakers, and a large share of the interest was being bestowed on Mr. Lyons, who was holding an impromptu reception. When at last Mrs. Earle had worked her way to within a few feet of him, her wheezing condition and bulk announced her approach, and procured her consideration from the others in the line, so that she was able to plant herself pervasively and firmly in front of her idol and take possession of him by the fervid announcement, "You were simply unanswerable. Eloquent, convincing, and unanswerable. And I have brought with me an old friend, Mrs. Littleton, who sympathizes with your superb utterances, and wishes to tell you so."

As Selma stepped forward in recognition of this introduction she vibrated to hear Mr. Lyons say, without a sign of hesitation, "A friend whom it is a pleasure to welcome back to Benham, Mrs. Littleton, I am pleased to meet you again."

Selma had hoped, and felt it her due, that he would recognize her. Still his having done so at once was a compliment which served to enhance the favorable opinion which she had already formed regarding him.

"I have been longing for months, Mr. Lyons," she said, "to hear someone say what you have said to-night. I am concerned, as we all are of course, in Miss Bailey's election, and your advocacy of her cause was most brilliant; but what I refer to—what interested, me especially, was the splendid protest you uttered against all movements to prevent the intelligence of the people from asserting itself. It gave me encouragement and made me feel that the outlook for the future is bright—that our truths must prevail."

It was a maxim with Lyons that it was desirable to remember everyone he met, and he prided himself on his ability to call cordially by name clients or chance acquaintances whom he had not seen for years. Nature had endowed him with a good memory for names and faces, but he had learned to take advantage of all opportunities to brush up his wits before they were called into flattering, spontaneous action. When his glance, attracted by Mrs. Earle's remote gesticulation, rested on Selma's face, he began to ask himself at once where he had seen it before. In the interval vouchsafed by her approach he recalled the incident of the divorce, that her name had been Babcock, and that she had married again, but he was still groping for the name of her husband when the necessary clew was supplied by Mrs. Earle, and he was able to make his recognition of her exhaustive. He noticed with approval her pretty face and compact figure, reflecting that the slight gain in flesh was to her advantage, and noticed also her widow's mourning. But her eager, fluent address and zealous manner had prevented his attention from secretly wandering with business-like foresight to the next persons in the line of those anxious to shake his hand, and led him to regard her a second time. He was accustomed to compliments, but he was struck by the note of discriminating companionship in her congratulation. He believed that he had much at heart the very issue which she had touched upon, and it gratified him that a woman whose appearance was so attractive to him should single out for sympathetic enthusiasm what was in his opinion the cardinal principle involved, instead of expatiating on the assistance he had rendered Miss Bailey. Lyons said to himself that here was a kindred spirit—a woman with whom conversation would be a pleasure; with whom it would be possible to discourse on terms of mental comradeship. He was partial to comely women, but he did not approve of frivolity except on special and guarded occasions.

"I thank you cordially for your appreciation," he answered. "You have grasped the vital kernel of my speech and I am grateful for your good opinion."

Even in addressing the other sex, Lyons could not forget the responsibility of his frock-coat and that it was incumbent upon him to be strictly serious in public. Nevertheless his august but glib demeanor suited Selma's mood better than more obvious gallantry, especially as she got the impression, which he really wished to convey, that he admired her. It was out of the question for him to prolong the situation in the face of those waiting to grasp his hand, but Lyons heard with interest the statement which Mrs. Earle managed to whisper hoarsely in his ear just as he turned to welcome the next comer, and they were swept along:

"She is one of our brightest minds. The poor child has recently lost her husband, and has come to keep Mr. Parsons company in his new house—an ideal arrangement."

The identity of Mr. Parsons was well known to Lyons. He had met him occasionally in the past in other parts of the State in connection with business complications, and regarded him as a practical, intelligent citizen whose name would be of value to an aspirant for Congressional honors. It occurred to him as he shook hands with those next in line and addressed them that it would be eminently suitable if he should pay his respects to this new-comer to Benham by a visit. By so doing he world kill two birds with one stone, for he had reasoned of late that he owed it to himself to see more of the other sex. He had no specific matrimonial intentions; that is, he was not on the lookout for a wife; but he approved of happy unions as one of the great bulwarks of the community, and was well-disposed to encounter a suitable helpmate. He should expect physical charms, dignity, capacity and a sympathetic mind; a woman, in short, who would be an ornament to his home, a Christian influence in society and a companion whose intelligent tact would be likely to promote his political fortunes. And so it happened that in the course of the next few days he found himself thinking of Mrs. Littleton as a fine figure of a woman. This had not happened to him before since the death of his wife, and it made him thoughtful to the extent of asking "Why not?" For in spite of his long frock-coat and proper demeanor, passion was not extinct in the bosom of the Hon. James O. Lyons, and he was capable on special and guarded occasions of telling a woman that he loved her.

CHAPTER III.

Miss Luella Bailey was not elected. The unenlightened prejudice of man to prefer one of his own sex, combined with the hostility of the Reform Club, procured her defeat, notwithstanding that the rest of her ticket triumphed at the polls. There was some consolation for her friends in the fact that her rival, Miss Snow, had a considerably smaller number of votes than she. Selma solaced herself by the reflection that, as she had been consulted only at the twelfth hour, she was not responsible for the result, but she felt nerved by the defeat to concentrate her energies against the proposed bill for an appointed school board.

Her immediate attention and sympathy were suddenly invoked by the illness of Mr. Parsons, who had seemed lacking in physical vigor for some weeks, and whose symptoms culminated in a slight paralysis, which confined him to his bed for a month, and to his house during the remainder of the autumn. Selma rejoiced in this opportunity to develop her capacities as a nurse, to prove how adequate she would have been to take complete charge of her late husband, had Dr. Page chosen to trust her. She administered with scrupulous regularity to the invalid such medicines as were ordered, and kept him cheerful by reading and conversation, so that the physician in charge complimented her on her proficiency. Trained nurses were unknown in Benham at this time, and any old or unoccupied female was regarded as qualified to watch over the sick. Selma appreciated from what she had observed of the conduct of Wilbur's nurse that there was a wrong and a right way of doing things, but she blamed Dr. Page for his failure to appreciate instinctively that she was sure to do things suitably. It seemed to her that he had lacked the intuitive gift to discern latent capabilities—a fault of which the Benham practitioner proved blameless.

From the large, sunny chamber in which Mr. Parsons slowly recovered some portion of his vitality, Selma could discern the distant beginnings of Wetmore College, pleasantly situated on an elevation well beyond the city limits on the further side of the winding river. An architect had been engaged to carry out Wilbur's plans, and she watched the outlines of the new building gradually take shape during the convalescence of her benefactor. She recognized that the college would be theoretically a noble addition to the standing of Benham as a city of intellectual and æsthetic interests, but it provoked her to think that its management was in the hands of Mrs. Hallett Taylor and her friends, between whom and herself she felt that a chasm of irreconcilable differences of opinion existed. Mrs. Taylor had not called on her since her return. She believed that she was glad of this, and hoped that some of the severely indignant criticism which she had uttered in regard to the Reform Club movement had reached her ears. Or was Mrs. Taylor envious of her return to Benham as the true mistress of this fine establishment on the River Drive, so superior to her own? Nevertheless, it would have suited Selma to have been one of the trustees of this new college—her husband's handiwork in the doing of which he had laid down his promising life—and the fact that no one had sought her out and offered her the honor as a fitting recognition of her due was secretly mortifying. The Benham Institute had been prompt to acknowledge her presence by giving a reception in her honor, at which she was able to recite once more, "Oh, why should the Spirit of Mortal be proud?" with old-time success, and she had been informed by Mrs. Earle that she was likely to be chosen one of the Vice-Presidents at the annual meeting. But these Reform Club people had not even done her the courtesy to ask her to join them or consider their opinions. She would have spurned the invitation with contempt, but it piqued her not to know more about them; it distressed her to think that there should exist in Benham an exclusive set which professed to be ethically and intellectually superior and did not include her, for she had come to Benham with the intention of leading such a movement, to the detriment of fashion and frivolity. With Mr. Parsons's money at her back, she was serenely confident that the houses of the magnates of Benham—the people who corresponded in her mind's eye to the dwellers on Fifth Avenue—would open to her. Already there had been flattering indications that she would be able to command attention there. She had expected to find this so; her heart would have been broken to find it otherwise. Still, her hope in shaking the dust of New York from her feet had been to find in Benham an equally admirable and satisfactory atmosphere in regard to mental and moral progress. She had come just in time, it is true, to utter her vehement protest against this exclusive, aristocratic movement—this arrogant affectation of superiority, and to array herself in battle line against it, resolved to give herself up with enthusiasm to its annihilation. Yet the sight of the college buildings for the higher education of women, rising without her furtherance and supervision, and under the direction of these people, made her sad and gave her a feeling of disappointment. Why had they been permitted to obtain this foothold? Someone had been lacking in vigilance and foresight. Thank heaven, with her return and a strong, popular spirit like Mr. Lyons in the lead, these unsympathetic, so-called reformers would speedily be confounded, and the intellectual air of Benham restored to its original purity.

One afternoon while Selma's gaze happened to be directed toward the embryo college walls, and she was incubating on the situation, Mr. Parsons, who had seemed to be dozing, suddenly said:

"I should like you to write to Mr. Lyons, the lawyer, and ask him to come to see me."

"I will write to-night. You know he called while you were ill."

"Yes, I thought him a clever fellow when we met two or three times on railroad matters, and I gather from what you told me about his speech at the political meeting that he's a rising man hereabouts. I'm going to make my will, and I need him to put it into proper shape."

"I'm sure he'd do it correctly."

"There's not much for him to do except to make sure that the language is legal, for I've thought it all out while I've been lying here during these weeks. Still, it's important to have in a lawyer to fix it so the people whom I don't intend to get my money shan't be able to make out that I'm not in my right mind. I guess," he added, with a laugh, "that the doctor will allow I've my wits sufficiently for that?"

"Surely. You are practically well now."

Mr. Parsons was silent for a moment. He prided himself on being close-mouthed about his private affairs until they were ripe for utterance. His intention had been to defer until after the interview with his lawyer any statement of his purpose, but it suddenly occurred to him that it would please him to unbosom his secret to his companion because he felt sure in advance that she would sympathize fully with his plans. He had meant to tell her when the instrument was signed. Why not now?

"Selma," he said, "I've known ever since my wife and

222

daughter died that I ought to make a will, but I kept putting it off until it has almost happened that everything I've got went to my next of kin—folk I'm fond of, too, and mean to remember—but not fond enough for that. If I give them fifty thousand dollars apiece—the three of them—I shall rest easy in my grave, even if they think they ought to have had a bigger slice. It's hard on a man who has worked all his days, and laid up close to a million of dollars, not to have a son or a daughter, flesh of my flesh, to leave it to; a boy or a girl given at the start the education I didn't get, and who, by the help of my money, might make me proud, if I could look on, of my name or my blood. It wasn't to be, and I must grin and bear it, and do the next best thing. I caught a glimpse of what that thing was soon after I lost my wife and daughter, and it was the thought of that more than anything which kept me from going crazy with despair. I'm a plain man, an uneducated man, but the fortune I've made has been made honestly, and I'm going to spend it for the good of the American people—to contribute my mite toward helping the cause of truth and good citizenship and free and independent ideas which this nation calls for. I'm going to give my money for benevolent uses."

"Oh, Mr. Parsons," exclaimed Selma, clasping her hands, "how splendid! how glorious! How I envy you. It was what I hoped."

"I knew you would be pleased. I've had half a mind once or twice to let the cat out of the bag, because I guessed it would be the sort of thing that would take your fancy; but somehow I've kept mum, for fear I might be taken before I'd been able to make a will. And then, too, I've been of several minds as to the form of my gift. I thought it would suit me best of all to found a college, and I was disappointed when I learned that neighbor Flagg had got the start of me with his seminary for women across the river. I wasn't happy over it until one night, just after the doctor had gone, the thought came to me, 'Why, not give a hospital?' And that's what it's to be. Five hundred thousand dollars for a free hospital in the City of Benham, in memory of my wife and daughter. That'll be useful, won't it? That'll help the people as much as a college? And, Selma," he added, cutting off the assuring answer which trembled on her tongue and blazed from her eyes, "I shan't forget you. After I'm gone you are to have twenty thousand dollars. That'll enable you, in case you don't marry, to keep a roof over your head without working too hard."

"Thank you. You are very generous," she said. The announcement was pleasant to her, but at the moment it seemed of secondary importance. Her enthusiasm had been aroused by the fact and character of his public donation, and already her brain was dancing with the thought of the prospect of a rival vital institution in connection with which her views and her talents would in all probability be consulted and allowed to exercise themselves. Her's, and not Mrs. Taylor's, or any of that censorious and restricting set. In that hospital, at least, ambition and originality would be allowed to show what they could do unfettered by envy or paralyzed by conservatism. "But I can't think of anything now, Mr. Parsons, except the grand secret you have confided to me. A hospital! It is an ideal gift. It will show the world what noble uses our rich, earnest-minded men make of their money, and it will give our doctors and our people a chance to demonstrate what a free hospital ought to be. Oh, I congratulate you. I will write to Mr. Lyons at once."

A note in prompt response stated the hour when the lawyer would call. On his arrival he was shown immediately to Mr. Parsons's apartments, with whom he was closeted alone. Selma managed to cross the hall at the moment he was descending, and he was easily persuaded to linger and to follow her into the library.

"I was anxious to say a few words to you, Mr. Lyons," she said. "I know the purpose for which Mr. Parsons sent for you. He has confided to me concerning his will—told me everything. It is a noble disposition of his property. A free hospital for Benham is an ideal selection, and one envies him his opportunity."

"Yes. It is a superb and generous benefaction."

"I lay awake for hours last night thinking about it; thinking particularly of the special point I am desirous to consult you in regard to. I don't wish to appear officious, or to say anything I shouldn't, but knowing from what I heard you state in your speech the other day that you feel as I do in regard to such matters, I take the liberty of suggesting that it seems to me of very great importance that the management of this magnificent gift should be in proper hands. May I ask you without impropriety if you will protect Mr. Parsons so that captious or unenthusiastic persons, men

224

or women, will be unable to control the policy of his hospital? He would wish it so, I am sure. I thought of mentioning the matter to him myself, but I was afraid lest it might worry him and spoil the satisfaction of his generosity or retard his cure. Is what I ask possible? Do I make myself clear?"

"Perfectly—perfectly. A valuable suggestion," he said. "I am glad that you have spoken—very glad. Alive as I am to the importance of protecting ourselves at all points, I might not have realized this particular danger had you not called it to my attention. Perhaps only a clever woman would have thought of it."

"Oh, thank you. I felt that I could not keep silence, and run the risk of what might happen."

"Precisely. I think I can relieve your mind by telling you—which under the circumstances is no breach of professional secrecy, for it is plain that the testator desires you to know his purpose—that Mr. Parsons has done me the honor to request me to act as the executor of his will. As such I shall be in a position to make sure that those to whom the management of his hospital is intrusted are people in whom you and I would have confidence."

"Ah! That is very satisfactory. It makes everything as it should be, and I am immensely relieved."

"Now that you have spoken," he added, meeting her eager gaze with a propitiating look of reflective wisdom, "I will consider the advisability of taking the further precaution of advising the testator to name in his will the persons who shall act as the trustees of his charity. That would clinch the matter. The selection of the individuals would necessarily lie with Mr. Parsons, but it would seem eminently natural and fitting that he should name you to represent your sex on such a board. I hope it would be agreeable to you to serve?"

Selma flushed. "It would be a position which I should prize immensely. Such a possibility had not occurred to me, though I felt that some definite provision should be made. The responsibility would be congenial to me and very much in my line."

"Assuredly. If you will permit me to say so, you are just the woman for the place. We have met only a few times, Mrs. Littleton, but I am a man who forms my conclusions of people rapidly, and it is obvious to me that you are thoughtful, energetic, and liberal-minded—qualities which are especially requisite for intelligent progress in semi-public work. It is essentially desirable to enlist the co-operation of well-equipped women to promote the national weal."

Lyons departed with an agreeable impression that he had been talking to a woman who combined mental sagacity and enterprise with considerable fascination of person. This capable companion of Mr. Parsons was no coquettish or simpering beauty, no mere devotee of fashionable manners, but a mature, well-poised character endowed with ripe intellectual and bodily graces. Their interview suggested that she possessed initiative and discretion in directing the course of events, and a strong sense of moral responsibility, attributes which attracted his interest. He was obliged to make two more visits before the execution of the will, and on each occasion he had an opportunity to spend a half-hour alone in the society of Selma. He found her gravely and engagingly sympathetic with his advocacy of democratic principles; he told her of his ambition to be elected to Congress—an ambition which he believed would be realized the following autumn. He confided to her, also, that he was engaged in his leisure moments in the preparation of a literary volume to be entitled, "Watchwords of Patriotism," a study of the requisites of the best citizenship, exemplified by pertinent extracts from the public utterances of the most distinguished American public servants.

Selma on her part reciprocated by a reference to the course of lectures on "Culture and Higher Education," which she had resolved to deliver before the Benham Institute during the winter. In these lectures she meant to emphasize the importance of unfettered individuality, and to comment adversely on the tendencies hostile to this fundamental principle of progress which she had observed in New York and from which Benham itself did not appear to her to be entirely exempt. After delivering these lectures in Benham she intended to repeat them in various parts of the State, and in some of the large cities elsewhere, under the auspices of the Confederated Sisterhood of Women's Clubs of America, the Sorosis which Mrs. Earle had established on a firm basis, and of which at present she was second vice-president. As a token of sympathy with this undertaking, Mr. Lyons offered to procure her a free pass on the railroads over which she would be obliged to travel. This pleased Selma greatly, for she had always regarded free passes as a sign of mysterious and enviable importance.

Two months later Selma, as secretary of the sub-committee of the Institute selected to oppose before the legislature the bill to create an appointed school board, had further occasion to confer with Mr. Lyons. He agreed to be the active counsel, and approved of the plan that a delegation of women should journey to the capital, two hours and a half by rail, and add the moral support of their presence at the hearing before the legislative committee.

The expedition was another gratification to Selma—who had become possessed of her free pass. She felt that in visiting the state-house and thus taking an active part in the work of legislation she was beginning to fulfil the larger destiny for which she was qualified. Side by side with Mrs. Earle at the head of a delegation of twenty Benham women she marched augustly into the committee chamber. The contending factions sat on opposite sides of the room. Through its middle ran a long table occupied by the Committee on Education to which the bill had been referred. Among the dozen or fifteen persons who appeared in support of the bill Selma perceived Mrs. Hallett Taylor, whom she had not seen since her return. She was disappointed to observe that Mrs. Taylor's clothes, though unostentatious, were in the latest fashion. She had hoped to find her dowdy or unenlightened, and to be able to look down on her from the heights of her own New York experience.

The lawyer in charge of the bill presented lucidly and with skill the merits of his case, calling to the stand four prominent educators from as many different sections of the State, and several citizens of well-known character, among them Babcock's former pastor, Rev. Henry Glynn. He pointed out that the school committee, as at present constituted, was an unwieldy body of twenty-four members, that it was regarded as the first round in the ladder of political preferment, and that the members which composed it were elected not on the ground of their fitness, but because they were ambitious for political recognition.

The legislative committee listened politely but coldly to these statements and to the testimony of the witnesses. It was evident that they regarded the proposed reform with distrust.

"Do you mean us to understand that the public schools of this State are not among the best, if not the best, in the world?"

asked one member of the committee, somewhat sternly.

"I recognize the merits of our school system, but I am not blind to its faults," responded the attorney in charge of the bill. He was a man who possessed the courage of his convictions, but he was a lawyer of tact, and he knew that his answer went to the full limit of what he could safely utter by way of qualification without hopelessly imperilling his cause.

"Are not our public schools turning out yearly hundreds of boys and girls who are a growing credit to the soundness of the institutions of the country?" continued the same inquisitor.

Here was a proposition which opened such a vista of circuitous and careful speech, were he to attempt to answer it and be true to conscience without being false to patriotism, that Mr. Hunter was driven to reply, "I am unable to deny the general accuracy of your statement."

"Then why seek to harass those who are doing such good work by unfriendly legislation?"

The member plainly felt that he had disposed of the matter by this triumphant interrogation, for he listened with scant attention to a repetition of the grounds on which, relief was sought.

Mr. Lyons's method of reply was a surprise to Selma. She had looked for a fervid vindication of the principle of the people's choice, and an eloquent, sarcastic setting forth of the evils of the exclusive and aristocratic spirit. He began by complimenting the members of the committee on their ability to deal intelligently with the important question before them, and then proceeded to refer to the sincere but mistaken zeal of the advocates of the bill, whom he described as people animated by conscientious motives, but unduly distrustful of the capacity of the American people. His manner suggested a desire to be at peace with all the world and was agreeably conciliatory, as though he deprecated the existence of friction. He said that he would not do the members of the committee the injustice to suppose that they could seriously favor the passage of a bill which would deprive the intelligent average voter of one of his dearest privileges; but that he desired to put himself on record as thinking it a fortunate circumstance, on the whole, that the well-intentioned promoters of the bill had brought this matter to the attention of the legislature, and had an opportunity to express their views. He believed that the hearing would be productive of benefit to both parties, in that on the one hand it would tend to make the voters more careful as to whom they selected for the important duties of the school board, and on the other would—he, as a lover of democratic institutions, hoped—serve to convince the friends of the bill that they had exaggerated the evils of the situation, and that they were engaged in a false and hopeless undertaking in seeking to confine by hard and fast lines the spontaneous yearnings of the American people to control the education of their children. "We say to these critics," he continued, "some of whom are enrolled under the solemn name of reformers, that we welcome their zeal and offer co-operation in a resolute purpose to exercise unswerving vigilance in the selection of candidates for the high office of guardians of our public schools. So far as they will join hands with us in keeping undefiled the traditions of our forefathers, to that extent we are heartily in accord with them, but when they seek to override those traditions and to fasten upon this community a method which is based on a lack of confidence in democratic theories, then I—and gentlemen, I feel sure that you—are against them."

Lyons sat down, having given everyone in the room, with the exception of a few discerning spirits on the other side, the impression that he had intended to be pre-eminently fair, and that he had held out the olive branch when he would have been justified in using the scourge. The inclination to make friends, to smooth over seamy situations and to avoid repellent language in dealing with adversaries, except in corporation cases before juries and on special occasions when defending his political convictions, had become a growing tendency with him now that he was in training for public office. Selma did not quite know what to make of it at first. She had expected that he would crush their opponents beneath an avalanche of righteous invective. Instead he took his seat with an expression of countenance which was no less benignant than dignified. When the hearing was declared closed, a few minutes later, he looked in her direction, and in the course of his passage to where she was sitting stopped to exchange affable greetings with assemblymen and others who came in his way. At his approach Mrs. Earle uttered congratulations so comprehensive that Selma felt able to refrain for the moment from committing herself. "I am glad that you were pleased," he said. "I think I covered the ground, and no one's feelings have been hurt." As though he divined what was passing through Selma's mind, he added in an aside intended only for their ears, "It was not necessary to use all our powder, for I could tell from the way the committee acted that they were with us."

"I felt sure they would be," exclaimed Mrs. Earle. "And, as you say, it is a pleasure that no one's feelings were hurt, and that we can all part friends."

"Which reminds me," said Lyons, "that I should be glad of an introduction to Mrs. Taylor as she passes us on her way out. I wish to assure her personally of my willingness to further her efforts to improve the quality of the school board."

"That would be nice of you," said Mrs. Earle, "and ought to please and encourage her, for she will be disappointed, poor thing, and after all I suppose she means well. There she is now, and I will keep my eye on her."

"But surely, Mr. Lyons," said Selma, dazed yet interested by this doctrine of brotherly love, "don't you think our school committee admirable as it is?"

"A highly efficient body," he answered. "But I should be glad to have our opponents—mistaken as we believe them to be—appreciate that we no less than they are zealous to preserve the present high standard. We must make them recognize that we are reformers and in sympathy with reform."

"I see," said Selma. "For, of course, we are the real reformers. Convert them you mean? Be civil to them at least? I understand. Yes, I suppose there is no use in making enemies of them." She was thinking aloud. Though ever on her guard to resent false doctrine, she was so sure of the loyalty of both her companions that she could allow herself to be interested by this new point of view—a vast improvement on the New York manner because of its ethical suggestion. She realized that if Mr. Lyons was certain of the committee, it was right, and at the same time sensible, not to hurt anyone's feelings unnecessarily—although she felt a little suspicious because he had asked to be introduced to Mrs. Taylor. Indeed, the more she thought of this attitude, on the assumption that the victory was assured, the more it appealed to her conscience and intelligence; so much so that when Mrs. Earle darted forward to detain Mrs. Taylor, Selma was reflecting with admiration on his magnanimity.

She observed intently the meeting between Mr. Lyons and Mrs. Taylor. He was deferential, complimentary, and genial, and he made a suave, impressive offer of his personal services, in response to which Mrs. Taylor regarded him with smiling incredulity—a smile which Selma considered impertinent. How dared she treat his courtly advances with flippant distrust!

"Are you aware, Mr. Lyons," Mrs. Taylor was saying, "that one of the present members of the school board is a milkman, and another a carpenter—both of them persons of very ordinary efficiency from an educational standpoint? Will you co-operate with us, when their terms expire next year and they seek re-election, to nominate more suitable candidates in their stead?"

"I shall be very glad when the time comes to investigate carefully their qualifications, and if they are proved to be unworthy of the confidence of the people, to use my influence against them. You may rely on this—rely on my cordial support, and the support of these ladies," he added, indicating Mrs. Earle and Selma, with a wave of his hand, "who, if you will permit me to say so, are no less interested than you in promoting good government."

"Oh, yes, indeed. We thought we were making an ideal choice in Miss Luella Bailey," said Mrs. Earle with effusion. "If Mrs. Taylor had seen more of her, I feel sure she would have admired her, and then our Institute would not have been dragged into politics."

Mrs. Taylor did not attempt to answer this appeal. Instead she greeted Selma civilly, and said, "I was sorry to hear that you were against us, Mrs. Littleton. We were allies once in a good cause, and in spite of Mr. Lyons's protestations to the contrary, I assure you that this is another genuine opportunity to improve the existing order of things. At least," she added, gayly but firmly, "you must not let Mr. Lyons's predilection to see everything through rose-colored spectacles prevent you from looking into the matter on your own account."

"I have done so already," answered Selma, affronted at the suggestion that she was uninformed, yet restrained from displaying her annoyance by the sudden inspiration that here was an admirable opportunity to practise the proselytizing forbearance suggested by Mr. Lyons. The idea of patronizing Mrs. Taylor from the vantage-ground of infallibility, tinctured by magnanimous

231

condescension, appealed to her. "I have made a thorough study of the question, and I never could look at it as you do, Mrs. Taylor. I sided with you before because I thought you were right—because you were in favor of giving everyone a chance of expression. But now I'm on the other side for the same reason—because you and your friends are disposed to deprive people of that very thing, and to regard their aspirations and their efforts contemptuously, if I may say so. That's the mistake we think you make—we who, as Mr. Lyons has stated, are no less eager than you to maintain the present high character of everything which concerns our school system. But if you only would see things in a little different light, both Mrs. Earle and I would be glad to welcome you as an ally and to co-operate with you."

Selma had not expected to make such a lengthy speech, but as she proceeded she was spurred by the desire to teach Mrs. Taylor her proper place, and at the same time to proclaim her own allegiance to the attitude of optimistic forbearance.

"I knew that was the way they felt," said Lyons, ingratiatingly. "It would be a genuine pleasure to us all to see this unfortunate difference of opinion between earnest people obviated."

Mrs. Taylor, as Selma was pleased to note, flushed at her concluding offer, and she answered, drily, "I fear that we are too far apart in our ideas to talk of co-operation. If our bill is defeated this year, we shall have to persevere and trust to the gradual enlightenment of public sentiment. Good afternoon."

Selma left the State-house in an elated frame of mind. She felt that she had taken a righteous and patriotic stand, and it pleased her to think that she was taking an active part in defending the institutions of the country. She chatted eagerly as she walked through the corridors with Mr. Lyons, who, portly and imposing, acted as escort to her and Mrs. Earle, and invited them to luncheon at a hotel restaurant. Excitement had given her more color than usual, to which her mourning acted as a foil, and she looked her best. Lyons was proud of being in the company of such a presentable and spirited appearing woman, and made a point of stopping two or three members of the legislature and introducing them to her. When they reached the restaurant he established them at a table where they could see everybody and be seen, and he ordered scolloped oysters, chicken-salad, ice-cream, coffee, and some bottles of sarsaparilla. Both women were in high spirits, and Selma was agreeably conscious that people were observing them. Before the repast was over a messenger brought a note to Mr. Lyons, which announced that the legislative committee had given the petitioners leave to withdraw their bill, which, in Selma's eyes, justified the management of the affair, and set the seal of complete success on an already absorbing and delightful occasion.

CHAPTER IV.

Her mourning and the slow convalescence of Mr. Parsons deprived Selma of convincing evidence in regard to her social reception in Benham, for those socially prominent were thus barred from inviting her to their houses, and her own activities were correspondingly fettered. Indeed, her circumstances supplied her with an obvious salve for her proper dignity had she been disposed to let suspicion lie fallow. As it was a number of people had left cards and sent invitations notwithstanding they could not be accepted, and she might readily have believed, had she chosen—and as she professed openly to Mr. Parsons—that everyone had been uncommonly civil and appreciative.

She found herself, however, in spite of her declared devotion to her serious duties, noting that the recognition accorded to Mr. Parsons and herself was not precisely of the character she craved. The visiting-cards and invitations were from people residing on the River Drive and in that neighborhood, indeed—but from people like the Flaggs, for instance, who, having acquired large wealth and erected lordly dwellings, were eager to dispense good-natured, lavish hospitality without social experience. Her sensitive ordeal in New York had quickened her social perceptions, so that whereas at the time of her departure from Benham as Mrs. Littleton she regarded her present neighborhood as an integral class, she was now prompt to separate the sheep from the goats, and to remark that only the goats seemed conscious of her existence. With the exception of Mrs. Taylor, who had called when she was out, not one of a certain set, the outward manifestations of whose stately being were constantly passing her windows, appeared to take the slightest interest in her. Strictly speaking, Mrs. Taylor was of this set, yet apart from it. Hers was the exclusive intellectual and æsthetic set, this the exclusive fashionable set—both alike execrable and foreign to the traditions of Benham. As Selma had discovered the one and declared war against it, so she promised herself to confound the other when the period of her mourning was over, and she was free to appear again in society. Once more she congratulated herself that she had come in time to nip in the bud this other off-shoot of aristocratic tendencies. As yet either set was small in number, and she foresaw that it would be an easy task to unite in a solid phalanx of offensive-defensive influence the friendly souls whom these people treated as outsiders, and purge the society atmosphere of the miasma of exclusiveness. In connection with the means to this end, when the winter slipped away and left her feeling that she had been ignored, and that she was eager to assume a commanding position, she began to take more than passing thought of the attentions of Mr. Lyons. That he was interested by her there could be no doubt, for he plainly went out of his way to seek her society, calling at the house from time to time, and exercising a useful, flattering superintendence over her lecture course in the other cities of the State, in each of which he appeared to have friends on the newspaper press who put agreeable notices in print concerning her performance. She had returned to Benham believing that her married life was over; that her heart was in the grave with Wilbur, and that she would never again part with her independence. The notice which Mr. Lyons had taken of her from the outset had gratified her, but though she contrasted his physical energy with Wilbur's lack of vigor, it had not occurred to her to consider him in the light of a possible husband. Now that a year had passed since Wilbur's death, she felt conscious once more, as had happened after her divorce, of the need of a closer and more individual sympathy than any at her command. Her relations with Mr. Parsons, to be sure, approximated those of father and daughter, but his perceptions were much less acute than before his seizure; he talked little and ceased to take a vital interest in current affairs. She felt the lack of companionship and, also, of personal devotion, such personal devotion as was afforded by the strenuous, ardent allegiance of a man. On the other hand she was firmly resolved never to allow the current of her own life to be turned away again by the subordination of her purposes to those of any other person, and she had believed that this resolution would keep her indifferent to marriage, in spite of any sensations of loneliness or craving for masculine idolatry. But as a widow of a year's standing she was now suddenly interested by the thought that this solid, ambitious, smooth-talking man might possibly satisfy her natural preference for a mate without violating her individuality. She began to ask herself if he were not truly congenial in a sense which no man had ever been to her before; also, to ask if their aspirations and aims were not so nearly identical that he would be certain as her husband to be proud of everything she did and said, and to allow her to work hand in hand with him for the furtherance of their common purpose. She did not put these questions to herself until his conduct suggested that he was seeking her society as a suitor; but having put them, she was pleased to find her heart throb with the hope of a stimulating and dear discovery.

Certain causes contributed to convince her that this hope rested on a sure foundation—causes associated with her present life and point of view. She felt confident first of all of the godliness of Mr. Lyons as indicated not only by his sober, successful life, and his enthusiastic, benignant patriotism, but by his active, reverent interest in the affairs of his church—the Methodist Church—to which Mr. Parsons belonged, and which Selma had begun to attend since her return to Benham. It had been her mother's faith, and she had felt a certain filial glow in approaching it, which had been fanned into pious flame by the effect of the ministration. The fervent hymns and the opportunities for bearing testimony at some of the services appealed to her needs and gave her a sense of oneness with eternal truth, which had hitherto been lacking from her religious experience. In judging Wilbur she was disposed to ascribe the defects of his character largely to the coldness and analyzing sobriety of his creed. She had accompanied him to church listlessly, and had been bored by the unemotional appeals to conscience and quiet subjective designations of duty. She preferred to thrill with the intensity of words which now roundly rated sin, now passionately called to mind the ransom of the Saviour, and ever kept prominent the stirring mission of evangelizing ignorant foreign people. It appeared probable to Selma that, as the wife of one of the leading church-members, who was the chairman of the local committee charged with spreading the gospel abroad, her capacity for doing good would be strengthened, and the spiritual availability of them both be enhanced.

Then, too, Mr. Lyons's political prospects were flattering. The thought that a marriage with him would put her in a position to control the social tendencies of Benham was alluring. As the wife of Hon. James O. Lyons, Member of Congress, she believed that she would be able to look down on and confound those who had given her the cold shoulder. What would Flossy say when she heard it? What would Pauline? This was a form of distinction which would put her beyond the reach of conspiracy and exclusiveness; for, as the wife of a representative, selected by the people to guard their interests and make their laws, would not her social position be unassailable? And apart from these considerations, a political future seemed to her peculiarly attractive. Was not this the real opportunity for which she had been waiting? Would she be justified in giving it up? In what better way could her talents be spent than as the helpmate and intellectual companion of a public man—a statesman devoted to the protection and development of American ideas? Her own individuality need not, would not be repressed. She had seen enough of Mr. Lyons to feel sure that their views on the great questions of life were thoroughly in harmony. They held the same religious opinions. Who could foretell the limit of their joint progress? He was still a young man—strong, dignified, and patriotic—endowed with qualities which fitted him for public service. It might well be that a brilliant future was before him—before them, if she were his wife. If he were to become prominent in the councils of the nation—Speaker of the House—Governor—even President, within the bounds of possibility, what a splendid congenial scope his honors would afford her own versatility! As day by day she dwelt on these points of recommendation, Selma became more and more disposed to smile on the aspirations of Mr. Lyons in regard to herself, and to feel that her life would develop to the best advantage by a union with him. Until the words asking her to be his wife were definitely spoken she could not be positive of his intentions, but his conduct left little room for doubt, and moreover, was marked by a deferential soberness of purpose which indicated to her that his views regarding marriage were on a higher plane than those of any man she had known. He referred frequently to the home as the foundation on which American civilization rested, and from which its inspiration was largely derived, and spoke feelingly of the value to a public man of a stimulating and dignifying fireside. It became his habit to join her after morning service and to accompany her home, carrying her hymn-books, and he sent her from time to time, through the post, quotations which had especially struck his fancy from the speeches he was collecting for his "Watchwords of Patriotism."

Another six months passed, and at its close Lyons received the expected nomination for Congress. The election promised to be close and exciting. Both parties were confident of victory, and were preparing vigorously to keep their adherents at fever pitch by rallies and torch-light processions. Although the result of the caucus was not doubtful, it was understood between Lyons and Selma that he would call at the house that evening to let her know that he had been successful. She was waiting to receive him in the library. Mr. Parsons had gone to bed. His condition was not promising. He had recently suffered another slight attack of paralysis, which seemed to indicate that he was liable at any time to a fatal seizure.

Lyons entered smilingly. "So far so good," he exclaimed.

"Then you have won?"

"Oh, yes. As I told you, it was a foregone conclusion. Now the fight begins."

Selma, who had provided a slight refection, handed him a cup of tea. "I feel sure that you will be chosen," she said. "See if I am not right. When is the election?"

"In six weeks. Six weeks from to-morrow."

"Then you will go to Washington to live?"

"Not until the fourth of March."

"I envy you. If I were a man I should prefer success in politics to anything else."

He was silent for a moment. Then he said, "Will you help me to achieve success? Will you go with me to Washington as my wife?"

His courtship had been formal and elaborate, but his declaration was signally simple and to the point. Selma noticed that the cup in his hand trembled. While she kept her eyes lowered, as women are supposed to do at such moments, she was wondering whether she loved him as much as she had loved Wilbur? Not so ardently, but more worthily, she concluded, for he seemed to her to fulfil her maturer ideal of strong and effective manhood, and to satisfy alike her self-respect and her physical fancy. A man of his type would not split hairs, but proceed straight toward the goal of his ambition without fainting or wavering. Why should she not satisfy her renewed craving to be yoked to a kindred spirit and companion who appreciated her true worth?

"I cannot believe," he was saying, "that my words are a surprise to you. You can scarcely have failed to understand that I admired you extremely. I have delayed to utter my desire to make you my wife because I did not dare to cherish too fondly the hope

238

that the love inspired in me could be reciprocated, and that you would consent to unite your life to mine and trust your happiness to my keeping. If I may say so, we are no boy and girl. We understand the solemn significance of marriage; what it imports and what it demands. Of late I have ventured to dream that the sympathy in ideas and identity of purpose which exist between us might be the trustworthy sign of a spiritual bond which we could not afford to ignore. I feel that without you the joy and power of my life will be incomplete. With you at my side I shall aspire to great things. You are to me the embodiment of what is charming and serviceable in woman."

Selma looked up. "I like you very much, Mr. Lyons. You, in your turn, must have realized that, I think. As you say, we are no boy and girl. You meant by that, too, that we both have been married before. I have had two husbands, and I did not believe that I could ever think of marriage again. I don't wish you to suppose that my last marriage was not happy. Mr. Littleton was an earnest, talented man, and devoted to me. Yet I cannot deny that in spite of mutual love our married life was not a success—a success as a contribution to accomplishment. That nearly broke my heart, and he—he died from lack of the physical and mental vigor which would have made so much difference. I am telling you this because I wish you to realize that if I should consent to comply with your wishes, it would be because I was convinced that true accomplishment—the highest accomplishment—would result from the union of our lives as the result of our riper experience. If I did not believe, Mr. Lyons, that man and woman as we are—no longer boy and girl—a more perfect scheme of happiness, a grander conception of the meaning of life than either of us had entertained was before us, I would not consider your offer for one moment."

"Yes, yes, I understand," Lyons exclaimed eagerly. "I share your belief implicitly. It was what I would have said only—"

Despite his facility as an orator, Lyons left this sentence incomplete in face of the ticklish difficulty of explaining that he had refrained from suggesting such a hope to a widow who had lost her husband only two years before. Yet he hastened to bridge over this ellipsis by saying, "Without such a faith a union between us must fall short of its sweetest and grandest opportunities."

"It would be a mockery; there would be no excuse for its

existence," cried Selma impetuously. "I am an idealist, Mr. Lyons," she said clasping her hands. "I believe devotedly in the mission and power of love. But I believe that our conception of love changes as we grow. I welcomed love formerly as an intoxicating, delirious potion, and as such it was very sweet. You have just told me of your own feelings toward me, so it is your right to know that lately I have begun to realize that my association with you has brought peace into my life—peace and religious faith—essentials of happiness of which I have not known the blessings since I was a child. You have dedicated yourself to a lofty work; you have chosen the noble career of a statesman—a statesman zealous to promote principles in which we both believe. And you ask me to share with you the labors and the privileges which will result from this dedication. If I accept your offer, it must be because I know that I love you—love you in a sense I have not loved before—may the dead pardon me! If I accept you it will be because I wish to perpetuate that faith and peace, and because I believe that our joint lives will realize worthy accomplishment." Selma looked into space with her wrapt gaze, apparently engaged in an intense mental struggle.

"And you will accept? You do feel that you can return my love? I cannot tell you how greatly I am stirred and stimulated by what you have said. It makes me feel that I could never be happy without you." Lyons put into this speech all his solemnity and all his emotional beneficence of temperament. He was genuinely moved. His first marriage had been a love match. His wife—a mere girl—had died within a year; so soon that the memory of her was a tender but hazy sentiment rather than a formulated impression of character. By virtue of this memory he had approached marriage again as one seeking a companion for his fireside, and a comely, sensible woman to preside over his establishment and promote his social status, rather than one expecting to be possessed by or to inspire a dominant passion. Yet he, too, regarded himself distinctly as an idealist, and he had lent a greedy ear to Selma's suggestion that mature mutual sympathy and comradeship in establishing convictions and religious aims were the source of a nobler type of love than that associated with early matrimony. It increased his admiration for her, and gave to his courtship, the touch of idealism which—partly owing to his own modesty as a man no longer in the flush of youth—it had lacked. He nervously stroked his beard with

240

his thick hand, and gave himself up to the spell of this vision of blessedness while he eagerly watched Selma's face and waited for her answer. To combine moral purpose and love in a pervasive alliance appealed to him magnetically as a religious man.

Selma, as she faced Lyons, was conscious necessarily of the contrast between him and her late husband. But she was attuned to regard his coarser physical fibre as masculine vigor and a protest against aristocratic delicacy, and to derive comfort and exaltation from it.

"Mr. Lyons," she said, "I will tell you frankly that the circumstances of married life have hitherto hampered the expression of that which is in me, and confined the scope of my individuality within narrow and uncongenial limits. I am not complaining; I have no intention to rake up the past; but it is proper you should know that I believe myself capable of larger undertakings than have yet been afforded me, and worthy of ampler recognition than I have yet received. If I accept you as a husband, it will be because I feel confident that you will give my life the opportunity to expand, and that you sympathize with my desire to express myself adequately and to labor hand in hand, side by side, with you in the important work of the world."

"That is what I would have you do, Selma. Because you are worthy of it, and because it is your right."

"On that understanding it seems that we might be very happy."

"I am certain of it. You fill my soul with gladness," he cried, and seizing her hand he pressed it to his lips and covered it with kisses, but she withdrew it, saying, "Not yet—not yet. This step represents so much to me. It means that if I am mistaken in you, my whole life will be ruined, for the next years should be my best. We must not be too hasty. There are many things to be thought of. I must consider Mr. Parsons. I cannot leave him immediately, if at all, for he is very dependent on me."

"I had thought of that. While Mr. Parsons lives, I realize that your first duty must be to him."

The reverential gravity of his tone was in excess of the needs of the occasion, and Selma understood that he intended to imply that Mr. Parsons would not long need her care. The same thought was in her own mind, and it had occurred to her in the course of her previous cogitations in regard to Lyons, that in the event of his death it would suit her admirably to continue to occupy the house as its real mistress. She looked grave for a moment in her turn, then with a sudden access of coyness she murmured, "I do not believe that I am mistaken in you."

"Ah," he cried, and would have folded her in his arms, but she evaded his onset and said with her dramatic intonation, "The knights of old won their lady-loves by brilliant deeds. If you are elected a member of Congress, you may come to claim me."

Reflection served only to convince Selma of the wisdom of her decision to try matrimony once more. She argued, that though a third marriage might theoretically seem repugnant if stated as a bald fact, the actual circumstances in her case not merely exonerated her from a lack of delicacy, but afforded an exhibition of progress—a gradual evolution in character. She felt light-hearted and triumphant at the thought of her impending new importance as the wife of a public man, and she interested herself exuberantly in the progress of the political campaign. She was pleased to think that her stipulation had given her lover a new spur to his ambition, and she was prepared to believe that his victory would be due to the exhaustive efforts to win which the cruel possibility of losing her obliged him to make.

This was a campaign era of torch-light processions. The rival factions expressed their confidence and enthusiasm by parading at night in a series of battalions armed with torches—some resplendently flaring, some glittering gayly through colored glass—and bearing transparencies inscribed with trenchant sentiments. The houses of their adherents along the route were illuminated from attic to cellar with rows of candles, and the atmosphere wore a dusky glow of red and green fire. To Selma all this was entrancing. She revelled in it as an introduction to the more conspicuous life which she was about to lead. She showed herself a zealous and enthusiastic partisan, shrouding the house in the darkness of Erebus on the occasion when the rival procession passed the door, and imparting to every window the effect of a blaze of light on the following evening—the night before election—when the Democratic party made its final appeal to the voters. Standing on a balcony in evening dress, in company with Mrs. Earle and Miss Luella Bailey, whom she had invited to view the procession from the River Drive, Selma looked down on the parade in an ecstatic mood. The torches, the music, the fireworks and the enthusiasm set her pulses astir and brought her heart into her mouth in melting appreciation of the sanctity of her party cause and her own enviable destiny as the wife of an American Congressman. She held in one hand a flag which she waved from time to time at the conspicuous features of the procession, and she stationed herself so that the Bengal lights and other fireworks set off by Mr. Parsons's hired man should throw her figure into conspicuous relief. The culminating interest of the, occasion for her was reached when the James O. Lyons Cadets, the special body of youthful torch-bearers devoted to advertising the merits of her lover, for whose uniforms and accoutrements he had paid, came in sight.

They proved to be the most flourishing looking organization in line. They were preceded by a large, nattily attired drum corps; their ranks were full, their torches lustrous, and they bore a number of transparencies setting forth the predominant qualifications of the candidate for Congress from the second district, the largest of which presented his portrait superscribed with the sentiment, "A vote for James O. Lyons is a vote in support of the liberties of the plain people." On the opposite end of the canvas was the picture of the king of beasts, with open jaws and bristling mane, with the motto, "Our Lyons's might will keep our institutions sacred." In the midst of this glittering escort the candidate himself rode in an open barouche on his way to the hall where he was to deliver a final speech. He was bowing to right and left, and constant cheers marked his progress along the avenue. Selma leaned forward from the balcony to obtain the earliest sight of her hero. The rolling applause was a new, intoxicating music in her ears, and filled her soul with transport. She clapped her hands vehemently; seized a roman-candle, and amid a blaze of fiery sparks exploded its colored stars in the direction of the approaching carriage. Then with the flag slanted across her bosom, she stood waiting for his recognition. It was made solemnly, but with the unequivocal demonstration of a cavalier or knight of old, for Lyons stood up, and doffing his hat toward her, made a conspicuous salute. A salvo of applause suggested to Selma that the multitude had understood that he was according to her the homage due a lady-love, and that their cheers were partly meant for her. She put her hand to her bosom with the

243

gesture of a queen of melodrama, and culling one from a bunch of roses Lyons had sent her that afternoon threw it from the balcony at the carriage. The flower fell almost into the lap of her lover, who clutched it, pressed it to his lips, and doffed his hat again. The episode had been visible to many, and a hoarse murmur of interested approval crowned the performance. The glance of the crowds on the sidewalk was turned upward, and someone proposed three cheers for the lady in the balcony. They were given. Selma bowed to either side in delighted acknowledgment, while the torches of the cadets waved tumultuously, and there was a fresh outburst of colored fires.

"I can't keep the secret any longer," she exclaimed, turning to her two companions. "I'm engaged to be married to Mr. Lyons."

CHAPTER V.

Lyons was chosen to Congress by a liberal margin. The Congressional delegation from his State was almost evenly divided between the two parties as the result of the election, and the majorities in every case were small. Consequently the more complete victory of Lyons was a feather in his cap, and materially enhanced his political standing.

The sudden death of Mr. Parsons within a week of the election saved Selma's conscience from the strain of arranging a harmonious and equitable separation from him. She had felt that the enlargement of her sphere of life and the opportunity to serve her country which this marriage offered were paramount to any other considerations, but she was duly conscious that Mr. Parsons would miss her sorely, and she was considering the feasibility of substituting Miss Bailey as his companion in her place, when fate supplied a different solution. Selma had pledged her friends to secrecy, so that Mr. Parsons need know nothing until the plans for his happiness had been perfected, and he died in ignorance of the interesting matrimonial alliance which had been fostered under his roof. By the terms of his will Selma was bequeathed the twenty thousand dollars he had promised her. She and Mr. Lyons, with a third person, to be selected by them, were appointed trustees of the Free Hospital with which he had endowed Benham, and Mr. Lyons was nominated as the sole executor under the will.

Selma's conception that her third betrothal was coincident with spiritual development, and that she had fought her way through hampering circumstances to a higher plane of experience, had taken firm hold of her imagination. She presently confessed to Lyons that she had not hitherto appreciated the full meaning of the dogma that marriage was a sacrament. She evinced a disposition to show herself with him at church gatherings, and to cultivate the acquaintance of his pastor. She felt that she had finally secured the opportunity to live the sober, simple life appropriate to those who believed in maintaining American principles, and in eschewing luxurious and effete foreign innovations; the sort of life she had always meant to live, and from which she had been debarred. She had now not only opportunity, but a responsibility. As the bride of a Congressman, it behooved her both to pursue virtue for its own sake and for the sake of example. It was incumbent on her to preserve and promote democratic conditions in signal opposition to so-called fashionable society, and at the same time to assert her own proper dignity and the dignity of her constituents by a suitable outward show.

This last subtlety of reflection convinced Selma that they ought to occupy the house on the River Drive. Lyons himself expressed some doubts as to the advisability of this. He admitted that he could afford the expense, and that it was just such a residence as he desired, but he suggested that their motives might not be understood, and he questioned whether it were wise, with the State so close, to give his political enemies the chance to make unjust accusations.

"Of course you ought to understand about this matter better than I," she said; "but I have the feeling, James, that your constituents will be disappointed if we don't show ourselves appreciative of the dignity of your position. We both agree that we should make Benham our home, and that it will be preferable if I visit Washington a month or two at a time during the session rather than for us to set up housekeeping there, and I can't help believing that the people will be better pleased if you, as their representative, make that home all which a beautiful home should be. They will be proud of it, and if they are, you needn't mind what a few fault-finders say. I have been thinking it over, and it seems to me that we shall make a mistake to let this house go. It just suits us. I feel sure that in their hearts the American people like to have their public men live comfortably. This house is small compared to many in New York, and I flatter myself that we shall be able to satisfy everyone that we are rootedly opposed to unseemly extravagance of living."

Lyons yielded readily to this argument. He had been accustomed to simple surroundings, but travel and the growth of Benham itself had demonstrated to him that the ways of the nation in respect to material possessions and comforts had undergone a marked change since his youth. He had been brought in contact with this new development in his capacity of adviser to the magnates of Benham, and he had fallen under the spell of improved creature comforts. Still, though he cast sheep's eyes at these flesh pots, he had felt chary, both as a worker for righteousness and an ardent champion of popular principles, of countenancing them

246

openly. Yet his original impulse toward marriage had been a desire to secure an establishment, and now that this result was at hand he found himself ambitious to put his household on a braver footing, provided this would do injury neither to his moral scruples nor to his political sincerity. The problem was but another phase of that presented to him by his evolution from a jury lawyer, whose hand and voice were against corporations, to the status of a richly paid chamber adviser to railroads and banking houses. He was exactly in the frame of mind to grasp at the euphemism offered by Selma. He was not one to be convinced without a reason, but his mind eagerly welcomed a suggestion which justified on a moral ground the proceeding to which they were both inclined. The idea that the people would prefer to see him as their representative living in a style consistent with the changes in manners and customs introduced by national prosperity, affording thereby an example of correct and elevating stewardship of reasonable wealth, by way of contrast to vapid society doings, came to him as an illumination which dissipated his doubts.

The wedding took place about three months after the death of Mr. Parsons. In her renovated outlook regarding matrimony, Selma included formal preparations for and some pomp of circumstances at the ceremony. It suited her pious mood that she was not required again to be married off-hand, and that she could plight her troth in a decorous fashion, suitably attired and amid conventional surroundings. Her dress was a subject of considerable contemplation. She guided her lover's generosity until it centred on a diamond spray for her hair and two rings set with handsome precious stones. She did not discourage Miss Luella Bailey from heralding the approaching nuptials in the press. She became Mrs. Lyons in a conspicuous and solemn fashion before the gaze of everybody in Benham whom there was any excuse for asking to the church. After a collation at the Parsons house, the happy pair started on their honeymoon in a special car put at their service by one of the railroads for which the bridegroom was counsel. This feature delighted Selma. Indeed, everything, from the complimentary embrace of her husband's pastor to the details of her dress and wedding presents, described with elaborate good will in the evening newspapers, appeared to her gratifying and appropriate.

They were absent six weeks, during which the Parsons house

was to be redecorated and embellished within and without according to instructions given by Selma before her departure. Their trip extended to California by way of the Yosemite. Selma had never seen the wonders of the far western scenery, and this appropriate background for their sentiment also afforded Lyons the opportunity to inspect certain railroad lines in which he was financially interested. The atmosphere of the gorgeous snow-clad peaks and impressive chasms served to heighten still further the intensity of Selma's frame of mind. She managed adroitly on several occasions to let people know who they were, and it pleased her to observe the conductor indicating to passengers in the common cars that they were Congressman Lyons and his wife on their honeymoon. She was looking forward to Washington, and as she stood in the presence of the inspiring beauties of nature she was prone to draw herself up in rehearsal of the dignity which she expected to wear. What were these mountains and canyons but physical counterparts of the human soul? What but correlative representatives of grand ideas, of noble lives devoted to the cause of human liberty? She felt that she was very happy, and she bore testimony to this by walking arm in arm with her husband, leaning against his firm, stalwart shoulder. It seemed to her desirable that the public should know that they were a happy couple and defenders of the purity of the home. On their way back the train was delayed on Washington's birthday for several hours by a wash-out, and presently a deputation made up of passengers and townspeople waited on Lyons and invited him to deliver an open-air address. He and Selma, when the committee arrived, were just about to explore the neighborhood, and Lyons, though ordinarily he would have been glad of such an opportunity, looked at his wife with an expression which suggested that he would prefer a walk with her. The eyes of the committee followed his, appreciating that he had thrown the responsibility of a decision on his bride. Selma was equal to the occasion. "Of course he will address you," she exclaimed. "What more suitable place could there be for offering homage to the father of our country than this majestic prairie?" She added, proudly, "And I am glad you should have the opportunity to hear my husband speak."

Some letters requiring attention were forwarded to Lyons at one of the cities where they stopped. As they lay on his dressing-table Selma caught sight of the return address, Williams &

Van Horne, printed on the uppermost envelope. The reminder aroused a host of associations. Flossy had not been much in her thoughts lately, yet she had not failed to plume herself occasionally with the reflection that she could afford now to snap her fingers at her. She had wondered more than once what Flossy would think when she heard that she was the wife of a Representative.

"Do you know these people personally?" she inquired, holding up the envelope.

"Yes. They are my—er—financial representatives in New York. I have considerable dealings with them."

Selma had not up to this time concerned herself as to the details of her husband's affairs. He had made clear to her that his income from his profession was large, and she knew that he was interested in a variety of enterprises. That he should have connections with a firm of New York brokers was one more proof to her of his common sense and capacity to take advantage of opportunities.

"Mr. Littleton used to buy stocks through Williams and Van Horne—only a few. He was not very clever at it, and failed to make the most of the chances given him to succeed in that way. We knew the Williamses at one time very well. They lived in the same block with us for several years after we were married."

"Williams is a capable, driving sort of fellow. Bold, but on the whole sagacious, I think," answered Lyons, with demure urbanity. It was rather a shock to him that his wife should learn that he had dealings in the stock market. He feared lest it might seem to her inconsistent with his other propensities—his religious convictions and his abhorrence of corporate rapacity. He preferred to keep such transactions private for fear they should be misunderstood. At heart he did not altogether approve of them himself. They were a part of his evolution, and had developed by degrees until they had become now so interwoven with his whole financial outlook that he could not escape from them at the moment if he would. Indeed some of them were giving him anxiety. He had supposed that the letter in question contained a request for a remittance to cover depreciation in his account. Instead he had read with some annoyance a confidential request from Williams that he would work for a certain bill which, in his capacity as a foe of monopoly, he had hoped to be able to oppose. It offended his

249

conscience to think that he might be obliged secretly to befriend a measure against which his vote must be cast. As has been intimated, he would have preferred that his business affairs should remain concealed from his wife. Yet her remarks were unexpectedly and agreeably reassuring. They served to furnish a fresh indication on her part of intelligent sympathy with the perplexities which beset the path of an ambitious public man. They suggested a subtle appreciation of the reasonableness of his behavior, notwithstanding its apparent failure to tally with his outward professions.

Selma's reply interrupted this rhapsody.

"I ought to tell you, I suppose, that I quarrelled with Mrs. Williams before I left New York. Or, rather, she quarrelled with me. She insulted me in my own house, and I was obliged to order her to leave it."

"Quarrelled? That is a pity. An open break? Open breaks in friendship are always unfortunate." Lyons looked grieved, and fingered his beard meditatively.

"I appreciate," said Selma, frankly, "that our falling out will be an inconvenience in case we should meet in Washington or elsewhere, since you and Mr. Williams have business interests in common. Of course, James, I wish to help you in every way I can. I might as well tell you about it. I think she was jealous of me and fancied I was trying to cut her out socially. At all events, she insinuated that I was not a lady, because I would not lower my standards to hers, and adopt the frivolous habits of her little set. But I have not forgotten, James, your suggestion that people in public life can accomplish more if they avoid showing resentment and strive for harmony. I shall be ready to forget the past if Mrs. Williams will, for my position as your wife puts me beyond the reach of her criticism. She's a lively little thing in her way, and her husband seems to understand about investments and how to get ahead."

They went direct to Washington without stopping at Benham. It was understood that the new session of Congress was to be very short, and they were glad of an opportunity to present themselves in an official capacity at the capital as a conclusion to their honeymoon, before settling down at home. Selma found a letter from Miss Bailey, containing the news that Pauline Littleton had accepted the presidency of Wetmore College, the buildings of which were now practically completed. Selma gasped as she read this. She had long ago decided that her sister-in-law's studies were unpractical, and that Pauline was doomed to teach small classes all her days, a task for which she was doubtless well fitted. She resented the selection, for, in her opinion, Pauline lacked the imaginative talent of Wilbur, and yet shared his subjective, unenthusiastic ways. More than once it had occurred to her that the presidency of Wetmore was the place of all others for which she herself was fitted. Indeed, until Lyons had offered himself she had cherished in her inner consciousness the hope that the course of events might demonstrate that she was the proper person to direct the energies of this new medium for the higher education of women. It irritated her to think that an institution founded by Benham philanthropy, and which would be a vital influence in the development of Benham womanhood, should be under the control of one who was hostile to American theories and methods. Selma felt so strongly on the subject that she thought of airing her objections in a letter to Mr. Flagg, the donor, but she concluded to suspend her strictures until her return to Benham. She sent, however, to Miss Bailey, who was now regularly attached to one of the Benham newspapers, notes for an article which should deplore the choice by the trustees of one who was unfamiliar and presumably out of sympathy with Benham thought and impulse.

Selma's emotions on her arrival in Washington were very different from those which she had experienced in New York as the bride of Littleton. Then she had been unprepared for, dazed, and offended by what she saw. Now, though she mentally assumed that the capital was the parade ground of American ideas and principles, she felt not merely no surprise at the august appearance of the wide avenues, but she was eagerly on the lookout, as they drove from the station to the hotel, for signs of social development. The aphorism which she had supplied to her husband, that the American people prefer to have their representatives live comfortably, dwelt in her thoughts and was a solace to her. Despite her New York experience, she had the impression that the doors of every house in Washington would fly open at her approach as the wife of a Congressman. She did not formulate her anticipations as to her reception, but she entertained a general expectation that their presence would be acknowledged as public officials in a notable way. She dressed herself on the morning after their arrival at the hotel with some showiness, so as to be prepared for flattering emergencies. She had said little to her husband on the subject, for she had already discovered that, though he was ambitious that they should appear well, he was disposed to leave the management of social concerns to her. His information had been limited to bidding her come prepared for the reception to be given at the White House at the reassembling of Congress. Selma had brought her wedding-dress for this, and was looking forward to it as a gala occasion.

The hotel was very crowded, and Selma became aware that many of the guests were the wives and daughters of other Congressmen, who seemed to be in the same predicament as herself—that is, without anyone to speak to and waiting in their best clothes for something to happen. Lyons knew a few of them, and was making acquaintances in the corridors, with some of whom he exchanged an introduction of wives. As she successively met these other women, Selma perceived that no one of them was better dressed than herself, and she reflected with pleasure that they would doubtless be available allies in her crusade against frivolity and exclusiveness.

Presently she set out with her husband to survey the sights of the city. Naturally their first visit was to the Capitol, in the presence of which Selma clutched his arm in the pride of her patriotism and of her pleasure that he was to be one of the makers of history within its splendid precincts. The sight of the stately houses of Congress, superbly dominated by their imposing dome, made them both walk proudly, lost, save for occasional vivid phrases of admiration, in the contemplation of their own possible future. What greater earthly prize for man than political distinction among a people capable of monuments like this? What grander arena for a woman eager to demonstrate truth and promote righteousness? There was, of course, too much to see for any one visit. They went up to the gallery of the House of Representatives and looked down on the theatre of Lyons's impending activities. He was to take his seat on the day after the morrow as one of the minority party, but a strong, vigorous minority. Selma pictured him standing in the aisle and uttering ringing words of denunciation against corporate monopolies and the money power.

"I shall come up here and listen to you often. I shall be able to tell if you speak loud enough—so that the public can hear you," she said, glancing at the line of galleries which she saw in her mind's eye crowded with spectators. "You must make a long speech very soon."

"That is very unlikely indeed. They tell me a new member rarely gets a chance to be heard," answered Lyons.

"But they will hear you. You have something to say."

Lyons squeezed her hand. Her words nourished the same hope in his own breast. "I shall take advantage of every opportunity to obtain recognition, and to give utterance to my opinions."

"Oh yes, I shall expect you to speak. I am counting on that."

On their way down they scanned with interest the statues and portraits of distinguished statesmen and heroes, and the representations of famous episodes in American history with which the walls of the landings and the rotunda are lined.

"Some day you will be here," said Selma. "I wonder who will paint you or make your bust. I have often thought," she added, wistfully, "that, if I had given my mind to it, I could have modelled well in clay. Some day I'll try. It would be interesting, wouldn't it, to have you here in marble with the inscription underneath, 'Bust of the Honorable James O. Lyons, sculptured by his wife?'"

Lyons laughed, but he was pleased. "You are making rapid strides, my dear. I am sure of one thing—if my bust or portrait ever is here, I shall owe my success largely to your devotion and good sense. I felt certain of it before, but our honeymoon has proved to me that we were meant for one another."

"Yes, I think we were. And I like to hear you say I have good sense. That is what I pride myself on as a wife."

On their return to the hotel Selma was annoyed to find that no one but a member of her husband's Congressional delegation had called. She had hoped to find that their presence in Washington was known and appreciated. It seemed to her, moreover, that they were not treated at the hotel with the deference she had supposed would be accorded to them. To be sure, equality was of the essence of American doctrine; nevertheless she had anticipated that the official representatives of the people would be made much of, and distinguished from the rest of the world, if not by direct attention, by being pointed out and looked at admiringly. Still, as Lyons showed no signs of disappointment, she forbore to express her own perplexity, which was temporarily relieved by an invitation from him to drive. The atmosphere was mild enough for an open carriage, and Selma's appetite for processional effect derived some crumbs of comfort from the process of showing herself in a barouche by the side of her husband. They proceeded in an opposite direction from the Capitol, and after surveying the outside of the White House, drove along the avenues and circles occupied by private residences. Selma noticed that these houses, though attractive, were less magnificent and conspicuous than many of those in New York—more like her own in Benham; and she pictured as their occupants the families of the public men of the country—a society of their wives and daughters living worthily, energetically, and with becoming stateliness, yet at the same time rebuking by their example frivolity and rampant luxury. She observed with satisfaction the passage of a number of private carriages, and that their occupants were stylishly clad. She reflected that, as, the wife of a Congressman, her place was among them, and she was glad that they recognized the claims of social development so far as to dress well and live in comfort. Before starting she had herself fastened a bunch of red roses at her waist as a contribution to her picturesqueness as a public woman.

While she was thus absorbed in speculation, not altogether free from worrying suspicions, in spite of her mental vision as to the occupants of these private residences, she uttered an ejaculation of surprise as a jaunty victoria passed by them, and she turned her head in an eager attempt to ascertain if her surprise and annoyance were well-founded. The other vehicle was moving rapidly, but a similar curiosity impelled one of its occupants to look back also, and the eyes of the two women met.

"It's she; I thought it was."

"Who, my dear?" said Lyons.

"Flossy Williams—Mrs. Gregory Williams. I wonder," she added, in a severe tone, "what she is doing here, and how she happens to be associating with these people. That was a private carriage."

"Williams has a number of friends in Washington, I imagine. I thought it likely that he would be here. That was another proof of your good sense, Selma—deciding to let bygones be bygones and to ignore your disagreement with his wife."

254

"Yes, I know. I shall treat her civilly. But my heart will be broken, James, if I find that Washington is like New York."

"In what respect?"

"If I find that the people in these houses lead exclusive, un-American, godless lives. It would tempt me almost to despair of our country," she exclaimed, with tragic emphasis.

"I don't understand about social matters, Selma. I must leave those to you. But," he added, showing that he shrewdly realized the cause of her anguish better than she did herself, "as soon as we get better acquainted, I'm sure you will find that we shall get ahead, and that you will be able to hold your own with anybody, however exclusive."

Selma colored at the unflattering simplicity of his deduction. "I don't desire to hold my own with people of that sort. I despise them."

"I know. Hold your own, I mean, among people of the right sort by force of sound ideas and principles. The men and women of to-day," he continued, with melodious asseveration, "are the grand-children of those who built the splendid halls we visited this morning as a monument to our nation's love of truth and righteousness. A few frivolous, worldly minded spirits are not the people of the United States to whom we look for our encouragement and support."

"Assuredly," answered Selma, with eagerness. "It is difficult, though, not to get discouraged at times by the behavior of those who ought to aid instead of hinder our progress as a nation."

For a moment she was silent in wrapt meditation, then she asked:

"Didn't you expect that more notice would be taken of our arrival?"

"In what way?"

"In some way befitting a member of Congress."

Lyons laughed. "My dear Selma, I am one new Congressman among several hundred. What did you expect? That the President and his wife would come and take us to drive?"

"Of course not." She paused a moment, then she said: "I suppose that, as you are not on the side of the administration, we cannot expect much notice to be taken of us until you speak in the House. I will try not to be too ambitious for you, James; but it

255

would be easier to be patient," she concluded, with her far-away look, "if I were not beginning to fear that this city also may be contaminated just as New York is."

CHAPTER VI.

The incidents of the next two days previous to her attendance at the evening reception at the White House restored Selma's equanimity. She had the satisfaction of being present at the opening ceremonies of the House of Representatives, and of beholding her husband take the oath of office. She was proud of Lyons as she looked down on him from the gallery standing in the aisle by his allotted seat. He was holding an improvised reception, for a number of his colleagues showed themselves desirous to make his acquaintance. She noticed that he appeared already on familiar terms with some of his fellow-members; that he drew men or was drawn aside for whispered confidences; that he joked knowingly with others; and that always as he chatted his large, round, smooth face, relieved by its chin beard, wore an aspect of bland dignity and shrewd reserve wisdom. It pleased her to be assisting at the dedication of a fresh page of national history—a page yet unwritten, but on which she hoped that her own name would be inscribed sooner or later by those who should seek to trace the complete causes of her husband's usefulness and genius.

Another source of satisfaction was the visit paid them the day before at the hotel by one of the United States Senators from their own State—Mr. Calkins. The two political parties in their own State were so evenly divided that one of the Senators in office happened to be a Republican and his colleague a Democrat. Mr. Calkins belonged to her husband's party, yet he suggested that they might enjoy a private audience with the President, with whom, notwithstanding political differences of opinion, Mr. Calkins was on friendly terms. This was the sort of thing which Selma aspired to, and the experience did much to lighten her heart. She enjoyed the distinction of seeing guarded doors open at their approach, and of finding herself shaking hands with the chief magistrate of the nation at a special interview. The President was very affable, and was manifestly aware of Lyons's triumph at the expense of his own party, and of his consequent political importance. He treated the matter banteringly, and Selma was pleased at her ability to enter into the spirit of his persiflage and to reciprocate. In her opinion solemnity would have been more consistent with his position as the official representative of the people of the United States, and his jocose manifestations at a time when serious conversation seemed to be in order was a disappointment, and tended to confirm her previous distrust of him as the leader of the opposite party. She had hoped he would broach some vital topics of political interest, and that she would have the opportunity to give expression to her own views in regard to public questions. Nevertheless, as the President saw fit to be humorous, she was glad that she understood how to meet and answer his bantering sallies. She felt sure that Lyons, were he ever to occupy this dignified office, would refrain from ill-timed levity, but she bore in mind also the policy of conciliation which she had learned from her husband, and concealed her true impressions. She noticed that both Lyons and Mr. Calkins forebore to show dissatisfaction, and she reflected that, though the President's tone was light, there was nothing else in his appearance or bearing to convict him of sympathy with lack of enthusiasm and with cynicism. It would have destroyed all the enjoyment of her interview had she been forced to conclude that a man who did not take himself and his duties seriously could be elected President of the United States. She was not willing to believe this; but her suspicions were so far aroused that she congratulated herself that her political opponents were responsible for his election. Nevertheless she was delighted by the distinction of the private audience, and by the episode at its close, which gave her opportunity to show her individuality. Said the President gallantly as she was taking leave:

"Will you permit me to congratulate Congressman Lyons on his good fortune in the affairs of the heart as well as in politics?"

"If you say things like that, Mr. President," interjected Lyons, "you will turn her head; she will become a Republican, and then where should I be?"

While she perceived that the President was still inclined to levity, the compliment pleased Selma. Yet, though she appreciated that her husband was merely humoring him by his reply, she did not like the suggestion that any flattery could affect her principles. She shook her head coquettishly and said:

"James, I'm sure the President thinks too well of American women to believe that any admiration, however gratifying, would make me lukewarm in devotion to my party."

This speech appeared to her apposite and called for, and she departed in high spirits, which were illuminated by the thought that the administration was not wholly to be trusted.

258

On the following evening Selma went to the reception at the White House. The process of arrival was trying to her patience, for they were obliged to await their turn in the long file of carriages. She could not but approve of the democratic character of the entertainment, which anyone who desired to behold and shake hands with the Chief Magistrate was free to attend. Still, it again crossed her mind that, as an official's wife, she ought to have been given precedence. Their turn to alight came at last, and they took their places in the procession of visitors on its way through the East room to the spot where the President and his wife, assisted by some of the ladies of the Cabinet, were submitting to the ordeal of receiving the nation. There was a veritable crush, in which there was every variety of evening toilette, a display essentially in keeping with the doctrines which Selma felt that she stood for. She took occasion to rejoice in Lyons's ear at the realization of her anticipations in this respect. At the same time she was agreeably stimulated by the belief that her wedding dress was sumptuous and stylish, and her appearance striking. Her hair had been dressed as elaborately as possible; she wore all her jewelry; and she carried a bouquet of costly roses. Her wish was to regard the function as the height of social demonstration, and she had spared no pains to make herself effective. She had esteemed it her duty to do so both as a Congressman's wife and as a champion of moral and democratic ideas.

The crowd was oppressive, and three times the train of her dress was stepped on to her discomfiture. Amid the sea of faces she recognized a few of the people she had seen at the hotel. It struck her that no one of the women was dressed so elegantly as herself, an observation which cheered her and yet was not without its thorn. But the music, the lights, and the variegated movement of the scene kept her senses absorbed and interfered with introspection, until at last they were close to the receiving party. Selma fixed her eyes on the President, expecting recognition. Like her husband, the President possessed a gift of faces and the faculty of rallying all his energies to the important task of remembering who people were. An usher asked and announced the names, but the Chief Magistrate's perceptions were kept hard at work. His "How do you do, Congressman Lyons? I am very glad to see you here, Mrs. Lyons," were uttered with a smiling spontaneity, which to his own soul meant a momentary agreeable relaxation of the nerves of memory, resembling the easy flourish with which a gymnast engaged in lifting heavy weights encounters a wooden dumb-bell. But though his eyes and voice were flattering, Selma had barely completed the little bob of a courtesy which accompanied her act of shaking hands when she discovered that the machinery of the national custom was not to halt on their account, and that she must proceed without being able to renew the half flirtatious interview of the previous day. She proceeded to courtesy to the President's wife and to the row of wives of members of the Cabinet who were assisting. Before she could adequately observe them, she found herself beyond and a part once more of a heterogeneous crush, the current of which she aimlessly followed on her husband's arm. She was suspicious of the device of courtesying. Why had not the President's wife and the Cabinet ladies shaken hands with her and given her an opportunity to make their acquaintance? Could it be that the administration was aping foreign manners and adopting effete and aristocratic usages?

"What do we do now?" she asked of Lyons as they drifted along.

"I'd like to find Horace Elton and introduce him to you. I caught a glimpse of him further on just before we reached the President. Horace knows all the ropes and can tell us who everybody is."

Selma had heard her husband refer to Horace Elton on several occasions in terms of respectful and somewhat mysterious consideration. She had gathered in a general way that he was a far reaching and formidable power in matters political and financial, besides being the president and active organizer of the energetic corporation known as the Consumers' Gas Light Company of their own state. As they proceeded she kept her eyes on the alert for a man described by Lyons as short, heavily built, and neat looking, with small side whiskers and a close-mouthed expression. When they were not far from the door of exit from the East room, some one on the edge of the procession accosted her husband, who drew her after him in that direction. Selma found herself in a sort of eddy occupied by half a dozen people engaged in observing the passing show, and in the presence of Mr. and Mrs. Gregory Williams. It was Mr. Williams who had diverted them. He now renewed his acquaintance with her, exclaiming—"My wife insisted that she had met you driving with some one she believed to be your husband. I had heard that Congressman Lyons was on his bridal tour, and now everything is clear. Flossy, you were right as usual, and it seems that our hearty congratulations are in order to two old friends."

Williams spoke with his customary contagious confidence. Selma noted that he was stouter and that his hair was becomingly streaked with gray. Had not her attention been on the lookout for his wife she might have noticed that his eye wore a restless, strained expression despite his august banker's manner and showy gallantry. She did observe that the moment he had made way for Flossy he turned to Lyons and began to talk to him in a subdued tone under the guise of watching the procession.

The two women confronted each other with spontaneous forgetfulness of the past. There was a shade of haughtiness in Selma's greeting. She was prepared to respect her husband's policy and to ignore the circumstances under which they had parted, but she wished Flossy to understand that this was an act of condescension on her part as a Congressman's wife, whose important social status was beyond question. She was so thoroughly imbued with this sense of her indisputable superiority that she readily mistook Flossy's affability for fawning; whereas that young woman's ingenuous friendliness was the result of a warning sentence from Gregory when Selma and her husband were seen approaching—"Keep a check on your tongue, Floss. This statesman with a beard like a goat is likely to have a political future."

"I felt sure it was you the other day," Flossy said with smiling sprightliness, "but I had not heard of your marriage to Mr. Lyons."

"We were married at Benham six weeks ago. We are to live in Benham. We have bought the house there which belonged to Mr. Parsons. We have just returned from visiting the superb scenery of the Yosemite and the Rocky Mountains, and it made me prouder than ever of my country. If Congressman Lyons had not been obliged to be present at the opening of Congress, we should have spent our honeymoon in Europe."

"Gregory and I passed last summer abroad yachting. We crossed on a steamer and had our yacht meet us there. Isn't it a jam to-night?"

"There seem to be a great many people. I suppose you came

261

on from New York on purpose for this reception?"

"Mercy, no. We are staying with friends, and we hadn't intended to come to-night. But we had been dining out and were dressed, so we thought we'd drop in and show our patriotism. It's destruction to clothes, and I'm glad I haven't worn my best."

Selma perceived Flossy's eye making a note of her own elaborate costume, and the disagreeable suspicion that she was overdressed reasserted itself. She had already observed that Mrs. Williams's toilette, though stylish, was comparatively simple. How could one be overdressed on such an occasion? What more suitable time for an American woman to wear her choicest apparel than when paying her respects to the President of the United States? She noticed that Flossy seemed unduly at her ease as though the importance of the ceremony was lost on her, and that they group of people with whom Flossy had been talking and who stood a little apart were obviously indulging in quiet mirth at the expense of some of those in the procession.

"Are the friends with whom you are staying connected with the Government?" Selma asked airily.

"Official people? Goodness, no. But I can point out to you who everybody is, for we have been in Washington frequently during the last three sessions. Gregory has to run over here on business every now and then, and I almost always come with him. To-night is the opportunity to see the queer people in all their glory—the woolly curiosities, as Gregory calls them. And a sprinkling of the real celebrities too," she added.

Selma's inquiry had been put with a view to satisfy herself that Flossy's friends were mere civilians. But she was glad of an opportunity to be enlightened as to the names of her fellow-officials, though she resented Flossy's flippant tone regarding the character of the entertainment. While she listened to the breezy, running commentary by which Flossy proceeded to identify for her benefit the conspicuous figures in the procession she nursed her offended sensibilities.

"I should suppose," she said, taking advantage of a pause, "that on such an occasion as this everybody worth knowing would be present."

Flossy gave Selma one of her quick glances. She had not forgotten the past, nor her discovery of the late Mrs. Littleton's real grievance against her and the world. Nor did she consider that her husband's caveat debarred her from the amusement of worrying the wife of the Hon. James O. Lyons, provided it could be done by means of the truth ingenuously uttered. She said with a confidential smile—

"The important and the interesting political people have other opportunities to meet one another—at dinner parties and less promiscuous entertainments than this, and the Washington people have other opportunities to meet them. Of course the President is a dear, and everyone makes a point of attending a public reception once in a while, but this sort of thing isn't exactly an edifying society event. For instance, notice the woman in the pomegranate velvet with two diamond sprays in her hair. That's the wife of Senator Colman—his child wife, so they call her. She came to Washington six years ago as the wife of a member of the House from one of the wild and woolly States, and was notorious then in the hotel corridors on account of her ringletty raven hair and the profusion of rings she wore. She used to make eyes at the hotel guests and romp with her husband's friends in the hotel parlors, which was the theatre of her social activities. Her husband died, and a year ago she married old Senator Colman, old enough to be her grandfather, and one of the very rich and influential men in the Senate. Now she has developed social ambition and is anxious to entertain. They have hired a large house for the winter and are building a larger one. As Mrs. Polsen—that was her first husband's name—she was invited nowhere except to wholesale official functions like this. The wife of a United States Senator with plenty of money can generally attract a following; she is somebody. And it happens that people are amused by Mrs. Cohnan's eccentricities. She still overdresses, and makes eyes, and she nudges those who sit next her at table, but she is good-natured, says whatever comes into her head, and has a strong sense of humor. So she is getting on."

"Getting on among society people?" said Selma drily.

Flossy's eyes twinkled. "Society people is the generic name used for them in the newspapers. I mean that she is making friends among the women who live in the quarter where I passed you the other day."

Selma frowned. "It is not necessary, I imagine, to make friends of that class in order to have influence in Washington,—the best kind of influence. I can readily believe that people of that sort would interest most of our public women very little."

"Very likely. I don't think you quite understand me, Mrs. Lyons, or we are talking at cross purposes. What I was trying to make clear is that political and social prominence in Washington are by no means synonimous. Of course everyone connected with the government who desires to frequent Washington society and is socially available is received with open arms; but, if people are not socially available, it by no means follows that they are able to command social recognition merely because they hold political office,—except perhaps in the case of wives of the Cabinet, of the Justices of the Supreme Court, or of rich and influential Senators, where a woman is absolutely bent on success and takes pains. I refer particularly to the wives, because a single man, if he is reasonably presentable and ambitious, can go about more or less, even if he is a little rough, for men are apt to be scarce. But the line is drawn on the women unless they are—er—really important and have to be tolerated for official reasons. Now every woman who is not *persona grata*, as the diplomats say, anywhere else, is apt to attend the President's reception in all her finery, and that's why I suggested that this sort of thing isn't exactly an edifying social event. It's amusing to come here now and then, just as it's amusing to go to a menagerie. You see what I mean, don't you?" Flossy asked, plying her feathery fan with blithe nonchalance and looking into her companion's face with an innocent air.

"I understand perfectly. And who are these people who draw the line?"

"It sometimes happens," continued Flossy abstractedly, without appearing to hear this inquiry, "that they improve after they've been in Washington a few years. Take Mrs. Baker, the Secretary of the Interior's wife, receiving to-night. When her husband came to Washington three years ago she had the social adaptability of a solemn horse. But she persevered and learned, and now as a Cabinet lady she unbends, and is no longer afraid of compromising her dignity by wearing becoming clothes and smiling occasionally. But you were asking who the people are who draw the line. The nice people here just as everywhere else; the people who have been well educated and have fine sensibilities, and who believe in modesty, and unselfishness and thorough ways of doing things.

264

You must know the sort of people I mean. Some of them make too much of mere manners, but as a class they are able to draw the line because they draw it in favor of distinction of character as opposed to—what shall I call it?—haphazard custom-made ethics and social deportment."

Flossy spoke with the artless prattle of one seeking to make herself agreeable to a new-comer by explaining the existing order of things, but she had chosen her words as she proceeded with special reference to her listener's case. There was nothing in her manner to suggest that she was trifling with the feelings of the wife of Hon. James O. Lyons, but to Selma's sensitive ear there was no doubt that the impertinent and unpatriotic tirade had been deliberately aimed at her. The closing words had a disagreeably familiar sound. Save that they fell from seemingly friendly lips they recalled the ban which Flossy had hurled at her at the close of their last meeting—the ban which had decided her to declare unwavering hostility against social exclusiveness. Its veiled reiteration now made her nerves tingle, but the personal affront stirred her less than the conclusion, which the whole of Flossy's commentary suggested, that Washington—Washington the hearth-stone of American ideals, was contaminated also. Flossy had given her to understand that the houses which she had assumed to be occupied by members of the Government were chiefly the residences of people resembling in character those whom she had disapproved of in New York. Flossy had intimated that unless a woman were hand in glove with these people and ready to lower herself to their standards, she must be the wife of a rich Senator to be tolerated. Flossy had virtually told her that a Congressman's wife was nobody. Could this be true? The bitterest part of all was that it was evident Flossy spoke with the assurance of one uttering familiar truths. Selma felt affronted and bitterly disappointed, but she chose to meet Mrs. Williams's innocent affability with composure; to let her see that she disagreed with her, but not to reveal her personal irritation. She must consider Lyons, whose swift political promotion was necessary for her plans. It was important that he should become rich, and if his relations with the firm of Williams & Van Horne tended to that end, no personal grievance of her own should disturb them. Even Flossy had conceded that the wives of the highest officials could not be ignored.

"I fear that we look at these matters from too different a standpoint to discuss them further," she responded, with an effort at smiling ease. "Evidently you do not appreciate that to the majority of the strong women of the country whose husbands have been sent to Washington as members of the Government social interests seem trivial compared with the great public questions they are required to consider. These women doubtless feel little inclination for fashionable and—or—frivolous festivities, and find an occasion like this better suited to their conception of social dignity."

A reply by Flossy to this speech was prevented by the interruption of Lyons, who brought up Mr. Horace Elton for introduction to his wife. Selma knew him at once from his likeness to the description which her husband had given. He was portly and thick-set, with a large neck, a strong, unemotional, high-colored face, and closely-shaven, small side whiskers. He made her a low bow and, after a few moments of conversation, in the course of which he let fall a complimentary allusion to her husband's oratorical abilities and gave her to understand that he considered Lyons's marriage as a wise and enviable proceeding, he invited her to promenade the room on his arm. Mr. Elton had a low but clear and dispassionate voice, and a concise utterance. His remarks gave the impression that he could impart more on any subject if he chose, and that what he said proceeded from a reserve fund of special, secret knowledge, a little of which he was willing to confide to his listener. He enlightened Selma in a few words as to a variety of the people present, accompanying his identification with a phrase or two of comprehensive personal detail, which had the savor of being unknown to the world at large.

"The lady we just passed, Mrs. Lyons, is the wife of the junior Senator from Nevada. Her husband fell in love with her on the stage of a mining town theatrical troupe. That tall man, with the profuse wavy hair and prominent nose, is Congressman Ross of Colorado, the owner of one of the largest cattle ranches in the Far West. It is said that he has never smoked, never tasted a glass of liquor, and never gambled in his life."

In the course of these remarks Mr. Elton simply stated his interesting facts without comment. He avoided censorious or satirical allusions to the people to whom he called Selma's attention. On the contrary, his observations suggested sympathetically that he

266

desired to point out to her the interesting personalities of the capital, and that he regarded the entertainment as an occasion to behold the strong men and women of the country in their lustre and dignity. As they passed the lady in pomegranate velvet, Selma said, in her turn, "That is Mrs. Colman, I believe. Senator Colman's child wife." She added what was in her thoughts, "I understand that the society people here have taken her up."

"Yes. She has become a conspicuous figure in Washington. I remember her, Mrs. Lyons, when she was Addie Farr—before she married Congressman Polsen of Kentucky. She was a dashing looking girl in those days, with her black eyes and black ringlets. I remember she had a coltish way of tossing her head. The story is that when she accepted Polsen another Kentuckian—a young planter—who was in love with her, drank laudanum. Now, as you say, she is being taken up socially, and her husband, the Senator, is very proud of her success. After all, if a woman is ambitious and has tact, what can she ask better than to be the wife of a United States Senator?" He paused a moment, then, with a gallant sidelong glance at his companion, resumed in a concise whisper, which had the effect of a disclosure, "Prophecies, especially political prophecies, are dangerous affairs, but it seems to me not improbable that before many years have passed the wife of Senator Lyons will be equally prominent—be as conspicuous socially as the wife of Senator Colman."

Selma blushed, but not wholly with pleasure. Socially conspicuous before many years? The splendid prophecy, which went beyond the limit of Horace Elton's usual caution—for he combined the faculty of habitual discretion with his chatty proclivities—was dimmed for Selma by the rasping intimation that she was not conspicuous yet. Worse still, his statement shattered the hope, which Flossy's fluent assertions had already disturbed, that she was to find in Washington a company of congenial spirits who would appreciate her at her full value forthwith, and would join with her and under her leadership in resisting the encroachments of women of the stamp of Mrs. Williams.

"I am very ambitious for my husband, Mr. Elton, and of course I have hoped—do hope that some day he will be a Senator. What you said just now as to the power of his voice to arouse the moral enthusiasm of the people seemed to be impressively true. I should be glad to be a Senator's wife, for—for I wish to help him. I wish to demonstrate the truth of the principles to which both our lives are dedicated. But I hoped that I might help him now—that my mission might be clear at once. It seems according to you that a Congressman's wife is not of much importance; that her hands are tied."

"Practically so, unless—unless she has unusual social facility, and the right sort of acquaintances. Beauty, wealth and ambition are valuable aids, but I always am sorry for women who come here without friends, and—er—the right sort of introduction. At any rate, to answer your question frankly, a Congressman's wife has her spurs to win just as he has. If you were to set up house-keeping, here, Mrs. Lyons, I've no doubt that a woman of your attractions and capabilities would soon make a niche for herself. You have had social experience, which Addie Farr, for instance, was without."

"I lived in New York for some years with my husband, Mr. Littleton, so I have a number of Eastern acquaintances."

"I remember you were talking with Mrs. Gregory Williams when I was introduced to you. The people with whom she is staying are among the most fashionable in Washington. What I said had reference to the wife of the every-day Congressman who comes to Washington expecting recognition. Not to Mrs. James O. Lyons."

Selma bit her lip. She recognized the death-knell of her cherished expectations. She was not prepared to acknowledge formally her discomfiture and her disappointment. But she believed that Mr. Elton, though a plain man, had comprehensive experience and that he spoke with shrewd knowledge of the situation. She felt sure that he was not trying to deceive or humiliate her. It was clear that Washington was contaminated also.

"I dare say I should get on here well enough after a time, though I should find difficulty in considering that it was right to give so much time to merely social matters. But Mr. Lyons and I have already decided that I can be more use to him at present in Benham. There I feel at home. I am known, and have my friends, and there I have important work—literary lectures and the establishment of a large public hospital under way. If the time comes, as you kindly predict, that my husband is chosen a United States Senator, I shall be glad to return here and accept the responsibilities of our position. But I warn you, Mr. Elton,—I warn the people of Washington," she added with a wave of her fan, while her eyes sparkled with a stern light "that when I am one of their leaders, I shall do away with some of the—er—false customs of the present administration. I shall insist on preserving our American social traditions inviolate."

Here was the grain of consolation in the case, which she clutched at and held up before her mind's eye as a new stimulus to her patriotism and her conscience. Both Mr. Elton and Flossy had indicated that there was a point at which exclusiveness was compelled to stop in its haughty disregard of democratic ideals. There were certain women whom the people who worshipped lack of enthusiasm and made an idol of cynicism were obliged to heed and recognize. They might be able to ignore the intelligence and social originality of a Congressman's wife, but they dared not turn a cold shoulder on the wife of a United States Senator. And if a woman—if she were to occupy this proud position, what a satisfaction it would be to assert the power which belonged to it; assert it in behalf of the cause for which she had suffered so much! Her disappointment tasted bitterly in her mouth, and she was conscious of stern revolt; but the new hope had already taken possession of her fancy, and she hastened to prove it by the ethical standard without which all hopes were valueless to her. Even now had anyone told her that the ruling passion of her life was to be wooed and made much of by the very people she professed to despise, she would have spurned the accuser as a malicious slanderer. Nor indeed would it have been wholly true. Mrs. Williams had practically told her this at their last meeting in New York, and its utterance had convinced her on the contrary of repugnance to them, and of her desire to be the leader of a social protest against them. Now here, in Washington of all places, she was confronted by the bitter suggestion that she was without allies, and that her enemies were the keepers of the door which led to leadership and power. Despondency stared her in the face, but a splendid possibility—aye probability was left. She would not forsake her principles. She would not lower her flag. She would return to Benham. Washington refused her homage now, but it should listen to her and bow before her some day as the wife of one of the real leaders of the State, whom Society did not dare to ignore.

CHAPTER VII.

At the close of the fortnight of her stay in Washington subsequent to the reception at the White House, Selma found herself in the same frame of mind as when she parted from Mr. Elton. During this fortnight her time was spent either in sight seeing or at the hotel. The exercises at the Capitol were purely formal, preliminary to a speedy adjournment of Congress. Consequently her husband had no opportunity to distinguish himself by addressing the house. Of Flossy she saw nothing, though the two men had several meetings. Apparently both Lyons and Williams were content with a surface reconciliation between their wives which did not bar family intercourse. At least her husband made no suggestion that she should call on Mrs. Williams, and Flossy's cards did not appear. Beyond making the acquaintance of a few more wives and daughters in the hotel, who seemed as solitary as herself, Selma received no overtures from her own sex. She knew no one, and no one sought her out or paid her attention. She still saw fit to believe that if she were to establish herself in Washington and devote her energies to rallying these wives and daughters about her, she might be able to prove that Flossy and Mr. Elton were mistaken. But she realized that the task would be less simple than she had anticipated. Besides she yearned to return to Benham, and take up again the thread of active life there. Benham would vindicate her, and some day Benham would send her back to Washington to claim recognition and her rightful place.

Lyons himself was in a cheerful mood and found congenial occupation in visiting with his wife the many historical objects of interest, and in chatting in various hotel corridors with the public men of the country, his associates in Congress. His solicitude in regard to the account which Williams was carrying for him had been relieved temporarily by an upward turn in the stock market, and the impending prompt adjournment of Congress had saved him from the necessity of taking action in regard to the railroad bill which Williams had solicited him to support. Moreover Selma had repeated to him Horace Elton's prophecy that it was not unlikely that some day he would become Senator. To be sure he recognized that a remark like this uttered to a pretty woman by an astute man of affairs such as Elton was not to be taken too seriously. There was no vacancy in the office of Senator from his state, and none was

270

likely to occur. At the present time, if one should occur, his party in the state legislature was in a minority. Hence prophecy was obviously a random proceeding. Nevertheless he was greatly pleased, for, after all, Elton would scarcely have made the speech had he not been genuinely well disposed. A senatorship was one of the great prizes of political life, and one of the noblest positions in the world. It would afford him a golden opportunity to leave the impress of his convictions on national legislation, and defend the liberties of the people by force of the oratorical gifts which he possessed. Elton had referred to these gifts in complimentary terms. Was it not reasonable to infer that Elton would be inclined to promote his political fortunes? Such an ally would be invaluable, for Elton was a growing power in the industrial development of the section of the country where they both lived. He had continued to find him friendly in spite of his own antagonism on the public platform to corporate power. A favorite and conscientious hope in his political outlook was that he might be able to make capital as well as labor believe him to be a friend without alienating either; that he might obtain support at the polls from both factions, and thus be left free after election to work out for their mutual advantage appropriate legislation. He had avowed himself unmistakably the champion of popular principles in order to win the confidence of the common people, but his policy of reasonable conciliation led him to cast sheep's eyes at vested interests when he could do so without exposing himself to the charge of inconsistency. Many of his friends were wealthy men, and his private ambition was to amass a handsome fortune. That had been the cause of his speculative ventures in local enterprises which promised large returns, and in the stock market. Horace Elton was a friend of but three years' standing; one of the men who had consulted him occasionally in regard to legal matters since he had become a corporation attorney. He admired Elton's strong, far-reaching grasp of business affairs, his capacity to formulate and incubate on plans of magnitude without betraying a sign of his intentions, and his power to act with lightning despatch and overwhelming vigor when the moment for the consummation of his purposes arrived. He also found agreeable Elton's genial, easy-going ways outside of business hours, which frequently took the form of social entertainment at which expense seemed to be no consideration and gastronomic novelties were apt to be presented. Lyons attended one of these private banquets while in Washington—a dinner party served to a carefully chosen company of public men, to which newspaper scribes were unable to penetrate. This same genial, easy-going tendency of Elton's to make himself acceptable to those with whom he came in contact took the form of a gift to Mrs. Lyons of a handsome cameo pin which he presented to her a day or two after their dialogue at the President's reception, and for which, as he confidentially informed Selma, he had been seeking a suitable wearer ever since he had picked it up in an out-of-the-way store in Brussels the previous summer.

On the day of their departure Selma, as she took a last look from the car window at the Capitol and the Washington Monument, said to her husband: "This is a beautiful city—worthy in many respects of the genius of the American people—but I never wish to return to Washington until you are United States Senator."

"Would you not be satisfied with Justice of the Supreme Court?" asked Lyons, gayly.

"I should prefer Senator. If you were Senator, you could probably be appointed to the Supreme Court in case you preferred that place. I am relying on you, James, to bring me back here some day."

She whispered this in his ear, as they sat with heads close together looking back at the swiftly receding city. Selma's hands were clasped in her lap, and she seemed to her lover to have a dreamy air—an air suggesting poetry and high ethical resolve such as he liked to associate with her and their scheme of wedded life. It pleased him that his wife should feel so confident that the future had in store for him this great prize, and he allowed himself to yield to the pathos of the moment and whisper in reply:

"I will say this, Selma. My business affairs look more favorable, and, if nothing unforeseen happens, I do not see why we shouldn't get on reasonably fast. Nowadays, in order to be a United States Senator comfortably, it is desirable in the first place to have abundant means."

"Yes."

"We must be patient and God-fearing, and with your help, dear, and your sympathy, we may live to see what you desire come to pass. Of course, my ambition is to be Senator, and—and to take you back to Washington as a Senator's wife."

Selma had not chosen to confide to Lyons in set terms her social grievance against the capital of her country. But she was glad to perceive from his last words that he understood she was not satisfied with the treatment accorded her, and that he also was looking forward to giving her a position which would enable her to rebuke the ungodly and presumptuous.

"Thank you, James," she answered. "When that time comes we shall be able to teach them a number of things. For the present though, I feel that I can be of best service to you and to the truths which we are living for by interesting myself in whatever concerns Benham. We believe in Benham, and Benham seems inclined to believe in us and our ideas."

The ensuing year passed uneventfully. Lyons was able to be at home from the first of April to the reassembling of Congress in the following December. He was glad to give himself up to the enjoyment of his handsome establishment. He resumed the tenor of his professional practice, feeling that as a sober-minded, married citizen he had become of more importance to the community, and he was eager to bear witness to his sense of responsibility. He took a more active part in soliciting contributions for evangelizing benighted countries, and he consented on several occasions to deliver an address on "Success in Life" to struggling young men of Benham and the surrounding towns. His easy flow of words, his dignity and his sober but friendly mien made him a favorite with audiences, and constantly broadened his circle of acquaintance.

Selma, on her side, took up the organization of the Free Hospital provided by Mr. Parsons. Her husband left the decision of all but legal and financial questions to her and Miss Luella Bailey, who, at Selma's request, was made the third member of the board of trustees. She decided to call in a committee of prominent physicians to formulate a programme of procedure in matters purely medical; but she reserved a right of rejection of their conclusions, and she insisted on the recognition of certain cardinal principles, as she called them. She specified that no one school of medicine should dictate the policy of the hospital as regards the treatment of patients. To the young physician whom she selected to assist her in forming this administrative board she stated, with stern emotion: "I do not intend that it shall be possible in this hospital for men and women to be sacrificed simply because doctors are unwilling to avail

273

themselves of the latest resources of brilliant individual discernment. I know what it means to see a beloved one die, who might have been saved had the physician in charge been willing to try new expedients. The doors of this hospital must be ever open to rising unconventional talent. There shall be no creeds nor caste of medicine here."

She also specified that the matron in charge of the hospital should be Mrs. Earle, whose lack of trained experience was more than counterbalanced by her maternal, humanitarian spirit, as Selma expressed it. She felt confident that Mrs. Earle would choose as her assistants competent and skilful persons, and at the same time that her broad point of view and sympathetic instincts would not allow her to turn a deaf ear to aspiring but technically ignorant ability. This selection of Mrs. Earle was a keen pleasure to Selma. It seemed to her an ideal selection. Mrs. Earle was no longer young, and was beginning to find the constant labor of lecture and newspaper work exhausting. This dignified and important post would provide her with a permanent income, and would afford her an attractive field for her progressive capabilities.

Selma's choice of young Dr. Ashmun as the head of the medical board was due to a statement which came to her ears, that he was reviled by some of the physicians of Benham because he had patented certain discoveries of his own instead of giving his fellow-practitioners the benefit of his knowledge. Selma was prompt to detect in this hostility an envious disposition on the part of the regular physicians to appropriate the fruits of individual cleverness and to repress youthful revolt against conventional methods. Dr. Ashmun regarded his selection as the professional chief of this new institution as a most auspicious occurrence from the standpoint of his personal fortunes. He was ambitious, ardent, and keen to attract attention, with an abundant fund of energy and a nervous, driving manner. He was, besides, good looking and fluent, and he quickly perceived the drift of Selma's intentions in regard to the hospital, and accommodated himself to them with enthusiasm. They afforded him the very opportunity which he most desired—the chance to assert himself against his critics, and to obtain public notice. The watchword of liberty and distrust of professional canons suited his purposes and his mood, and he threw himself eagerly into the work of carrying out Selma's projects.

As a result of the selection of Dr. Ashmun and of the other members of the administrative board, who were chosen with a view to their availability as sympathetic colleagues, letters of protest from several physicians appeared in the newspapers complaining that the new hospital was being conducted on unscientific and shallow principles, disapproved of by the leading men of the profession. Selma was indignant yet thrilled. She promptly took steps to refute the charge, and explained that the hostility of these correspondents proceeded from envy and hide-bound reluctance to adopt new and revolutionizing expedients. Through the aid of Mrs. Earle and Miss Luella Bailey a double-leaded column in the Benham *Sentinel* set forth the merits of the new departure in medicine, which was cleverly described as the revolt of the talented young men of the profession from the tyranny of their conservative elders. Benham became divided in opinion as to the merits of this controversy, and Selma received a number of anonymous letters through the post approving her stand in behalf of advanced, independent thought. Among the physicians who were opposed to her administration of the hospital she recognized with satisfaction the name of a Dr. Paget, who, as she happened to know, was Mrs. Hallett Taylor's medical adviser.

Another matter in which Selma became interested was the case of Mrs. Hamilton. She was a woman who had been born in the neighborhood of Benham, but had lived for twenty years in England, and had been tried in England by due process of law for the murder of her husband and sentenced to imprisonment for life. Some of the people of the state who had followed the testimony as reported in the American newspapers had decided that she ought not to have been convicted. Accordingly a petition setting forth the opinion of her former neighbors that she was innocent of the charge, and should as an American citizen be released from custody, was circulated for signature. A public meeting was held and largely attended, at which it was resolved to send a monster petition to the British authorities with a request for Mrs. Hamilton's pardon, and also to ask the government at Washington to intercede on behalf of the unfortunate sufferer. The statement of the case appealed vividly to Selma, and at the public meeting, which was attended chiefly by women, she spoke, and offered the services of her husband to lay the matter before the President. It was further resolved to obtain the names of influential persons all over the country in order that the petition might show that the sentiment that injustice had been done was national as well as local.

Selma espoused the case with ardor, and busied herself in obtaining signatures. She called on Miss Flagg and induced her to sign by the assurance that the verdict was entirely contrary to the evidence. She then had recourse to her former sister-in-law, conceiving that the signature of the President of Wetmore College would impress the English. She and Pauline had already exchanged visits, and Pauline had shown no umbrage at her marriage. The possibility of being rebuffed on this occasion did not occur to Selma. She took for granted that Pauline would be only too glad to give her support to so deserving a petition, and she considered that she was paying her a compliment in soliciting her name for insertion among the prominent signers. Pauline listened to her attentively, then replied:

"I am sorry for the woman, if she is innocent: and if she has been falsely accused, of course she ought to be released. But what makes you think she is innocent, Selma?"

"The testimony did not justify her conviction. Every one is of that opinion."

"Have you read the testimony yourself, Selma?"

"No, Pauline."

"Or your husband?"

"My husband is satisfied from what others have told him, just as I am, that this poor American woman is languishing in prison as the result of a cruel miscarriage of justice, and that she never committed the crime of which she has been found guilty. My husband has had considerable legal experience."

Pauline's questions were nettling, and Selma intended by her response to suggest the presumptuousness of her sister-in-law's doubts in the face of competent authority.

"I realize that your husband ought to understand about such matters, but may one suppose that the English authorities would deliberately allow an innocent woman to remain in prison? They must know that the friends of Mrs. Hamilton believe her innocent. Why should we on this side of the water meddle simply because she was born an American?"

"Why?" Selma drew herself up proudly. "In the first place I

276

believe—we believe—that the English are capable of keeping her in prison on a technicality merely because she is there already. They are worshippers of legal form and red tape, my husband says. And as to meddling, why is it not our duty as an earnest and Christian people to remonstrate against the continued incarceration of a woman born under our flag and accustomed to American ideas of justice? Meddling? In my opinion, we should be cowards and derelict in our duty if we did not protest."

Pauline shook her head. "I cannot see it so. It seems to me an interference which may make us seem ridiculous in the eyes of the English, as well as offensive to them. I am sorry, Selma, not to be able to do as you wish."

Selma rose with burning cheeks, but a stately air. "If that is your decision, I must do without your name. Already we have many signatures, and shall obtain hundreds more without difficulty. We look at things differently, Pauline. Our point of view has never been the same. Ridiculous? I should be proud of the ridicule of people too selfish or too unenlightened to heed the outcry of aspiring humanity. If we had to depend on your little set to strike the note of progress, I fear we should sit with folded hands most of the time."

"I do not know what you mean by my little set," said Pauline with a smile. "I am too busy with my college duties to belong to any set. I see my friends occasionally just as you see yours; and as to progress—well, I fear that you are right in your statement that we shall never look at things alike. To me progress presupposes in the individual or the community attaining it a prelude of slow struggle, disheartening doubts, and modest reverence for previous results—for the accumulated wisdom of the past."

"I mean by your set the people who think as you do. I understand your point of view. I should have liked," she added, "to ask you to share with me the responsibility of directing the policy of the Benham Free Hospital, had I not known that you would listen to the voice of conservative authority in preference to that of fearless innovation."

"I certainly should have hesitated long before I overruled the experience of those who have devoted their lives to conscientious effort to discover truth."

"That illustrates admirably the difference between us, Pauline. No one is more eager to aid the discovery of truth than I, but I believe that truth often is concealed from those who go on, day after day, following hum-drum routine, however conscientious. I recognized that Dr. Ashmun was a live man and had fresh ideas, so I chose him as our chief of staff, notwithstanding the doctors were unfriendly to him. As a result, my hospital has individuality, and is already a success. That's the sort of thing I mean. Good-by," she said, putting out her hand. "I don't expect to convert you, Pauline, to look at things my way, but you must realize by this time that it is the Benham way."

"Yet the leading physicians of Benham disapprove of your plans for the management of the hospital," said Pauline firmly.

"But the people of Benham approve of them. I prefer their sanction to that of a coterie of cautious, unenthusiastic autocrats."

Selma, true to her intentions, did not return to Washington with her husband when Congress reassembled in December. While she was absorbed with her philanthropic plans in Benham, Lyons was performing his public duties; seeking to do the country good service, and at the right moment to attract attention to himself. The opportunity to make a speech along the line of his public professions in behalf of labor against corporate monopoly did not offer itself until late in the session. He improved the few minutes allowed him to such advantage that he was listened to with close attention, and was at once recognized as one of the persuasive and eloquent speakers of the minority. Before Congress adjourned he obtained another chance to take part in debate, by which he produced an equally favorable impression. The newspapers of the country referred approvingly to his cogent gift of statement and dignified style of delivery. Both the bills against which he spoke were passed by the Republican majority, but echoes of his words came back from some of their constituents, and Lyons was referred to as certain to be one of the strong men of the House if he returned to Congress. He went home at the close of the session in a contented frame of mind so far as his political prospects were concerned, but he was not free to enjoy the congratulations accorded him for the reason that his business ventures were beginning to give him serious solicitude. The trend of the stock market was again downward. In expectation of a rise from the previous depression, he had added to the line of shares which Williams & Van Horne were carrying for him. A slight rise had

278

come, sufficient to afford him a chance to escape from the toils of Wall street without loss. But he needed a profit to rehabilitate his ventures in other directions—his investments in the enterprises of his own state, which had now for some months appeared quiescent, if not languishing, from a speculative point of view. Everything pointed, it was said, to a further advance as soon as Congress adjourned. So he had waited, and now, although the session was over, the stock market and financial undertakings of every sort appeared suddenly to be tottering. He had not been at home a month before prices of all securities began to shrink inordinately and the business horizon to grow murky with the clouds of impending disaster. To add to his worry, Lyons was conscious that he had pursued a fast and loose mental coarse in regard to the railroad bill in which his broker, Williams, was interested. He had given Williams to understand that he would try to see his way to support it; yet in view of his late prominence in Washington, as a foe of legislation in behalf of moneyed interests, he was more than ever averse to casting a vote in its favor. The bill had not been reached before adjournment, a result to which he had secretly contributed, but it was certain to be called up shortly after Congress reassembled. It disturbed him to feel that his affairs in New York were in such shape that Williams could embarrass him financially if he chose. It disturbed him still more that he appeared to himself to be guilty of bad faith. His conscience was troubled, and his favorite palliative of conciliation did not seem applicable to the case.

CHAPTER VIII.

Until this time the course of financial events in Benham since its evolution from a sleepy country town began had been steadily prosperous. There had been temporary recessions in prices, transient haltings in the tendency of new local undertakings to double and quadruple in value. A few rash individuals, indeed, had been forced to suspend payments and compound with their creditors. But there had been no real set back to commercial enthusiasm and speculative gusto. Those who desired to borrow money for progressive enterprises had found the banks accommodating and unsuspicious, and to Benham initiative it yet appeared that the development of the resources of the neighborhood by the unwearying, masterful energy of the citizens was still in its infancy.

But now, after a few months of inactivity, which holders of speculative securities had spoken of as another healthy breathing spell, the tendency of prices had changed. Had not merely halted, but showed a radical tendency to shrink; even to tumble feverishly. Buyers were scarce, and the once accommodating banks displayed a heartless disposition to scrutinize collateral and to ask embarrassing questions in regard to commercial paper. Rates of interest on loans were ruthlessly advanced, and additional security demanded. A pall of dejection hung over Benham. Evil days had come; days the fruit of a long period of inflation. A dozen leading firms failed and carried down with them diverse small people. Amid the general distrust and anxiety all eyes were fixed on Wall street, the so-called money centre of the country, the Gehenna where this cyclone had first manifested itself. The newspapers, voicing Benham public opinion, cast vituperation at the bankers and brokers of Wall street, whose unholy jugglings with fortune had brought this commercial blight on the community. Wall street had locked up money; consequently funds were tight in Benham, and the plans of its honest burghers to promote enterprise and develop the lawful industries of the country were interrupted. So spoke public opinion, and, at the same time, hundreds of private letters were being despatched through the Benham Post Office in response to requests for more margins on stocks held for the honest burghers by the fraternity of Wall street gamblers. There was private wailing and gnashing of teeth also, for in the panic a few of these bankers and brokers had been submerged, and the collateral of Benham's leading citizens had been swept away.

The panic itself was brief as panics always are, but it left behind it everywhere a paralyzed community. So far as Benham was concerned, only a few actually failed, but, in a host of instances, possessors of property who had thought themselves wealthy a year before found that they were face to face with the knotty problem of nursing their dwarfed resources so as to avoid eventual insolvency. Everything had shrunk fifty—often one hundred—per cent., for the basis of Benham's semi-fabulous development had been borrowed money. Many of Benham's leading citizens were down to hard pan, so to speak. Their inchoate enterprises were being carried by the banks on the smallest margins consistent with the solvency of those institutions, and clear-headed men knew that months of recuperation must elapse before speculative properties would show life again. Benham was consequently gloomy for once in despite of its native buoyancy. It would have arisen from the ashes of a fire as strenuous as a young lion. But, with everybody's stocks and merchandise pledged to the money lenders, enterprise was gripped by the throat. In the pride of its prosperity Benham had dreamed that it was a law unto itself, and that even Wall street could not affect its rosy commercial destinies. It appeared to pious owners of securities almost as though God had deserted his chosen city of a chosen country.

Lyons was among those upon whom the harrow of this fall in prices and subsequent hand-to-mouth struggle with the banks pressed with unpleasant rigor. In business phraseology he was too much extended. Consequently, as the margins of value of the securities on which he had borrowed dropped away, he was kept on tenter-hooks as to the future. In case the process of shrinkage went much further, he would be required to supply more collateral; and, if the rate of money did not fall, the banks would refuse to renew his notes as they became due, unless he could furnish clear evidence of his solvency. He was owing over one hundred and fifty thousand dollars on paper secured only by the stock and bonds of brand-new enterprises, which had no market negotiability. From the money which he had borrowed he had sent, from time to time, to Williams and Van Horne an aggregate of forty thousand dollars to protect some two thousand shares of railroad stocks. Williams had especially commended the shares of the coal-carrying roads to his attention, and the drop in prices had been uniformly severe in these properties. Instead of being the possessor of a stable quarter of a million, which he considered to be the value of his property at the time of his election to Congress, Lyons suddenly realized that he was on the brink of a serious financial collapse through which he might lose everything before he could discharge his liabilities. It seemed cruel to him, for he believed that all his ventures were sound, and that if he were not forced to sacrifice his possessions, their future value would attest his sagacity. But at present the securities of speculative enterprises were practically worthless as procurers of ready money. The extreme circumstances had come upon him with startling rapidity, so that he found himself in the unpleasant predicament of having used for temporary relief some of the bonds belonging to the Parsons estate which he held as executor. He had forwarded these to Williams merely as a matter of convenience before he had become anxious, expecting to be able to replace them with funds coming to him within thirty days from a piece of real estate for which he had received an offer. He had held off in the hope of obtaining a higher price. The following week, when signs of danger were multiplying, he had found the would-be purchaser unwilling to buy at any price. Realizing the compromising position in which he had placed himself by his action, he had cast about feverishly for the means to redeem the hypothecated securities, but all his resources were taxed of a sudden by the advent of the panic. It occurred to him to ask Selma to allow substitution of the twenty thousand dollars, which had been apportioned, to her as her legacy, for the bonds, but at first he had shrunk from the mortification of disclosing his condition to her, and now that the situation had developed, he feared that he might be obliged to borrow this money from her for the protection of his other interests. It gave him sore concern that he, a champion of moral ideas, a leading church member, and a Representative of the Federal Government should be put in such an equivocal position. Here again there was no opportunity for conciliation, and dignified urbanity was of no avail. If the condition of drooping prices and general distrust, a sort of commercial dry-rot, which had succeeded the panic, continued much longer he would be driven to the wall unless relief were forthcoming. Nor was it much consolation that many others were on the verge of failure. Financial insolvency for him would mean the probable loss of his seat in Congress, and the serious interruption of his political career. From what source could he hope for relief? The preparations for the autumn campaign were already being considered, and there was likelihood of another close contest between the two political parties. But for the worry occasioned by his plight, he would have resumed the contest with hopeful ardor, appreciating that the pecuniary distress of the community would be likely to work to his advantage. His own nomination was assured; his re-election appeared probable. But after it what could he expect but the deluge?

One source of the effectiveness of Horace Elton was that he was wont to exercise foresight, and make his plans in advance while other men were slumbering. He had been prepared for the panic because he had been expecting it for more than a year, and the ship of his financial fortunes was close reefed to meet the fury of the overdue gale. Also he was quick to recognize that the wide-spread depreciation of values would inevitably be followed by a period of business inactivity which would throw out of employment a large number of wage earners whose ballots as a consequence would be cast against the political party in power. As far back as the time when he made the acquaintance of Selma at Washington and selected her as the wearer of his cameo pin, he had been incubating on a scheme for the consolidation of the gas companies in the cities and towns of the state into one large corporation. For this corporation he required a liberal charter, which the next legislature would be invited to grant. He expected to be able to procure this franchise from the legislature, but he judged that the majority in favor of the bill would not be large enough to pass it over the Governor's veto. Accordingly it was of the first importance that the Governor should be friendly to the measure.

This was the year of the Presidential election. Both political parties were seeking to nominate their strongest candidates for the various federal and state offices. A promoter of large business schemes was at a disadvantage in a campaign where party feelings ran high and national issues were involved, and Elton knew it. He commonly chose an off year in politics for the consummation of his business deals. But he had chosen to push his bill this year for the reason that he wished to be in a position to buy out the sub-companies cheaply. The community was pressed for ready money, and many men who would be slow in prosperous times to extract gas shares from their tin boxes and stockings would be glad to avail themselves of a reasonable cash offer. Elton was a Republican on national issues. His experience had been that the Republican Party was fundamentally friendly to corporations, in spite of occasional pious ejaculations in party platforms to the contrary. He had a Republican candidate for Governor in mind who would be faithful to his interests; but this candidate was put aside in the convention in deference to the sentiment that only a man of first-rate mental and moral calibre could command the allegiance of independent voters, whose co-operation seemed essential to party success. The Republican state convention was held three weeks prior to the date fixed for that of their opponents. Within twenty-four hours subsequent to the nomination of Hon. John Patterson as the Republican candidate for Governor, while the party organs were congratulating the public on his selection, and the leaders of the party were endeavoring to suppress the murmurs of the disappointed lower order of politicians who, in metaphorical phrase, felt that they were sewed up in a sack for another two years by the choice of this strong citizen, one of the most widely circulated democratic newspapers announced in large type on its front page that Hon. James O. Lyons was the only Democrat who could defeat him in the gubernatorial contest. Behind the ledger sheet of this newspaper—which was no other than the Benham *Sentinel*—lurked the keen intelligence of Horace Elton. He knew that the candidate of his own party would never consent to indicate in advance what his action on the gas bill would be, and that he would only prejudice his chances of obtaining favorable action when the time arrived by any attempt to forestall a decision. This did not suit Horace Elton. He was accustomed to be able to obtain an inkling before election that legislation in which he was interested would not encounter a veto. His measures were never dishonest. That is, he never sought to foist bogus or fraudulent undertakings upon the community. He was seeking, to be sure, eventual emolument for himself, but he believed that the franchise which he was anxious to obtain would result in more progressive and more effectual public service. He had never before felt obliged to refrain from asking direct or indirect assurance that his plans would be respected by the

Governor. Yet he had foreseen the possibility of just such an occurrence. The one chance in a hundred had happened and he was ready for it. He intended to contribute to the Republican national campaign fund, but he did not feel that the interests of his State would suffer if he used all the influences at his command to secure a Governor who would be friendly to his scheme, and Congressman Lyons appeared to him the most available man for his purpose.

It had already occurred to Lyons that his nomination as Governor was a possibility, for the leaders of the party were ostensibly looking about for a desirable Democrat with whom to confront Patterson, and had shown an intention to turn a cold shoulder on the ambition of several aspirants for this honor who might have been encouraged in an ordinary year as probable victors. He knew that his name was under consideration, and he had made up his mind that he would accept the nomination if it were offered to him. He would regret the interruption of his Congressional career, but he felt that his election as Governor in a presidential year after a close contest would make him the leader of the party in the State, and, in case the candidate of his party were chosen President, would entitle him to important recognition from the new administration. Moreover, if he became Governor, his financial status would be strengthened. The banks would be more likely to accommodate one in such a powerful position, and he might be able to keep his head above water until better times brought about a return of public confidence and a recovery in prices. Yet he felt by no means sure that even as Governor he could escape betraying his financial embarrassment, and his mind was so oppressed by the predicament in which he found himself that he made no effort on his own part to cause the party leaders to fix their choice on him. Nor did he mention the possibility of his selection to Selma. Mortification and self-reproach had made him for the moment inert as to his political future, and reluctant to confide his troubles to her.

The clarion declaration of the Benham *Sentinel* in favor of Lyons evoked sympathetic echoes over the State, which promptly convinced the political chieftains that he was the strongest candidate to pit against Patterson. The enthusiasm caused by the suggestion of his name spread rapidly, and at the end of a week his nomination at the convention was regarded as certain.

The championship of the *Sentinel* was a complete surprise to

Selma. She had assumed that her husband would return to Washington, and that political promotion for the present was out of the question. When she saw her husband's features looking out at her from a large cut on the front page of the morning newspaper, and read the conspicuous heading which accompanied it—"The *Sentinel* nominates as Governor the Hon. James O. Lyons of Benham, the most eloquent orator and most public-spirited citizen of the State"—her heart gave a bound, and she eagerly asked herself, "Why not?" That was just what they needed, what she needed to secure her hold on the social evolution of Benham. As the wife of the Governor of the State she would be able to ignore the people who held aloof from her, and introduce the reforms in social behavior on which her heart was set.

"James, have you seen this?" she asked, eagerly.

Lyons was watching her from across the breakfast table. He had seen it, and had laid the newspaper within her reach.

"Yes, dear. It is very complimentary, isn't it?"

"But what does it mean? Are you to be Governor? Did you know of it, James?"

"I knew that my name, with others, had been mentioned by those who were looking for a candidate whom we can elect. But this nomination of the *Sentinel* comes from a clear sky. Would you like to have me Governor, Selma?"

"Yes, indeed. If the chance is offered you, James, you will surely accept it. It would please me immensely to see you Governor. We should not be separated then part of the year, and—and I should be able here in Benham to help you as your wife ought to help you. I know," she added, "that you have been looking forward to the next session of Congress, in the hope of distinguishing yourself, but isn't this a finer opportunity? Doesn't it open the door to splendid possibilities?"

Lyons nodded. His wife's eager presentation of the case confirmed his own conclusions. "It is an important decision to make," he said, with gravity. "If I am not elected, I shall have lost my place in the Congressional line, and may find difficulty in recovering it later. But if the party needs me, if the State needs me, I must not think of that. I cannot help being gratified, encouraged by the suggestion that my fellow-citizens of my political faith are turning to me as their standard-bearer at this time when great public issues are involved. If I can serve God and my country in this way, and at the same time please you, my wife, what can I ask better?"

He spoke with genuine feeling and reverence, for it was in keeping with his religious tendencies to recognize in advance the solemn responsibilities of high office, and to picture himself as the agent of the heavenly powers. This attitude of mind always found Selma sympathetic and harmonious. Her eyes kindled with enthusiasm, and she replied:

"You view the matter as I would have you view it, James. If this trust is committed to us by Providence, it is our duty to accept it as lovers of our country and promoters of true progress."

"It would seem so. And in some ways," he said, as though he felt the impulse to be reasonably frank toward Providence in his acceptance of the trust, "my election as Governor would be advantageous to my political and business interests. I have not sought the office," he added with dignified unction, "but my knowledge of local conditions leads me to believe that this action of the *Sentinel* signifies that certain powerful influences are working in my favor. I shall be able to tell you more accurately in regard to this before long."

Lyons happened to know that the Benham *Sentinel* had enlarged its plant two years previous, and that Horace Elton was still the holder of its notes for borrowed money. The transaction had passed through his bank, and in the course of his mental search for reasons to account for the sudden flat-footed stand of the newspaper, the thought came into his mind and dwelt there that Elton was at the bottom of it. If so, what was Elton's reason? Why should Elton, a Republican, desire his nomination? Surely not to compass his defeat.

In this connection Elton's friendship and the prophecy made to Selma as to his political future occurred to him and forbade an invidious supposition. "Glamis thou art, and Cawdor, and thou shalt be what thou art promised!" Lyons left Selma with the conviction that he would find Elton to be mainly responsible for what had taken place. Shortly after reaching his office he received a note from him asking for an appointment. Punctually at twelve o'clock Elton arrived and was shown into Lyons's private room. Lyons gave orders that he was not to be disturbed, for he believed that the results of the interview were likely to have a serious bearing on his career as a statesman.

Both men were of heavy physique, but as they sat facing each other an observer would have remarked that Elton's visage possessed a clean-cut compactness of expression despite its rotund contour. His closely trimmed whiskers, his small, clear, penetrating eyes, and the effect of neatness conveyed by his personal appearance were so many external indications of his mental lucidity and precision.

In contrast Lyons's moon-shaped face, emphasized by its smooth-shaven mobile mouth, below which his almost white chin beard hung pendent, expressed a curious interplay of emotional sanctity, urbane shrewdness, and solemn self-importance.

"Governor Lyons, at your service," said Elton, regarding him steadily.

"Do you think so?"

"I know so, if you desire it."

"The nomination, you mean?"

"The election by a comfortable majority."

Lyons breathed hard with satisfaction. "If the people of the State choose to confide their interests to my custody, I shall not refuse to serve them."

"So I supposed. You may be wondering, Lyons, why I, a Republican, should be talking like this. I will tell you. Observation has led me to believe that the people of this State will elect a Democratic Governor this year. The hard times will hurt the administration. Consequently, as your friend and my own friend, I have taken the liberty to indicate to the managers of your party their strongest man. I am responsible for what you saw on the front page of the *Sentinel* this morning. There need not be much difficulty," he added, significantly, "in securing emphatic endorsement throughout the State of the *Sentinel's* preference."

Lyons looked grave. "You must be aware that our views on public questions—especially those which concern the relations of capital and labor—are not the same."

"Certainly. I tell you frankly that while, from a humanitarian point of view, I respect your desire to relieve the inequalities of modern civilization, as a business man and a man of some property I do not regard the remedies presented by your party platform as just or adequate. I recognize that your opinions are hostile to

288

corporate interests, but I have gathered also that you are disposed to be reasonable and conciliatory; that you are not inclined to regard all men and all measures as dangerous, merely because they have means or are introduced in the name of capital."

"It has always seemed to me that a conciliatory spirit secures the most definite results for the public," assented Lyons.

"Precisely. See here, Lyons," Elton said, leaning forward across the table at which they were sitting, "I wish to be entirely frank with you. You know me well enough to understand that I have not offered you my support in any philanthropic spirit. I could not have deceived you as to this had I tried. I am a practical man, and have an axe to grind. I am urging your election as Governor because I believe you to possess intelligent capacity to discriminate between what is harmful to the community and what is due to healthy, individual enterprise—the energy which is the sap of American citizenship. We capitalists have no fear of an honest man, provided he has the desire and the ability to protect legitimate business acumen against the slander of mere demagogues. I have a bill here," he added, drawing a printed document from his pocket, "which I am desirous to see passed by the next legislature. It embodies a charter authorizing the acquisition and merger in one corporation of all the gas companies of this State, and an extension of corporate powers so as to cover all forms of municipal lighting. Were your hands not tied by your prospective election, I should be glad to offer you an opportunity to become one of the incorporators, for I believe that the undertaking will be lucrative. That, of course, is out of the question. Now then, this is a perfectly honest bill. On its face, to be sure, it secures a valuable franchise for the petitioners, and consequently may encounter some opposition. But, on the other hand, no one who considers the matter candidly and closely can fail to recognize that the great public will secure cheaper gas and more efficient service as the result of the consolidation. And there is where I felt that I could count on your intelligence. You would not allow the plea that capitalists were interested in obtaining a profitable franchise to obscure the more vital consideration that the community will be the true gainers."

Lyons bowed graciously, and stroked his beard. "What is it you wish me to do?" he asked.

"To read the bill in the first place; to convince yourself that what I have told you is true; to satisfy yourself that the measure is essentially harmless. The bill is not long. Read it now and let me hear your objections. I have some papers here to look over which will occupy me a quarter of an hour, if you can spare me the time."

Lyons acquiesced, and proceeded to peruse slowly the document. When he had finished it he folded it solemnly and returned it to Elton. "It is a bill framed in the interest of capital, but I cannot say that the public will be prejudiced by it. On the contrary, I should judge that the price of gas in our cities and towns would be lowered as a consequence of the reduction in running expenses caused by the projected consolidation. What is it that you wish me to do?"

"Agree to sign the bill as it now stands if it passes the legislature."

Lyons rested his head on his hand and his mouth moved tremulously. "If I am elected governor," he said, "I wish to serve the people honestly and fearlessly."

"I am sure of it. I ask you to point out to me in what manner this bill trenches upon the rights of the people. You yourself have noted the crucial consequence: It will lower the price of gas. If at the same time I am benefited financially, why should I not reap the reasonable reward of my foresight?"

"I will sign the bill, Elton, if it comes to me for signature. I may be criticised at first, but the improved public service and reduction of the gas bills will be my justification, and show that I have not been unmindful of the interests of the great public whose burdens my party is seeking to lighten."

"I shall count on you, then," said Elton, after a pause. "The failure of the bill at the last stage when I was expecting its passage might affect my affairs seriously."

"If the legislature does its part, I will do mine," responded Lyons, augustly. "I will sign the bill if it comes to me in the present form."

"I thank you, Governor."

Lyons looked confused but happy at the appellation.

"By the way," said Elton, after he had returned the papers to his pocket, "these are trying times for men with financial obligations. It is my custom to be frank and not to mince matters where important interests are concerned. A candidate for office in this campaign will need the use of all his faculties if he is to be successful. I should be very sorry for the sake of my bill to allow your mind to be distracted by solicitude in regard to your private affairs. Some of the best and most prudent of our business men are pressed to-day for ready money. I am in a position to give you temporary assistance if you require it. In justice to my interests you must not let delicacy stand in the way of your accepting my offer."

Lyons's bosom swelled with the tide of returning happiness. He had scarcely been able to believe his ears. Yet here was a definite, spontaneous proposition to remove the incubus which weighed upon his soul. Here was an opportunity to redeem the bonds of the Parsons estate and to repair his damaged self-respect. It seemed to him as though the clouds of adversity which had encompassed him had suddenly been swept away, and that Providence was smiling down at him as her approved and favorite son. His emotion choked his speech. His lip trembled and his eyes looked as though they would fill with tears. After a brief pause he articulated that he was somewhat pressed for ready money. Some explanation of his affairs followed, the upshot of which was that Elton agreed to indorse Lyons's promissory notes held by the banks to the amount of $60,000, and to accept as collateral for a personal loan of $40,000 certain securities of new local enterprises which had no present marketable value. By this arrangement his property was amply protected from sacrifice; he would be able to adjust his speculative account in New York; and he could await with a tranquil soul the return of commercial confidence. Lyons's heart was overflowing with satisfaction. He pressed Elton's hand and endeavored to express his gratitude with appropriate grandiloquence. But Elton disclaimed the obligation, asserting that he had acted merely from self-interest to make the election of his candidate more certain.

The loan of $40,000 was completed within forty-eight hours, and before the end of another week Lyons had rescued the bonds of the Parsons estate from pawn, and disposed of his line of stocks carried by Williams & Van Horne. They were sold at a considerable loss, but he made up his mind to free his soul for the time being from the toils and torment of speculation and to nurse his dwarfed resources behind the bulwark of Elton's relief fund until the financial situation cleared. He felt as though he had grown ten years younger, and without confiding to Selma the details of these transactions he informed her ecstatically that, owing to certain important developments, due partly to the friendliness of Horace Elton, the outlook for their future advancement had never been so bright. When a month later he was nominated as Governor he threw himself into the contest with the convincing ardor of sincere, untrammelled faith in the reforms he was advocating. His speeches reflected complete concentration of his powers on the issues of the campaign and evoked enthusiasm throughout the State by their eloquent arraignment of corporate rapacity at the expense of the sovereign people. In several of his most telling addresses he accused the national administration of pandering to the un-American gamblers who bought and sold stocks in Wall street.

CHAPTER IX.

Lyons was chosen Governor by a large majority, as Elton had predicted. The Republican Party was worsted at the polls and driven out of power both at Washington and in the State. Lyons ran ahead of his ticket, receiving more votes than the presidential electors. The campaign was full of incidents grateful to Selma's self esteem. Chief among these was the conspicuous allusions accorded her by the newspapers. The campaign itself was a fervid repetition of the stirring scenes of two years previous. Once more torch-light processions in vociferous serried columns attested the intensity of party spirit. Selma felt herself an adept through her former experience, and she lost no opportunity to show herself in public and bear witness to her devotion to her husband's cause. It pleased her to think that the people recognized her when she appeared on the balcony or reviewing stand, and that her presence evoked an increase of enthusiasm.

But the newspaper publicity was even more satisfying, for it centred attention unequivocally on her. Columns of descriptive matter relative to her husband's personality began to appear as soon as it became obvious that he was to be Governor. These articles aimed to be exhaustive in their character, covering the entire scope of his past life, disclosing pitiless details in regard to his habits, tastes, and private concerns. Nothing which could be discovered or ferreted out was omitted; and most of these biographies were illuminated by a variety of more or less hideous cuts showing, for example, his excellency as he looked as a school boy, his excellency as a fledgling attorney, the humble home where his excellency was born, and his excellency's present stately but hospitable residence on Benham's River Drive. Almost every newspaper in the State took its turn at contributing something which it conceived to be edifying to this reportorial budget. And after the Governor, came the turn of the Governor's lady, as she was called.

Selma liked best the articles devoted exclusively to herself; where she appeared as the special feature of the newspaper issue, not merely as an adjunct to her husband. But she liked them all, and she was most benignant in her reception of the several newspaper scribes, principally of her own sex, who sought an interview for the sake of copy. She withheld nothing in regard to her person, talents, household, or tastes which would in her opinion be effective in print. She had a photograph of herself taken in simple, domestic matronly garb to supplement those which she already possessed, one of which revealed the magnificence of the attire she wore at the President's Reception; another portrayed Littleton's earnest bride, and still a fourth disclosed her as the wistful, aspiring school-mistress on the threshold of womanhood. These, and the facts appropriate to them, she meted out to her biographers from time to time, lubricating her amiable confidences with the assertion that both she and her husband felt that the people were entitled to be made familiar with the lives of their public representatives. As the result of her gracious behavior, her willingness to supply interesting details concerning herself, and her flattering tendency to become intimate on the spot with the reporters who visited her, the newspaper articles in most cases were in keeping with Selma's prepossessions. Those which pleased her most emphasized in the first place her intellectual gifts and literary talents, intimating delicately that she had refused brilliant offers for usefulness with her pen and on the lecture platform in order to become the wife of Congressman Lyons, to whom her counsel and high ideals of public service were a constant stimulus. Emphasized in the second place her husband's and her own pious tastes, and strong religious convictions, to which their constant church attendance and the simple sanctity of their American home bore testimony. Emphasized in the third place—reproducing ordinarily a sketch and cut of her drawing-room—her great social gifts and graces, which had made her a leader of society in the best sense of the word both in Benham and in New York. A few of the articles stated in judicious terms that she had been twice a widow. Only one of them set this forth in conspicuous and opprobrious terms: "Her Third Husband! Our Chief Magistrate's Wife's Many Marriages!" Such was the unsympathetic, alliterative heading of the malicious statement which appeared in an opposition organ. It did no more than recall the fact that she had obtained a divorce from her first husband, who had in his despair taken to drink, and intimate that her second husband had not been altogether happy. Selma wept when she read the article. She felt that it was cruel and uncalled for; that it told only half the truth and traduced her before the American people. She chose to conceive that it had been inspired by Pauline and Mrs. Hallett Taylor, neither of whom had sent her a word of congratulation on her promotion to be the Governor's wife. Who but Pauline knew that her marriage with Littleton had not been completely harmonious? Who but Mrs. Taylor or one of her set would have the malice to insinuate that she had been merciless to Babcock? This was one libel in a long series of complimentary productions. The representation of the family group was made complete by occasional references to the Governor elect's mother—"Mother Lyons, the venerable parent of our chief magistrate." Altogether Selma felt that the picture presented to the public was a truthful and inspiring record of pious and enterprising American life, which showed to the community that its choice of a Governor had been wise and was merited.

Close upon the election and these eulogistic biographies came the inauguration, with Lyons's eloquent address. Selma, of course, had special privileges—a reserved gallery in the State House, to which she issued cards of admission to friends of her own selection. Occupying in festal attire the centre of this conspicuous group, she felt that she was the cynosure of every eye. She perceived that she was constantly pointed out as the second personage of the occasion. To the few legislators on the floor whom she already knew she took pains to bow from her seat with gracious cordiality, intending from the outset to aid her husband by captivating his friends and conciliating the leaders of the opposition party. On her way to and from the gallery she was joined by several members, to each of whom she tried to convey subtly the impression that she purposed to take an earnest interest in legislative affairs, and that her husband would be apt to consult her in regard to close questions. On the morning after the inauguration she had the satisfaction of seeing her own portrait side by side with that of her husband on the front page of two newspapers, a flattering indication, as she believed, that the press already recognized her value both as a helpmate to him and an ornament to the State. She took up her life as the Governor's lady feeling that her talents and eagerness to do good had finally prevailed and that true happiness at last was in store for her. She was satisfied with her husband and recognized his righteous purpose and capacity as a statesman, but she believed secretly that his rapid success was due in a large measure to her genius. Her prompting had inspired him to make a notable speech in his first Congress. Her charms and clever conversation had magnetized Mr. Elton so that he had seen fit to nominate him for Governor. A fresh impulse to her self-congratulation that virtue and ability were reaping their reward was given a few weeks later by the announcement which Lyons read from the morning newspaper that the firm of Williams & Van Horne had failed disastrously. The circumstances attending their down-fall were sensational. It appeared that Van Horne, the office partner, who managed the finances, had shot himself as the culmination of a series of fraudulent hypothecations of securities and misrepresentations to which it was claimed that Williams was not a party. The firm had been hopelessly insolvent for months, and had been forced to the wall at last by a futile effort on the part of Van Horne to redeem the situation by a final speculation on a large scale. It had failed owing to the continuation of the state of dry rot in the stock market, and utter ruin followed.

The regret which Lyons entertained as he read aloud the tragic story was overshadowed in his mind by his own thankfulness that he had redeemed the bonds and settled his account with them before the crash came. He was so absorbed by his own emotions that he failed to note the triumphant tone of his wife's ejaculation of amazement. "Failed! Williams & Van Horne failed! Oh, how did it happen? I always felt sure that they would fail sooner or later."

Selma sat with tightly folded hands listening to the exciting narrative, which Lyons read for her edification with the urbanely mournful emphasis of one who has had a narrow escape. He stopped in the course of it to relieve any solicitude which she might be feeling in regard to his dealings with the firm, by the assertion that he had only two months previous closed out his account owing to the conviction that prudent investors were getting under cover. This assurance gave the episode a still more providential aspect in Selma's eyes. In the first flush of her gratitude that Flossy had been superbly rebuked for her frivolous existence, she had forgotten that they were her husband's brokers. Moreover the lack of perturbation in his manner was not calculated to inspire alarm. But the news that Lyons had been shrewd enough to escape at the twelfth hour without a dollar's loss heightened the justice of the situation. She listened with throbbing pulses to the particulars. She could scarcely credit her senses that her irrepressible and light-hearted enemy had been confounded at last—confronted with bankruptcy and probable disgrace. She interrupted the reading to express her scepticism regarding the claim that Williams had no knowledge of the frauds.

"How could he be ignorant? He must have known. He must have bribed the reporters to put that in so as to arouse the sympathy of some of their fashionable friends. Van Horne is dead, and the lips of the dead are sealed."

Selma spoke with the confidence born of bitterness. She was pleased with her acumen in discerning the true inwardness of the case. Her husband nodded with mournful acquiescence. "It would seem," he said, "as if he must have had an inkling, at least, of what was going on."

"Of course he had. Gregory Williams, with all his faults, was a wide-awake man. I always said that."

Lyons completed the reading and murmured with a sigh, which was half pity, half grateful acknowledgment of his own good fortune—"It's a bad piece of business. I'm glad I had the sense to act promptly."

Selma was ruminating. Her steel bright eyes shone with exultation. Her sense of righteousness was gratified and temporarily appeased. "They'll have to sell their house, of course, and give up their horses and steam-yacht? I don't see why it doesn't mean that Flossy and her husband must come down off their pedestal and begin over again? It follows, doesn't it, that the heartless set into which they have wormed their way will drop them like hot coals?"

All these remarks were put by Selma in the slightly interrogative form, as though she were courting any argument to the contrary which could be adduced in order to knock it in the head. But Lyons saw no reason to differ from her verdict. "It means necessarily great mortification for them and a curtailment of their present mode of life," he said. "I am sorry for them."

"Sorry? Of course, James, it is distressing to hear that misfortune has befallen any person of one's acquaintance, and so far as Gregory Williams himself is concerned I have no wish to see him punished simply because he has been worldly and vainglorious. You thought him able in a business way, and liked to meet him. But as for her, Flossy, his wife," Selma continued, with a gasp, "it would be sheer hypocrisy for me to assert that I am sorry for her. I should deem myself unworthy of being considered an earnest-minded American woman if I did not maintain that this disgrace which has befallen them is the logical and legitimate consequence of their godless lives—especially of her frivolity and presumptuous indifference to spiritual influences. That woman, James, is utterly hostile to the things of the spirit. You have no conception—I have never told you, because he was your friend, and I was willing to let bygones be bygones on the surface on your account—you have no conception of the cross her behavior became to me in New York. From almost the first moment we met I saw that we were far apart as the poles in our views of the responsibilities of life. She sneered at everything which you and I reverence, and she set her face against true progress and the spread of American principles. She claimed to be my friend, and to sympathize with my zeal for social truth, yet all the time she was toadying secretly the people whose luxurious exclusiveness made me tremble sometimes for the future of our country. She and her husband were prosperous, and everything he touched seemed to turn to gold. It may sound irreverent, James, but there was a time during my life in New York when I was discouraged; when it seemed as though heaven were mocking me and my husband in our homely struggle against the forces of evil, and bestowing all its favors on a woman whose example was a menace to American womanhood! Sorry? Why should I be sorry to see justice triumph and shallow iniquity rebuked? I would give Florence Williams money if she is in want, but I am thankful, very thankful, that her heartless vanity has found its proper reward."

Lyons fingered his beard. "I didn't know she was as bad as that, Selma. Now that they have come to grief, we are not likely to be brought in contact with them, and in all probability they will pass out of our lives. Williams was smart and entertaining, but I never liked his taking advantage of the circumstances of my having an account in his office to urge me to support a measure at variance with my political convictions."

"Precisely. The trouble with them both, James, is that they have no conscience; and it is eminently just they should be made to realize that people who lack conscience cannot prosper in this country in the long run. They have loosed the awful lightnings of his terrible swift sword.'"

"I say 'amen' to that assuredly, Selma," Lyons answered. His predilection to palliate equivocal circumstances was never proof against clear, evidence of moral delinquency. When his religious scruples were finally offended, he was grave and unrelenting.

The downfall of the Williamses continued to be a sweet solace and source of encouragement to Selma. It made her, when taken in conjunction with her own recent progress, feel that the whirligig of time was working in her behalf after all; and that if she persevered, not merely Flossy, but all those who worshipped mammon, and consequently failed to recognize her talents, would be made to bite the dust. At the moment these enemies seemed to have infested Benham. Numerically speaking, they were unimportant, but they had established an irritating, irregular skirmish line, one end of which occupied Wetmore College, another held secret midnight meetings at Mrs. Hallett Taylor's. Rumors of various undertakings, educational, semi-political, artistic, or philanthropic, agitated or directed by this fringe of society, came to her ears from time to time, but she heard them as an outsider. When she became the Governor's wife she had said to herself that now these aristocrats would be compelled to admit her to their counsels. But she found, to her annoyance, that the election made no difference. Neither Pauline nor Mrs. Taylor nor any of the coterie had asked her to join them, and she was unpleasantly conscious that there were people on the River Drive who showed no more desire to make her acquaintance than when she had been Mrs. Lewis Babcock. What did this mean? It meant simply—she began to argue—that she must hold fast to her faith and bide her time. That if she and her friends kept a bold front and resisted the encroachments of this pernicious spirit, Providence would interfere presently and confound these enemies of social truth no less obviously than it had already overwhelmed Mrs. Gregory Williams. As the wife of the Governor, she was clearly in a position to maintain this bold front effectively. Every mail brought to her requests for her support, and the sanction of her signature to social or charitable enterprises. Her hospital was flourishing along the lines of the policy which she had indicated, and was feeling the advantage of her political prosperity. She was able to give the petition in behalf of Mrs. Hamilton, which contained now twenty-five thousand signatures, fresh value and solemnity by means of an autograph letter from the Governor's wife, countersigned by the Governor. This, with the bulky list of petitioners, she addressed and despatched directly to Queen Victoria. Her presence was in constant demand at all sorts of functions, at many of which she had the opportunity to make a few remarks; to express the welcome of the State, or to utter words of sympathy and encouragement to those assembled. In the second month of her husband's administration, she had the satisfaction of greeting, in her double capacity as newly-elected President of the Benham Institute and wife of the Governor, the Federation of Women's Clubs of the United States, on the occasion of its annual meeting at Benham. This federation was the incorporated fruit of the Congress of Women's Clubs, which Selma had attended as a delegate just previous to her divorce from Babcock, and she could not refrain from some exultation at the progress she had made since then as she sat wielding the gavel over the body of women delegates from every State in the Union. The meeting lasted three days. Literary exercises alternated with excursions to points of interest in the neighborhood, at all of which she was in authority, and the celebration was brought to a brilliant close by a banquet, to which men were invited. At this Selma acted as toastmaster, introducing the speakers of the occasion, which included her own husband. Lyons made a graceful allusion to her stimulating influence as a helpmate and her executive capacity, which elicited loud applause. Succeeding this meeting of the Federation of Women's Clubs came a series of semi-public festivities under the patronage of women—philanthropic, literary or social in character—for the fever to perpetuate in club form every congregation, of free-born citizens, except on election day, had seized Benham in common with the other cities of the country in its grasp, to each of which the Governor's wife was invited as the principal guest of honor. Selma thus found a dozen opportunities to exhibit herself to a large audience and testify to her faith in democratic institutions.

On the 22d of February, Washington's birthday, she held a reception at their house on River Drive, for which cards had been issued a fortnight previous. She pathetically explained to the reporters that, had the dimensions and resources of her establishment permitted, she and the Governor would simply have announced themselves at home to the community at large; that they would have preferred this, but of course it would never do. The people would not be pleased to see a rabble confound the hospitality of the chief magistrate and his wife. The people

300

demanded proper dignity from their representatives in office. The list of invitations which Selma sent out was, however, comprehensive. She aimed to invite everyone of social, public, commercial or political importance. A full band was in attendance, and a liberal collation was served. Selma confided to some of her guests, who, she thought, might criticise the absence of wine, that she had felt obliged, out of consideration for her husband's political prospects, to avoid wounding the feelings of total abstainers. The entertainment lasted from four to seven, and the three hours of hand-shaking provided a delicious experience to the hostess. She gloried in the consciousness that this crush of citizens, representing the leaders of the community in the widest sense, had been assembled by her social gift, and that they had come to offer their admiring homage to the clever wife of their Governor. It gratified her to think that Pauline and Mrs. Taylor and the people of that class, to all of whom she had sent cards, should behold her as the first lady of the State, and mistress of a beautiful home, dispensing hospitality on broad, democratic lines to an admiring constituency. When Mr. Horace Elton approached, Selma perpetrated a little device which she had planned. As they were in the act of shaking hands a very handsome rose fell—seemingly by chance—from the bouquet which she carried. He picked it up and tendered it to her, but Selma made him keep it, adding in a lower tone, "It is your due for the gallant friendship you have shown me and my husband." She felt as though she were a queen bestowing a guerdon on a favorite minister, and yet a woman rewarding in a woman's way an admirer's devotion. She meant Elton to appreciate that she understood that his interest in Lyons was largely due to his partiality for her. It seemed to her that she could recognize to this extent his chivalrous conduct without smirching her blameless record as an American housewife.

Meantime the Governor was performing his public duties with becoming dignity and without much mental friction. The legislature was engaged in digesting the batch of miscellaneous business presented for its consideration, among which was Elton's gas consolidation bill. Already the measure had encountered some opposition in committee, but Lyons was led to believe that the bill would be passed by a large majority, and that its opponents would be conciliated before his signature was required. Lyons's reputation

301

as an orator had been extended by his term in the House of Representatives and his recent active campaign, and he was in receipt of a number of invitations from various parts of the country to address august bodies in other States. All of these were declined, but when, in the month of April, opportunity was afforded him to deliver a speech on patriotic issues on the anniversary of the battle of Lexington, he decided, with Selma's approval, to accept the invitation. He reasoned that a short respite from the cares of office would be agreeable; she was attracted by the glamour of revisiting New York as a woman of note. New York had refused to recognize her superiority and to do her homage, and New York should realize her present status, and what a mistake had been made. The speech was a success, and the programme provided for the entertainment of the orator and his wife included the hospitality of several private houses. Selma felt that she could afford to hold her head high and not to thaw too readily for the benefit of a society which had failed to appreciate her worth when it had the chance. She was the wife now of one of the leading public men of the nation, and in a position to set fashions, not to ask favors. Nevertheless she chose on the evening before their return to Benham to show herself at dinner at Delmonico's, just to let the world of so-called fashion perceive her and ask who she was. There would doubtless be people there who knew her by sight, and who, when they were told that she was now the wife of Governor Lyons, would regret if not be ashamed of their short-sightedness and snobbery. She wore a striking dress; she encouraged her husband's willingness to order an elaborate dinner, including champagne (for they were in a champagne country), and she exhibited a sprightly mood, looking about her with a knowing air in observation of the other occupants of the dining-room.

While she was thus engaged the entrance of a party of six, whom the head waiter conducted with a show of attention to a table which had evidently been reserved for them, fettered Selma's attention. She stared unable to believe her eyes, then flushed and looked indignant. Her attention remained rivetted on this party while they laid aside their wraps and seated themselves. Struck by the annoyed intensity of his wife's expression, Lyons turned to follow the direction of her gaze.

"What is the matter?" he said.

302

For a few moments Selma sat silent with compressed lips, intent on her scrutiny.

"It's an outrage on decency," she murmured, at last. "How dare she show herself here and entertain those people?"

"Of whom are you talking, Selma?"

"The Williamses. Flossy Williams and her husband. The two couples with them live on Fifth Avenue, and used to be among her exclusive friends. Her husband has just ordered the dinner. I saw him give the directions to the waiter. It is monstrous that they, who only a few months ago failed disgracefully and were supposed to have lost everything, should be going on exactly as if nothing had happened."

"People in New York have the faculty of getting on their feet again quickly after financial reverses," said Lyons, mildly. "Like as not some of Williams's friends have enabled him to make a fresh start."

"So it seems," Selma answered, sternly. She sat back in her chair with a discouraged air and neglected her truffled chicken. "It isn't right; it isn't decent."

Lyons was puzzled by her demeanor. "Why should you care what they do?" he asked. "We can easily avoid them for the future."

"Because—because, James Lyons, I can't bear to see godless people triumph. Because it offends me to see a man and woman, who are practically penniless through their own evil courses, and should be discredited everywhere, able to resume their life of vanity and extravagance without protest."

While she was speaking Selma suddenly became aware that her eyes had met those of Dr. George Page, who was passing their table on his way out. Recognition on both sides came at the same moment, and Selma turned in her chair to greet him, cutting off any hope which he may have had of passing unobserved. She was glad of the opportunity to show the company that she was on familiar terms with a man so well known, and she had on her tongue what she regarded as a piece of banter quite in keeping with his usual vein.

"How d'y do, Dr. Page? We haven't met for a long time. You do not know my husband, Governor Lyons, I think. Dr. Page used to be our family physician when I lived in New York, James. Everyone here knows that he has a very large practice."

Selma was disposed to be gracious and sprightly, for she felt that Dr. Page must surely be impressed by her appearance of prosperity.

"I had heard of your marriage, and of your husband's election. I congratulate you. You are living in Benham, I believe, far from this hurly-burly?"

"Yes, a little bird told me the other day that a no less distinguished person than Dr. Page had been seen in Benham twice during the last three months. Of course a Governor's wife is supposed to know everything which goes on, and for certain reasons I was very much interested to hear this bit of news. I am a very discreet woman, doctor. It shall go no further."

The physician's broad brow contracted slightly, but his habitual self-control concealed completely the inclination to strangle his bright-eyed, over-dressed inquisitor. He was the last man to shirk the vicissitudes of playful speech, and he preferred this mood of Selma's to her solemn style, although his privacy was invaded.

"I should have remembered," he said, "that there is nothing in the world which Mrs. Lyons does not know by intuition."

"Including the management of a hospital, Dr. Page. Perhaps you don't know that I am the managing trustee of a large hospital?"

"Yes, I was informed of that in Benham. I should scarcely venture to tell you what my little bird said. It was an old fogy of a bird, with a partiality for thorough investigation and scientific methods, and a thorough distrust of the results of off-hand inspiration in the treatment of disease."

"I dare say. But we are succeeding splendidly. The next time you come to Benham you must come to see me, and I will take you over our hospital. I don't despair yet of converting you to our side, just as you evidently don't despair of inducing a certain lady some day to change her mind. I, for one, think that she is more fitted by nature to be a wife than a college president, so I shall await with interest more news from my little bird." Selma felt that she was talking to greater advantage than almost ever before. Her last remark banished every trace of a smile from her adversary's face, and he stood regarding her with a preternatural gravity, which should have been appalling, but which she welcomed as a sign of serious feeling on his part. She felt, too, that at last she had got the better of the ironical doctor in repartee, and that he was taking his leave tongue-tied. In truth, he was so angry that he did not trust himself to speak. He simply glared and departed.

"Poor fellow," she said, by way of explanation to Lyons, "I suppose his emotion got the better of him, because he has loved her so long. That was the Dr. Page who has been crazy for years to marry Pauline Littleton. When he was young he married a woman of doubtful character, who ran away from him. I used to think that Pauline was right in refusing to sacrifice her life for his sake. But he has been very constant, and I doubt if she has originality enough to keep her position as president of Wetmore long. He belongs to the old school of medicine. It was he who took care of Wilbur when he died. I fancy that case may have taught him not to mistrust truth merely because it isn't labelled. But I bear him no malice, because I know he meant to do his best. They are just suited for each other, and I shall be on his side after this."

The interest of this episode served to restore somewhat Selma's serenity, but she kept her attention fixed on the table where the Williamses were sitting, observing with a sense of injury their gay behavior. To all appearances, Flossy was as light-hearted and volatile as ever. Her attire was in the height of fashion. Had adversity taught her nothing? Had the buffet of Providence failed utterly to sober her frivolous spirit? It seemed to Selma that there could be no other conclusion, and though she and Lyons had finished dinner, she was unable to take her eyes off the culprits, or to cease to wonder how it was possible for people with nothing to continue to live as though they had everything. Her moral nature was stirred to resentment, and she sat spell-bound, seeking in vain for a point of consolation.

Meantime Lyons, like a good American, had sent for an evening paper, and was deep in its perusal. A startled ejaculation from him aroused Selma from her nightmare. Her husband was saying to her across the table:

"My dear, Senator Calkins is dead." He spoke in a solemn, excited whisper.

"Our Senator Calkins?"

"Yes. This is the despatch from Washington: 'United States Senator Calkins dropped dead suddenly in the lobby of the Senate chamber, at ten o'clock this morning, while talking with friends. His age was 52. The cause of his death was heart-failure. His decease has cast a gloom over the Capital, and the Senate adjourned promptly out of respect to the memory of the departed statesman.'"

"What a dreadful thing!" Selma murmured.

"The ways of Providence are inscrutable," said Lyons. "No one could have foreseen this public calamity." He poured out a glass of ice-water and drank it feverishly.

"It's fortunate we have everything arranged to return to-morrow, for of course you will be needed at home."

"Yes. Waiter, bring me a telegram."

"What are you going to do?"

"Communicate to Mrs. Calkins our sympathy on account of the death of her distinguished husband."

"That will be nice," said Selma. She sat for some moments in silence observing her husband, and spell-bound by the splendid possibility which presented itself. She knew that Lyons's gravity and agitation were not wholly due to the shock of the catastrophe. He, like herself, must be conscious that he might become the dead Senator's successor. He poured out and drained another goblet of ice-water. Twice he drew himself up slightly and looked around the room, with the expression habitual to him when about to deliver a public address. Selma's veins were tingling with excitement. Providence had interfered in her behalf again. As the wife of a United States Senator, everything would be within her grasp.

"James," she said, "we are the last persons in the world to fail in respect to the illustrious dead, but—of course you ought to have Senator Calkins's place."

Lyons looked at his wife, and his large lips trembled. "If the people of my State, Selma, feel that I am the most suitable man for the vacant senatorship, I shall be proud to serve them."

Selma nodded appreciatively. She was glad that her husband should approach the situation with a solemn sense of responsibility.

"They are sure to feel that," she said. "It seems to me that you are practically certain of the party nomination, and your party has a clear majority of both branches of the Legislature."

Lyons glanced furtively about him before he spoke. "I don't see at the moment, Selma, how they can defeat me."

306

CHAPTER X.

The body of Senator Calkins was laid to rest with appropriate ceremonies in the soil of his native State, and his virtues as a statesman and citizen were celebrated in the pulpit and in the public prints. On the day following the funeral the contest for his place began in dead earnest. There had been some quiet canvassing by the several candidates while the remains were being transported from Washington, but public utterance was stayed until the last rites were over. Then it transpired that there were four candidates in the field; a Congressman, an ex-Governor, a silver-tongued orator named Stringer, who was a member of the upper branch of the State Legislature and who claimed to be a true defender of popular rights, and Hon. James O. Lyons. Newspaper comment concerning the candidacy of these aspirants early promulgated the doctrine that Governor Lyons was entitled to the place if he desired it. More than one party organ claimed that his brilliant services had given him a reputation beyond the limit of mere political prestige, and that he had become a veritable favorite son of the State. By the end of a fortnight the ex-Governor had withdrawn in favor of Lyons; while the following of the Congressman was recognized to be inconsiderable, and that he was holding out in order to obtain terms. Only the silver-tongued orator, Stringer, remained. On him the opposition within the party had decided to unite their forces. To all appearances they were in a decided minority. There was no hope that the Republican members of the Legislature would join them, for it seemed scarcely good politics to rally to the support of a citizen whose statesmanship had not been tested in preference to the Governor of the State. It was conceded by all but the immediate followers of Stringer that Lyons would receive the majority vote of either house, and be triumphantly elected on the first joint ballot.

And yet the opposition to the Governor, though numerically small, was genuine. Stringer was, as he described himself, a man of the plain people. That is he was a lawyer with a denunciating voice, a keen mind, and a comprehensive grasp on language, who was still an attorney for plaintiffs, and whose ability had not yet been recognized by corporations or conservative souls. He was where Lyons had been ten years before, but he had neither the urbanity, conciliatory tendencies, nor dignified, solid physical properties of the Governor. He was pleased to refer to himself as a tribune of the people, and his thin, nervous figure, clad in a long frock-coat, with a yawning collar and black whisp tie, his fiery utterance and relentless zeal, bore out the character. He looked hungry, and his words suggested that he was in earnest, carrying conviction to some of his colleagues in the Legislature. The election at which Lyons had been chosen chief magistrate had brought into this State government a sprinkling of socialistic spirits, as they were called, who applauded vigorously the thinly veiled allusions which Stringer made in debate to the lukewarm democracy of some of the party leaders. When he spoke with stern contempt of those who played fast and loose with sacred principles—who were staunch friends of the humblest citizens on the public platform, and behind their backs grew slyly rich on the revenues of wealthy corporations, everyone knew that he was baiting the Governor. These diatribes were stigmatized as in wretched taste, but the politicians of both parties could not help being amused. They admitted behind their hands that the taunt was not altogether groundless, and that Lyons certainly was on extremely pleasant terms with prosperity for an out and out champion of popular rights. Nevertheless the leading party newspapers termed Stringer a demagogue, and accused him of endeavoring to foment discord in the ranks of the Democracy by questioning the loyalty of a man who had led them to notable victory twice in the last three years. He was invited to step down, and to season his aspirations until he could present a more significant public record. What had he done that entitled him to the senatorship? He had gifts undeniably, but he was young and could wait. This was a taking argument with the legislators, many of whom had grown gray in the party service, and Lyons's managers felt confident that the support accorded to this tribune of the people would dwindle to very small proportions when the time came to count noses.

Suddenly there loomed into sight on the political horizon, and came bearing down on Lyons under full sail, Elton's bill for the consolidation of the gas companies. The Benham *Sentinel* had not been one of the promoters of Lyons's senatorial canvass, but it had not espoused the cause of any of his competitors, and latterly had referred in acquiescent terms to his election as a foregone conclusion. He had not happened to run across Elton during these intervening weeks, and preferred not to encounter him. He cherished an ostrich-like hope that Elton was in no haste regarding the bill, and that consequently it might not pass the legislature until after his election as Senator. If he were to come in contact with Elton, the meeting might jog the busy magnate's memory. It was a barren hope. Immediately after the *Sentinel* announced that Governor Lyons was practically sure to be the next United States Senator, the gas bill was reported favorably by the committee which had it in charge, and was advanced rapidly in the House. Debate on its provisions developed that it was not to have entirely plain sailing, though the majority recorded in its favor on the first and second readings was large. It was not at first regarded as a party measure. Its supporters included most of the Republicans and more than half of the Democrats. Yet the opposition to it proceeded from the wing of the Democracy with which Stringer was affiliated. Elton's interest in the bill was well understood, and the work of pledging members in advance, irrespective of party, had been so thoroughly done, that but for the exigencies of the senatorial contest it would probably have slipped through without notice as a harmless measure. As it was, the opposition to it in the lower branch was brief and seemed unimportant. The bill passed the House of Representatives by a nearly two-thirds vote and went promptly to the Senate calendar. Then suddenly it became obvious to Lyons not merely that Elton was bent on securing its passage while the present Governor was in office, but that his rival, Stringer, had conceived the cruel scheme of putting him in the position, by a hue and cry against monopoly and corporate interests, where his election to the senatorship would be imperilled if he did not veto the measure. By a caustic speech in the Senate Stringer drew public attention to the skilfully concealed iniquities of the proposed franchise, and public attention thus aroused began to bristle. Newspapers here and there throughout the state put forth edicts that this Legislature had been chosen to protect popular principles, and that here was an opportunity for the Democratic party to fulfil its pledges and serve the people. Stringer and his associates were uttering in the Senate burning words against the audacious menace of what they termed the franchise octopus. Did the people realize that this bill to combine gas companies, which looked so innocent on its face, was a gigantic scheme to wheedle them out of a valuable franchise for nothing? Did they understand that they were deliberately putting their necks in the grip of a monster whose tentacles would squeeze and suck their life-blood for its own enrichment? Stringer hammered away with fierce and reiterated invective. He had no hope of defeating the bill, but he confidently believed that he was putting his adversary, the Governor, in a hole. It had been noised about the lobbies by the friends of the measure earlier in the session that the Governor was all right and could be counted on. Stringer reasoned that Lyons was committed to the bill; that, if he signed it, his opponents might prevent his election as Senator on the plea that he had catered to corporate interests; that if he vetoed it, he would lose the support of powerful friends who might seek to revenge themselves by uniting on his opponent. Stringer recognized that he was playing a desperate game, but it was his only chance. One thing was evident already: As a result of the exposure in the Senate, considerable public hostility to the bill was manifesting itself. Petitions for its defeat were in circulation, and several Senators who had been supposed to be friendly to its passage veered round in deference to the views of their constituents. Its defeat had almost become a party measure. A majority of the Democrats in the Senate were claimed to be against it. Nevertheless there was no delay on the part of those in charge in pushing it to final action. They had counted noses, and their margin of support had been so liberal they could afford to lose a few deserters. After a fierce debate the bill was passed to be engrossed by a majority of eleven. The Democrats in the Senate were just evenly divided on the ballot.

What would the Governor do? This was the question on everyone's lips. Would he sign or veto the bill? Public opinion as represented by the newspapers was prompt to point out his duty. The verdict of a leading party organ was that, in view of all the circumstances, Governor Lyons could scarcely do otherwise than refuse to give his official sanction to a measure which threatened to increase the burdens of the plain people. The words "in view of all the circumstances" appeared to be an euphemism for "in view of his ambition to become United States Senator." Several journals declared unequivocally that it would become the duty of the party to withdraw its support from Governor Lyons in case he allowed this undemocratic measure to become law. On the other hand, certain party organs questioned the justice of the outcry against the bill, arguing that the merits of the case had been carefully examined in the Legislature and that there was no occasion for the Governor to disturb the result of its action. On the day after the bill was sent to the chief magistrate, an editorial appeared in the Benham *Sentinel* presenting an exhaustive analysis of its provisions, and pointing out that, though the petitioners might under certain contingencies reap a reasonable profit, the public could not fail in that event to secure a lower price for gas and more effective service. This article was quoted extensively throughout the State, and was ridiculed or extolled according to the sympathies of the critics. Lyons received a marked copy of the *Sentinel* on the morning when it appeared. He recognized the argument as that which he had accepted at the time he promised to sign the bill if he were elected Governor. In the course of the same day a letter sent by messenger was handed to him in the executive chamber. It contained simply two lines in pencil in Elton's handwriting—"It continues to be of vital importance to my affairs that the pending bill should receive your signature." That was obviously a polite reminder of their agreement; an intimation that the circumstances had not altered, and that it was incumbent on him to perform his part of their compact. Obviously, too, Horace Elton took for granted that a reminder was enough, and that he would keep his word. He had promised to sign the bill. He had given his word of honor to do so, and Elton was relying on his good faith.

The situation had become suddenly oppressive and disheartening. Just when his prospects seemed assured this unfortunate obstacle had appeared in his path, and threatened to confound his political career. He must sign the bill. And if he signed it, in all probability he would lose the senatorship. His enemies would claim that the party could not afford to stultify itself by the choice of a candidate who favored monopolies. He had given his promise, the word of a man of honor, and a business man. What escape was there from the predicament? If he vetoed the bill, would he not be a liar and a poltroon? If he signed it, the senatorship would slip through his fingers. The thought occurred to him to send for Elton and throw himself on his mercy, but he shrank from such an interview. Elton was a business man, and a promise was a promise. He had enjoyed the consideration for his promise; his notes were secure and the hypothecated bonds had been redeemed. He was on his feet and Governor, thanks to Elton's interposition, and now he was called on to do his part—to pay the fiddler. He must sign the bill.

Lyons had five days in which to consider the matter. At the end of that time if he neither signed nor vetoed the bill, it would become law without his signature. He was at bay, and the time for deliberation was short. An incubus of disappointment weighed upon his soul and clouded his brow. His round, smooth face looked grieved. It seemed cruel to him that such an untoward piece of fortune should confront him just at the moment when this great reward for his political services was within his grasp and his opportunities for eminent public usefulness assured. He brooded over his quandary in silence for twenty-four hours. On the second day he concluded to speak of the matter to Selma. He knew that she kept a general run of public affairs. Not infrequently she had asked him questions concerning measures before the Legislature, and he was pleasantly aware that she was ambitious to be regarded as a politician. But up to this time there had been no room for question as to what his action as Governor should be in respect to any measure. It had happened, despite his attitude of mental comradeship with his wife, that he had hitherto concealed from her his most secret transactions. He had left her in the dark in regard to his true dealings with Williams & Van Horne; he had told her nothing as to his straitened circumstances, the compact by which he had been made Governor, and his relief at the hands of Elton from threatened financial ruin. Reluctance, born of the theory in his soul that these were accidents in his life, not typical happenings, had sealed his lips. He was going to confide in her now not because he expected that Selma's view of this emergency would differ from his own, but in order that she might learn before he acted that he was under an imperative obligation to sign the bill. While he was sitting at home in the evening with the topic trembling on his tongue, Selma made his confession easy by saying, "I have taken for granted that you will veto the gas bill."

Selma had indeed so assumed. In the early stages of the bill she had been ignorant of its existence. During the last fortnight, since the controversy had reached an acute phase and public sentiment had been aroused against its passage, she had been hoping that it would pass so that Lyons might have the glory of returning it to the Legislature without his signature. She had reasoned that he would be certain to veto the measure, for the bill was clearly in the

312

interest of monopoly, and though her nerves were all on edge with excitement over the impending election of a Senator, she had not interfered because she took for granted that it was unnecessary. Even when Lyons, after reading the article in the *Sentinel*, had dropped the remark that the measure was really harmless and the outcry against it unwarranted, she had supposed that he was merely seeking to be magnanimous. She had forgotten this speech until it was recalled by Lyons's obvious state of worry during the last few days. She had noticed this at first without special concern, believing it due to the malicious insinuations of Stringer. Now that the bill was before him for signature there could be no question as to his action. Nevertheless her heart had suddenly been assailed by a horrible doubt, and straightway her sense of duty as a wife and of duty to herself had sought assurance in a crucial inquiry.

"I was going to speak to you about that this evening. I wish to tell you the reasons which oblige me to sign the bill," he answered. Lyons's manner was subdued and limp. Even his phraseology had been stripped of its stateliness.

"Sign the bill?" gasped Selma. "If you sign it, you will lose the senatorship." She spoke like a prophetess, and her steely eyes snapped.

"That is liable to be the consequence I know. I will explain to you, Selma. You will see that I am bound in honor and cannot help myself."

"In honor? You are bound in honor to your party—bound in honor to me to veto it."

"Wait a minute, Selma. You must hear my reasons. Before I was nominated for Governor I gave Horace Elton my word, man to man, that I would sign this gas bill. It is his bill. I promised, if I were elected Governor, not to veto it. At the time, I—I was financially embarrassed. I did not tell you because I was unwilling to distress you, but—er—my affairs in New York were in disorder, and I had notes here coming due. Nothing was said about money matters between Elton and me until he had agreed to support me as Governor. Then he offered to help me, and I accepted his aid. Don't you see that I cannot help myself? That I must sign the bill?"

Selma had listened in amazement. "It's a trap," she murmured. "Horace Elton has led you into a trap." The thought that Elton's politeness to her was a blind, and that she had been

313

made sport of, took precedence in her resentment even of the annoyance caused her by her husband's deceit.

"Why did you conceal all this from me?" she asked, tragically.

"I should not have done so, perhaps."

"If you had told me, this difficulty never would have arisen. Pshaw! It is not a real difficulty. Surely you must throw Elton over. Surely you must veto the bill."

"Throw him over," stammered Lyons. "You don't understand, Selma. I gave my word as a business man. I am under great obligations to him." He told briefly the details of the transaction; even the hypothecation of the Parsons bonds. For once in his life he made a clean breast of his bosom's perilous stuff. He was ready to bear the consequences of his plight rather than be false to his man's standard of honor, and yet his wife's opposition had fascinated as well as startled him. He set forth his case—the case which meant his political checkmate, then waited. Selma had risen and stood with folded arms gazing into distance with the far away look by which she was wont to subdue mountains.

"Have you finished?" she asked. "What you are proposing to do is to sacrifice your life—and my life, James Lyons, for the sake of a—er—fetish. Horace Elton, under the pretence of friendship for us, has taken advantage of your necessities to extract from you a promise to support an evil scheme—a bill to defraud the plain American people of their rights—the people whose interests you swore to protect when you took the oath as Governor. Is a promise between man and man, as you call it, more sacred than everlasting truth itself? More binding than the tie of principle and political good faith? Will you refuse to veto a bill which you know is a blow at liberty in order to keep a technical business compact with an over-reaching capitalist, who has no sympathy with our ideas? I am disappointed in you, James. I thought you could see clearer than that."

Lyons sighed. "I examined the bill at the time with some care, and did not think it inimical to the best public interest; but had I foreseen the objections which would be raised against it, I admit that I never would have agreed to sign it."

"Precisely. You were taken in." She meant in her heart that they had both been taken in. "This is not a case of commercial give

314

and take—of purchase and sale of stocks or merchandise. The eternal verities are concerned. You owe it to your country to break your word. The triumph of American principles is paramount to your obligation to Elton. Whom will this gas bill benefit but the promoters? Your view, James, is the old-fashioned view. Just as I said to you the other day that Dr. Page is old-fashioned in his views of medicine, so it seems to me, if you will forgive my saying so, you are, in this instance, behind the times. And you are not usually behind the times. It has been one of the joyous features of my marriage with you that you have not lacked American initiative and independence of conventions. I wish you had confided in me. You were forced to give that promise by your financial distress. Will you let an old-fashioned theory of private honor make you a traitor to our party cause and to the sovereign people of our country?"

Lyons bowed his head between his hands. "You make me see that there are two sides to the question, Selma. It is true that I was not myself when Elton got my promise to sign the bill. My mind had been on the rack for weeks, and I was unfit to form a correct estimate of a complicated public measure. But a promise is a promise."

"What can he do if you break it? He will not kill you."

"He will not kill me, no; but he will despise me." Lyons reflected, as he spoke, that Elton would be unable to injure him financially. He would, be able to pay his notes when they became due, thanks to the improvement in business affairs which had set in since the beginning of the year.

"And your party—the American people will despise you if you sign the bill. Whose contempt do you fear the most?"

"I see—I see," he murmured. "I cannot deny there is much force in your argument, dear. I fear there can be no doubt that if I let the bill become law, public clamor will oblige the party to throw me over and take up Stringer or some dark horse. That means a serious setback to my political progress; means perhaps my political ruin."

"Your political suicide, James. And there is another side to it," continued Selma, pathetically. "My side. I wish you to think of that. I wish you to realize that, if you yield to this false notion of honor, you will interfere with the development of my life no less than your own. As you know, I think, I became your wife because I felt that as a public woman working, at your side in behalf of the high purposes in which we had a common sympathy, I should be a greater power for good than if I pursued alone my career as a writer and on the lecture platform. Until to-day I have felt sure that I had made no mistake—that we had made no mistake. Without disrespect to the dead, I may say that for the first time in my life marriage has meant to me what it should mean, and has tended to bring out the best which is in me. I have grown; I have developed; I have been recognized. We have both made progress. Only a few days ago I was rejoicing to think that when you became a United States Senator, there would be a noble field for my abilities as well as yours. We are called to high office, called to battle for great principles and to lead the nation to worthy things. And now, in a moment of mental blindness, you are threatening to spoil all. For my sake, if not for your own, James, be convinced that you do not see clearly. Do not snatch the cup of happiness from my lips just as at last it is full. Give me the chance to live my own life as I wish to live it."

There was a brief silence. Lyons rose and let fall his hand on the table with impressive emphasis. His mobile face was working with emotion; his eyes were filled with tears. "I will veto the bill," he said, grandiloquently. "The claims of private honor must give way to the general welfare, and the demands of civilization. You have convinced me, Selma—my wife. My point of view was old-fashioned. Superior ethics permit no other solution of the problem. Superior ethics," he repeated, as though the phrase gave him comfort, "would not justify a statesman in sacrificing his party and his own powers—aye, and his political conscience—in order to keep a private compact. I shall veto the bill."

"Thank God for that," she murmured.

Lyons stepped forward and put his arm around her. "You shall live your own life as you desire, Selma. No act of mine shall spoil it."

"Superior ethics taught you by your wife! Your poor, wise wife in whom you would not confide!" She tapped him playfully on his fat cheek. "Naughty boy!"

"There are moments when a man sees through a glass, darkly," he answered, kissing her again. "This is a solemn decision for us, Selma. Heaven has willed that you should save me from my own errors, and my own blindness."

"We shall be very happy, James. You will be chosen Senator, and all will be as it should be. The clouds on my horizon are one by one passing away, and justice is prevailing at last. What do you suppose I heard to-day? Pauline Littleton is to marry Dr. Page. Mrs. Earle told me so. Pauline has written to the trustees that after the first of next January she will cease to serve as president of Wetmore; that by that time the college will be running smoothly, so that a successor can take up the work. There is a chance now that the trustees will choose a genuine educator for the place—some woman of spontaneous impulses and a large outlook on life. Pauline's place is by the domestic hearth. She could never have much influence on progress."

"I do not know her very well," said Lyons. "But I know this, Selma, you would be just the woman for the place if you were not my wife. You would make an ideal president of a college for progressive women."

"I am suited for the work, and I think I am progressive," she admitted. "But that, of course, is out of the question for me as a married woman and the wife of a United States Senator. But I am glad, James, to have you appreciate my strong points."

On the following day Lyons vetoed the gas bill. His message to the Legislature described it as a measure which disposed of a valuable franchise for nothing, and which would create a monopoly detrimental to the rights of the public. This action met with much public approval. One newspaper expressed well the feeling of the community by declaring that the Governor had faced the issue squarely and shown the courage of his well-known convictions. The Benham *Sentinel* was practically mute. It stated merely in a short editorial that it was disappointed in Governor Lyons, and that he had played into the hands of the demagogues and the sentimentalists. It suggested to the Legislature to show commendable independence by passing the bill over his veto. But this was obviously a vain hope.

The vote in the House against the veto not merely fell short of the requisite two-thirds, but was less than a plurality, showing that the action of the chief magistrate had reversed the sentiment of the Legislature. The force of Stringer's opposition was practically killed by the Governor's course. He had staked everything on the chance that Lyons would see fit to sign the bill. When the party caucus for the choice of a candidate for Senator was held a few days later, his followers recognized the hopelessness of his ambition and prevailed on him to withdraw his name from consideration. Lyons was elected Senator of the United States by a party vote by the two branches of the Legislature assembled in solemn conclave. Apparently Elton had realized that opposition was useless, and that he must bide his time for revenge. Booming cannon celebrated the result of the proceedings, and Selma, waiting at home on the River Drive, received a telegram from the capital announcing the glad news. Her husband was United States Senator, and the future stretched before her big with promise. She had battled with life, she had suffered, she had held fast to her principles, and at last she was rewarded.

Lyons returned to Benham by the afternoon train, and a salute of one hundred guns greeted him on his arrival. He walked from the station like any private citizen. Frequent cheers attended his progress to his house. In the evening the shops and public buildings were illuminated, and the James O. Lyons Cadets, who considered themselves partly responsible for his rapid promotion, led a congratulatory crowd to the River Drive. The Senator-elect, in response to the music of a serenade, stepped out on the balcony. Selma waited behind the window curtain until the enthusiasm had subsided; then she glided forth and showed herself at his elbow. A fresh round of cheers for the Senator's wife followed. It was a glorious night. The moon shone brightly. The street was thronged by the populace, and glittered with the torches of the cadets. Lyons stood bareheaded. His large, round, smooth face glistened, and the moonbeams, bathing his chin beard, gave him the effect of a patriarch, or of one inspired. He raised his hand to induce silence, then stood for a moment, as was his habit before speaking, with an expression as though he were struggling with emotion or busy in silent prayer.

"Fellow citizens of Benham," he began, slowly, "compatriots of the sovereign State which has done me to-day so great an honor, I thank you for this precious greeting. You are my constituents and my brothers. I accept from your hands this great trust of office, knowing that I am but your representative, knowing that my mission is to bear constant witness to the love of liberty, the love of progress, the love of truth which are enshrined in the hearts of the great American people. Your past has been ever glorious; your future looms big with destiny. Still leaning on the God of our fathers, to whom our patriot sires have ever turned, and whose favors to our beloved country are seen in your broad prairies tall with fruitful grain, and your mighty engines of commerce, I take up the work which you have given me to do, pledged to remain a democrat of the democrats, an American of the Americans."

Selma heard the words of this peroration with a sense of ecstasy. She felt that he was speaking for them both, and that he was expressing the yearning intention of her soul to attempt and perform great things. She stood gazing straight before her with her far away, seraph look, as though she were penetrating the future even into Paradise.

Printed in Great Britain
by Amazon

79542980R00183